Finger

A SHAAR PRESS PUBLICATION

print

A NOVEL BY
CHAIM GREENBAUM
author of The Will *and* The Mexico File

© Copyright 2015 by Shaar Press

First edition – First impression / August 2015

ALL RIGHTS RESERVED
No part of this book may be reproduced in any form, *photocopy, electronic media, or otherwise without* written *permission from the copyright holder, except by a reviewer who wishes to quote brief passages in connection with a review written for inclusion in magazines or newspapers.*
THE RIGHTS OF THE COPYRIGHT HOLDER WILL BE STRICTLY ENFORCED.

This is a work of fiction. Names, characters, places, and incidents are either the product of the author's imagination or are used fictitiously. Any resemblance to actual persons, living or dead, or locales is entirely coincidental.

Published by **SHAAR PRESS**
Distributed by MESORAH PUBLICATIONS, LTD.
4401 Second Avenue / Brooklyn, N.Y 11232 / (718) 921-9000

Distributed in Israel by SIFRIATI / A. GITLER
Moshav Magshimim / Israel

Distributed in Europe by LEHMANNS
Unit E, Viking Business Park, Rolling Mill Road / Jarrow, Tyne and Wear, NE32 3DP/ England

Distributed in Australia and New Zealand by GOLDS WORLD OF JUDAICA
3-13 William Street / Balaclava, Melbourne 3183 / Victoria Australia

Distributed in South Africa by KOLLEL BOOKSHOP
Northfield Centre / 17 Northfield Avenue / Glenhazel 2192, Johannesburg, South Africa

ISBN 10: 1-4226-1622-3 / ISBN 13: 978-1-4226-1622-2

Printed in the United States of America
Custom bound by Sefercraft, Inc. / 4401 Second Avenue / Brooklyn N.Y. 11232

Jerusalem, 5772 / 2011

THE ELEGANTLY DRESSED MAN STANDING IN THE DOORWAY of the Kohlberg house of mourning looked as though he had wandered there by mistake.

The stranger's appearance contrasted sharply with the atmosphere in the grieving home, where the family was still reeling from the tragedy. Clean-shaven, he exuded a fresh scent of after-shave. His garments were impeccable: hand-tailored suit, matching tie, and fine leather shoes. The most conspicuous detail of all was his bare head. No *kippah* atop the meticulous haircut—a fact that elicited some low-voiced grumbling among several of those present.

The man hovered on the landing in front of the door, which stood wide open during this *shivah* week. He seemed completely at a loss over the spectacle that met his eyes. Several sorrowful-looking people were in the living room, but they were neither seated around a table nor relaxing on the couches. Instead, they were perched on a row of very low chairs ranged along one wall of the room.

Facing them, on a standard-height bench and a few ordinary chairs, sat other people. Those occupying the low chairs—they all appeared to be young, the man noted—were serving as the focal point for all those present. All eyes were watching them, and when one of them opened his mouth to speak, everyone listened with interest and empathy.

What added to the stranger's discomfort were the many pairs of curious eyes fixed on *him*. The people in the room were finding it impossible to ignore his unusual presence, radically different from those who had filled the Kohlberg home since Sunday night…

The loudspeakers that had blared their message through the quiet Jerusalem streets just before evening three days earlier had stunned her residents. "The funeral of *Harav Hachassid* R' Shlomo Kohlberg, *zt"l*, will leave at ten p.m. tonight from the Shamgar Funeral Home, going to Har HaMenuchos," the announcer had shouted.

"Shlomo Kohlberg?" Yaakov Levy, longtime owner of the neighborhood's grocery, had turned pale. "I don't believe it… How could this have happened?" Tears welled in his eyes and his lower lip began to tremble. "He was just here this morning, buying bread and milk. What happened all of a sudden?"

"Shloimeh Kohlberg?" The men in shul stared at one another with stricken eyes. "How did this happen? What did he die of?"

"How old is… was he?" asked Srulik Shapir, switching to the past tense in mid-sentence. "Only fifty-something, it seems to me. Not even sixty yet! He only married off two of his children so far. Was he sick or something?"

"Not that I know of," answered Nachman Greenwald, looking equally shocked. "How awful… Just terrible! A *rachmanus* on the family…"

Minchah, for which the regular *minyan* convened at twenty minutes before sunset, resembled Tishah B'Av *davening* that day. The worshipers' faces were drawn and downcast. The same thoughts seemed to be passing through the minds of all the *mispallelim*: Never again would R' Shlomo stand for *Shemoneh Esrei* in his usual corner near the bookcase. Never again would he bring his young children to the *"Avos u'Banim"* learning program—exactly on time, never late. No longer would R' Shlomo sit with complete concentration, learning his regular half-hour of *Shaarei Teshuvah*… It was terrible… Just terrible. The poor widow… How would she support her large family? He had left behind a houseful of children: two sons married, another who had just reached marriageable age, a daughter in high school, and a whole slew of younger children. Who would take care of them now? Who would educate them? Who would marry them off?

When R' Zerach, the *maggid shiur*, arrived at the shul, additional details were provided about the tragedy. R' Shlomo had left his workplace on Har HaChotzvim as usual, R' Zerach said, and headed to Geulah. At 2:30, he had been seen by his *mechutan*, Muttel Hershkowitz, on Malchei Yisrael Street, and they'd chatted for a few minutes. At ten minutes to three, the first call came in to Magen David Adom about a man who had collapsed at the corner of Ashtorei HaParchi and Reishis Chachmah streets. A team of Hatzalah paramedics had arrived on the scene first and initiated resuscitation efforts, but the situation—so they said afterward—was hopeless from the start. They were not even able to stabilize him enough to transport him to Bikkur Cholim Hospital, only a few hundred meters away. Instead, they had worked on him in the street for more than an hour until, at last, they gave up and established the time of his demise.

The *maggid shiur* finished speaking, tears clogging his throat. "*Nu, rabbosai*," he said in an encouraging voice. "Let's open our Gemaras and begin the *shiur*. And let today's learning be an elevation for the soul of our dear friend R' Shlomo, *zichrono livrachah*, who passed away in the prime of his life."

Silently, the members of the *shiur* took their seats around the table. R' Zerach opened his Gemara, but he did not start the *shiur*. Instead, he paused for a few moments as though debating the wisdom of saying something. He looked around the room, focusing at random on one of the men at the table, and then dropped back to the lines of the Gemara.

Finally, as though he had reached a decision, R' Zerach sighed and added—half to himself and half to his listeners: "People don't know who Shlomo Kohlberg was. They have no idea… Ah! If people knew who he really was…"

"Who's that?" Avreimi whispered to Chezky, indicating the doorway with his glance.

Chezky looked in that direction, and shrugged. "I don't have a clue," he hissed back. So many unfamiliar people had been coming by… And they'd been hearing such stories about their father that it suddenly seemed as if they'd hardly known him at all. Still, the fellow at the door was really strange. He wasn't religious—that much was certain. In fact, he didn't even appear to be Jewish. He looked like some sort of diplomat or wealthy businessman.

Avreimi and Chezky, R' Shlomo Kohlberg's two oldest sons, sat side by side on low plastic chairs, brought over by a local *gemach* that supplied the necessities of mourning. Their father's sudden death, which had stunned everyone who knew him, had found his family equally unprepared. The anguish was overwhelming, their hearts practically shredded with pain, but bitter reality had forced the two oldest brothers to pull themselves together within a short time and begin coping. All at once, they had become the acting heads of the family, responsible for seeing to a great many things.

Their mother was in a different world. Her agony made it difficult to speak with her about anything. Teachers and students from the high school where she worked as a secretary had been flocking to the house, but her shock was simply too onerous. There were no relatives to help bear the burden, for their father had been an only son and their mother's entire family lived in the States and hardly kept in touch.

Their brother Ari, 21, had also been lost inside himself since being summoned from his yeshivah in Bnei Brak, and Miri and the other little ones were certainly no help. Avreimi and Chezky, 23 and 25 years old respectively, had found themselves dealing with the Chevra Kaddisha, informing their younger siblings' teachers of the tragedy, and of course sitting for long hours, early morning to late night, receiving the throngs of people who streamed in to comfort the mourners.

The bareheaded man had not yet entered. He lingered on the landing, gazing in astonishment at the scene taking place inside the apartment.

Facing the row of mourners at present were two men who represented both sides of their father's life. One of them was the head of the morning *kollel* where Shlomo Kohlberg went to learn before Shacharis; the second was the division manager in the high-tech company where Kohlberg had worked. Both of them described the same quality in his personality: despite the fact that Shlomo Kohlberg had been past fifty, he had competed honorably with much younger men—and often surpassed them.

"In our *kollel*," the Rosh Kollel said, "most of the *avreichim* are in their thirties. Your father was the oldest there—and his diligence served as an outstanding example to all the others. He never came late, not even on the mornings after your family weddings."

"As you probably know, in the high-tech world, anyone past forty is considered old," the division manager added. "But there was no one like your father. Do you realize that I, his supervisor, am more than 20 years younger than he was? If he had wanted, he could have been a senior executive. But he preferred to do his job, quietly and dependably—and, especially, with original thinking that was incomparable. He was truly a genius with computers, and he'll be very much missed in our division. We all join in your sorrow."

As the manager and two of his father's colleagues took their leave, Chezky kept track of what was happening in the doorway. R' Chaim Pines, their next-door neighbor, who had been spending long hours in their apartment helping in every way he could, approached the stranger and asked what he wanted.

The stranger, apparently, did not understand Hebrew. His eyes darted around the room, seeking help.

"Does anyone here know English?" he whispered.

No one volunteered.

What was going on over there? With a subtle hand gesture, Chezky motioned for R' Chaim Pines to come closer. R' Chaim leaned in and said, "He only speaks English. I don't understand him."

"Why doesn't he come in?"

"He doesn't want to come inside," R' Chaim said. "It doesn't look like he came to pay a *shivah* call…"

Then, from his left, Chezky heard his older brother Avreimi say, "*You* know English, don't you? Go see what he wants."

Chezky lifted a puzzled brow. Something in this situation was odd. After a moment, he realized what it was. Avreimi's comment —and others like it which obliquely touched on Chezky's law studies—had always before been said in a mocking tone. *You know English…* And *why* did Chezky know English? Because he had gone to study law, and had learned English at the same time. Such observations were usually made in a spirit of criticism. This time, however, the remark had been surprisingly matter-of-fact and to the point: "*You* know English, don't you? Go see what he wants."

A fleeting thought popped into his mind: this *shivah* week had improved the strained relationship between himself and his brother. He suddenly realized that three days had passed without a single eruption of the usual quarrels that never seemed to lead anywhere: debates about *kollel* versus work, Torah or *parnassah*, *hishtadlus* or *emunah*. For three days they had been functioning as a team, seeing eye to eye and working shoulder to shoulder. What a pity their father had to leave the world in order for that to happen…

The Rosh Kollel and several others rose to their feet, murmured the traditional words of comfort to the mourners and left. The numbers in the room were dwindling. Chezky forced himself to get up from his seat and move toward the door.

"How can I help you?" he asked in English.

The stranger's face lit up. Finally, someone who spoke his language! He didn't want to interrupt anything, he told Chezky. He was just looking for Mr. Shlomo Kohlberg.

A minute later, the man's face filled with distress and discomfort when he heard Chezky's answer: Mr. Shlomo Kohlberg had passed away suddenly, three days earlier.

"Oh—I'm sorry! I am very sorry," the man stammered.

"Would you like to come in?" Chezky asked. He was very curious to know why the stranger had come to see his father—and who he was. But the man merely mumbled a few more words of apology and commiseration, and quickly turned to retreat down the stairs.

Had it not been in the middle of his week of mourning, Chezky would have simply run after him. But that was clearly not an option under present conditions. Even getting up and going to the door had not been exactly acceptable. So Chezky returned to his seat, a thousand questions racing through his brain: Who was that man? What did he want with Abba? And why did he rush away like that when he heard that Abba had passed away?

Before he sat down, Chezky glanced out the window at the street below. The man was just emerging from the building's main entrance, three floors below. He walked rapidly toward a large, opulent car idling on the other side of the street. With his right hand he held a cell phone to his ear. And—judging by his sharp, excited gestures—the call was not a relaxed conversation between friends.

The man approached the passenger door of the car, making it obvious that someone else was sitting in the driver's seat. Just before he was swallowed up inside the vehicle, the man lifted his head. For a brief moment his eyes met Chezky's, looking down at him through the window.

The man dropped his glance. Hastily he slipped into the car, which sped away.

France, 5704 / 1944

The five men were exhausted to death. They followed one another through the forest, drawing on their last reserves of strength. For six days they had been walking almost continuously, stopping only for a few hours' sleep in twenty-four.

Their feet were swollen and painful, their hands cut and scratched, and their faces covered with grime. Over the last day, hunger had also begun to be a problem. As the food they had with them on the road dwindled, they were forced to satisfy their hunger with fruit plucked from the trees they passed, and two loaves of bread they found as they passed near one of the villages.

The man who'd prepared their route across the conquered land, east to west, knew every trail through France's forests and hills. Over the course of hundreds of kilometers, the five rarely encountered a living soul. Their winding course, carefully marked on a map, took them far from any place of habitation. Their only difficulty arose when they reached a main road or thoroughfare that they had no choice but to cross. They always did so at night, under cover of darkness, after checking and re-checking to make sure the area was clear of German soldiers and French collaborators.

The last leg of the journey was the most dangerous. They were approaching the coast of the Atlantic, an area under German control. The region was sprinkled with numerous small villages. They might be spotted by farmers and laborers going out to the fields and vineyards, greedy for the huge prize that the occupying authorities had promised to anyone who aided in their capture. Danger loomed and exhaustion threatened to get the better of them—but the knowledge that they would soon be in a safe place infused the five refugees with renewed strength.

Their route ran through a hilly district carpeted with vine-covered slopes. The grapevines, planted in long rows, were laden with heavy clusters of blue-black grapes. The fertile valley spread out at their feet looked like something out of a picture postcard: golden wheat fields, dotted with red-roofed cottages and flourishing orchards, and threaded with sparkling canals of water.

But the tranquility was deceptive. Occupied France lay crushed under the cruel German boot, subdued and choking with pain. Terror floated through the village streets. Degradation was the people's lot from morning to night. French pride had been shattered under the conqueror's heel, blown away by the brown-uniformed troops that swarmed everywhere.

And if such was the situation in the last few years, it had been magnified this past week with the onset of the Germans' pursuit of the fugitives. The Nazi authorities had been gripped with a kind of madness. They were sparing no effort to lay their hands on the fleeing terrorist cell. There were house-to-house searches, arrests, and interrogations based on the flimsiest of suspicion. The most senior of the officers went out into the field to encourage their men in conducting an all-out hunt.

And yet, six days had passed, and the fugitives had managed to cross France without being apprehended.

An hour before sunset, they reached their destination. They stood at the edge of a dense copse of trees and looked down at the hiding place that had been prepared for them. It was an isolated house nestled in the side of a mountain. On the first and second floors lived a local family whose father was lame, and they'd been told that they could stay in the basement until the danger was past. The house was encircled by a tidy courtyard. A clothesline, stretched across it, featured two pairs of white socks.

"What day is this?" one of the men asked his companions, though he already knew the answer.

"Monday," someone said.

The first man nodded to himself with satisfaction.

The socks were not dangling from the line in order to dry in the sun. They were a signal that had been arranged in advance: black socks meant that there was a problem; white socks would indicate that all was well. The number of pairs corresponded to the day of the week on which the socks had been hung. If today was Monday and two pairs of white socks hung there, then everything was all right.

Neatly made beds awaited the five fugitives in the cellar of the house, along with plenty of food and hot water with which to remove the dirt of their long journey.

In the interim, someone had gone to the clothesline and removed the white socks and hung six other pairs in their stead: five pairs of blue socks and one pair of red socks.

The villager who rode past on his bicycle each morning would immediately notice them and pass the information on. Of the six original members of the Resistance cell, five had reached the hiding place safely. One fighter did not make it.

THURSDAY, THE FOURTH DAY OF *SHIVAH* IN THE KOHLBERG home, was an especially moving one for the two older brothers, Avreimi and Chezky. Early that afternoon, the illustrious head of the yeshivah where they had both learned came to console them.

The Rosh Yeshivah was a figure that inspired admiration in all who saw him, and mourners and comforters alike listened intently as he spoke. From what he said, the brothers learned to their surprise how very closely their father had interested himself in and tracked the progress of their learning and spiritual growth. Even more surprising was the way he had managed to do this without either of them suspecting a thing.

The Rosh Yeshivah's visit left a deep impression on the household—especially on the younger boys, on whom he showered warmth and attention. Chezky, however, received another pair of visitors that deserved mention. Before Minchah, two men in crocheted *kippot* came into the house. Both were lecturers at the Givat Shmuel Institute where Chezky was pursuing his studies: Attorney Safrid, lecturer on legal jurisprudence, and Dr. Marcus, who taught contracts. Chezky Kohlberg was one of the most talented and successful students in the school, and a favorite of the staff. His grade on the psychometric exam had been one of the highest ever recorded in the annals of the institute, which had been founded just a few years earlier. Chezky had been granted every available scholarship and stipend to help him defray the high cost of tuition.

Attorney Safrid told Chezky that, because of his bereavement, he was eligible to postpone the work he had been due to hand in the following week. Dr. Marcus contributed a number of minor anecdotes from the school. Chezky labored under a pronounced sense of discomfort throughout the visit, and was secretly relieved that Avreimi, his big brother, was giving his attention to other visitors and not to this specific conversation. Although several other ultra-Orthodox friends with whom he studied had come to comfort him, they'd been dressed in the customary hat and jacket. These two lecturers—one of whom was moderately observant, while the other kept a *kippah* in his car for funerals and weddings—made Chezky cringe.

It was near midnight when the last of the visitors left the house, despite the fact that R' Chaim Pines had hung a sign on the door stating explicitly that visits were to end by 11 p.m. The mourners stood up, stretching to relieve the discomfort of muscles that ached from sitting for so long. At long last they could close the door, remove their jackets and hats, and rest a bit after the exhausting effort—both emotional and physical—of the long day that had begun at 6:30 that morning.

The younger children had already gone to bed. Ari was beginning to emerge from the traumatic shock that had descended on him since he had learned of his father's sudden death. To Avreimi's and Chezky's vast relief, their mother, too, was beginning to come back to herself after the initial three days of mourning.

This was the family's time to go into the kitchen and eat something hot that one of the neighbors had cooked, swap impressions, and sum up the day's events. And it was also the time to loosen their tongues a bit, after a full day of focusing on conversations with streams of people who came and went, accepting their condolences and answering their repetitive questions, when all they really wanted to do was find a quiet corner and have a good cry.

Avreimi had never reconciled himself to the fact that his brother had left the *kollel* to study law—or, as he liked to mockingly refer to it, *chukas hagoyim*.* Not even the fact that Chezky had consulted with a *rav* before taking that step had softened his brother's opposition. Chezky still remembered the bitter arguments they'd had when he first gathered the courage to discuss the topic at home.

Actually, no one had expected him to continue with full-time learning for a long period after his marriage, as his older brother had done. Chezky had always been the undisputed *"macher"* of his yeshivah, as opposed to Avreimi, who remained completely immersed in his spiritual pursuits. While Avreimi sat before his *shtender* even outside the regular learning *sedarim*, Chezky would be organizing transportation to fellow students' weddings and lending a hand with various yeshivah operations, such as running a *gemach* with a net worth of several thousand shekels.

Each brother had his weaknesses. And Chezky's weakness—what was he to do?—was money. Everyone knew it. Even as a child, he had loved to sit on the balcony and watch the big, shiny cars go by. He would promise himself that, when he grew up, he would have a car just like those. The family would recall, with a smile, the Shabbos they'd spent in a neighborhood of upscale private homes in Bnei Brak. Chezky, then a boy of seven, had looked around as though mesmerized, and then remarked that it was a pity a person could live in only one house, because he wished he had *all* of them!

And Avreimi? Such things never interested him. He always toed the line: the best student in his class, the one who always did his homework on time, earned the best grades on tests, and gave his parents and teachers plenty of *nachas*. That was the way it had been in *yeshivah ketanah*, and the story repeated itself in *yeshivah gedolah*. It was no surprise, then, that at the very start of his foray into the world of *shidduchim*, he had been snatched up by Muttel Hershkowitz, a prominent member of the community who was also, *baruch Hashem*, not lacking for money.

---

*Chukas hagoyim — literally, *the laws of the nations* — generally refers to prohibited non-Jewish practices. The term is used, in a play on words, to refer to secular law in contradistinction to Torah law.

It had been Abba, Chezky mused, who'd served as the balanced paradigm of Torah and *derech eretz*. He did not waste a minute that he could spend learning, and at the same time he worked for his living. Though in the parlance of the times he was known as a *"balebus"*—a householder, as opposed to one who dwelled in the halls of Torah full-time—he had lived every minute with a consciousness of his mission in this world and what Hashem wanted from him.

Now that their father had passed away—Chezky continued his train of thought—he and Avreimi were going to have to find a way to coexist.

"I noticed that R' Zerach came again today," Ari said, in an attempt to thaw the atmosphere.

R' Zerach, the *maggid shiur* in shul and a good friend of their father's, had come for Minchah and Ma'ariv nearly every day that week. Afterward, he had been in no hurry to leave. Instead, he had lingered for half an hour, sitting silently on one side of the living room, listening to the conversations, shaking his head sorrowfully and occasionally releasing a groan of pain from an aching heart.

"Itzik came today, too. Did you see him?" Chezky asked. "How he was crying! I had to comfort him…"

Itzik was a man of about sixty who had begun to return to his Jewish roots several years earlier, after being befriended by their father. Ever since, they'd remained in close contact.

"And did you see the Russian?" Avreimi asked.

"What Russian?"

"Some Russian Jew was here this morning—looked like a *ba'al teshuvah*. He didn't talk much. Just said that Abba was a great *tzaddik*…"

"Okay, that's what everyone's saying." They all shared a sad smile.

"He asked something strange: if Abba was ever involved in archeology," Avreimi added with a grin.

"Archeology?" Chezky echoed with a bark of surprised laughter.

"Archeology. Do you know anything about that?"

Chezky was amused. "You mean, like a grave robber? A skeleton snatcher?"

"Come on. Stop talking nonsense," Avreimi chided.

Chezky sobered. "Okay. I don't know anything about this. But who knows? The more I hear about Abba, the more I realize that we hardly knew him."

"And do you know what else he said?" Avreimi asked.

"Who—the Russian Jew?"

"Yes."

"What did he say?"

"He said that Abba could have been a very rich man today."

"Is that what he said?" Chezky's eyes opened wide.

Avreimi chuckled. "I knew that would get you excited. But, yes—that's exactly what he said."

Chezky did not take well to the implied criticism. "You know something?" he said in sudden umbrage. "Abba never said a negative word about my studies. He never threw it in my face the way you keep doing."

"True." Avreimi was unyielding. "But you heard the Rosh Yeshivah say how Abba would call him to find out how we were coming along. For some reason, I have a feeling Abba never called your lecturers in law school to hear how his dear son was progressing in his studies..."

Ari, as usual, continued eating in silence, careful not to become embroiled in his brothers' ongoing contention. But Miri, at seventeen the fourth in line, could not keep quiet any longer. "You should both be ashamed of yourselves!" she said, as tears welled in her eyes. "Abba was *niftar*... and you're continuing to fight like two little children."

France, 5704 / 1944

The winter sun sent its first rays across the countryside. Drops of last night's rain sparkled in the grass like scattered diamonds. The peace of the village night slowly dissipated to the sounds of a gradually awakening new day. From the door of the house burst little Pierre, racing on bare feet to the well in the center of the courtyard, an empty tin pail dangling from his hand.

Pierre set the pail down under the lip of the pump, grasped the rusted metal lever with both hands and began pumping with a steady rhythm. A stream of water burst out and filled the bucket to its brim.

As the nine-year-old started for the house, weighed down by the heavy pail, he noticed a German military vehicle climbing the narrow road leading up the hill. Pierre averted his eyes so as not to attract the soldiers' attention. For nearly half of his life, Pierre had lived under Nazi rule. He had been five when the Germans had invaded and conquered his native France, and the four ensuing years had taught him that the less contact he had with them, the better.

Neither Pierre nor his brothers and sisters had the slightest idea that they were harboring five guests, strangers who had arrived at their home the night before from the direction of the vineyards and entered the deep cellar beneath their house. No one else in the village knew that lame Antoine, in his remote house at the top of the hill, was engaged in aiding and abetting French Resistance fighters against the Nazis.

The stone cellar—which, in better times, had been used to store wine and to age cheese—was devoid of windows. Only the winding staircase, carved from stone, let in a smidgen of light from the courtyard. Two thick wooden doors, one at the head of the staircase and a second at its foot, separated the cellar from the outside world. A hidden chute descended from the scullery off the kitchen, leading down to the cellar deep below. It was through this chute, originally designed for bringing up bottles of wine, that Antoine and his wife—the only person who shared his secret—sent food and other necessities down to the underground resistance fighters who had come to shelter under their roof.

At that hour of the morning, all five men were deep in slumber. The night before they had managed to bathe and to bandage the wounds and scrapes they'd absorbed up on their long trek. Then they'd sat down to eat the meal that was sent down to them in a reed basket attached to a long rope: a dish consisting of potatoes and beets, along with two bottles of cheap wine. Afterward they'd dispersed to the straw pallets that had been prepared for them and surrendered their bodies at last to the fatigue of a week of excruciating effort.

During the past few days, a single step had separated them from death. All of France was searching for them. German military units and local collaborators had been recruited to join the country-wide hunt. The fugitives' names and pictures were sent to every police station and military base; roadblocks were set up, trains halted, and their passengers checked. A large bounty had been promised to anyone who would provide information leading to the men's capture, but they had managed to cross the country in safety and reach secure refuge in the cellar of Antoine's home.

Pierre walked along the path leading to his house as quickly as his legs would carry him. As he opened the door, he heard the squeak of the iron gate opening behind him. From the corner of his eye he caught a glimpse of German soldiers descending from their army vehicle and entering the courtyard. He hastened into the house and closed the door behind him, his little heart thudding in fear.

THE WEEK OF MOURNING IN THE KOHLBERG HOUSE CAME TO an end. On Sunday morning, the last of the *shivah*, men still came to *daven* in their house. Afterward the family sat for a short time, receiving the last of the comforters. And then they got up. A van, hired in advance, took them to Har HaMenuchos to visit their father's grave for the first time. The custom in Jerusalem is for women not to attend funerals, and even the deceased's sons do not join the procession to the cemetery.

And then it was time to try to return to routine life. The boys would attend their *cheders* and the girls their schools. Their mother would go back to her job at the high school and the older sons to their respective pursuits. But nothing, of course, would ever be the way it had been before. The family's heart and soul had been abruptly ripped out, and they now had to learn how to live with the reality of something forever missing, a constant loss for which there was no comfort, a tear always in the corner of the eye, threatening to glide down the cheek.

Without making any conscious decision to do so, Avreimi and

Chezky undertook the burden of running the household. As early as Sunday evening, after Ari returned from his yeshivah in Bnei Brak and the little ones had been put to bed, they came to talk with their mother about "what happens next." To their surprise, the distraught widow they'd come to know during the week of *shivah* had vanished. They found themselves facing a strong woman determined to cope with every obstacle and to continue managing her home and raising her children "exactly the way Abba would have wanted."

Perhaps she would need some help in certain areas, she admitted, and she would not be shy about asking them for it. For example, she certainly would not be able to learn with the boys on Shabbos; that would be their job. "But neither your father nor I were spoiled," she said thoughtfully, stirring a full cup of tea that had already gone cold. "Listen, children: we never had it easy. There were difficult times and less difficult times, but Hashem always helped. Abba will watch over us from *Shamayim*. We are not alone."

This, the two older sons thought, was the right moment to clarify the mysteries that had arisen during the week of mourning.

"Ima," said Chezky, "maybe you didn't notice, but one day last week a stranger came to the house. He looked like a businessman. He said that he was looking for Abba. He spoke English, and when I told him that Abba was *niftar* a few days before, he seemed to get upset and left in a hurry."

"Well?" his mother asked.

"We thought… maybe you know what it was all about." Chezky felt slightly disappointed at his mother's lack of interest.

"I have no idea," she said. "So many people came…"

"And there was someone else," Avreimi added. "Some sort of strange Russian—he looked like a *ba'al teshuvah*—who asked if Abba had ever been involved in archeology."

"Enough, boys!" their mother said in sudden anger. Her eyes filled with tears. "I don't know who they were, and that's that. Abba was *niftar*, and you're busy with nonsense…"

Avreimi and Chezky were taken aback. They had certainly not intended to distress their mother, heaven forbid. Hastily they returned to the previous topic of conversation, though the strained atmosphere lingered for several long moments.

"Did you see how Ima started crying?" Avreimi asked his brother in a remorseful tone as they waited for the bus some ninety minutes later. "We'll have to drop the whole subject. It only distresses her."

"Her reaction surprised me," Chezky agreed. But he had come to a different conclusion than his brother. "It was a mistake to bring up the subject so soon. Everything is still too raw, and the wounds are still open. We'll have to wait a little."

Avreimi didn't answer, but he understood all too well what Chezky was saying. His brother did not intend to stand down. He would investigate this matter to his satisfaction.

Chezky had smelled money. And when it came to things like that, "attorney" Chezky Kohlberg was not in the habit of giving up that easily.

France, 5704 / 1944

German soldiers arrived at the house in remarkably short order. They knocked on the front door powerfully and rapidly, leaving those within no choice but to respond. Leaning on his stick, Antoine limped toward the door and opened it halfway.

"*Bonjour*," he said in French. His expression was shuttered.

There were three of them: Gestapo soldiers armed with submachine guns. Their leader had a long, narrow face and steel-cold eyes. Antoine hoped that his own face did not betray the deathly fright that filled every cell in his body. He felt as if he were suffocating. His right hand, the one that grasped the doorknob, trembled uncontrollably.

"*Guten morgen*," the Nazi officer replied in haughty German.

Antoine waited fearfully for the uninvited visitor to speak further. He was acutely aware of the enormous danger into which he had placed himself and his family these past four years. Though his aid to the Resistance was capable of plunging them all into terrible tragedy, there was no question in his mind that he was doing the right thing. The despised Germans had invaded his beloved country and were ruling it with a heavy hand. Many Frenchmen had chosen to bow their heads, go on with their comfortable lives, and hope for better days. There were others who actively cooperated with the conquerors in the most degraded and treasonous fashion. Only a few dared raise the banner of rebellion, to fight the enemy and safeguard the tattered remnant of national pride.

The Gestapo—Germany's secret police—had been relentless in hunting down members of this underground movement. But now, in the wake of the successful action outside Lyon, the Nazis had gone truly berserk and had launched a manhunt of unprecedented proportions.

"We are searching for a band of five terrorists," the Gestapo officer said, exhibiting an unexpected knowledge of French. "We have information that says they were in this region. Have you seen them?"

Antoine shook his head in the negative.

"Have you heard anything about them? Is anyone talking about them in the village?"

"No."

"Are you aware of the punishment for concealing or aiding enemies of the regime?"

Antoine tightened his jaw and did not reply.

"The punishment is death, for himself and his entire family." The Gestapo captain raised his voice and leveled an icy look at the Frenchman.

Antoine did not say a word. In the kitchen, his wife continued with shaking hands to chop vegetables for a salad. The children huddled close together in fear.

"I will ask you again." The officer lowered his voice and spoke with menacing slowness. "Did you see the five terrorists who blew up the railroad bridge near Lyon a week ago, or do you have knowledge of their whereabouts?"

"No," said Antoine. "I have neither seen them nor heard anything about them."

"With your kind permission, Monsieur, we will search the house," the captain said. Antoine moved slightly away from the door, and the soldiers passed him to go inside.

The Gestapo men went through every room, even climbing up to the empty attic that had once housed Antoine's sister. They maintained a polite demeanor, punctuating their remarks with *"bitte"* ("please") or *"antschuldigung"* ("pardon"). But Antoine knew that this courtesy was just a thin veneer covering a bestial cruelty that might burst forth at any moment, without warning, to destroy everything within reach.

For ten long, nerve-wracking minutes, the armed soldiers circulated through the house and found nothing. They checked the courtyard and peered over the side of the seaward cliff. Finally, the captain ordered his men to return to their truck. He himself remained standing near the well. He addressed Antoine, who stood with his back to the front door.

"People have mentioned your name in connection with the fugitives," the officer said. "The name 'Antoine' has been turning up in more and more reports from the Paris branch. Did you know that?"

Antoine leaned on his stick with both hands and lifted his eyes to the German. "That's simply not true," he said.

"So there is no truth in all these rumors?" the Nazi asked with ominous dryness.

"I am an honest French citizen," Antoine said. "It's no secret that I am not happy that you conquered my country, but I am not acting against the law."

The long line of socks—one red pair and five blue pairs—still hung on the clothesline. The Nazi stuck out his hand and toyed with them abstractedly, making them sway lightly. "Then you are not hiding the fugitives anywhere, and you do not know where they are? Is that true?"

The Frenchman gazed bravely into the Nazi's frightening eyes. "I did not see five fugitives, and I've heard nothing about them," he said woodenly.

The German inclined his head, his face devoid of expression. "Have a pleasant day." And he left the courtyard, closing the iron gate behind him.

The army vehicle started up with a noisy roar. Antoine stayed where he was a bit longer, watching the truck retreat into the distance in a cloud of smoke. Then he turned and went back into the house.

His wife was still standing in the same frozen position near the counter. Though she heard her husband open the door and walk in, she did not turn toward him. She was held fast in the grip of shock, eyes staring at a fixed point through the kitchen window.

She wholeheartedly supported her husband's activities. Her hatred for the Germans was no less potent than his, but the past few minutes had frightened her to death. This was not the first time Gestapo and SS men had visited their home. But it was the first time they'd come when, mere meters beneath their feet, in the cellar, five "dangerous terrorists" were hidden.

With a sigh, Antoine sank into a chair. What did the Nazis know? What was the reason behind the room-to-room search, so different from the other occasions? The officer had mentioned hearing a rumor that Antoine aided the underground Resistance. People said all sorts of things. The five men would be leaving soon, but this was beginning to pose a serious danger not only to himself, but also to his wife and children. The Nazis would have no pity on anyone if, heaven forbid, his actions ever came to light…

It was the Resistance group that secretly made sure he had a steady supply of gasoline for the Citroen, which was designated not for family outings but for operational needs. When fighting a hopeless battle against a cruel invading force, mobility could spell saved lives. Such as right now, for example, Antoine thought as he drove down the sloping road that led to the center of the village.

Jean's small smithy was located in an ancient stone building right behind the LaMarse family's dairy. The blacksmith's motorcycle was resting against the fence, announcing that he was in his workshop.

Antoine parked his car and went in. He was greeted by the sound of a hammer pounding an anvil. Jean was trying to straighten out a twisted cartwheel. The furnace emitted enormous heat, and from time to time he paused to mop his brow.

"*Bonjour!*" Antoine called from the doorway.

Jean turned slowly to face him. "*Bonjour*," he said in a surprised tone. Clearly, he wondered why his friend had come to him today. The two were careful not to meet or to be seen in one another's company—especially in sensitive times like these, with five of France's most wanted fugitives hiding in one of their cellars.

Jean had already passed the house on his motorcycle and seen the six pairs of socks fluttering on the clothesline. Now they must wait patiently for instructions to arrive. Papers might be prepared, providing the fugitives with new identities that would allow them to remain in France and blend into the population. Or the organization's leaders might prefer to smuggle them out through the Pyrenees mountain range into Spain, where the Nazis were not in power. Or, as they had done on other occasions, they might be sent by boat across the Channel to England.

"Some Germans paid me a visit today," Antoine said.

The blacksmith looked at his friend in alarm.

"They didn't find anything," Antoine reassured him. "But the captain said that there are rumors that I've been aiding the Resistance. He said that people are saying all sorts of things."

"That's not good," Jean muttered.

"Tell them that things have to move faster. The ground is starting to burn beneath our feet," Antoine said, ending their talk.

Hundreds of kilometers from Antoine's village, on a cold, stone floor between thick walls that oozed with moisture, sat a young man with a tormented expression on his face. The cold and the pain were making him shiver uncontrollably. The thin straw pallet on which his jailers had tossed him eons ago was soaked with his blood. His mind was foggy and he kept sinking into nightmares. He appeared far older than his 25 years.

The past week, since his arrest by the Gestapo, had been filled with harsh interrogations and nonstop torture.

"Maurice!" his interrogators screamed. "Where did your friends go? Where are they planning to hide?"

There was no point in hiding the identities of his five friends. The Germans were well aware of the Resistance terror cell, which struck from time to time in places calculated to cause maximum damage. The cell—comprised of six members, the oldest 27 years of age and the youngest only 19—had quickly instilled fear into the German authorities. It excelled in its choice of targets, in the accuracy of its attack, and in the preparation of its escape routes. Its operatives would appear as though out of a fog, strike with surgical precision, and disappear without a trace. They derailed trains filled with German soldiers. They set fire to grain silos that had been confiscated from French farmers, slated for transportation to Germany. They blew up gasoline depots that served the Wehrmacht—German army—tanks.

This was the first time that a member of the daring cell had been captured, and the Nazis were sparing no pains in their attempts to extract information from him. Maurice's left leg was fractured, but his captors had neither had it set nor provided medical treatment. On the contrary, they directed their blows at the injured leg in order to maximize the prisoner's suffering.

"Maurice!" the interrogators screamed in his ear. "Which direction did they take? Who helped them escape? Start talking!"

The prison in southeast Paris was one of the largest in France and resembled a well-fortified garrison. With the German conquest, it had been turned into the Gestapo's primary incarceration center, into which they tossed captured British agents, Allied pilots whose planes had been downed, and members of the French underground Resistance. Conditions in the prison were horrific, and executions were a matter of course. Maurice's agonized cries could be heard night and day. His Nazi interrogators tortured him until he lost consciousness, and then waited until he had recovered to start all over again.

"Where were you supposed to run to? Who helped you in planning the attack? Who found you a place to hide?"

The cell's last attack had been bigger than any of its predecessors, and caused the Germans not only tremendous damage but also significant loss of face. The Germans regularly robbed and took advantage of France in every possible way: they had taken control of the coal and iron industry, confiscated huge quantities of farmers' crops, and used French political prisoners as a form of cheap forced labor. Trains made their way daily from the mines near Lyon, headed for Germany, filled with ore and minerals to feed the German industrial war machine.

And then, a week ago, all that had stopped. The sole railroad track exiting the area of the mines was demolished. It would take long months to restore it to functionality.

The members of the Resistance cell had managed to reach the bridge despite the heavy patrol units guarding the area, attach a large pack of explosives to it, and then vanish as though the earth had swallowed them up. Maurice, who had broken his leg, urged his companions to leave without him. He had attempted to find concealment in the area, but was quickly spotted and thrown into jail.

"Where are your friends? Which direction did they escape to? Give us a direction, give us the name of someone who helped them, and we'll stop this torture."

Maurice bit his lips until they ran with blood, but he didn't say a word. He preferred to die rather than betray his friends. The Nazis knew this, and they knew, too, that even they were incapable of extracting information from a corpse. They were careful, therefore, to keep Maurice alive. They explained to him that he would not have the privilege of being redeemed by death. They would continue torturing him until he decided to open his mouth and tell them everything he knew.

The old Citroen climbed the mountain slope easily. Antoine returned home with a perceptible sense of relief. Jean the blacksmith would pass his message on to the Resistance people, and they would come up with a new hiding place for the terror cell. The noose was beginning to tighten around their necks, and that wasn't healthy for anyone.

A herd of cows crossed the narrow road, forcing Antoine to brake and wait patiently. The war would end soon, he mused. And then he would take his whole family on a big trip around the country. When the Nazis departed, France would once again be a proud, free nation. That would be the time to bring to justice all the traitors and collaborators, and to raise high all the patriots who loved their land and had spilled their blood in battle against the cruel conqueror.

At long last, the road was clear and Antoine continued on his way. Two hours had passed since he had left home. He had grabbed the opportunity of being in the village to stock up on some staples.

Some twenty meters before he reached the house, he began to have a sense that something wasn't right. An eerie silence reigned. There was no sound of children playing. An icy tentacle of fear stole into his heart.

Antoine sped up and took the last curve. The sight that met his eyes curdled the blood in his veins. His hands turned to stone as they gripped the steering wheel in a panic. A sense of terrible tragedy began to consume him. The courtyard of his home was filled with Nazi soldiers, all of them armed with bayoneted rifles.

A second glance showed him that they were standing in a tightly-packed circle around the house, as though forming a human blockade. In the courtyard entrance, near the iron gate, stood the Gestapo captain with the cold-as-steel eyes. He watched the approaching Citroen through narrowed eyes. He wore a faint, sarcastic smile, like a bloodthirsty hunting dog with the scent of prey in its nostrils.

Jerusalem, 5772 / 2011

The bombshell fell on the Kohlberg family on Motzaei Shabbos.

It had been their first Shabbos since the *shivah*. All the children had come to Yerushalayim to spend it in their parents' home—which, sadly, would henceforth be known as "Ima's house."

At the Shabbos meals, everyone tried to maintain a joyous atmosphere. And they were fairly successful, though their father's absence was keenly felt. They sang *zemiros*, listened to *divrei Torah* from their little brothers, and kept up a lively conversation around the table, just as they used to do in the good old days…eons ago… just two weeks ago.

Avreimi, it seemed to Chezky, had already forgotten the surprising events that had cropped up during their days of mourning: the weird visit by the English-speaking stranger, the Russian *ba'al te-shuvah's* assertion that their father could have been a very rich man, and his question about whether their father had ever interested himself in archeology. But Chezky had not forgotten.

He was waiting for the right moment to raise the issue for discussion, but knew that he must proceed with caution and patience. If Avreimi sensed his excitement over getting to the bottom of this, it would arouse his immediate opposition. The rare spirit of trust and cooperation that had sprung up between them during this painful period in their lives was fragile and delicate, and liable to shatter from the slightest pressure.

He wondered if Avreimi, steeped as he was in the world of Torah, had an inkling about the future that faced them. From now on, the family would require every possible source of income that it could find. Expenses would rise and income would diminish. Their father's salary would no longer be deposited in their bank account each month, and their mother, too, was considering cutting back her work hours in order to devote more time to the children. There were, *baruch Hashem*, people willing to concern themselves with weddings for Ari, Miri, and the other children, as per the well-known maxim — all of Israel are responsible for one another. But the household's daily needs would grow, and it was still unclear how much debt remained from his wedding, and Avreimi's. Besides, what justification did they have for using charity funds if there existed a property or source of income that the family could use?

In the end, it was Avreimi who broached the subject. As they walked home from shul after Shacharis, he asked Chezky to refrain from raising the topic that had caused their mother so much distress—to the point of tears. "Chezky, I don't think it's worthwhile asking Ima about all those things again," he said, speaking quietly so that their younger brothers wouldn't hear.

They walked on without a word for a few minutes. Chezky was lost in a thoughtful silence.

"The whole story sounds very strange," Avreimi said at last.

"Which one?" Chezky aimed for a matter-of-fact tone, but his heart leaped.

"I don't know… that Russian *ba'al teshuvah*, and the man who came looking for Abba and then ran away… It was all so strange…"

"Want to hear something?" Ari broke in. "I suddenly realize that we didn't—I mean, we *really* didn't—know Abba."

"Believe me…" Avreimi and Chezky said in one voice.

"Not only just now," Ari went on. "Much more than that. Where was he from? Where did he grow up? Who were his parents? Do you realize that we simply do not know a thing about him?"

"Well, Abba wasn't a big talker…"

"We had no aunts and uncles, no cousins—just one distant relative who'd already passed away. Doesn't that seem a little odd to you?"

"What is odd is that, until today, we didn't think it was odd," Avreimi remarked.

"Maybe it's time to find out," said Ari.

"Leave Ima out of it," Avreimi warned.

"Ima is definitely out," Chezky agreed. "But maybe one of Abba's friends knew him when he was young…"

"Ai, ai, ai, R' Shlaimeleh, R' Shlaimeleh," R' Zerach chanted in a sorrowful voice to the three brothers.

The idea of asking him had been Avreimi's. "You know who knew Abba well?" he had told his brothers on their way to shul for Minchah. "R' Zerach."

"R' Zerach, the *maggid shiur* at the *shtiebel*?"

"Yes. He knew Abba for many years. Abba once told me that they learned together in *kollel* after he was married."

"Ai, ai, ai… Your father was the kind of Jew you don't see every day," R' Zerach continued in a tone of eulogy. "He really didn't talk much about himself."

"When did you first meet him?" Avreimi asked.

R' Zerach calculated quickly in his head. "If I'm not mistaken, it's been nearly thirty years. We learned together in *kollel* after he got married. I was a bit older than he was. I was actually the one who got him into the *kollel* and helped him get acclimated. After all, he had come without…"

"Without what?" Chezky prompted, as R' Zerach searched for the word he wanted.

"Without a home, without a family, without roots," R' Zerach finished uncomfortably.

"What do you mean?"

"Listen," R' Zerach said, as though justifying something. "A child who comes from an orphanage…"

"An orphanage?" Three pairs of eyes grew round.

Now it was R' Zerach's turn to be surprised. "What—you didn't know that he grew up in a children's home?"

France, 5704 / 1944

ANTOINE BRAKED ABRUPTLY, SEIZED BY A DEATHLY FEAR. Dreadful questions flitted through his mind, one after the other: What had they done with his wife? And the children? What about the five fugitives? Had the Nazis uncovered their hiding place?

The Gestapo officer, in his long coat and hat with the distinctive swastika, approached Antoine with a face that gave nothing away but boded ill.

"Once again, for the second time today: *bonjour*," he said, with a cold courtesy that sent a shiver down Antoine's back.

"*Bonjour*," Antoine replied almost inaudibly. His face was white as death and his heart was pounding with terror.

"Would you be so kind as to invite me into your home?" the Nazi asked with a haughty smile, enjoying the Frenchman's distress. "As a proper German, I didn't want to enter before the master of the house returned."

Antoine moved toward the door on shaky legs, with the officer right behind him. Three armed soldiers accompanied them, the staccato of their footsteps menacing.

"They tell me that you have a most interesting house," the captain told Antoine as they walked inside, his manner as nonchalant as if they were discussing the weather. "I understand that you have a very unusual cellar under the floor."

Antoine did not answer. His face froze and his lips began to tremble.

The officer strode ahead toward the kitchen. "And they tell me that there is even a chute leading from the cellar up to the larder beside the kitchen. What is it used for?"

"It's... for bringing up bottles of wine, and cheese," Antoine said hoarsely.

The Nazi swiveled abruptly around on his heel and stared directly into Antoine's eyes. "Is there wine and cheese in the cellar?" he barked.

"Yes... And pickled olives, and raisins..."

"Is there anything down there apart from food?"

"No."

The officer leaned on the wooden table and studied Antoine through narrowed eyes. "I would be pleased, monsieur, if you would honor me and my soldiers with a bottle of fine wine," he said at last.

"You may t-take whatever you wish," Antoine stammered.

"No, no, no." The Nazi's steely eyes laughed. "As a self-respecting Frenchman—a Frenchman who knows how to receive his guests—I'd expect *you* to choose the bottle for us. After all, we Germans are not as expert regarding wines as are you, our French neighbors."

"I don't have especially fine wines," Antoine said. "This has not been a good year in the vineyards. Grapevines don't like war."

A flash of anger showed momentarily in the German's eyes. At once, he regained control of himself. "I insist that you choose the wine for us," he said, raising his voice. "Come, let us go down to the cellar. I understand that the entrance is at the edge of the courtyard, near the cliff that faces the sea. Correct?"

Maurice, the prisoner in cell number 542 in the men's division, woke up and opened his swollen eyes a crack. A rare ray of sunlight had found its way through the aperture near the cell's ceiling and crept down the damp wall opposite. He closed his eyes again. Something was odd, but his sense of surprise was soon lost among the clouds of his confusion.

Several hours later, he woke again. The stray line of sun had traveled to a different corner of his cell.

Maurice's mind was foggy. Pain wracked him without a stop and a feverish delirium blurred the lines between reality and illusion. Nevertheless, he sensed that something was different. He tried with all his might to focus—and finally realized what it was. It was mid-afternoon, and he was still in his cell.

This was something that had not occurred since his arrival. Each day, he had been dragged out before dawn and taken to the interrogation chamber in the prison's basement. He had routinely been tossed back into his cell, tortured and bleeding, late at night. Today, no one had come for him. He had spent all day in his cell.

He fell back into a blessed sleep that helped him forget all pain and sorrow. Sometime later, there was a loud knock on the metal door. One of the jailers brought him a bowl of thin soup, two slices of black bread and a full jug of water—a distinct improvement over the meager menu that had been his lot in recent days.

The night passed, punctuated by nightmares and terrors. The next morning, a doctor entered his cell. He set the prisoner's broken leg, bandaged his wounds, and injected him with painkillers.

Maurice spent two more days alone in his cell. The jailer who brought his food was the only living soul he saw. The ache in his body began to subside, and his tortured mind cleared slightly. The male nurse who worked in the prison clinic—a Belgian political prisoner—revealed the bitter truth when he came to change Maurice's bandages: the five members of his Resistance cell had been murdered by Gestapo men who had discovered their hiding place in a cellar in a small village near the Atlantic Coast. The Resistance member who'd provided the place of concealment, a man by the name of Antoine, lost his life as well—but not before he managed to kill a Gestapo officer and two other Nazi soldiers.

Antoine's wife had been arrested and shipped to a concentration camp. Their four children were placed in a local orphans' home under German supervision, where they would merit an "education" far better than their criminal parents had provided until now.

Israel, 5772 / 2011

The old strip mall in the southern town, situated between the municipal building and the post office, appeared particularly shabby in the waning light of the setting sun. A few of its stores were abandoned, locked and barred, but even those that remained open showed no appreciable signs of customer activity. The slanted metal lattice that was meant to protect the customers from the harsh Negev sun was peeling and spotted with rust, and the nearby sprinkler had long since dried up. On a bench in the almost moribund square sat several old men with downcast eyes, trying to kill time with the aid of cigarette smoke and cheap alcohol.

The silver Mazda 3 formed a sharp contrast to the glaring poverty on every side. The rented car advanced hesitantly around the square, as though seeking something. Finally, it pulled up near the bench-sitters. The window rolled down with a silent electric sigh.

"Excuse me. Where can I find the 'Ohr Dovid' shul?" Avreimi Kohlberg asked from the passenger seat.

One of the men lifted tired eyes, taking brief pleasure in the blast of cool air from the car's air-conditioning system. "Ohr Dovid?" he repeated. "Go straight on until after the municipal building, yes? There you'll see a community center, okay? Continue on a little after that… and you'll see Ohr Dovid."

Avreimi thanked the man, and the car started forward again. "I told you it was there," said Chezky, at the wheel.

Ohr Dovid was not the main synagogue, but one of dozens of smaller shuls scattered throughout the town, most of whose residents were mitzvah-observant and lovers of tradition. It was obvious that the shul was not blessed with means, but it had been tended with devoted hands. A strip of red velvet was carefully spread over the neatly-arranged wooden benches. Gilded sconces with memorial plaques were suspended from the ornate ceiling, and embroidered tapestries hung on the walls. Here, too, an air of sadness clung to the worshipers. Long years of life under threat of missile attack, combined with the difficulties of scratching out a living and the travails of day-to-day existence, had left their mark on the veteran residents.

The *chazzan* warbled at the front of the room, and the congregation offered its throaty response. Minchah in this place looked very different from the energetic version to be found in the *shtieblach* of Jerusalem. The Kohlberg brothers had come in search of a man known as "Chacham Reuven." His wife had told them on the phone, in an accent that they'd struggled to understand, that he worked all day but could be found in the evenings at the Ohr Dovid *beit knesset*.

When Minchah was over, the *gabbai*—an elderly fellow with a large crocheted *kippah* that covered his balding crown—called: "Chacham Reuven—*b'kavod*!"

One of the worshipers stood up. He was a man of advanced years, wearing an ancient suit and a hat that had seen better days. He took his place at the head of one of the tables and began reading and explaining *mishnayos* to his drowsy audience in a thick Iraqi accent. Immediately after the *shiur*, Ma'ariv commenced. Later, Avreimi and Chezky approached the man and introduced themselves.

"*Shalom Aleichem*," Chacham Reuven said, smiling warmly. "You are R' Shlomo's sons? My wife told me that you called."

The shul emptied. A sorrowful expression appeared on Chacham Reuven's lined face. "I heard that your father passed from this world in the prime of his life," he said. "Hashem gives, and Hashem takes away... May Hashem's Name be blessed. And may Heaven comfort you."

Avreimi and Chezky accepted the consoling words with a nod.

"How many children did he have?"

"There are eight of us," Avreimi replied.

"Ah, *bli ayin hara*!" Chacham Reuven exclaimed. "May His Name be extolled forever! Your father merited seeing a righteous and blessed generation. I remember traveling to his wedding in Yerushalayim, many, many years ago. It was a long trip—several hours. What did he die from? Was he ill, *rachamana litzlan?*"

"No. He died suddenly of a heart attack."

"Ah! May Hashem have mercy… What did he do? Did he learn Torah?"

"Our father worked in computers and had set times to learn Torah."

"As it says: *Yafeh Talmud Torah im derech eretz, she'yegias sheneihem meshakachas avon,*" Chacham Reuven chanted in a musical voice. "Your father was always a good and likeable child."

"Actually, we wanted to hear a bit about his childhood," Chezky said. "Where did he come from, did he have any family…"

Chacham Reuven—R' Reuven Dalel—had, in his younger years, worked as a counselor in a Jerusalem orphan's home during the period that the boy Shlomo Kohlberg resided there.

The *gabbai* began turning off lights, preparatory to locking the shul. Chacham Reuven invited the two brothers to his home nearby. He walked slowly, showing them the crater where a Kassam rocket had fallen in his yard. Miraculously, it had caused no injuries.

"Your father was a polite and engaging child," Chacham Reuven told the brothers, after his wife had set cups of tea and a plate of cookies on the table. "He didn't fight with the other boys and didn't talk back to me or the housefather. He went to bed on time and woke up early."

"He had no relatives?" Avreimi asked. "Did anyone come visit him?"

"He had no one, and that gave him great pain. You should know that not all the children in the home were orphans. There were some who had a father or mother, and others who had two parents at home who were unable to raise them. Those children would go home occasionally, or the parents would come see them. Your father would look at them in anguish. No one ever visited him. He was alone in the world."

"What else can your honor remember about him?" Chezky asked.

"He loved to learn Torah." A good-natured smile spread across the elderly man's face. "He read the *pesukim* nicely, in a clear voice. *Baruch Hashem*, he merited being *chozer b'teshuvah*."

A moment of electrified silence filled the room.

"What do you mean, 'merited being *chozer b'teshuvah?*'" Avreimi asked apprehensively.

"He returned wholeheartedly to his Father in Heaven. Perhaps because of the things he learned as a child."

"What do you mean, *'chozer b'teshuvah'*?" Chezky echoed his brother's question. "Until what age did you know him?"

"He was with us until the age of five," said Chacham Reuven. "And then they took him away. I didn't see him for several years. He went someplace else. One day, he stopped me in the street. He said, 'Mr. Dalel, don't you recognize me?' I looked at him and didn't know who he was. He said, 'I'm Shlomo Kohlberg. How are you, Mr. Dalel?' After that, I didn't see him for many years. Then, suddenly, an invitation came in the mail. He was getting married. I went to his wedding in Yerushalayim. Suddenly I saw that he was religious, with a beard. How happy that made me!"

"Just a second," Avreimi asked in agitation. "Your honor said that Abba was not religious before he got married?"

"No, he was not *dati*," said Chacham Reuven, oblivious to the turmoil his words were rousing in the two brothers. "He was a soldier. In uniform. Without a *kippah*."

"A soldier? In uniform?" Chezky was floored. "And he was not religious?"

"Certainly not. How could he be? They took him to a kibbutz."

"Enough! Enough! I can't take anymore," Avreimi whispered to Chezky. "Let's go home."

M<small>AURICE SPENT ANOTHER WEEK IN PRISON. MERCIFULLY,</small> his jailers' attitude toward him improved somewhat. The interrogations did not resume, the food came in reasonable quantities and he was taken out every day to walk in the courtyard, for a breath of fresh air and the feel of the sun on his face.

One morning, his cell door opened and a jailer tossed him a set of clean clothes. "Get dressed and follow me," he ordered. In the prison's administrative office waited a slender man in a gray suit. His sharp, narrow features made him resemble a rodent. The man introduced himself as a local attorney and told Maurice that he had been assigned to represent him at his upcoming trial.

"I'm glad to see that the Germans are treating you well," the lawyer said. "I understand that you are receiving medical attention and reasonable treatment, as befits a political prisoner."

Maurice threw a contemptuous glance at the French rat, but didn't bother correcting him. Now he understood the reason behind the sudden improvement in the conditions of his imprisonment. The Germans simply wanted to make sure he would appear to advantage at the show trial they were preparing for him. And this lawyer was cooperating with them... yet another despicable Frenchman who'd sold his soul to the Nazi ruler. Why did he need a lawyer? To enable the accursed Nazis to show the French populace that they afforded ostensible justice to members of the Resistance?

The lawyer seemed unimpressed by Maurice's attitude. He explained the situation: Because all his fellow cell members were dead, the Germans intended to saddle him with the full blame for the explosion—despite the fact that Maurice had only stood watch from afar and had not participated in blowing up the railroad bridge.

"And finally," the lawyer concluded, "the fact that you are a Jew, and not only that but also a German citizen who emigrated from Germany to France, does not play in your favor and may make your sentence more severe."

Maurice chuckled bitterly. "So if I'm sentenced to just one death sentence, does that mean I got off easy? I don't think I'll need your assistance to get to the gallows, sir. I believe I can manage alone."

"The court consists of German judges, but it is administered in accordance with international wartime law," the attorney said, ignoring the barb. "If we can cobble together some sort of defense, there's a chance—albeit a slim one—that instead of the firing squad, you'll receive a life sentence with hard labor or something along those lines."

"I prefer to die with my head high than to be defended by a traitor to his country and his countrymen," Maurice spat back in sudden anger.

The meeting in the prison office lasted for more than an hour. Maurice's open hostility toward the lawyer gradually abated, but he was still filled with a contempt that he did not hesitate to express from time to time toward this collaborator and all his ilk. The rat-faced Frenchman aroused his disgust. He was the Germans' indentured servant, a servile, obsequious tool being used by them to crush his country's pride and the pride of freedom-loving people everywhere.

This was the type of person with whom France would have to

deal later, Maurice thought—after she achieved victory over the Nazi beast. He would not be alive to see those days, but the heirs to the Resistance, the citizens of free France, would know how to lay their hands on those despicable traitors and make sure they received their just desserts.

The meeting ended, and the attorney began collecting his papers. Suddenly, his manner became different, more discreet. He looked directly into Maurice's eyes and whispered two short sentences.

Maurice stared at him in total shock.

The lawyer continued to whisper, as the prisoner watched him with a strange expression. Maurice froze for an instant, and then recovered. He stood up and moved away from the lawyer in loathing.

"You scum!" he screamed. "You and all collaborators. You should be ashamed of yourselves! Traitor!"

The lawyer snapped his briefcase shut and began striding rapidly toward the door, shoulders hunched defensively. Maurice followed in a fury. "Get out of here!" He pushed him with both hands. "I don't want to see you again!"

The lawyer hastened into the corridor. The two German jailers, watching through a small window in the door, burst out laughing at the diverting spectacle of the prisoner pushing and beating his ridiculous lawyer, while the latter did his best to ward off his client's blows.

The jailers returned Maurice to his cell, prodding him with their cudgels all the way. Tomorrow they'd have the pleasure of a repeat performance, they assured one another. There was another meeting with his attorney scheduled for the prisoner then. It would be worth their while peeking in again for some more free entertainment.

Maurice's night in his narrow cell passed like all the others before it: in bone-chilling cold. The thin blanket with which he had been provided did virtually nothing to retain his body heat. His fractured leg, which had just begun to knit, had received a powerful kick from one of the jailers and again ached unbearably.

But it was neither the cold nor the pain that kept him awake that night. The collaborator-lawyer's last sentences ran through his head repeatedly, giving him no rest. He turned them over and over in his mind and made feverish plans. He had attacked the Frenchman with the rat face and sent him off with curses, but the matter didn't end there. On the contrary—the main event still lay ahead.

Early the next morning, Maurice woke to the sound of a key turning in the iron door. Apparently, he had dropped off to sleep at some point during the night. The jailer shoved his breakfast tray into the cell, marking the start of another day of preparation for his trial. At noon, he would be taken out for his twenty-minute stroll through the prison courtyard, and in the afternoon his lawyer would be back to confer with him about his defense.

Or rather, that was the day the Germans had planned for him.

Jerusalem, 5772 / 2011

The Kohlberg brothers returned to Jerusalem in early evening. Their spirits were low. A gloomy silence had filled the car for most of the journey up from the south.

This was a huge mistake, Avreimi thought. *Why did we ever start digging into Abba's life? With whose permission? Why expose what he had chosen to conceal all his life?*

It was Chezky who was to blame—as usual. He had pushed them both into this doubtful adventure. The smell of money always made him lose all sense of proportion. Another thing that he had doubtless learned over there, in his school of *"chukas hagoyim"*...

Chezky, too, chose silence. His hands gripped the wheel and his gaze remained riveted on the road, but his thoughts were on the chain of troubling revelations about their father. It seemed as if every stop they made along the road of Abba's life came with another disturbing surprise. It had started yesterday, on Motzaei Shabbos, when R' Zerach, the *maggid shiur*, unwittingly let drop the information that their father had been reared in an orphans' home. And now Chacham Reuven had innocently revealed that he had met Abba in his army years without a *kippah*. Had his father

---
* See earlier note, pg. 16.

really been a *chiloni*—a secular Jew? Had he done *teshuvah*? It made no sense! Could Chacham Reuven's mind have become confused? Maybe he had confused Abba with someone else. Abba, growing up on a kibbutz… how absurd!

And where was Ima in all of this? How much did *she* know about Abba's life? Add it all to that Russian who'd come to see them as they sat *shivah*, with a story about archeology… and the English-speaking stranger who fled when he heard that Abba had died. And that wasn't all. To the list of mysterious events could be added what had happened that morning at the Jerusalem Orphans' Home… Had it really happened today? Yes, it was only this morning! It had been the home's administrator who'd directed them to Chacham Reuven and provided his address.

Wow! Hard to believe the meeting had occurred only that morning. So many things had happened since then…

Twelve hours earlier, at 8 a.m., Chezky had called Avreimi to tell him that he would pick him up in the car at nine. There were no law-school classes on Sunday. The night before, in the wake of their conversation with R' Zerach, the brothers had decided to devote the day to a deeper investigation of their father's life.

"Car?" Avreimi had asked on the phone. "Since when do you have a car?"

At that hour of the morning, neither of them had had a clue that their investigation would take them to a southern town in the afternoon. Their plan was to stay in Jerusalem, where the orphanage was located.

"I rented a car for the day," Chezky replied.

"What for? Do you have a problem with taking a bus?"

"Time is too valuable to waste on buses."

"Really, Chezky," Avreimi had scoffed. "It seems to me you simply want to have some fun. Don't forget that we're still in our *sheloshim*. What will people say if they see Kohlberg's sons riding around in rental cars?"

"Do me a favor." Chezky's voice hardened. "It's been a long time since I've cared what people say about me, okay?"

"Yes. I know that," Avreimi said bitterly.

Chezky tried to soften his tone. "Don't be like that, Avreimi. Stop making such a fuss over everything. This won't cost you a shekel, okay? I'm paying for the car."

"What am I going to do with you?" Avreimi asked in resignation.

Several hours later, when the pair found themselves driving south in the heat of the day, Chezky naturally did not ignore the sterling opportunity to tease his brother. "Well, did we need a car or not?"

Avreimi, of course, had a ready response: "As far as I know, there's public transportation available to take us anywhere."

"So get on the bus, if you want. I'll take the car!"

But at nine a.m., when Chezky reached Modiin Illit and honked outside Avreimi's house, he had been wearing a smile.

"They didn't have any small cars, so they upgraded me to a Mazda-3," he announced. "There's not even 500 kilometers on this car. Practically brand-new!"

His older brother scanned the vehicle with the usual frown, but he was honest enough to admit to himself that he, too, preferred a drive in an air-conditioned new car to a swaying, crowded, sweltering ride in a bus.

"Okay. Let's go to Yerushalayim." Avreimi slipped into the passenger seat, buckled himself in and leaned back.

"Full speed ahead," Chezky said, and pressed on the gas.

A PALE WINTER SUN SHONE OVER FROZEN PARIS. THE PRISON courtyard was completely deserted. The jailers, interrogators, and administration preferred to remain in their well-heated offices and to avoid as far as possible setting foot outdoors.

At precisely noon, Maurice was taken from his cell for his daily walk. He paced the well-worn route, from the door of the prison laundry to the northern watchtower and back again.

At 12:15, a powerful blast shook the prison compound. An explosive device had detonated behind the concrete walls, opening up a large hole. The shock wave was felt throughout the area. A thick cloud of dust and smoke lifted into the air, covering everything with a layer of debris and fragments of concrete.

For a few seconds, a deathlike silence held. Then, all at once, the air was filled with an ear-splitting cacophony of sound: the screams of the wounded, orders barked in German, and the thunder of submachine gunfire.

A moment later, a siren began to wail through the courtyard—a signal to all the jailers and guards to take up defensive positions in the face of a possible attack. Total chaos reigned in the smoke-filled courtyard. Soldiers and officers ran in all directions, out of control.

But before that, in the first seconds of confusion, there was one man who operated with complete calm. That man was Maurice. For him, the blast had come as no surprise. He had known about it since yesterday, when "rodent man"—the French lawyer assigned by the Germans—had met with him.

For a full hour, throughout their meeting, the attorney had absorbed Maurice's insults in silence. Near its conclusion, however, as he had begun collecting his papers, he had lowered his voice and told Maurice in a whisper: "I've come to rescue you. I am going to give you a number of instructions now. Afterward, you are to chase me out of here with blows and curses."

Maurice had gaped at him in utter bewilderment. The lawyer continued, "Tomorrow, when they let you out for your walk, there will be a large explosion behind the walls. Escape immediately to the small gate near the northern watchtower. Someone will be there to get you away."

Maurice had frozen in shock—but quickly recovered and did as the Frenchman had ordered. He began kicking and beating him, and chased him from the room to the amusement of his German jailers.

And now the explosion had taken place. A thought flashed through his mind: *Must reach the gate*! Under cover of the thick smoke, dust, and general confusion, Maurice limped the short distance. To his surprise—or perhaps not—the narrow gate stood wide open. Three German guards had been neutralized during the first few seconds after the blast, at the hands of two armed French Resistance fighters who, with perfect synchronization, had emerged from the stairwell of the building across the street.

There was no time for hellos or emotional reunions. The Resistance men, noting that Maurice was finding it difficult to walk, lifted him up and ran with him in their arms. A car was waiting for them, engine running. They opened the rear door, set Maurice inside and pushed in after him. The driver, a young Frenchman with blazing eyes, slammed his foot on the gas and the car shot forward.

Maurice's mind was empty of thought. He closed his eyes, letting his arms dangle limply at his sides as weakness engulfed him. The tension of the past 24 hours had imposed an enormous strain that had sapped every last ounce of his energy.

"Don't faint on me now." He heard, as though from a great distance, the voice of one of his Resistance friends. The fellow sprinkled water on Maurice's face, which revived him slightly.

The young driver was an expert at his job. The car moved with reckless speed, swallowing up the narrow streets and taking the sharp corners with a squeal of the brakes. Gripping the wheel with an iron hand, he navigated easily between the other vehicles and pedestrians. Every minute was critical. It would not take the jailers long to discover that the bird had flown from its cage. Within a short time, the Nazis would surround all of Paris with a tight ring of soldiers, and the streets would swarm with Gestapo and SS men who would scrupulously inspect every car.

"It's not possible to get you out of the city right now," the driver shouted at Maurice over the noise of the engine. "We're taking you to a hiding place that's been prepared for you. There's enough food, drink, and medicine for a week. You must not turn on a light or make a sound. If we can, we'll send you a doctor in a day or two; depends on the conditions of the search. We'll be back in a week. If they don't find you till then, we'll try to smuggle you out of France. Is all of that clear?"

Maurice nodded his head, and suddenly winced. A bump in the road had banged his broken leg against the door and sent a wave of pain shooting up to his brain.

The car swerved sharply into a narrow street and braked near an old and partially abandoned apartment building. The drive had indeed been short: this building was no more than two or three kilometers from the prison. The wailing sirens of police vehicles and ambulances racing toward the site of the explosion reached their ears clearly from every direction.

"Let's get you upstairs," one of the Resistance men said.

The two men and the driver carried Maurice to a squealing, ancient elevator that took him up to the building's sixth floor. There were no flats on this floor, only a low door that led into a small, concealed attic. The staircase stopped at the fifth floor, where it was sealed off by thick planks of lumber and reinforced steel bars. The approach to the attic, therefore, was only possible via elevator.

The Resistance fighters carried Maurice into the attic. This was a low space with a slanted ceiling. It contained a neatly made bed, several enamel jugs of water, and a large pile of fresh baguettes.

Only after he had been set down on the bed did Maurice realize that there was another person in the attic. It was the lawyer in the checked suit with the face of a rodent—the man who'd risked his life to free him from jail.

Tears of emotion filled Maurice's eyes. He tried to say something, but the Frenchman did not allow him to pour out what was in his heart. "Take care of yourself, and try not to get caught," he told Maurice with an affectionate thump on the shoulder, as he prepared to leave. "We can't go through this rigmarole a second time."

"*Merci beaucoup* (thank you very much)," said Maurice. The two words were far from sufficient to express the strength of his feelings. "And... I'm sorry about all the curses and insults."

A brief smile touched the attorney's troubled face. "That's all right, son," he said softly. "Watch out for yourself. *Vive la France* (long live France)!"

The lawyer and the three Resistance men went out, locking the attic door behind them. They descended the six floors, but before exiting the building one of them made sure to turn off the electricity for the elevator, to prevent anyone else from using it. Now there was no approach to the attic; the staircase was sealed and the elevator was out of order. If luck smiled on them, the boy would survive the next week.

"Drive a few blocks and then abandon the car," the attorney instructed the driver. He himself would return to the prison now, to the German lions' den, where he would continue to do what he had been doing for the past three years: pretending to collaborate with the conquering authorities.

He would, of course, have to feign surprise and shock at the escape of the prisoner he had been meant to represent. He would have to act furious over the success of the criminal Resistance fighters to rescue their friend from the gallows at the last moment. He would join his curses and tirades to those of the Germans—and hope that no Gestapo officer suspected him and decided to put him in the cell that had suddenly become available in the most unexpected way...

Iran, 5753 / 1993

Reza was exhausted and played out. For the past five hours, since seven that morning, he had been staring at the harbor through a pair of binoculars. His eyes were stinging and watery, and his back ached from sitting hunched over for so long. But despite the difficulty, he continued to watch the loading dock with great attention.

The Iranian student had been given a crash course in ships in advance of this mission, but he had learned much more over the past few days simply by watching. A complete and fascinating world had opened up before his eyes. The port operated like a well-oiled machine whose parts were synchronized to perfection.

He learned, for example, that it was not the ship's captain who sailed it into the harbor, but the navigator or pilot. This was usually a senior employee of the port authority, a sea captain by profession who had formerly been in charge of big ships. The pilot knew the harbor intimately. He knew the changing depths of its waters and its natural obstacles, and his job was to bring the ship safely to anchor in its proper berth. The pilot went out to meet the incoming ship in a speedboat that carried him quickly across the stretch of open water, and climbed aboard with the help of a rope ladder. Then he made his way to the bridge and took the wheel from the captain. From that point until the ship was securely tied up at the pier, he was in command.

During the final stage of the ship's approach, the engines were cut. The powerful engines were built for crossing an ocean, not for the slow and careful maneuvering necessary in a crowded harbor, which called for delicate adjustments and sharp turns. For this purpose, every port had a fleet of tugboats—extraordinarily strong and speedy motorboats. The big vessel was tied to one of these boats. In the case of an exceptionally large ship, two tugboats might be put into play, one at the bow and the other at the stern, to pull and push the ship alongside its proper platform. The sight never failed to enthrall Reza—seeing two tiny tugboats succeed in moving vessels tens or even hundreds of times larger than they were.

"Because we are searching for a shipping container," his handler had told him over the phone, "you will be able to disregard ships carrying bulk items such as wheat, millet, or coal, or ships bringing what is known in harbor lingo as 'general cargo' such as cars, lumber, machinery—anything not packed into a container. You are to focus only on ships carrying metal storage containers. Track these very well, so that you do not miss the specific cargo container that we're seeking."

And that was exactly what Reza was doing. The unloading dock for storage containers was directly ahead of him—about seven kilometers away. Except for several tall, narrow minarets poking into the sky, there was nothing blocking his line of vision. The surveillance called for enormous concentration, as the containers were unloaded rapidly despite the fact that each weighed many tons. A giant crane lifted the containers from the ship's deck or cargo hold with astonishing ease, as though they were a child's marbles, and placed them one by one on flatbed trucks waiting in a row on the pier. The trucks then drove them to the rear of the harbor, and the storage area where the containers would await their owners.

"I cannot be certain," the handler told Reza, "but it is reasonable to assume that 'our' ship will not be forced to wait at sea, but will sail directly into the dock."

Reza learned a new concept in the shipping world: the "operating line" that formed when the number of vessels waiting outside the harbor exceeded the number of docking slips available to absorb them. Each day of waiting at sea meant a monetary loss for the shipping companies. Entry into the harbor was determined not only by order of arrival, but also by the type of cargo the ship was carrying. Steel pipes or rolls of paper, for instance, would not suffer from an additional day or two at sea, while fruit, vegetables, or other perishables would be given preferential treatment to avoid spoilage.

"There is an international protocol that establishes the operating line in every harbor," the handler said. "But the people waiting for this particular shipment have enough power and connections to avoid having the ship wait even a minute longer than necessary."

"So what exactly am I looking for?" Reza asked.

"You must identify a specific container. It will be a pale blue in color, with three letters painted in red on the side: SRT, the initials of a large German shipping company. There are probably a million containers like that, but ours will have a sign. Underneath the middle letter, the 'R,' there is a white stain. That is the only way to recognize the container. Unless someone bothered to wipe the stain off—and let us pray that that is not the case—you are to call me the minute you identify the container and take a few good pictures of it. At the same time, mark down which vessel it was unloaded from and at precisely what time, where it was taken, and any other detail you may notice."

"Very good," Reza said.

"Ah… one more thing," the handler remembered. "We're talking about a forty-foot container."

"Pardon?"

"Containers come in various standard sizes. The most common are twenty-foot containers—about six meters—and those that are forty feet in length, or about twelve meters. We know that the container in question is a forty-footer. That will limit the possibilities and make your job easier."

The handler did not tell Reza, or the others who'd spelled him in watching the loading dock over the past twenty-four hours, what was inside the container, who had sent it, or why it was so important that it be located. What they didn't know could not be extracted from them. After all, he was in a secure location, while they, the watchers, were in the middle of the lions' den. Bandar-Abbas was a pleasant coastal city with palm-lined streets and a lovely boardwalk, but it also served as a focal point for members of the Iranian intelligence community. They would definitely not like the fact that someone was spying secretly on the port and reporting on its activities to foreign entities.

And there was another reason why the handler did not tell Reza or the others what the shipment contained: He simply didn't know. All his efforts to discover the answer had been in vain. There was only one thing that he knew with certainty: The container held something that personally involved the highest echelons of Iran's government. A trustworthy source in Teheran had reported that the supreme leader, the Ayatollah, had issued instructions that he be informed the instant the container arrived at Bandar-Abbas—adding that he wished to see its contents with his own eyes.

Jerusalem, 5772 / 2011

The old orphans' home was located in a largely secular section of Jerusalem. The weathered building boasted four stories that were utterly lacking in grace or beauty. The steel gate and barred windows gave it the appearance of a prison and raised the inevitable specter of child abuse, neglect, and malnutrition.

Before they rang the bell, Avreimi and Chezky glanced around them. They had not told their mother about the investigative journey they'd undertaken, and the last thing they needed was for her to see them by chance, knocking at the gates of the orphanage in which their father had been raised.

When the guard opened the gate for them, the brothers were surprised. Inside, the place looked a great deal better than it had on the outside. If anyone was harming the children of this institution, he was hiding it well. It was a square building surrounding a large, well-tended courtyard. Several children sat on benches, reading books or chatting, while others ran around in the throes of a seemingly enjoyable activity. The pupils appeared happy and content. Still, Chezky and Avreimi could not help but think, their hearts broken, that a few decades earlier it had been their own father walking around this courtyard. The place made a good impression—at least today—but any institution, however professional and well-run, was no substitute for a warm home and loving family.

The home's administrator was young, ultra-Orthodox, and energetic. He wore a neat suit and a fashionable tie. *Someone else who has succeeded in life*, Chezky thought with a stab of envy. The administrator welcomed them pleasantly in his ground-floor office.

"We're looking for details about… our father," Avreimi said with obvious discomfort. "That is… he… grew up here…"

"He recently passed away," Chezky added.

The young administrator did not seem surprised. This was not the first time, and it would presumably not be the last, that people had come to him with such a request.

"I'm sorry for your loss," he said formally. "What was his name?"

"Kohlberg. R' Shlomo Kohlberg—*hareini kapparas mishkavo*," Avreimi said, careful to enunciate the formula recited by children in the first year after their father's death.

"How old was he?"

"Around fifty-nine."

"Born in '52," the administrator announced, after a rapid calculation on his obviously up-to-date phone. "When did he pass away?"

"Two weeks ago."

"Ah, yes, I heard. Died suddenly, no?"

"It's always sudden…" Avreimi said. "Someone mentioned during the *shivah* that he grew up here. We didn't even know that he was an orphan. Actually… we're missing a lot of details. So we thought we'd ask if you have a list of children who were raised here."

"No problem." The young man swiveled on his chair and pulled a thick, ancient-looking volume from the shelf behind him. He placed the book on his desk carefully, as though it were very valuable, and opened it at random.

"This is our registry of all the children who were in the home since its founding and up until the seventies."

The pages of the book were blank forms, with lines and spaces to be filled in by hand. "This is how they used to do things, once upon a time," the administrator remarked with the trace of a grin. "Today, everything is computerized and you can pull up any detail you want with the push of a button."

The page that lay open before them happened to deal with an orphan by the name of Rahamim Agioff, pupil #108, a member of the Bucharim community. His picture had been affixed to the top corner of the page—in black-and-white, of course. The rest of the form had been filled in the old style, with a fountain pen and ink. It said that the boy had entered the orphanage in the year 1941, after his father lost his life to a British bullet and his mother remarried a man who did not wish to have the boy in his home.

Rahamim had been only 5½ when he had joined the home, in reasonably good health except for a chronic eye infection. He was sent to be educated at a Bucharim school located near the Bava Tama shul, where his teachers testified that he was a diligent and well-behaved student. His birth mother came to visit him from time to time, when her new husband was away on business, and she paid the home's administration half the sum needed for his maintenance. When he reached the age of twelve, the orphan was sent to learn a trade with R' Nissim, the silversmith, on Rehov HaChavashim. His salary: a half-lira per month. The money was saved in the institution's coffers until he married. The orphan left the home in the year 1953, upon his marriage to a fine, modest girl who'd grown up in a different orphanage. The match was made with the help of the home's counselor, Reuven Dalel. After the wedding, Rahamim received the money he had earned—a total of 30 *lirot*—for which he signed a receipt.

"How is it possible to locate our father?" Chezky asked.

"Fortunately, we can get a little assistance from modern technology," the administrator said, facing his computer monitor. "A few years ago, we made an index of all the orphans who've passed through here since the home's founding, to help us pinpoint the page on which each one appears. Let me check... Kohlberg... Kohlberg... Here it is! Shlomo Kohlberg. Pupil #1065."

The administrator returned to the book and began turning its pages, quickly at first and then, as he neared the one he wanted, at a slower pace.

Avreimi and Chezky watched him with mounting tension. What would they discover? What details would their father's page hold? What surprises lay in store for them? Avreimi's mouth was strangely dry; Chezky tried to be alert and detached, but he, too, felt tension rise in his throat.

A surprised look crossed the administrator's face. He turned another page, and then went one back. To and fro he turned the pages, muttering to himself, "What's going on here?"

"What? What happened?" both brothers asked in unison.

"It's very strange," the administrator said. "I don't know how, but your father's page seems to be missing…"

A BLESSED SILENCE FELL OVER THE TINY ATTIC.

Only thirteen minutes had passed since the explosion behind the prison walls—thirteen minutes of nonstop action at a dizzying pace. Now everyone else was gone, leaving Maurice alone with his thoughts.

He curled up in the bed and pulled the covers over his head. Tears gathered at the corners of his eyes and his heart seemed to swell with the force of his powerful emotions. At first, he felt an overwhelming relief: He had been given his life back, saved from certain death. He could have the privilege of seeing the return of good times after the war.

Then a wave of gratitude filled him: to the lawyer who'd risked his life to have him rescued, to the Resistance friends who had pulled him from the gate, to the men who'd arranged the explosion and supplied a car for their escape and this attic for his refuge … So many good men had invested time and effort on his behalf. So many had courted danger for his sake. Could he ever thank them? Could he ever repay them for what they'd done?

Why had he merited being spared? His five fellow cell members had been captured and murdered by the Nazis, along with the brave farmer who had let them hide in his house. Why did they deserve that? They'd been young, in the prime of life: golden-haired Martin, chubby, good-hearted Jean, sensitive Francoise of the philosophical bent, and the others. Why had *he* remained alive, while they would stay young forever? Maurice had lost his entire family. There would have been no one to grieve for him. While they had left behind fathers and mothers, brothers and sisters…

They'd been so idealistic, brimful of values, believing in the righteousness of what they were doing. No one had forced them to join the Resistance. Nothing had prevented them from behaving as thousands of young French people had done: simply bowing their heads in the face of an ugly reality and continuing on with the routine of life. The Resistance fighters had sacrificed their jobs and their educations because they could not bear a life of degradation and oppression. They preferred death to a life without honor under a foreign power. They knew that they would never be able to look themselves in the mirror if they did not raise the banner of revolt and go out to battle for their country's honor and freedom.

After his initial exultation came the fear. The Germans were no fools, Maurice knew. They must have already ascertained that he had escaped, and figured out who had rigged the blast. There was nothing that motivated the Nazis more than the sting of humiliation. They would go on a rampage now. They would abandon every other aim in their effort to recapture him. Was this hiding place safe enough? Was it only a matter of time before he was discovered? Would this whole daring escapade grant him no more than a few hours of freedom, at the end of which he would be back in enemy hands?

Maurice listened with beating heart to the confusion of noise rising up from the street: emergency vehicles wailing on their way to the site of the explosion, speeding army jeeps and urgent orders blaring from loudspeakers mounted on the watchtowers. From his room, he could hear soldiers roughly stopping cars and trucks, making their passengers get out, and conducting thorough searches. Regiments of soldiers went from house to house, combing every centimeter. Frightening sounds from the nearest homes penetrated the attic and reached his ears beneath the blanket: a loud thumping on doors, the tinkle of shattering glass, hoarse shouts in German demanding that they be let in at once, and then the sounds of falling furniture and hurled objects.

They searched his building as well. They did not skip a single apartment on the floors below him. These were the moments of his greatest terror. Maurice froze in place, afraid to breathe. Would the Germans be content with the five lower stories, or would they check to see what lay above? It was not difficult to imagine what would happen the moment they found him...

Only at nightfall did the clamor begin to subside. Maurice assumed that the Nazis had exhausted their efforts in the radius closest to the prison and had broadened the search. The greatest danger, then, had passed. The first part of the rescue operation had been crowned with success. Now he must survive here for a week and wait patiently until someone came for him.

The next days were quieter. The Germans continued searching diligently throughout France. They never dreamed that the escaped prisoner was hiding a mere six-minute drive from the prison.

It was the very quiet that unnerved Maurice. The days were long and empty. The pain in his fractured leg returned to trouble him, and the food and drink he had been left was quickly becoming depleted. He ate his last morsel of bread on the evening of the fifth day, and then he remained hungry. Nights in the attic were freezing, leaving Maurice shivering in his bed. The loneliness and the difficult living conditions left him feeling depressed and despairing. The optimism of the first days dissipated, and nightmares took its place. In his blackest visions, all his fellow Resistance members were killed by the Nazis, while he was sentenced to die a slow and agonizing death in the sealed attic.

Seven days after the escape, at a late hour of the night, Maurice suddenly heard the elevator hum to life. His heart lifted and he was engulfed by a powerful joy.

A moment later, it dropped again. Wait! What if these were not his friends? What if someone had given him away? Might not someone have broken under torture and revealed his hiding place?

Maurice heard the old elevator slowly creak its way up. The sound was like the step of a cruel killer, approaching him in the dark. A cold sweat covered his trembling body as his eyes darted in every direction, trying to find a way out.

The elevator stopped with a muffled thud on the sixth floor. Maurice tensed in fear, hugging himself with trembling arms. He heard the elevator door open. His teeth chattered uncontrollably. He squeezed his eyes shut, bracing himself for the worst.

Iran, 5753 / 1993

The huge vessel, approaching from the southwest, in the direction of the Straits of Oman, flew the yellow-and-blue flag of Ukraine. It was a new ship, and a fast one. On her flank, the name *Odessa* was proudly evident in both Cyrillic and Latin letters. The ship's deck was crammed with containers, stacked six deep.

Reza whistled with excitement. This was without doubt the largest ship he had seen since he had begun spying on the harbor—a veritable steel monster. The vessel measured 300 meters in length and at least 40 across. Most of the ships that had come to the port on his watch were the equivalent of six to ten cargo containers in width, while this one was sixteen! Multiply 16 by 25—the number of containers ranged along the deck—and you had 400. With six stories stacked that way, the total was a staggering 2,400 containers—and that did not take into account a similar quantity of containers stored in the ship's belly. Yalla! How did that thing stay afloat? It was simply unbelievable!

The Ukrainian ship did not linger at sea. It sailed at full speed until the harbor mouth, where a guide boat darted forward without delay to meet it. Two motorized tugboats quickly attached themselves to the huge vessel and led it confidently to slip number seven.

A great deal of frenetic activity began taking place at the foot of the *Odessa*. Harbor personnel secured her quickly to the pier while others climbed up to the bridge to complete the necessary paperwork with the captain and his crew. Additional workers used a crane to lift themselves up to the top of the gigantic pile of cargo containers, where they set to work untying the lashings that held them together.

Having witnessed the arrival of a large number of ships, it was obvious to Reza that the *Odessa* was receiving preferential treatment. The work was generally done at a leisurely pace; now, not a second was wasted. Someone was very anxious to unload the ship as soon as possible—or, at any rate, to unload *something* from it.

Actually, it required no circumstantial evidence to tell him that this was not an ordinary vessel. On other occasions, security personnel had appeared at random around the harbor. But never before had four big *Pasderan*—Revolutionary Guard—jeeps been on hand to supervise the unloading. Armed soldiers leaped from the vehicles to fan out along the platform. The senior officer among them issued loud cries to spur on the man in charge of the unloading, who appeared suitably cowed.

Reza sensed his heartbeat speed up as tension spread through all his limbs. This was the ship he had been waiting for. By all indications, he was about to locate the desired container.

A tow truck appeared alongside platform seven to haul away the containers—a "port horse," in harbor lingo. It pulled up near the vessel. The crane went into action. Its arm moved until it was poised above a specific point on the deck. Then it began to slowly loosen the metal cables, under which the "spreader" was positioned. This was a special fastener encircling the container, its arms attached to the container's four upper corners for the purpose of lifting it.

Breathlessly, Reza followed the scene. He knew the drill by heart. First the operator seated in the crane's compartment above would tug gently on the cables, lifting the container slightly to make sure it was securely fastened. Only then would he raise the container fully into the air.

And that's exactly the way it happened. The spreader latched onto one of the containers, the fourth from the left in the third row. The cables were tightened, and after a moment the container was drawn from the mountain of cargo cubes and hoisted into the air, where it dangled at the end of the powerful metal cables.

Reza's breath caught in his chest. This was it! The container was pale blue in color, with three red letters—SRT—painted on its side.

At first, he did not notice any white stain. But then the crane began moving the container through the air until it hovered over the platform, and then set it down, gently and precisely, on the bed of the waiting truck.

The "port horse" began to move along the platform, accompanied by the four jeeps, each with its complement of soldiers. It made a full revolution until it faced the exit from the harbor. Now, with the opposite side of the container facing Reza, the white blotch was revealed in all its glory.

His heart swelled with pride. The fatiguing mission had not been in vain. His handler would shower Reza with praise: he had pinpointed the container.

He had waited a full week for this moment. He had memorized his handler's instructions and planned the order of his actions meticulously. But now, at the moment of truth, a feverish excitement confused him and made him work with an inefficiency that cost him valuable seconds.

The first thing to do, he remembered, was to make sure it was the correct container.

Reza adjusted his grip on the binoculars and studied the container again. Suddenly, he experienced a pang of doubt. Was that really the white stain he had been told about? It was only a spray of white, as if someone had taken a can of paint and tossed it at the container's side. The blotch of color began beneath the letter "R," forming a white circle about the size of a basketball before trailing off in a downward direction as it dried, forming a spray of long, thin lines. This was not the way he had imagined it would look. But it certainly fit the description of a "white stain."

Now… what was he supposed to do? *Take a picture! Get proof!*

He pressed the binoculars to the camera he had been provided along with it. It was a strange camera. It had not been made by Kodak, Nikon, or any other firm he recognized. An unfamiliar logo appeared on its underside: a letter in some foreign alphabet, embedded in a triangle. The camera's great advantage was the device that linked it to the binoculars, enabling him to take sharp photos from a distance.

Enough thinking! Enough wasting time! Take the picture!

The tow truck moved slowly through the harbor, escorted by the Revolutionary Guard jeeps. Reza took photo after photo. Later, he would have to withdraw the film from the camera and develop the pictures himself. After all, he couldn't very well hand the spool in to be developed at a store in town. Not if he was interested in staying alive…

And now, what was the next step? *Call the handler.*

The phone was on the table at his side. Reza lifted the receiver and dialed the international code for Oman, followed by a number he had worked hard to memorize this past week, until he could have said it in his sleep. If anyone in the Iranian security service checked the call's destination, he would find that it was a phone number belonging to a roofing company in Muscat, capital of the small kingdom of Oman on the other side of the Strait.

The phone rang several times before someone at the other end picked up.

"*Dobroya utra* (good morning)," the man said.

"*Dobroya utra*," Reza replied eagerly. "The container has arrived. I see it."

"Are you sure?"

"Yes, yes! It's a light-blue container with the letters 'SRT.' And it has a white stain."

"Which ship was it unloaded from?"

"A ship called the *Odessa*. From Ukraine."

"What are they doing with it? Where are they taking it?"

"A group of *Pasderan* soldiers came in jeeps. They're escorting it out of the harbor now."

"Did you take pictures?"

"Yes, yes. Beautiful pictures. I used a whole roll of 36 shots."

Reza would have been considerably less eager had he known that, just two hours later, he would be captured by the men of the Revolutionary Guard, who burst into the office and found him just as he finished developing the incriminating roll of film.

9

In his terror, Maurice's soul nearly left his body. He heard the heavy elevator door open and then shut with a thud. Footsteps sounded, approaching the attic door. A key was inserted in the keyhole from the outside and turned once...

...This is what had happened. The rodent-faced attorney had returned to the prison after the explosion, to continue in his role as legal counsel appointed to represent the captured Resistance fighter. He had tried to appear astonished at his client's daring escape, but the Nazis were not that naïve. They'd already been harboring a suspicion that the lawyer was not truly loyal to them but had been planted by the Resistance. Just minutes after he reached the prison offices, he was taken to the interrogation chamber. Two jailers tied him to a chair and left the room. Not long afterward, an interrogator entered. As an ice-breaker, he knocked the lawyer over, kicking him in the ribs for good measure.

"Where is Maurice?" he asked, standing over the lawyer, who was sprawled on the floor still tied to his chair.

"I know as much as you do," the attorney replied, groaning with pain.

The Nazi's reply was another kick, this time directed at the Frenchman's stomach.

Over the course of the next few days, the French lawyer bravely withstood the torture. Then the Germans introduced a particularly Satanic twist.

"I have a surprise for you," the interrogator announced with an evil smile. He ordered two jailers to cover the lawyer's eyes and drag him into the next room. When his eyes were uncovered, the first thing the Frenchman saw were his wife and children, trembling and afraid.

"Animals!" he screamed. Then he fainted dead away on the floor.

The Nazis revived him without undue gentleness, so that he might see an officer move closer to the family and place the barrel of his gun against the head of one of the children. "I'm going to count to five," the Nazi said in a frigid voice. "If you don't tell me where Maurice is, I will shoot—and then move on to the next child."

"Rodent man" broke down in tears. "Leave the boy alone!" he shouted. "I'll tell you everything. Maurice is in an attic at 35 Victor Hugo Street. Very close to here."

"You're lying," the Nazi spat out, without moving the barrel of his gun from the boy's temple. "We checked all the buildings in the area."

"I swear it!" the lawyer wailed. "There's a locked door that leads to a small attic. There's no access from the stairs."

"Then how does one reach it?"

"You have to reconnect the elevator to the electricity and go up to the sixth floor."

"And where is the key?"

"In my house."

The Nazi returned the gun to its holster and roughly shoved the weeping boy into the arms of his equally distraught mother.

"Your wife and children will stay here. You will come with me, to fetch the key and show me the hiding place. And if you're lying…" He left the rest unsaid.

Half an hour later, dozens of soldiers and Gestapo men quietly surrounded the building on Victor Hugo Street. The poor lawyer could hardly stand on his feet, and two soldiers held him up. With shaking fingers he reconnected the elevator to the electrical system, and the engine whirred to life. He was dragged into the elevator, where the interrogator and three armed Gestapo thugs joined him.

The key to the attic was in the lawyer's hand. As the elevator approached the sixth floor, the interrogator motioned for his men to be silent. They stepped out of the elevator without a sound. The lawyer inserted the key in the hole, turned it once and opened the door…

Maurice huddled under the covers, paralyzed with fear. He covered his head with his hands, closed his eyes, and pressed his face into the mattress in an effort to calm his chattering teeth.

He heard cautious footsteps moving in his direction.

"Maurice?" It was the lawyer's hesitant voice. "Maurice, are you all right?"

Maurice didn't move.

The lawyer lifted the edge of the blanket slightly, to reveal a Maurice who was alive and breathing. "Oh, thank G-d," he sighed with relief. "I didn't know what state I'd find you in."

Maurice lifted his head slightly and peeked out through his fingers. The lawyer stood beside his bed, healthy and unharmed. No one stood behind him—neither Gestapo men nor armed soldiers. It had simply been a wild fantasy that had consumed him. He broke down in bitter tears. The terrible tension and deathly fear dissipated abruptly, leaving a storm of emotion in its wake.

The attorney sat down and patted the young man's back with compassion, the way one might comfort a small child.

"Maurice, calm down," he said in a soft voice. "Everything's all right. And everything *will* be all right."

Maurice did not calm down. The long days of fear and loneliness had stretched his nerves to the breaking point. The nightmarish visions had seemed so real that they had, in his mind, turned into a bitter reality.

"They didn't arrest you?" he asked through a flood of tears, still shaking.

"No, no. I'm here. Everything's okay. Everything's okay."

The lawyer poured some hot, sweet tea that he had brought in a thermos. Maurice couldn't hold the cup, so the lawyer fed him sips of tea. Slowly, Maurice regained his equilibrium and stopped crying.

"Now, listen." The lawyer's tone grew businesslike again. "I've brought you something to eat and drink. In about two hours, a couple of our boys will come to get you out of here. If all goes according to plan, in a few days you'll be in England."

Maurice's eyes were still red and damp. "England?"

"Yes. Right now, yours is the most famous face in France. The entire country is looking for you. There's not a single Gestapo man or French *gendarme* who wouldn't recognize you the minute you set foot in the street."

The journey to England, which in peacetime took no longer than a day, lasted nearly a week for Maurice. He made his way there with the help of a few dedicated and courageous Frenchmen, in the cargo holds of trucks and the engine rooms of ships, hidden from sight.

The search for him was still on. More than once, he was forced to hide with thudding heart as German soldiers and French collaborators stood just a step away. But, in the end, he set foot on secure British soil, where the Nazis had no power.

English friends of the Resistance brought Maurice to a small guesthouse near the city of Leeds, in Yorkshire, some 300 kilometers north of London. There, in a peaceful country village that the war seemed to have skipped over, they hoped that his tortured body would recover and his injured spirit revive.

Several years passed. The Second World War had ended in Germany's defeat. Maurice, his strength restored, chose to remain in England. He had no desire to return to his native Germany, and he had no roots in France. The small Jewish community in Leeds welcomed him with open arms. He found work in a local automobile factory and settled into a blessed, routine life. In time, he married a young woman from the community.

Maurice felt that he had found his place. He was the only one left of his family. The rest had been cut down—while he had merited continuing the line and establishing a Jewish home. There was no one happier on the day his wife gave birth to a beautiful baby boy.

But the measure of Maurice's suffering, it appeared before too long, was not yet full.

Jerusalem, 5772 / 2011

On Monday afternoon, Chezky Kohlberg presented himself at the orphan home again—this time, without bothering to tell his brother. He was not obligated to give Avreimi advance notice of all his plans. In any case, Avreimi would not have joined him, as that would have meant missing another day at the *kollel*. He undoubtedly would also have turned up his nose and said that it was time to end this unpleasant pursuit into their father's life. Even sadder, he would likely have joined him anyway, if only to keep a close eye on things and make sure his feckless brother did not do anything foolish…

That morning, after returning the Mazda to the car-rental firm, Chezky had phoned the home's administrator. Yesterday, when he and Avreimi had visited with him in his office, the administrator had been merely polite. But after discovering that their father's page was mysteriously missing from the institution's registry, he had begun to evince more interest. This had become a fascinating riddle. "I have several meetings in town," he had apologized, handing them his business card. "Call me tomorrow and I'll see how I can help."

And then, just before they left his office, he had suddenly remembered "Chacham" Reuven Dalel, who'd worked as a counselor in the home many years before. Perhaps he could provide more details about their father.

"He lives somewhere in the south," the administrator had said, thumbing through his phone's memory until he found the number. The rest was history. They'd called Chacham Reuven's wife, who'd told them that they could find him at the Ohr Dovid shul that evening. Wasting no time, they'd immediately traveled south, where they were rewarded with some important facts: Their father had been a well-behaved and likeable child who had not fought with the other children. He had been obedient and had gone to bed on time. Oh, yes, and two other details: at the age of five he was taken to a kibbutz, and at 19, Chacham Reuven had met him in the street, wearing a soldier's uniform but not a sign of a *kippah* on his head…

"Chezky Kohlberg?" the administrator had repeated on the phone. Then he remembered. "Ah, you were here yesterday, with your brother. About your father's missing page."

"That's right. You said you might be able to help us look into the matter."

"Okay," he heard. "I'm in yeshivah now, but come see me at the office at noon. I've thought of an idea for you."

10

H E WAS ALWAYS AT MEETINGS, OR YESHIVAHS, OR EVENTS, Chezky thought to himself. Always busy, always running from place to place, bursting with energy and action.

He had managed to learn a good number of details about the home's administrator. There were no secrets these days. All he'd had to do was type in "Yoni Schlusserman"—the name on the business card he had given them—and all the information was spread out before him on the computer screen.

Schlusserman, 33, had attended a good yeshivah and then studied business administration in the Givat Shmuel Institute. He had tried his hand at journalism and eventually served as communications adviser to the city's deputy mayor. His name had found its way onto the list of the "thirty most promising young businessmen" in the holiday issue of one of the city's freebie newspapers.

In short, Yoni Schlusserman was a *chareidi* celebrity, Chezky concluded—not without a twinge of envy. Schlusserman's face had starred in more than a few events, beginning with a ceremony to mark the donation of eyeglasses to the orphanage's children by a well-known optical chain, through the opening of a new fish restaurant, where he had been photographed with a group of haughty media and businesspeople thoroughly enjoying the fare, and ending with a visit by the orphans to receive a blessing for the new year in the home of one of Israel's great Torah luminaries. *Standing at the rear is noted activist R' Yonasan Schlusserman, who works tirelessly for the benefit of the orphans under his care and the development of the venerable institution whose fame has already spread far and wide*, and so on, and so on, and so on.

The orphanage, for some reason, appeared less menacing to Chezky today than it had the day before. The guard opened the gate and he crossed the inner expanse with a light step.

The office door stood open. The energetic administrator was engaged in a loud phone conversation with a bureaucrat in some government office or other. He noticed Chezky in the doorway and gestured in a friendly way for him to come in. As the phone call stretched on, Chezky's discomfort grew. He did not take a seat because he had not been invited to do so, but stood facing Schlusserman's big desk like one of the institution's charges obediently waiting for the man to speak.

"So, how are you?" Yoni Schlusserman addressed Chezky after he had finally completed his call.

"*Baruch Hashem*," Chezky replied, in a voice that was weaker than he would have liked.

"Did you and your brother go see that... Chacham Reuven yesterday?" the administrator asked curiously, as he summoned his secretary from the next room and gave her several documents.

"Yes, we went there. He didn't tell us much."

Chezky was disappointed in himself. Picturing this meeting, he had envisioned conducting a friendly, flowing conversation with the man. After all, they did have one thing in common: both of them had been students at the same academy. But now he found himself attacked by a paralyzing sense of inadequacy. All the spontaneous remarks he had prepared had fled, leaving him with the sense of confusion and inferiority that he always experienced when in the company of famous or successful people.

Yoni Schlusserman, of course, had no self-confidence problems. He oozed with radiant smiles and friendly winks.

"Listen, Kohlberg," he said. "I had an idea that may be able to give you a clue. In the basement of this building there's a large archive containing documents and certificates dating back to the institution's founding. To tell you the truth, I would have tossed it all a long time ago and built a gym and swimming pool in its place. But the previous administrator—who's half-senile today, but what can you do?—is the one who signs the checks, and he insists on holding onto every piece of paper. Someone ought to tell him that they've invented the computer… Anyway, there are documents down there from the beginning of time. If you want to go down and rummage around, I have no problem with that. Just make sure to leave the place neat, because the old man visits the place to look things up now and then. Who knows? Maybe you'll find something interesting."

The basement level was far less well-maintained and much dirtier than other parts of the orphanage. The vaunted archive was actually no more than a large, dusty vestibule, the lion's share of which had been pressed into use as a storage area for all sorts of broken furniture, lifeless electrical appliances, *succah* boards, and other items that had no other home. In a distant corner of the room were several metal bookcases whose shelves were filled from floor to ceiling with boxes of documents.

Chezky, moving along the shelves, was impressed. The previous administrator might be half senile, but he was certainly organized. The boxes were arranged chronologically. Each had a year marked on its side, starting with the year 1941, when the orphanage was presumably founded, and up until the most recent years. Chezky pulled a box from one of the lower shelves and opened it. His eyes darkened. The carton was filled with documents and forms, crammed so densely as to leave no space at all.

Where in Heaven's name to begin? There was an endless quantity of material in here. A sea of paperwork. A pity, after all, that he hadn't brought Avreimi. The two of them could have divided the task and made it that much easier.

But there was no undoing what had been done. He was here, and he must handle things on his own. Maybe he should simply focus on the relevant time period. From what they'd learned, his father had apparently been born in the year 1952. Chacham Reuven had told them yesterday that he had arrived at the orphans' home at the age of four—that is, in the year 1956. He began searching the shelves.

He soon found the year he wanted. It consisted of five cartons of documents perched on the uppermost shelf of one of the bookcases. Chezky dragged over a ladder he had noticed in a corner of the vestibule and took down the first box. It was surprisingly heavy. This, too, was filled to the brim with papers. Chezky made a rapid mental calculation: if a 500-page book was approximately four or five centimeters wide, then this 60-centimeter box must contain several thousand documents. At this rate, he would not find anything until his father's *yahrzeit*!

Thrusting a finger and thumb into the mass of papers, Chezky extracted a sheaf of them from one side. They were yellowed and flaking with age. He began to leaf through them carefully, scanning the writing. He saw the results of medical tests and hospital release forms, correspondence with Talmud Torahs and trade schools regarding the home's pupils, forms from previous institutions from which the orphans had come and copies of letters given to the pupils when they transferred to other places.

The filing system quickly became clear to Chezky: all the paperwork pertaining to a particular child was gathered in one place, with the orphans filed in rising order by the number that was listed in the registry in the upstairs office. This box contained documents from the year 1956. Other boxes contained documents from other years, but all of them used the same internal filing system based on the pupil number. *Bless that half-senile administrator*, Chezky thought with relief. All he had to do was locate the file belonging to his father, and the mystery would be solved.

What was his father's number? 1065. That was what Yoni Schlusserman had told them yesterday. The carton open before him contained documents through Pupil 924. His father's file must be in the next box.

Chezky climbed back up the ladder, returned the first

box—marked 1956a—to its place and took down the second one, labeled 1956b. Here, the papers were a little less crowded, unlike those of the first box, where the files had been so densely crammed together that it had been hard to pull them out.

For the first time, Chezky began to feel the tug of his emotions. He turned page after page with his fingertips, his heart hammering in his chest. In just a few seconds, the great secret would be revealed. What would he find? What had his father so zealously concealed all his life? Would the knowledge rock the entire family?

"Why continue digging?" Avreimi had asked him the day before, in an effort to persuade Chezky to drop the investigation. "Abba was successful in making two *shidduchim*. Both your father-in-law and mine undoubtedly made inquiries. Ima must know something, too, though she hasn't shared it with us. Why not let sleeping dogs lie? What's the good of this? Just to satisfy our curiosity?"

Yesterday, he had not agreed with Avreimi. And now, it was too late. He had not come this far only to turn back at the last instant. Perhaps it was for the best that his older brother wasn't here. Based on what he discovered in these files, he would have to decide whether or not to share the information with him. Avreimi said he didn't want to know? Then let him not know…

Chezky continued moving through the pages. Here was orphan number 1063—a secular boy, aged six. Most of the paperwork on him revolved around medical issues. The last two documents were a death certificate and a burial receipt from the Chevra Kaddisha. Poor kid.

Moving on…

Number 1064. Zalman Berkovitz, the son of Holocaust survivors whose emotional stability had been undermined in the war. There was a correspondence with the Welfare Ministry, psychiatric exams, letters of complaint from the boy's school about his wild behavior, and so on. Just a few more pages… Where are you, young Shlomo Kohlberg?

An instant later, Chezky froze in shock and disappointment. Pupil 1065, better known as Shlomo Kohlberg, had vanished. There was not a single paper or document regarding him!

It required only another second for Chezky to understand. What a genius he was… He should have known the minute he had opened the box. Why were all the other cartons packed to the hilt, while number 1956b had some breathing space? Simple. Someone had taken a file from there.

It was excruciatingly clear: whoever had smuggled his father's page from the book of orphans in the office upstairs had taken the trouble to make all his paperwork in the basement archive vanish as well.

S**EVERAL WEEKS BEFORE REZA BEGAN SPYING ON THE** Bandar-Abbas harbor and spotted the container arrive safely in Iran, it left its original port at Hamburg.

The big German port city of Hamburg perches on the estuary of the Elbe River on the North Sea. Tens of thousands of containers pass through there every day. Many of them belong to the SRT shipping concern and can be recognized by their pale-blue hue and by the three letters—the firm's initials—emblazoned in red on the container's side.

Although the container's final destination was the port of Bandar-Abbas, there was no indication of this on any of the official documentation. According to the official cargo manifest, it was filled with office supplies, writing implements, and toys, and its destination was the port of Kherson, in Ukraine.

No one suspected that things were not as they seemed. Trade between Germany and Ukraine—since the latter had been privileged to gain independence from the Soviet Union—was flourishing. Many goods and cargos regularly made their way to the new state.

But one of England's most experienced informers in Teheran—a source known only as "the Clerk"—had told his handler in the British intelligence service that it would be very much worth their while to locate this particular container and to lay their hands on it.

There are numerous ways in which people who choose to betray their native country can establish initial contact with the country on whose behalf they wish to serve. All of these contacts take place far from prying eyes. No spy worth his salt will walk through the front door of a foreign embassy and inform the stunned reception clerk that he has classified information, and could he please be connected to one of the spies in the building? No way. Such encounters take place in secret, and in hidden places: a quiet corner of the public library, the lower level of an underground parking lot, or a remote field outside city limits. The Clerk, however, had done the unthinkable.

The incident had occurred three years earlier, in 1990, during the big commercial fair that took place in Teheran in the days when Iran had not yet been ostracized from the international community and its leaders were not yet considered the insane and unpredictable men they would reveal themselves to be in the coming years.

Numerous Iranian entrepreneurs came to the fair, with the goal of establishing contacts with representatives of firms from all over the globe. Iranian security personnel swarmed over the place as well, some of them openly and the majority in the guise of businessmen, to keep an eye on local merchants and make sure that they did not succumb to the temptation of conducting business other than honest commerce.

Not only traders visited the fair. Well-connected citizens sought admission as well, just to sniff the international fragrance, to enjoy the stunning exhibits and to return home with a wealth of gifts and souvenirs that had been distributed with a lavish hand.

The British booth was optimally situated in the center of the fair. It was attractively decorated in the colors of the Union Jack, and along the walls were pictures highlighting the achievements of industry and technology in the United Kingdom.

The basic operation was done by members of the Office of

Business and Industry, who'd come from London, as well as several local sales representatives. Many members of the British Embassy were also on hand at the fair to provide assistance where needed. One of them was Sean Mackenzie, the embassy's vice-attaché for commercial affairs. Though his job called for him to be present at the fairgrounds, international trade and commercial networks were the last things on his mind. Sean Mackenzie was a secret agent with MI6, the British intelligence service.

Intelligence agencies often have representatives serving in official, recognized capacities in other countries, and these men and women act openly out of the embassy. Russia's secret service, for example, might have a declared representative in Israel to stand in for his agency in dealing with the country's security and governing bodies. This representative will not act against the host country or harm her interests. However, in addition to these declared agents, there are also agents operating under a diplomatic or other guise. Outwardly, they are attached to the consulate, as administrators or low-level secretaries. But secretly—under the radar, so that few members of the staff are even aware of it—they are engaged in actively spying on the country which is hosting them, and recruiting agents from the local populace.

This was precisely Sean Mackenzie's role.

For many years, he had worked on the fifth floor of MI6's central branch in London, manning the agency's Iranian desk. He had outlasted several leaders: His career began when the Persian Shah, Reza Pahlavi, was still in power; he went through Khomeini's Islamic revolution and was still around when Ali Khameini came to power. At a certain point, when Iran began to take a leading role in the cast of characters constituting a threat to world peace, Mackenzie decided to go out into the field and work from the "inside." The British Foreign Office, which is in charge of Great Britain's foreign embassies, authorized the move and he was assigned to a suitable position. Over the course of a busy two months, Sean Mackenzie took a crash course in business and commerce, then flew out to Iran to serve as the ostensible economic attaché to the British Embassy in northern Teheran.

Agents who operate under diplomatic cover face a certain drawback: they are always under surveillance. In countries such as Iran, every Western diplomat is suspected of spying as a matter of course, and the authorities keep a gimlet eye on their activities. However, there is also a great advantage: The agent operates under the protective umbrella of his diplomatic status. Were he to be caught in the act of spying on his host country, he would be neither arrested nor detained, but merely expelled back to his native land. Iran knew full well that a number of the embassy staff were spies wearing the mask of diplomats, but there was nothing she could do except grind her teeth, track their movements, and wait for evidence that would allow her to send them back home. From time to time an agent would make a mistake serious enough to expose his true role, and he would be forced to leave the country post-haste.

The Clerk's first contact fell squarely into this category.

It was the evening of the third day of the commercial fair. Sean Mackenzie stood just outside the British booth, sipping a cold drink. Teheran was especially sweltering that day. Suddenly, a man who appeared to be a local approached him. He wore a suit that was old but well-preserved. He was very thin, and a narrow mustache adorned his upper lip. The Iranian asked if Mackenzie worked in the British Embassy, and Mackenzie told him that he did.

"I'd like to work with you people," the man said simply. "I am a government clerk. I have information that will interest you."

Sean Mackenzie thought he would faint on the spot. But years of British reserve came to his rescue and helped him keep the astonishment from his face. "You've come to the wrong person," he said with a chuckle, careful to reject the proposition without insulting the proposer. "I work in the financial sector. I do business. Besides, Great Britain does not engage in spying on Iran."

The Iranian persisted. Ignoring the last part of Mackenzie's speech, he thrust a slip of paper in the Englishman's hand. "So pass my name on to someone who does deal with this," he said, and turned away to circulate among the exhibits.

The economic attaché watched the retreating Iranian without expression, though his mind whirled with questions. After a moment, he signaled one of the other young men who supposedly was a sales rep, and with a gesture indicated that he stick with the man. The Iranian continued to walk from booth to booth, and then moved on to the pavilions of other countries. After about two hours, he left the fairgrounds and boarded a bus. He did not establish contact with any Iranian security people, and none of them approached him to see what he had wanted from the British. Not once did he turn around to see whether anyone was following him. He returned to his home in one of Teheran's suburbs. After two additional hours, the "sales rep" ended his surveillance and returned to the embassy. The slender Iranian, reported the agent, appeared to be an ordinary family man. He had gone home, eaten dinner, helped put the kids to bed, stepped out to the local mosque for evening prayers, and gone to bed.

Lengthy discussions took place on secure lines between London headquarters and the embassy in Teheran, debating the question of whether to respond to the Iranian's strange request. If this was a trap designed to get Sean Mackenzie out of Iran, it was an insultingly obvious one.

On the other hand, continuing investigation brought to light the fact that the Iranian with the thin mustache worked in an extremely sensitive area. The man—whose name, as he had written on the slip of paper he had pushed into Mackenzie's hand, was Hatib Maharani—worked as a low-level clerk in the "Shahid Fund"—the organization responsible for transmitting payments to the families of young people killed in service to the Islamic revolution throughout the world. While the organization had no direct ties to political or security groups, to underscore its symbolic importance its offices had been established in close proximity to those of the Supreme Leader, the Ayatollah Khomeini.

Hatib Maharani, then, was in the position of a fly on the wall. He circulated near the centers of power and decision-making—while at the same time remaining an unnoticed, unexceptional underling in the least significant department in the building.

Finally, the resolution was made to take "the Clerk" up on his offer. To contact him and hear what he had to say. His alarming lack of caution was a testimony to his innocence and his intemperate haste. It was even possible, someone remarked in one of the debates, that some Iranian security officer had actually witnessed Hatib's brief conversation with the ostensible diplomat, but Hatib's naively direct approach had removed all suspicion from his mind. Who would be foolish enough to engage in espionage in the middle of a fair swarming with members of the Revolutionary Guard and the Iranian Intelligence Ministry?

To be on the safe side, it was decided that his handler would be a minor covert agent. If that agent were "burned" and ousted from the country, Sean Mackenzie would still be able to remain. He could always claim that he had innocently passed on the note the Iranian had given him to someone else on the embassy staff, without grasping its significance...

Over the next two months, the Clerk underwent a strict training program, particularly with regard to caution and covert methods of communication, so that next time, when he "happened" to come across a detailed plan of Iran's nuclear program, he would be able to pass it all the way to the British Embassy.

For three years, the Clerk supplied information rated middling or below. The intelligence world does not disdain any source. First of all, even tangential and seemingly trivial details may be combined with information received from other sources, to complete a picture. Even more important, Hatib Maharani was able to describe which way the winds were blowing in the higher echelons of Iran's ruling circle. He could tell them when the corridors of power were grim and despondent, and when there was a sense of relief.

In return, he received a bit of cash and some favors. He tried his best to please his handlers. And now, for the first time in three years, it looked as if he had finally supplied information that justified the investment. This time it looked like he had some really noteworthy merchandise for them.

The "Clerk" had heard it in the building's elevator, in a conversation between two senior men in Khomeini's own office. The powers that be, Hatib understood from their talk, were extremely excited. They were expecting some sort of shipment from Ukraine.

He even managed a peek at the documents the pair were holding, and remembered the number of the container.

No, they had not mentioned what it contained. They'd only said that the Supreme Leader himself was treating it very seriously, and had issued an order to be informed the minute the container arrived.

CHEZKY'S DISAPPOINTMENT WAS HUGE—IN DIRECT proportion to his expectation. For the past hour, since his descent into the orphanage basement, he'd had the sense that he was poised at the edge of discovery. He was finally about to unravel the riddle of his father's life. Step after step, he had moved toward the longed-for solution… until, at the last moment, he found himself once again facing a dead end. Back to square one.

But even beyond the destruction of his hopes, he was beginning to believe that something about this whole story was odd—or even worse. The documents had not disappeared on their own. Someone was trying to hide something. For some reason, the trail had been carefully erased.

Who could it be? What interest did that person have in all of this? And, no less important: when had this happened? Had all the documentation relating to the young Shlomo Kohlberg vanished in recent days, or had it happened while his father was still alive? What was there in his father's past to motivate someone to extract pages from books and documents from boxes? What had his father been involved in? And how was it linked to all the surprising events that had taken place during the *shivah*?

Chezky was still seated on the floor with the carton of papers open before him. He sat back, leaning on his arms and tilting his head upward to gaze thoughtfully at the ceiling.

Or maybe, he thought suddenly, the correct question was: what had his father been *embroiled* in?

He sat up in alarm. The thought was frightening.

But the next idea that flitted through his mind was even more so. Chezky tried to banish it, but it refused to leave. Could… could his father's demise be somehow connected to all of this? Was it possible… that his death had not been natural?

He stood up, seized with panic. His entire body was shaking. His heart pounded powerfully in his chest as fear threatened to engulf him. The fear was so real, so tangible, that he looked over his shoulder to make sure he was alone. To reassure himself that no one was stalking him, waiting to ambush him in the dim basement, plotting evil against him…

After a moment, he regained some of his composure and began berating himself. What were these wild imaginings? But thoughts, once born, take on a life of their own. This one continued inexorably to develop: Abba had never suffered from heart trouble. He had not been overweight and had been completely healthy. Perhaps someone had killed him and disguised the act as a heart attack? Such things did happen… Until two days ago, the possibility would never have entered his mind. But today—right now, right here, in this subterranean archive—nothing seemed beyond the realm of possibility.

A cold sweat covered his body. He wished now that Avreimi had come with him. He found himself walking to the door, to make sure it wasn't locked. That no one had locked him in this windowless archive…

The door, of course, was unlocked. The wave of fear subsided. Chezky shook his head, as though to chase away these suspicions. *Enough*, he told himself. *Get a grip. Start thinking logically.*

The decision to remain in the basement and return to the shelves of boxes restored a sense of control and calmed him. He was embarrassed at the childish terror that had nearly overwhelmed him. This was no time for emotion, but for action. He must search all avenues. There was no telling if he would ever have another chance to spend time down here. What to do? Which direction to turn?

The first thing, he thought, was to search the cartons of the adjacent years. According to Chacham Reuven his father had lived in the orphans' home for less than a year, but twelve months could very well be spread out over two calendar years. After all, Abba had not landed here on the first day of 1956.

Chezky returned the 1956b carton to its place on the top shelf and took down 1957b. That half-senile administrator, bless him, had left this box as organized as the others, but Chezky was not surprised to find that this one, too, held no remnant of his father. There was paperwork relating to #1064, Zalman Berkovitz, the poor kid with the two unstable parents, and then to pupil 1066, Yaakov Barshai. But 1065, Shlomo Kohlberg, seemed to have been swallowed up by the earth. This carton, too, had a gap where the relevant files had been.

Chezky returned the box to its shelf and stood facing the shelves, arms crossed, as he mustered his thoughts. He needed a creative idea. He had to think out of the box… in this case, literally.

Suddenly, he remembered a lecture that he had once heard from one of his law professors—a man whose name had appeared in connection with almost every high-profile case in the country.

The lawyer had driven up to the institute in a shiny Jaguar, and he told the students all about his exploits in the halls of justice—but not before he depressed them by saying that most of their professional lives were destined to be spent in tedious and routine requests for continuances, filing documents in triplicate, and other procedural tasks.

"All the great dramas that you see in the movies—or, in your case, that you read in books," he corrected himself, suddenly remembering that he was lecturing to an ultra-religious crowd, "are one in a million. Forget about suddenly producing an amazing argument that will turn the whole case on its head and make the plaintiff ask the judge to drop all charges. The courtroom is a lot more boring than it seems… Nevertheless, one must seek proofs in the most unlikely places. If you dig deep into a case, checking every document and every iota of evidence, you can discover treasure." Here, the attorney had offered a few stories of stunning arguments that he had developed from the most miniscule and deeply-buried facts, and the revolutions he had set in motion in court—tales that clarified for those who still needed it why he billed his famous clients at a rate of five hundred dollars an hour.

So, what to do now? Chezky asked himself. *How to think out of the box? Where to find the elusive evidence? Where was it hiding?*

Perhaps it would be worth his while to go back and check the other boxes labeled "1956." There were five cartons dating from that year. Maybe his father's papers had simply been misfiled for some reason.

Carton 1956c was arranged in the same way as the first two had been. It contained documents pertaining to pupils 1833 to 2470. This carton was only two-thirds full, with old newspapers taking up the rest of the space. Chezky pulled out the last pupil's file. Pupil 2470 had entered the orphanage at the end of Elul. It was easy to conclude that this was the last box of personal paperwork for that year. The two remaining boxes contained something else.

Chezky felt a slight lifting of the heart as he opened the fourth box and saw that his guess had been correct. As he had hoped, this one, marked 1956d, did contain documents of a different kind. They did not pertain directly to specific children, but were part of a general correspondence between the home and various other parties.

He pulled out a group of papers at random and began to read. There were letters to government and municipal authorities with regard to moving the orphanage from its previous location to its current one. There were letters from donors, both in Israel and abroad, with a copy of a thank-you note attached to each. And there were letters to rabbis and halachic experts with queries regarding the running of the orphans' home, and the rabbis' handwritten answers.

At this point, Chezky reflected, Avreimi would have forgotten everything else and immersed himself in devouring this rare correspondence. But Avreimi wasn't here. Chezky continued going through the documents. He saw a letter from a childless couple who were interested in adopting an orphan, one from a well-known Agudah activist who wanted to put a child into the home, a list of monthly food and kerosene purchases, and so on and so forth.

Here and there, children's names cropped up in these papers as well. There were, for instance, monthly reports sent to the relevant committee in the Sephardic community, demanding payment for the upkeep of various Sephardic orphans, listed by name. There were also reports to the Health Ministry regarding infectious ailments that children had contracted, and an exchange of letters with the Security Ministry regarding three children whose fathers had fallen while serving in the IDF during Israel's War of Independence, and whom the state had entrusted to the orphanage.

Well, there was no choice, Chezky sighed. He had to start at the beginning and go through all these documents, page by page. He glanced at his watch. It was nearly two p.m. *To work!*

At three, he paused for some rest. It was an exhausting job, and he had hardly been through half the carton. Now he understood the reality: Behind that famous attorney's dazzling successes, behind every decisive argument, lay long hours of dull, Sisyphean labor, combing through documents and studying boring texts.

Chezky stretched his muscles and then sat back down to work. He was growing impatient. If, at first, he had perused each document thoroughly, now he scanned them rapidly, trying to assess whether its contents were relevant to his search or could be dismissed.

And then, without any warning, the word "Kohlberg" appeared before his eyes.

It was a page that he had already glanced at, with little interest. A delayed second later, his brain absorbed what his eyes had seen and he took a second look.

Chezky stopped breathing. A tremendous excitement gripped him. Here, at long last, was the first reference to his father! Suddenly, he was sorry that Avreimi wasn't with him to share the moment.

He read the letter from start to finish, and then read it again.

It was directed to the orphanage's management, and contained a request that the honored institution accept the orphan Shlomo Kohlberg. The date on the letter was January 1956, and it had been typed on an old-fashioned typewriter.

The roots of his family were exposed in the letter—and they were less awful than he had feared. At least he knew now that his father had been born a Jew. There were still unanswered questions about the kibbutz and why Abba had been taken there after a year, but at least now there was a thread to follow.

As he re-read for a third time, Chezky pressed 5 on his phone—his brother's speed-dial number.

"Chezky? How are you doing?" Avreimi asked.

"Baruch Hashem."

"What's new?"

"Listen, I'm at the orphanage…"

"What? You went back there? Why didn't you tell me?"

"Let it go. It doesn't matter now; we can fight about it another time. I found something here about Abba."

"How long have you been there?"

"Since noon. Anyway, there's an archive of old documents, and I've been going through them for the past three hours. Just this minute, I finally found something."

"What?"

"It's a letter that some rabbi in England sent the orphanage, asking them to accept Abba."

"What else does it say?"

"Let me read it to you: 'The orphan, Shlomo Kohlberg, is the only son of a member of our community, a Mr. Maurice Kohlberg, *zichrono livrachah*. The boy's father was born in Germany and escaped to France before the Second World War, where he joined the partisans known as the Resistance. He was smuggled into England, where he settled in our city and married a girl by the name of Miriam Kleinman. When the boy was only four, his parents, *z"l*, were killed in a train crash. He has no known relatives on his father's side, and his grandfather on his mother's side cannot raise the child. Your wonderful institution is known to me, which is why I've turned to you…"

"So," Avreimi said, when Chezky had finished reading the letter. "Abba is the son of a French partisan named Maurice, who was born in Germany and escaped to England. What do we do now?"

UKRAINE, LIKE THE OTHER FORMER SOVIET UNION STATES, IS a paradise for smugglers, tax-evaders, and lawbreakers. In the years following her emancipation from the suffocating Soviet grip and her detachment from the central government in Moscow, total anarchy reigned in the country. The ruling political and economic oligarchy expropriated national treasures and turned into millionaires practically overnight. They maintained their authority with the help of powerful criminal organizations that obeyed their demands.

In this fruitful but unfortunate land, which had been dubbed "the breadbasket of the Soviet Union" but whose children went to bed hungry, bribery was the only way to survive. It had been so during the Soviet era. Then, one could obtain almost anything in exchange for a half-kilo of potatoes or a loaf of bread. If caught in the act, one was whisked off for interrogation in the notorious KGB cellars. Now, one had to pay in cash—with a definite preference for dollars—and, if caught, merely greased the police officer's palm with some greenbacks as well. The average monthly salary in

Ukraine in those days was the equivalent of about thirty American dollars, and only about one-third of the men worked on a regular basis. It was not surprising, therefore, that what other countries viewed as criminal corruption was accepted practice here, and anyone who could find a way to add a little bit extra to his income did so without hesitation.

Sergei Arkady was a prime example. An employee of the port of Kherson, he waited near the harbor's rear gate, in the area where the containers were stored, bundled in his coat. Tonight's job promised to be an especially easy one. He would let the men who had phoned him that afternoon into the harbor in return for a twenty-dollar bill, take them to their desired destination, wait for them to finish their business, and receive another thirty dollars after bringing them back out again.

The hour was one a.m. The city slumbered, and the harbor area was empty and dark. At precisely the pre-arranged time, an old car approached the gate, halting some distance away. Three men got out.

The driver was a local agent who'd been working with British Intelligence since the Soviet era. The two others had just flown in direct from London. They possessed a unique expertise in gaining entry to all sorts of things, and then closing them again so that no one would suspect they'd ever been there.

The harbor's storage area, which held thousands of sealed containers, was surrounded only by a shaky fence less than five feet high. The two Englishmen could have opened the simple lock on the fence at the rear in four seconds, with their eyes closed and hands tied behind their backs. Sophisticated alarm systems had not yet reached remote Kherson. But the port employee had one very important asset: access to the huge catalogue index that would help the British agents locate what they were seeking—a certain container that had arrived that morning from Hamburg, Germany, and which was scheduled to be loaded the next day on board another ship bound for Bandar-Abbas, Iran.

The financial aspect of the night's work was speedily transacted. The local agent handed Sergei Arkady a green bill, and Arkady took a large ring of keys out of his coat pocket, opened the gate, and quickly let the three men inside.

The night was warm and the darkness was thick. Spotlights were scattered over the harbor area, but their bulbs had long since been stolen. The four men walked in single file, with the port employee first, the local agent next, and the two Englishmen bringing up the rear. They passed several single-story stone buildings. In the spaces between the buildings they glimpsed the pale shapes of ships tied up to their slips and the enormous cranes, silent now, their metal arms hanging down. The mingled odors of salt water, rust, kerosene and grease reached their nostrils. Distant noises occasionally disturbed the silence of the night.

After ten minutes, Arkady stopped outside a small booth. He opened the door with another key he had selected from his ring and entered the booth with the three men hard on his heels.

The Ukrainian agent made sure that the door was shut behind them and that all the windows were well-covered with thick curtains. "Turn on the light," he instructed, gesturing at the switch near the door.

The meager light afforded by the lone bulb made the agent's precautions in covering the widows seem almost superfluous. By its dim illumination, the Britishers scanned the room. It was a typical Soviet office, its furniture gray and nondescript. Only one wall displayed a surprising burst of color. A pair of large, framed pictures hung there, of the two Leonids: Ukraine's president Leonid Kravchuk and prime minister Leonid Kuchma.

Literally under the noses of these government leaders was a wide desk made of coarse wood, on which stood a large index composed of many square compartments divided by pieces of metal. It would be a good few years and a good few government turnovers before the news about computers reached the port of Kherson.

"What's the number?" the Ukrainian barked. The local agent translated the question into broken English.

One of the Englishmen rattled off the container's number from memory: a single letter followed seven numerals. This made its way back, via the local agent, to the port employee.

With nimble fingers, Arkady began searching through the thousands of cards in the index. Afterward, he perused a large logbook that was on an adjoining desk.

"It's at the edge of the storage area," he said finally, copying several numbers and figures onto a slip of paper.

He turned off the light and moved aside the curtains, so that those who entered the office in the morning would not guess that someone had visited in their absence. They all left the office, with Arkady bringing up the rear and locking the door behind him.

He began striding energetically toward the section that housed the container in question. The others followed at the same clip. Hundreds of containers in a rainbow of colors and sizes were crowded together, piled three or four layers high, with the aisles between them serving as narrow streets for passage.

There was not a living soul in the port apart from the four men. The moon, rising in the black sky, obviated the necessity of using flashlights. After twenty minutes' walking, Arkady halted.

"Walk another thirty meters and turn right," he told his fellow countryman. "It's the fifth container—the one in the corner." By the rules that they'd arranged beforehand, he was forbidden to come any closer or to see what the Englishmen were doing.

When the two English agents had covered the thirty meters, they could see the container they sought: pale blue, with three familiar letters in red belonging to the German shipping company, SRT. But here an unanticipated problem arose.

Of all of Ukraine's neglected and pothole-filled streets, of all the byways in need of urgent repairs, it was the road near the harbor that was slated to be repaved tonight. A number of workers worked there at a snail's pace, languidly pushing wheelbarrows filled with asphalt, pouring it along the length of the road and raking it smooth. A spasmodic, hand-held ramp pushed by two other workers moved slowly along, painting the black lines of a straight new road.

Of all the ill-lit locations throughout Ukraine, it was here that the contractor—who had probably earned the right to the job through a hefty bribe to one bureaucrat or another—had decided to rig powerful spotlights to illuminate the work zone. And of all the work sites in a country whose laws were so amazingly flexible, it was here that two sleepy patrol officers stood directing the sparse traffic along the road.

"We've got a problem," one of the Englishmen whispered to his companion. The rear of the container, where it opened, faced directly onto the road. The mesh fence would not completely conceal them. They had the equipment they needed to remove the container's seal, open it to check the contents, and close it again in such a way that no one would ever know it had been opened—but they had no means to blind possible spectators to their work. The moment they set to work on the container, the workers—and, more importantly, the policemen—would notice and start asking questions.

An hour passed, and then another. The repaving progressed slowly. Though the workers took advantage of the night, when there was little traffic, as is the usual practice in developed countries, they did so at a Ukrainian pace notable for its lack of alacrity. Arkady, the port employee, grumbled continuously behind them until he was finally silenced by another twenty American dollars. The sky began to lighten in the east. The road workers finished their job but planted themselves on the curb to have some breakfast while waiting for their transport to arrive.

"In half an hour, the harbor opens for business," the port worker told the local agent, who passed the message on to the British agents.

Cars began to move along the newly-paved road. A new morning was dawning in Kherson.

"We have to get out of here," Arkady said forcefully. "If you aren't coming, I'll go alone."

One of the Englishmen looked around in dismay. Suddenly, he recalled several buckets of paint he had noticed some meters behind them, apparently left behind from a paint job that had been conducted at the port. He ran back to the spot and returned with a bucket of paint. The container's opening was exposed to the road, but its side wall was better hidden. The English agent pried the bucket open and hurled its contents at the shipping container. The white paint hit the space beneath the middle letter, "R," first creating a circular splotch about the size of a basketball and then trickling slowly downward, tracking long, thin lines of paint to the base of the container.

The two Englishmen and the two Ukrainians hastened toward the exit. Their mission had failed, the two British agents thought bitterly, and all because of an unexpected spurt of Ukrainian energy. They had not managed to find out what the container held. They had not succeeded in destroying, neutralizing, sabotaging, or even photographing those contents. And the failure was all theirs. The valuable information had reached them from Iran; the London branch had flown them, along with all their illegal equipment, to Kherson; the seasoned local agent had brought them to the spot. But they had failed to provide the goods.

At least there was now some way of identifying the container, they tried to console themselves. It would be possible to continue tracking it as it continued its journey.

Two weeks later, from a window of the tall office tower in Bandar-Abbas, an Iranian student armed with a pair of binoculars succeeded in pinpointing the container as it reached its destination. And two hours after that, he was screaming in pain in a Revolutionary Guard subterranean interrogation chamber.

He had managed to pass on the information that the container had arrived to his handler, who was presently in Muscat, Oman. But the MI6 and other Western intelligence operatives were left with the largest riddle unsolved: What, in heaven's name, was inside the "innocent" container that had merited such personal interest by the top hierarchy of Iran's government?

"TELL ME, CHEZKY, DO YOU NEED HELP WITH ALL THOSE papers? Do you want me to come to Yerushalayim?" Avreimi asked.

Chezky was taken aback. His brother sounded sincere. Avreimi was not holding it against him that he had concealed his return to the orphanage and was simply offering his help.

"That's not necessary," Chezky answered. "It would take you over an hour to get here. There are only two or three boxes left for me to go through. I'll handle them myself."

"So how exactly did you find that letter?"

Chezky told him how the home's administrator had sent him down to the archive in the basement, and how Chezky had figured out that the documents were arranged by year and pupil ID number, and how surprised he had been to find that all the papers relating to their father had disappeared here, as well, and how he had continued searching through the cartons containing the institution's general correspondence until he had come across the letter from a rabbi in England requesting that the orphan home accept their father after the tragic deaths of his parents, Maurice the Resistance partisan and his wife, the former Miriam Kleinman.

"Who are actually our grandparents," Avreimi said.

"The grandparents we never had," Chezky agreed. "Anyway, I'm going to continue looking. Let's hope I come across something else about Abba."

After two hours, he called Avreimi again, only to update him that he was leaving the archive empty-handed. He had looked through the remaining cartons and found not a single mention of their father or the transfer of any child to a kibbutz. What he had found, in rummaging through the box labeled 1956d, was a passport photo of their father at the age of four.

The photo had apparently fallen out of the envelope bearing that English rabbi's letter, perhaps in the hopes that the orphan's big, sad eyes would induce the home's administration to offer him their protection.

"So we're stuck again," Avreimi concluded.

"You could say that."

"Maybe we can learn something through the kibbutzim."

"What's that supposed to mean? Do we call every kibbutz in the country and ask if they ever had a boy there named Shlomo Kohlberg? Be realistic…"

"Maybe there's an umbrella organization for all the kibbutzim in the country," Avreimi suggested. "A central administration or something."

"Hmm… you know what? I'll check that out later."

"How will you check?"

"How else? On the Internet."

"What?!" Avreimi was shocked. His tone filled with condemnation. "You have… *Internet*… in your house?"

It needed nothing more than this to inflame Chezky. The truth was that he had been planning to use the Internet in his law institute in Givat Shmuel, not at home, but he chose not to let Avreimi know that.

"Yes," he said forcefully. "I have Internet. And, by the way, I also have electricity, cooking gas, and running water!"

"What's the connection?"

"The connection," Chezky fumed, "is that it's impossible to live the way we did a hundred years ago. *That's* the connection."

"Nonsense." Avreimi was adamant. "I have no Internet, and I don't live the way they did a century ago. I actually live quite well, and very much in the present."

Chezky was fed up. "Avreimi," he said, raising his voice, "leave me alone, okay? Even Abba, if you don't mind, worked on the Internet."

"Why are you confusing the issue? Abba worked with computers, but we *never* had Internet at home!"

"Well, I do, okay?" Chezky—who did not have Internet in his home—permitted himself this untruth for the sake of making war. "Call it *yeridas hadoros*… ever heard of that idea?"

"This is not about *Yiddishkeit*," Avreimi said. "It simply destroys a home."

Chezky's voice dripped with mockery. "Ah, now you're worried about me. Thanks a lot, really. I'm touched…"

Avreimi sighed in despair, regretting the moment he had allowed himself to be dragged into this argument.

"All right, Chezky. I don't want to fight with you." He lowered his voice. "See what you can find out, and we'll talk."

Three hours later, Chezky realized that he would find no answers on the Internet. There were nearly 300 kibbutzim in Israel, but no central body through which one could glean information about individuals who'd lived in one kibbutz or another. It was a royal mess: There were kibbutzim that had been privatized, kibbutzim that had split up, those that had been closed and abandoned and others whose population had changed entirely. There were also many groups that had focused on children and their adoption in those days, such as "Aliyat HaNoar," agricultural schools, Zionist women's organizations, and political offshoots. In conjunction with all of these there were huge, crowded archives of various kibbutz and other authorities.

"Briefly," Chezky told Avreimi in their third phone conversation of the day, which was far calmer than its predecessor had been, "this is not taking us anywhere."

"We have to think," Avreimi said. "Let's talk again tomorrow."

"Just a minute," said Chezky. "Do you want me to fax you the letter? Do you have a neighbor with a fax machine?"

"What?" Avreimi laughed in surprise. "Don't tell me you smuggled the letter out of the archive?"

"Why not?"

"Listen… you can't just take things without permission."

"Who said I can't? Have you ever tried?"

"Chezky, be serious…"

"Okay. Relax: your little brother is no thief. He asked the administrator politely for permission, and the administrator said that, while documents can't be taken out of the archive, he could photocopy it for me."

Hearing Avreimi breathe a sigh of relief, Chezky couldn't resist. Mischievously, he added, "What the honored administrator *doesn't* know is that I put the copy in the archive and kept the original!"

"You… are something else." Avreimi had no words.

In their next phone call—the fourth that day—after Chezky faxed the letter to Avreimi, they discussed several details that might serve as starting points for further investigation: the Jewish community in Leeds where their father was born; the Kleinman family in Leeds to which their grandmother Miriam had belonged; R' Shabsai HaKohen Gordonsky, the community's *rav* and the name signed on the letter to the orphans' home. They might also take a deeper look into the partisans in France and the Resistance fighters during World War II.

"But none of this gets us any further," Avreimi said, in a hurry to get to his regular *minyan*, where he would lead the service. "The question of *'me'ayin basa*—from where have you come?' has been answered—I'll admit, thanks to you. Now we have to find out *'le'an atah holeich*—where are you going?' Who transferred Abba to a kibbutz… which kibbutz was it… and why?"

Chezky's cellphone rang at 6:40 the next morning, rousing him from sleep. He peered at the caller screen through bleary eyes and quickly picked up. It was Avreimi.

"What's the matter?" he asked in alarm. This was not a usual time for his brother to call.

"Oh, did I wake you? I'm sorry… It's just that I had an idea."

"That's okay. What's the idea?"

"It occurred to me that we might be able to get more information from other children who were in the orphanage with Abba."

All at once, Chezky was wide awake. "Wow! That's a great idea!" He spoke with appreciation—and a twinge of envy that *he* hadn't been the one to think of it.

"Do you remember the names of any of the kids you noticed when you were looking through the files?" Avreimi asked.

"Two of them, for sure: the boy right before Abba—number 1064, Zalman Berkovitz. And the boy after Abba—number 1066, Yaakov Barshai."

"The question is how to locate them," Avreimi mused out loud. "How about dialing 144 for directory information? Though it's very expensive. Every call costs a fortune…"

"Leave that to me," Chezky said, stifling a chuckle. His brother was really stuck somewhere in the Middle Ages. He probably had a rotary-dial phone, and his righteous wife no doubt still cooked on a kerosene stove…

Tracking down Yaakov Barshai turned out to be ridiculously simple. Before Chezky could blink an eye, the computer's search engine had supplied a wealth of encouraging information.

There were eight people in the country who bore that name, but Chezky was quickly able to pinpoint the Yaakov Barshai he wanted. He was a wealthy contractor who lived in a luxury villa on Moshav Beit Zayit, near Jerusalem.

Yaakov Barshai, it seemed from the material Chezky read, was not concerned about keeping a low profile. He had been interviewed multiple times by financial, professional, and local periodicals, as well as anyone else who agreed to come over with a recorder and camera. He loved to boast about the fact that he had started out as a penniless orphan in a Jerusalem orphans' home. By dint of hard work and never giving up, he had built a financial empire with his own two hands. He donated generously to causes aimed at assisting impoverished or otherwise afflicted youths. One magazine displayed a photo of Barshai at a lavish donors' dinner, arm-in-arm with none other than a beaming Yoni Schlusserman.

Reaching him by phone was also easy. Chezky punched in the number of the "Barshai and Sons" executive offices and simply asked for the boss. Yaakov Barshai proved to be a friendly, amiable fellow, ready and eager to be of assistance.

"Of course I remember him—the English boy!" he said in a tone of nostalgia. "So you're his son? No kidding! Truth is, he was pretty miserable with us. It's no wonder they moved him someplace else so soon. He simply didn't adjust—practically the only Ashkenazi among all the Kurds and Bucharim and Iraqis. I don't know who even sent him to us. There were Ashkenazi orphanages around in those days… You say they took him to a kibbutz? I don't remember. We forgot about him in less than a day. You know how children are…"

"What about Zalman Berkovitz?" Avreimi asked, when Chezky called to tell him of the meager crop he had harvested in Yaakov Barshai's fields.

"There are seven people by that name in the country, and none of them grew up in an orphans' home. I spoke with them all, or with their families. Maybe he's not alive any more, or left Israel…"

"Or he could have changed his name."

"We'll have to go back to the orphanage and copy a few more names from that period," Chezky said.

"Chezky, wait a minute," Avreimi said suddenly. "I have a 'call waiting' from Ima's house. Let's talk later." With a push of a button, Avreimi took the other call.

"Avreimi, how are you?" It was Miri, his seventeen-year-old sister—the fourth child in the family, who came right after Ari.

"*Baruch Hashem.* Why are you home? No school today?"

"I had a dentist's appointment and there's a test at school tomorrow, so I stayed home a little longer to go over the material."

"How's Ima?"

"*Baruch Hashem.* She's at work."

"How are her spirits?"

"Actually, pretty good."

"And how are you?"

"My friends get on my nerves… they pity me, but don't know how to act with me…"

"Well, people really *are* at a loss and don't always know what to say. So why did you call? Did you want anything special?"

"I went to the *makolet* (grocery store) today, and Yaakov asked me, quietly, who's taking care of money matters for our family. I didn't know what to tell him."

"Is there an outstanding debt at the *makolet*? What exactly is the problem?"

"I don't know. I felt uncomfortable, so I just mumbled something and got out of there. I didn't want to tell Ima…"

"You did well," Avreimi said. "You know what? I'm planning to come into Yerushalayim this afternoon. I'll drop in at Yaakov's and speak to him."

"Good. Thanks."

Less a minute passed before Chezky was back on the line, wanting to know what their mother had said.

"It wasn't Ima. It was Miri," Avreimi told him.

"Miri?"

Suddenly, they both realized for whom she had been named.

"Yaakov, from the *makolet*, asked her who takes care of the family's finances. Apparently, there's some outstanding debt."

Chezky took a deep breath. "And now the problems begin," he said in a hollow voice.

Tel Aviv, 5772 / 2011

It was one a.m. A sleepy silence reigned all around. Only the murmur of the black Grand Cherokee's broad wheels on the asphalt of the internal hospital road broke the nighttime quiet.

"Doron, it's here," the driver's wife said from the back seat. A sign on the double doors confirmed her statement: *Emergency Room*.

Doron gently pressed on the jeep's brakes and halted directly in front of the doors. He got out. He was about sixty. He looked young for his age and was neatly dressed. It was very late, and he looked around helplessly. In private life he ran a successful high-tech firm. This was the first time that he had ever set foot in a psychiatric hospital.

The ER's automatic doors parted at his approach, revealing a modest entrance area and a reception desk. Hesitantly, Doron stepped inside. A young receptionist sat behind the desk, apparently very busy with a personal phone call.

"Excuse me… Can someone help me? I have a patient in the car… right outside…"

The receptionist rattled off a few more sentences into the phone before he deigned to glance at the older man. "Ambulatory?"

"What?"

"The patient. Can he walk on his own?"

"No, he's not walking. He's simply not moving…"

"Then take a wheelchair." The young man pointed languidly at several wheelchairs that had been pushed into a far corner of the room, and returned to his phone call.

"*I* should bring him in?" Doron burst out.

The reception clerk gave him a surprised look. "What do you think this is—a hotel?" He went back to his business.

Doron looked around and saw that there was no one to talk to. He took one of the wheelchairs and pushed it toward the automatic doors, cursing himself for listening to his wife, who loved to help others, and volunteering for this mission. He should have respectfully told their neighbor to call an ambulance, or take a taxi, or phone her brother. Why should he have to take the boy to the Emergency Room? What was he, a psychiatric nurse? What did he owe his neighbor? They merely happened to live in the same building—and not even on the same floor…

On his return to the front of the hospital, he found that his wife and their neighbor had already emerged from the jeep's back seat and were waiting for him.

"What's that?" the neighbor asked, spotting the wheelchair. "How will I get him into it?"

Doron shrugged, and threw a reproving glance at his wife.

The neighbor opened the front passenger door. The boy sat immobile, his arms dangling limply at his sides and his head inclined sharply downward. Only the seatbelt prevented his body from sliding right out of the seat.

"Come, Barak," the woman told her son. "Get out of the car."

Though she was trying to control herself, it was clear that her nerves had been rubbed raw. The boy didn't react at all.

"Barak, get out already!" She raised her voice. "We can't keep Doron and Dalia here all night."

The teenager's only reaction was a single, slow blink.

"Come on!" she screamed, shaking his shoulder.

The boy still didn't move.

Doron, who had stood aside till now, stepped forward to help. "Leora, let me talk to him," he said quietly.

With tears gathering in her eyes, his neighbor stepped away to let him approach the vehicle.

"Barak," the older man said patiently. "Please come. Let's go inside."

Barak kept staring at the same fixed point, as though he were in another world.

"Barak, let me help you. Okay?"

Doron put a hand under the boy's armpit and pulled him carefully from the car, supporting his weight so he didn't fall. The boy neither resisted nor cooperated. He was completely passive.

"Bring the wheelchair," Doron told the neighbor. But it was Dalia, his wife, who hastened to roll the chair over. She positioned it behind the boy's back, so that her husband could slowly and gently deposit him onto the seat.

Here, too, the boy was utterly limp and passive.

"Take his shoulders so he won't fall forward," Doron instructed his wife and Barak's mother. He gripped the chair's handles and began rolling it toward the ER entrance.

The reception clerk was apparently still immersed in his riveting conversation. He took information from the boy's mother and typed it up on the computer with the phone still tucked into his shoulder. A noisy printer spat out a set of forms and a sheet of stickers. He handed these to the mother.

"Take a seat inside. Someone will be right out," he said. "Just make sure to put the wheelchair back from where you took it."

Doron, good neighbor that he was, wheeled the boy through another door and into the ER itself, and left him sitting in the wheelchair.

"Doron and Dalia, I don't know how to thank you," the boy's mother said emotionally. "I could not have managed this alone."

"Never mind, Leora. It's all right," they both said. "The important thing is for Barak to feel better."

They went out to the shiny new jeep waiting at the door, and drove home in a thoughtful silence. Doron no longer regretted having extended a helping hand to his neighbor. He felt a sense of satisfaction over the good deed he had done. Leora Altman was really to be pitied. Imagine having a son suddenly go crazy without any warning! While he hadn't known seventeen-year-old Barak personally, he had seen him from time to time, in the stairwell or the yard. He had been a sweet boy who'd grown up into a sturdy, handsome youth. What had happened to him so suddenly? It was frightening! Yesterday he had been a teenager filled with life, and now he was one of the walking dead, unable to move a limb.

Half an hour passed but no one came to tend to Barak. Half an hour in which Leora, his mother, gazed at her son, who sat unmoving in the exact position in which Doron had left him. His eyes were vacant and his expression unreadable. This was all she needed now, on top of all her other troubles! As though her husband's illness weren't enough, or the sharp drop in their standard of living since he had been forced to stop working, or their nonexistent bank balance despite her own two jobs. Now her son seemed to have lost his mind.

What was going on? Why wasn't anyone coming? Leora sat on a plastic chair, her eyes fixed on Barak and her thoughts wandering disconsolately. In her absorption, the hubbub of the ER did not reach her ears. She heard none of the cries, wails, or arguments. One man sang at the top of his voice while a girl, thin as a skeleton, rocked to and fro declaiming a string of senseless sentences in perfect monotony.

What was wrong with Barak? And when would a doctor come to see him?

Jerusalem, 5772 / 2011

"Problems?" Avreimi asked. "What problems are starting? What are you talking about?"

"What do you think?" Chezky retorted. "How, exactly, is the family going to live from now on? On Ima's part-time job? Abba's salary is no longer going to show up in their bank account—and you know that he was earning a nice amount. It's just two weeks later, and already there's a bill at the *makolet*. Did you think that money was going to drop down from the sky?"

"Maybe we should talk to Ima."

"I don't know…"

"You're right," Avreimi said, after a moment's thought. "Ima will say that everything's all right. She doesn't want to involve us, or maybe she's simply incapable of it. Abba and Ima never spoke to us about such things. On the other hand, we can't leave everything on her shoulders. Things could get even more complicated. Are there loans that need paying off? And what about our apartments?"

This, indeed, was a big riddle: Where had their father found the money to pay half the cost of an apartment for each of them? Had he incurred debts for that purpose? Had he saved up? Until two weeks ago, they would never have dreamed of asking such questions at home. Their father was not one for involving his children in his financial affairs. But everything had changed now. Perhaps it was time to plunge into the thick of things.

"So what do we do?" Chezky wondered aloud.

"I'm going to Yerushalayim to talk to Yaakov, the grocer," Avreimi decided.

"When?"

"This afternoon. Why?"

"I want to come along."

"What for? There's no need for both of us."

"That's all right. I have other errands to run in Yerushalayim."

"You don't have classes?"

Chezky burst out laughing. "*Oy*, Avreimi, you are so transparent! Suddenly you're worried about my classes?"

Avreimi was silent for a moment, as though caught out in an error. He recovered at once: "Tell me, Chezky—don't you trust me? Do you think I'm hiding things from you?"

"Oh, don't make such a big deal out of everything. Don't be so negative, Avreimi."

"I'm not easy in my mind," Avreimi confessed. "I'm not comfortable with this investigation of ours."

Yaakov's ancient grocery store was one of the last survivors of a world that was fast disappearing, trampled without mercy beneath the giant, conquering food chains and supermarkets. Nothing appeared to have changed in the store's forty years of existence. Cans were still lined up on the same rusting, paper-lined shelves. Dairy products were still kept in the same old refrigeration unit beneath the counter, its front made of glass that was stained with the passage of time and its stainless-steel doors opening with difficulty. Above the unit rested the thick marble counter that was the heart of the store. Yaakov and his wife stood behind that counter from morning to night, faithfully serving their customers and providing entertainment for the neighborhood children.

As boys, Avreimi and Chezky used to love watching Yaakov slice a large block of cheese in his "guillotine," the thin slices falling one after another onto a sheet of waxed paper balanced on the palm of his hand, or how he scooped olives from a large tin can into a plastic bag lying on the scale, adding another olive or two until it reached the desired weight. On Fridays, if they'd learned well during the week, they would come here to buy a gumball, which Yaakov would pluck out of a clear plastic jar. The gum was sweet and tasty, though he never let them choose the color, saying that they would have to accept the luck of the draw.

"Avreimi! Chezky!" Yaakov was happy to see the two brothers when they walked in that afternoon. He had known them since the day they were born, and had watched them and the other neighborhood children as they grew into boys, then youths, and then young men. "How's your mother? How is she feeling?"

"*Baruch Hashem*. Little by little, you know…"

After a few more polite exchanges, Avreimi got to the point of their visit. "Miri said that our father still had an outstanding debt here."

"Debt?" Yaakov recoiled. "*Chas v'chalilah*! Your father never ran up a bill. He always paid on time."

"So what's the problem?" The brothers were surprised. "You

said there's some matter concerning money."

"Oh, that." Yaakov suddenly understood. "Just a minute. Wait here…"

He moved back to his accustomed place to ring up a customer's purchase. Then he returned to them, his face filled with his secret.

"I wanted to tell you during the *shivah*," he said diffidently, "but I thought it might embarrass people."

"What? What did you want to say?"

"I wanted to talk about your father, *zichrono livrachah*. His whole thing with the money."

"What whole thing? What money?!"

"You mean you don't know?"

16

L EORA ALTMAN LOOKED AT HER WATCH. NEARLY TWO A.M., and no one from the hospital staff had seen to her son yet. She was just gearing up to find someone to yell at when a white-coated doctor finally approached. He was an older, heavyset man with salt-and-pepper hair.

"Hello," he said in a Russian accent, and began perusing the medical file in his hand.

Leora lifted weary eyes to him. *These Russians*, she thought in sudden anger, *have taken over the country*.

"Yes, madam," the psychiatrist said when he had finished reading. "What is the problem?"

She gestured at Barak, as though to say, *There. That's the problem.*

The doctor looked at the teenager slumped in the wheelchair. "What is your name?" he asked, leaning slightly toward him.

No answer was forthcoming.

"Barak Altman—is that you?" the doctor tried again.

The boy did not react. There was no sign that he had even heard the question.

The doctor dragged a chair over and sat down near Barak. "My name is Dr. Yevgeny Yompolsky. I am a doctor and I want to help you."

Barak continued to huddle in his place without reacting.

"I will now ask your mother a few questions, okay?" the psychiatrist said. "You are welcome to join in the conversation whenever you like."

For a long moment, his gaze remained fixed on Barak. Then he turned to Leora. "What condition does Barak have?"

"You can see for yourself."

"What I see is that he is not talking," Dr. Yompolsky said with a pleasant smile. "It is every person's right to remain silent. That does not hurt anyone. I even know some people who would be much better off if they were quieter. What are his symptoms, Mrs. Altman?"

The mother's voice broke. "Look at him. A boy of seventeen, closed up in his room all the time, doesn't eat, doesn't drink, doesn't shower—doesn't do anything! Just lies in his bed all day and cries."

"What about school?"

"It's summer vacation."

"Ah. And friends?"

"I don't know. I go out in the morning and come back late at night. I work at two jobs. My husband has been in Beit Levenstein for the past half-year. A vegetable."

"And what happened now? What brought you here?"

"Barak suddenly stopped moving. He won't react, won't answer me. See for yourself. I called our family doctor and he told me to take him to the psychiatric emergency room. I... I can't believe I'm in a place like this." She started crying.

"You've come to the right place. I hope that we will be able to help Barak here," the psychiatrist said. He studied the boy and jotted a few notes in his file. The boy's weight appeared normal for his age; he was dressed appropriately for the season; his hygiene seemed slightly less than ideal; his fingernails were uncut but not torn off; there were no outward indications of his having been harmed by himself or others.

"Does he drink alcohol or use illegal substances?"

"No. Heaven forbid!" Leora said with a shudder. Dr. Yompolsky hid a smile. Another Tel-Aviv mother who thought she knew everything her son was up to…

"Has he had treatment in the past?"

"Too much. I must have supported half the psychologists in Tel Aviv."

"Medications?"

"You mean, does he take pills?"

"Yes."

"Of course not!" The mother appeared shaken at the thought.

"Suicidal tendencies?"

"What do you mean?"

"Has he ever tried to harm himself, or talked about doing so?"

"No. Not that I know of."

"Good. Thank you." The psychiatrist turned back to the boy. "Barak, I want to examine you now. Are you okay with that?"

No answer.

"I will wheel you to a cubicle and examine you, and if anything bothers you, just tell me," said Dr. Yompolsky.

The physical exam was conducted without the slightest reaction from the patient. The doctor shone a flashlight into his eyes, looked at his arms to check for cuts or injection-marks and checked Barak's reflexes, all the while making notations in the file.

"Barak, I am going to talk to your mother now, okay? We'll be right back."

Even when the psychiatrist and Barak's mother disappeared from view—despite the fact that they could see him through a crack in the curtain—he did not move a muscle but remained exactly as before.

"What does he have, doctor?" Leora asked.

Dr. Yompolsky sighed. "Right now, the boy appears to be in a catatonic state. That means a significant drop in reactiveness to surrounding stimuli. Such symptoms may come from several conditions—ranging from clinical depression or bi-polar disease, to dissociative disruption or even an outbreak of schizophrenia."

"I didn't understand a word of that."

"The important thing is that he is not a danger right now, neither to himself nor to others," the psychiatrist said. "But I would recommend leaving him here for observation for at least a few days."

The mother's permission was quickly obtained.

Dr. Yompolsky went off to deal with the admissions paperwork. But before that, he went into a quiet corner and dialed a number that did not appear in his phone's memory, but was firmly engraved on his own.

"*Tak* (yes)?" the man at the other end of the line said in their native Ukrainian tongue. In other words, *What led you to call me after two a.m.?*

The man listened to the psychiatrist's answer. Five minutes later, he was in his car and speeding to the hospital.

Jerusalem, 5772 / 2011

Avreimi and Chezky were apprehensive. What "whole thing with the money" was Yaakov the grocer referring to? What new bombshell was about to descend on their unsuspecting heads on top of all the other recent surprises?

"What, you don't know?" Yaakov said. "Your father, *z"l*, used to pay other people's accounts here in my store. They would sign for groceries, and at the end of the month he would come and pay part of the bill."

"Are you serious?" Avreimi and Chezky stared at one another in astonishment.

"He wouldn't pay it all," Yaakov clarified. "Maybe that was to prevent the people from realizing what was happening. A few hundred shekels for each family."

It was a long minute before the two brothers could properly absorb this new and moving information about their father.

"How… how many such families were there?" Chezky asked.

"Four or five. Really needy families: *bnei Torah*, some of them *ba'alei teshuvah*."

"Families from the neighborhood?"

"Yes."

"How long did this go on?"

"Years. Ten, maybe. It could be more."

"And how much did it all add up to?"

"Two or three thousand shekels every month. It varied."

Another customer walked into the grocery store and asked Yaakov for several dairy items. Chezky and Avreimi stood rooted in place, in the grip of deep emotion. No words were necessary. *Oy, Abba, zichrono livrachah…* Their dear, good father whom no one, it seemed, had really known…

A few minutes later, Yaakov returned, pulling them back into the here and now.

"So what do we do?" Avreimi asked his brother. It was obvious to both of them that they ought to carry on their father's custom, but where would they find the money? One of them learned in *kollel* and the other would make his millions only after he completed his studies. The sums Yaakov had mentioned had been their father's *"ma'aser* money." For them, it was a fortune.

"Tell me, Yaakov," Chezky said. "All those families? Where did he know them from?"

"I don't have a clue," Yaakov replied. "He sent them to me, but asked me not to tell anyone. There were also a few individuals, sad cases that no one cared about except him."

"I'm simply—stunned," Avreimi told Chezky. The same emotion was stamped on Chezky's face.

"There's one person you may know," Yaakov said. "An old man who wanders the streets in dirty clothes, a little mixed-up in his head. He's from Zichron Moshe. They call him Zalman. Do you know him?"

"No."

"You'd definitely recognize his face. The whole city knows him. It was very important to your father that the guy never know where the money came from. He warned me many times not to tell him who was paying the bill."

"So how did he get to you?"

"Your father told me where he lived. I went to him and told him that he could come buy food at my *makolet*. Believe me, I would not have done such a thing for anyone but your father. He lives in a filthy basement, and…"

"Just a second," Chezky interrupted sharply. "What did you say his name was?"

"Zalman."

"Is he an Ashkenazi?"

Yaakov sent Chezky a reproving look through his enlarging spectacles. "What does it matter whether he's Ashkenazi or Sephardi?" he asked in an insulted tone. "Are Sephardim not Jews?"

"No, no, you got me wrong," Chezky laughed, both amused and contrite at the accusation. "We're simply looking for someone by the name of Zalman who once had a connection with our father. What is his last name? Is it Berkovitz?"

"How would I know?"

"Where does he live?"

"Back then, a few years ago, he lived in Bucharim. I don't know if he's still there today."

"Okay, Reb Yaakov. We'll figure out what can be done about the money," Avreimi said. "Thank you very much—and *tizkeh l'mitzvos!*"

Yaakov's eyes filled with sudden, hot tears. "Ah, what a *tzaddik* your father was… It's such a pity. Really a pity."

Avreimi and Chezky lingered a moment in silence, respecting Yaakov's pain. Then, with a word of farewell, they left the store.

"Are we going to Bucharim?" Chezky asked.

"We're going to Bucharim. Do we have a choice?" Avreimi replied in seeming resignation. For two days he had been urging his brother to abandon his obsessive hunt for facts about their father's life. Now, though, he had to admit that his heart burned with the same curiosity.

The few details that Yaakov had succeeded in dredging from his memory brought the brothers to an old building not far from the Bucharim *shuk*. It was actually a large courtyard surrounded by residential flats, built in the style typical of the older Jerusalem neighborhoods. They had to enter the courtyard through the main entrance and cross it on the diagonal until they reached a narrow gate which would lead them out to the area behind the flats. There, on the left, a narrow staircase led to a tiny hallway—only a meter or two in all—with a peeling door at one end, its doorknob missing.

Chezky knocked on the door. No one responded.

"I don't think anyone lives here," Avreimi said nervously. The evening shadows had begun to gather, and the situation was not at all to his liking. There was no way of knowing who might dwell in this hole in the ground, or who might suddenly open the door.

Chezky pushed it lightly with his foot. To his surprise, the door opened a crack. Inside they saw a cluttered and messy room.

"Hello? Is anyone here? Anyone home?" Chezky called into the void.

No sound answered him.

"Enough, Chezky. Let's go!" Avreimi pleaded. "There's no one here."

Chezky pushed the door slightly more ajar. "Zalman! Zalman, are you here?" he shouted. But no Zalman appeared.

The door was wide open now, revealing the entire basement flat in all its disarray. It consisted of one room, long and narrow. At the far end, covered by a jumble of clothing, towels, and bedclothes, stood a bed. Nearby was a large table piled high with books. Chezky took a step inside, despite his brother's frantic, hissed disapproval, and took a closer look at the books. They were volumes of philosophy and science, astronomy and physics. Some were closed, while others lay open as though someone had been reading them. Bits of old, leftover food lay on what was supposed to be a counter. There was a sink in the center whose faucet dripped without surcease. Did anyone live here? It was hard to tell based on what he was seeing.

"Chezky," Avreimi whispered shakily. "Come out!"

Chezky emerged with his fingers over his nose. "What a foul odor," he said, taking a deep breath of the relatively clean air outside.

"Well, did you see anything?" Avreimi asked.

"No Zalman, no Berkovitz. I didn't see any name."

"So what do we do?"

Chezky looked around and shrugged his shoulders. "Maybe we should wait for him."

"What do you mean, 'wait'? Who says he'll come? Who even says that this is 'our' Zalman?"

"Let's ask the neighbors."

"And where do you see any neighbors?"

Chezky stuck his hands in his pockets and leaned against the stone fence. "So, we'll wait," he said.

"I am not waiting here till it's pitch dark," Avreimi informed him.

"You can go. I'm staying." In a mocking voice, Chezky taunted, "Now you'll definitely stay, right?"

Avreimi's mouth turned down. Chezky knew how to sting when he wanted to.

The toe of Avreimi's shoe nudged an envelope that lay abandoned on the ground. An old, stained envelope bearing the logo of the Israeli electric company.

Suddenly, his eyes registered something. He stooped and picked up the envelope. A broad smile broke out on his face. The name on the front of the envelope was a very familiar one.

"What's that you have there?" Chezky asked.

"Apparently, this *is* our Zalman," Avreimi announced. "Zalman Berkovitz."

"How do you know?"

Avreimi held out the envelope. "Look. Now you'll see why we haven't succeeded in finding him till now. See how it's spelled? Your dumb computer was looking for a 'Zalman Berkovitz.' It didn't have the sense to understand that 'Berkovitch' is also 'Berkovitz.'"

A S THE HOUR APPROACHED SEVEN A.M., THE EMERGENCY room began its usual noisy shift change. The day-shift nurses came in fresh and energetic, while the night staff waited, bleary-eyed, for the transport that would take them home. In a regular hospital, most nurses tend to be female; here, in the psychiatric hospital, by the nature of things a big percentage of the nursing staff was male.

Svetlana, the supervising nurse in charge of the night shift, made the usual rounds before handing over the reins. She passed among the beds accompanied by three male nurses from the day shift, briefly summarizing each patient's condition.

"We've admitted two stars in the last couple of hours," Svetlana said dryly. One of them was an Arab youth from Yafo who'd come directly from Abu Kabir where, according to the police report, he "suddenly went crazy." In the opinion of the head nurse, this was all a nice bit of playacting for legal purposes. The second was an elderly man from an upscale old-age home in Herzeliya who was spotted in the middle of the night walking on the building's roof.

When asked what he was looking for up there, he had been unable to supply a coherent answer. The home's staff averred that the old man had lately been complaining that he was sick and tired of life. In the morning, the psychiatrist on duty would be in touch with the man's attending physician. It was doubtless nothing more than the effect of an unfortunate combination of medications.

"And I see that Her Majesty, Queen Elizabeth, is with us again," one of the male nurses said with a cynical grin. He gestured at a fragile-looking woman in a tiara who'd been released from the locked ward just two months earlier, after her condition had stabilized and she had allowed herself to be persuaded at long last that she was not the Queen of England. As usual, she had stopped taking her meds, and within a few days her condition had deteriorated again. She had been brought to the psychiatric emergency room the day before, after she was found wandering through the lanes of a busy highway, stopping cars and demanding imperiously that their drivers take her home to Buckingham Palace.

"And this is Barak Altman," Svetlana said. "Seventeen years old, brought here during the night by his mother. He is nonresponsive and noncommunicative, doesn't pose a danger to himself or others. He was admitted for observation by Dr. Yompolsky. They'll decide what happens to him next at morning rounds."

The three male nurses studied the handsome youth rather sadly. Barak lay in the bed, unmoving, still in the clothes he had come in. A thread of saliva drooled from the corner of his half-open mouth and his blank stare was fixed on the ceiling. Long years of work in the psychiatric hospital had shown them so much suffering that their emotions had more or less shut down. Still, the sight of a young boy or girl newly plunged into the cycle of emotional sickness was bound to arouse a certain pain and compassion.

"Did something happen to him last night?" asked Ahmed, one of the nurses.

Svetlana picked up the case chart dangling at the end of the bed. There was nothing written on it except some sort of scrawl in Dr. Yompolsky's atrocious handwriting.

"Nothing special," she said, and continued her tour.

Her last remark was not strictly true. Though nothing at all appeared on his chart, a number of things had definitely happened to the boy during the night.

At 3:30 a.m., shortly after his weeping mother took a taxi home, a shiny black Buick with tinted windows had pulled into the psychiatric parking lot. The driver who stepped out of the car was sturdy though not tall, with a very short haircut that exposed his rather flattened skull. If not for the good suit he wore, one would have guessed that he was a boxer or wrestler. His step was bouncy and energetic, but beneath his low, broad forehead a pair of sharp eyes peered out of deep sockets.

The stranger passed by the reception clerk, now dozing in his chair, and dialed Dr. Yompolsky's number as he walked.

"Yevgeny, where are you?" he asked with a touch of impatience.

"I just stepped down to the cafeteria," Dr. Yompolsky said without a trace of apology. "He's in Room 18. I'll be up in a minute."

When the psychiatrist entered the room rapidly, holding a cardboard cup full of coffee, the visitor was already standing beside Barak Altman's bed and regarding him intently.

"Do you think he's...?" the stranger asked, carefully omitting the last word.

"Looks that way," replied Dr. Yompolsky. "He's definitely..."

"Good," said the muscular, short-statured man. He took a few pictures of Barak with his cell phone, while Dr. Yompolsky peered through the room's keyhole to make sure no one was coming.

"Details?" asked the visitor, after checking to make sure that the pictures had emerged successfully.

"Barak Altman, male, age 17½," the psychiatrist began reading, as the other man typed the facts in with his stubby fingers. "Came last night with acute catatonic rigidity, apathy, and paralysis. No specific traumas known. No knowledge of previous morbidity. An only child, living for the past six months only with his mother."

Dr. Yompolsky concluded his recitation and fell silent. The visitor stopped typing and lifted his eyes questioningly.

"That's all?"

"At this stage. When he starts talking, we'll know more."

"Keep me updated." The stranger returned his phone to his pocket.

Yevgeny Yompolsky looked at the other man's expensive suit and late-model phone and smiled inwardly. He remembered the two of them as students in Kiev, when that city had been part of the Soviet Union. In those days they hadn't had fashionable briefcases or sophisticated computers. Computers? Sometimes they hadn't had anything to write with at all! When a shipment of paper reached the university, there was sure to be a dearth of pens—and when the pens finally arrived, the paper had run out...

"When are you taking him up for an MRI?" the visitor asked in Ukrainian.

"Irina arranged a slot for me at 4:30," Yevgeny said.

For the first time, a satisfied expression crossed the visitor's face. Irina Plotkov, another faithful partner from the Soviet era. It was good to have friends, and good to have them placed in strategic positions. Irina was the technician in the hospital's only magnetic resonance imagining office, and she had proved herself very useful there. Like right now, for instance, when it was necessary to bring the boy up for an MRI before dawn, without too many people knowing about it.

"I'm going," he said, jangling his car keys. "Send me the results the minute you get them."

"Of course," Dr. Yevgeny Yompolsky said obediently.

And so, about an hour and a half before Svetlana declared at the changing of the shifts that nothing had occurred to Barak Altman in the course of the night, the results of his brain scan were already in the stranger's email inbox in his penthouse apartment in north Tel Aviv. He ran an eye over the pictures with satisfaction. He was no neurologist and had never studied medicine, but he had learned how to look at an MRI and find what was important to him.

As Dr. Yompolsky believed, the boy was definitely a candidate. Yevgeny did good work, he thought. He would definitely throw in a good word for him in Kiev.

The low-browed fellow opened a new file on his personal computer, named it "Barak Altman" and saved it along with dozens of other files that bore names such as "Guy Hardof," "Tamar Toledano," "Noam Hadar," "Yaniv Kahanowich," "Sahar Stern," "Meital Cohen-Aharonov" and "Orit Talmor"—all of them Israeli teenagers between the ages of 16 and 18, most of them from the Gush Dan area. For several years now, he had been assiduously gathering the facts and performing the follow-up, with the help of faithful partners such as Yevgeny Yompolsky, Irina Plotkov, and a few other old friends.

The first signs of morning had appeared in the sky over Tel Aviv when the man who looked like a boxer turned off his personal computer. At six, he would begin the new day with an hour of vigorous swimming, followed by another hour of exercise in the gym.

The elevator descended the twenty floors to the private parking lot in speedy silence. Instinctively, from the habit of long years, he checked his car to make sure no one had broken into it, sabotaged it, or wired it with explosives. Many dangers stalked a man in his profession. Most of his friends, who had been less cautious, rested today under marble monuments—in the best cases—or on river bottoms, in the worst ones.

The ride was short. Tel-Aviv was not yet crowded with traffic at a quarter to six. On Rechov Yirmiyahu, his destination, all the parking spots were taken. But he didn't have to worry about that. There was a space reserved for him, as there were for all diplomatic embassy vehicles.

The sun continued to climb, and the soft air of morning enveloped the city. The driver of the black Buick could already make out the colors of the national flag flying proudly over his workplace: the yellow-and-blue flag of Ukraine.

Jerusalem, 5772 / 2011

Avreimi and Chezky were excited. This was Zalman Berkovitch's house—pupil #1064, who had lived in the orphanage alongside their father for a year and could certainly supply new details about him.

"The documents in the archive," Chezky recalled, "said that he was an intelligent boy, but disturbed. There were several letters from a psychiatrist and admittance forms from the Kfar Shaul psychiatric hospital. Both his parents were Holocaust survivors, who, the file said, were emotionally disturbed."

"The question is: How close was he with Abba?" Avreimi said. "It's not logical to expect Abba to have kept up with the children in the orphans' home after he was taken away to the kibbutz. He was only five years old."

"True," Chezky agreed. "Not even Chacham Reuven laid eyes on him until that chance meeting in the street, when Abba was already about twenty."

"Abba probably met Zalman again after he married Ima and returned to Yerushalayim," Avreimi speculated. "He probably recognized him as one of the kids from the orphanage and made sure to add his name to the list of those he was helping out financially."

"So why was Abba so insistent that Zalman not know who was paying for him?" Chezky asked. "Yaakov said that this was especially important to Abba in Zalman's case."

Avreimi was silent. What could he say? There were so many questions and so few answers. It seemed as though each new snippet that was revealed only brought additional mysteries.

"So what do we do?" he asked after a long moment. "Do you really want to wait until he gets back?"

Chezky looked at his watch doubtfully. He, too, was not enamored of the idea of wasting hours in this hole.

"Yaakov from the *makolet* said that Zalman is well-known in Zichron Moshe," Avreimi said. "Should we go there? It's not far."

Chezky grinned dismissively. "And do what? Go over to each beggar and ask what his name is? That's no good."

Another silence fell between them. Chezky sat down on the stone wall and passed the time scrolling through his cell phone. Avreimi clasped his hands behind his back and paced back and forth, sunk in thought. Chezky called a friend to ask something about a class they were taking. Ten minutes crawled by.

"Well, we can't wait here till Moshiach comes!" he snapped suddenly.

Avreimi turned to face him, surprised by his brother's outburst.

"Let's wait a little longer," he suggested. "We'll make our effort and Hashem will help. You can see how we were led to this place… real *siyata d'Shmaya*. What are the chances that Yaakov from the *makolet* would remember Zalman's name, out of all the people Abba was giving money to?"

Chezky regarded his brother suspiciously. "What happened to you?" he asked. "Changed your mind? Yesterday you were against this whole investigation."

Avreimi took one step toward him, and stopped. "True," he admitted. "But this is something I learned from Abba: Always think about what Hakadosh Baruch Hu wants from you right now. Chezky, let Hashem guide us. Believe me, we won't lose out."

Chezky lowered his eyes and wrapped himself in a baleful silence. It always made him angry when his big brother talked in this vein. For Avreimi, Hashem was in the picture 24 hours a day. He lived with a kind of constant, righteous devotion to Him. True, Abba had been that way, too—but Abba was *Abba*. On him, it had sat naturally. Who was Avreimi trying to fool? Let him save these performances for his wife.

It wasn't that Chezky didn't believe, *chas v'shalom*. But enough of this all-devouring *frumkeit*. With all respect to *emunah*, you didn't have to wave it around all the time.

Chezky felt his heart constrict at a sudden memory that surfaced out of nowhere. He, too, had been this way in *yeshivah ketanah*. He, too, had once been innocent and righteous and striving for the spiritual. But that was long ago. How very long ago…

You can't go out into the cynical academic world and remain a "yearner." You can't hang around with ambitious law students and speak the language of the *mussar va'ad*. If the gang down at the Institute could see Avreimi… they'd gobble him up without salt. *Kollel* men like him were the frequent target of mockery and haughtiness, even contempt. In the halls of academia, they were not too keen on those for whom the peak of ambition was to have one good *davening* or a total immersion in Torah.

"How cold you've become," Avreimi would tell him sometimes,

when he caught a look of disdain on Chezky's face at the sound of some halachic or *hashkafic* argument. "Where did it come from? From your friends at the Institute for *'Chukas Hagoyim'*?"

The truth was—yes. Chezky admitted as much to himself in rare moments of introspection. *But I brought some of it with me…*

"Hey, did you *daven* Minchah?" Avreimi asked suddenly.

"Yes, early this afternoon."

"I haven't yet. I'm going to find a shul. I have plenty to *daven* for," Avreimi said, with total seriousness.

It doesn't take a scientific mind or complex statistical computation to figure out that Minchah, in the first eleven months after a parent's passing, takes longer than at any other time. First you wait for the previous *minyan* to finish, hoping that there's no one else with a similar obligation lurking in a corner and plotting to take the *amud* that you've had your eye on for the past ten minutes. And at the end of *davening*, there's no slipping away after *Kedushah* or making an elegant getaway while saying *Aleinu L'shabe'ach*. You stand right there like a good boy, in front of the congregation, until the last word of the last Kaddish.

While Avreimi was *davening*, Chezky remained in the small clearing, strewn with stones and thistles, and went slowly crazy with boredom. A mischievous wish flashed through his mind that Zalman Berkovitch would appear right now, while Avreimi was gone, if only for the sight of his brother's surprised face on his return from shul. But not even this thought was capable of entertaining him for more than a few seconds out of the forty minutes he waited with nothing to do.

"Well? He never showed up?" Avreimi had finally returned.

"No."

Dusk was falling, and the blue sky was turning dark.

"I have to get home," Avreimi said. "What should we do?"

Chezky shrugged.

There was a sudden noise from the courtyard. It came again, closer this time. The brothers fixed their eyes on the courtyard's inner entrance. They still couldn't see anyone, but their ears told them that a person was walking, or rather schlepping himself, toward them. He would set down one foot and then drag the second; put down one foot and drag the other. Was it him? Had Zalman Berkovitch arrived at last?

Something clattered to the ground in the courtyard. The foot-dragger paused for a moment, perhaps to rest. Then the sounds of his approach began anew, and a familiar figure slowly filled the entrance.

18

So *this* was Zalman Berkovitch? The same thought passed through Avreimi's and Chezky's minds. A little disappointing, to be sure… Indeed, there was no one in Zichron Moshe who didn't know this eccentric, strange, oversized pauper, with his dirty, ancient cap and eyes perpetually downcast.

The man continued to drag himself toward the door to his abode. Then, at a precise instant, Avreimi and Chezky's feet entered his line of sight. He froze in place and lifted his head slightly, studying them with rheumy eyes.

"What do you want?" He waved the bag he carried in their direction, as though shooing away a couple of pesky flies.

"*Shalom aleichem*, Reb Yid," Avreimi said.

The pauper was momentarily taken aback. Then he began advancing again, dragging his leg toward his home. In the clear plastic bag in his hand was a loaf of bread, a bag of milk, a container of cheese, and a thick book written in English.

"What do you want?" he asked again. He obviously did not expect an answer.

"Are you Reb Zalman Berkovitch?" Avreimi asked, speaking slowly and clearly.

"Get out of here. What do you want?" The beggar repeated his mantra without stopping.

"We are looking for Reb Zalman Berkovitch."

"What do you want?"

It required a sensitive ear to pick up the slight change in his tone. His meaning was definitely still *get out of here*. But now there was also a hint of *who are you, and what do you want*?

Avreimi took a single cautious step forward. "We are the sons of R' Shlomo Kohlberg, who passed away two weeks ago. Do you know him? You were together as children."

Zalman Berkovitch remained still. No reaction.

"Were you in an orphanage?" Chezky tried. "Was there a boy there by the name of Shlomo Kohlberg?"

Zalman Berkovitch had already begun limping down the four steps leading to his door.

Avreimi looked at Chezky in despair. What to do now? The fellow refused to answer their questions. In a moment he would reach the door and bolt it behind him.

I have an idea, Chezky signaled to his brother. "Yaakov, from the *makolet*, sent us," he called after the retreating figure. "Do you know Yaakov?"

It worked. The beggar stopped walking.

"He told us to ask you if you know Shlomo Kohlberg."

Zalman Berkovitch turned slowly to face them. His eyes still held suspicion, but it had diminished.

"Yaakov is a good man," he said finally, and held up the bag with the grocery items.

"Yes, Yaakov is a *tzaddik*," Avreimi agreed.

"He gives bread and milk. But not cigarettes," Zalman Berkovitch complained.

"Why not?"

"It's not healthy."

"Do you want cigarettes?"

"Yes."

"What brand?"

"Parliament Long," the beggar said, with surprisingly refined taste.

"Tell me if you knew Shlomo Kohlberg, and I'll buy them for you," Chezky declared.

Zalman Berkovitch responded with silence.

"Were you in an orphanage as a child?"

Zalman Berkovitch mumbled something.

"There was a boy there named Shlomo Kohlberg. Do you remember him?"

The beggar shrugged his shoulders, longing for cigarettes but unwilling to supply the desired answer.

"He was an English boy. He was there only a few months and then was sent to a kibbutz. Do you know him? Do you remember someone like that?"

"What do you want?" Zalman Berkovitch retreated to his former line of defense.

"Yaakov said that you should try to remember," Chezky said.

"Yaakov is a good man," repeated Zalman Berkovitch.

"Yaakov said that you should try to remember if you knew a boy named Shlomo Kohlberg," Chezky tried again.

"But he doesn't give cigarettes. Only bread and milk." The man continued bemoaning his bitter lot.

Avreimi and Chezky exchanged a discouraged glance. They were out of ideas.

Berkovitch turned toward his door.

At the last instant, a notion popped into Chezky's mind. He stuck his hand in his back pocket and withdrew his wallet.

Zalman Berkovitch had stiffened at the sudden movement. A moment later, his eyes lit up at the sight of the thing from which people usually took out coins for him. Or even, if he was lucky, a bill or two.

"Money?!" Avreimi whispered into Chezky's ear. If a pack of Parliament Longs hadn't helped, why should a few shekels wake up Zalman's memory?

Without taking his eyes from the pauper, Chezky opened his

wallet. He rummaged among the compartments until he found what he wanted and drew it out. It was a small passport picture, wrapped in plastic—the photograph of his father at the age of four, which had arrived at the orphans' home together with the letter from the English rabbi, R' Shabsai Gordonsky. The picture Chezky had found in carton 1956d in the orphanage's archive.

"Nice!" Avreimi whispered approvingly. Despite the situation, Chezky's heart swelled with pleasure for a second.

He balanced the picture between the pads of his thumb and forefinger and extended his hand to Zalman Berkovitch. "This is Shlomo Kohlberg," he said. "Do you remember him? Was he with you in the orphanage?"

The man took a step back in reaction to Chezky's outstretched arm, so that he stood with his back pressed to the door of his flat. But his interest had been piqued, and his eagerness to receive the promised pack of cigarettes overcame his fears. From the protection of his doorway, he leaned forward. He wrinkled his nose and creased his brows in an effort to see the picture.

"Do you remember this boy? Was he in the orphanage with you?" Chezky asked again.

At first, either the picture was too far away or the pauper's poor eyesight made it impossible for him to focus on it. Chezky walked slowly forward, bringing the photo closer and encouraging him to try harder. When he was about three steps away, the picture was at the point where Zalman could see it clearly.

His eyes rested on the photograph for a moment. Suddenly, as though he had seen a monster, a look of pure terror crossed his face. He retreated in alarm until his back touched the door of his home. His hand groped feverishly for the knob, trying to open an escape hatch.

Avreimi and Chezky's hearts skipped a beat. This reaction was completely unexpected.

Gradually, the initial panic subsided from Zalman Berkovitch's face. His teeth clashed together angrily. "*Yemach shemoinik! Yemach shemoinik!*" he screamed hoarsely, his accusing eyes riveted to the picture in Chezky's hand. His former apathy had vanished.

Fury agitated his whole body. Advancing toward them, his hands shook as he began to spew an incomprehensible diatribe aimed at the childish, innocent face of Shlomo Kohlberg peering out from behind its plastic cover.

Chezky took a hasty step back and exchanged a look with his brother, who seemed equally stunned. Zalman raised his eyes to them, as though he had suddenly realized that they were somehow connected to the figure in the photograph. He stomped toward them with open menace, spitting and roaring, "Wicked ones! Communists! Go back to Russia! Go to the KGB!"

The brothers recoiled. This was a new and frightening Zalman Berkovitch. From the shell of the passive pauper had burst a completely different figure, forceful and filled with fury.

Zalman Berkovitch regained his composure—or as much composure as his damaged spirit allowed. Wheeling abruptly, he limped as quickly as he could to his flat, like an animal escaping to its lair.

The two brothers remained rooted in place in the small clearing in front of the house, frozen in shock. "Get out of here!" they heard from inside the flat. "What do you want?"

Zalman Berkovitch paced his dark hovel in turmoil, shouting and cursing. Suddenly, the window opened and a cup flew out at them—followed a moment later by a spoon. The man's face appeared at the window. "Get out of here! Go back to Russia! Go to the KGB!" he screamed. More than anything, he appeared to be afraid.

"Let's go," Avreimi told Chezky. "It's a pity about that poor guy."

"What could be so frightening about this picture of Abba?" Chezky asked as they walked rapidly back to the courtyard and out to the street.

Avreimi did not say what he was thinking.

"Do you think Abba did something to him as a child?" Chezky pressed.

"I don't think that's it," Avreimi said briefly.

"On the one hand, he didn't remember Abba's name. But, on the other, the picture made him go out of his mind. It seemed to remind him of something very traumatic."

Avreimi turned aside and entered one of the small shops in the Bucharim shuk. "Give me a pack of Parliament Longs," he asked the shopkeeper, and took out his wallet.

Chezky gaped at him in astonishment.

"For Zalman Berkovitch," Avreimi explained. "We promised."

"Are you crazy? He spat at me!"

"I don't recall that you made the cigarettes conditional on our liking the information he supplied us," Avreimi said sarcastically.

"What did he even say? Nothing!"

"A great deal." Avreimi smiled sadly. "Communists, KGB, Russia. He said a great deal."

Chezky looked at his brother. All at once, he absorbed what had really happened back there.

"He also told us—in case we hadn't known it yet—that there were portions of Abba's life that were not so nice," Avreimi said in a lowered voice. After a moment's thought, he added, "We should never have become involved in this."

They left the shop. Avreimi headed back toward the courtyard and Zalman's home.

"You're not going to knock on his door and give him the cigarettes, I hope," Chezky said, looking askance at his brother.

"Actually, I thought I'd give you the honor." Avreimi's lips turned up in a half-smile. "A chance to see what good aim you really have."

"I'm still not sure he deserves it. But okay…" Chezky took the cigarette pack and crossed the courtyard on the diagonal until he reached the entrance of the small, open area from which Zalman's door could be seen. He hurled the pack right onto the small paved area in front of the door. When he returned to his waiting brother, his brow was creased in thought.

"What?" asked Avreimi.

"I have an idea," Chezky said slowly.

Avreimi looked at him expectantly.

"He spoke of Communists, and Russia," Chezky said in a thoughtful tone. "And that reminds me of something. When I checked out kibbutzim, there was one that was considered a

Communist kibbutz. 'The first and only Communist kibbutz in Israel.' I just don't remember what it was called."

"Aren't all kibbutzim Communist?"

"Oh, no. Kibbutzim belong to the *Socialist* movement—Mapai, Mapam, and that sort. Only one kibbutz was openly Communist, which is a far more radical approach. They admired Stalin and the Soviet Union even when others had already wised up. Why can't I remember the name of the kibbutz?"

"Is there any way you could find out?"

A spark of mischief rose to Chezky's eyes, but he immediately suppressed it. This was not the time to debate the merits of the Internet with his brother again.

"I'll try to check," he said. "It's late. You have to get home. I'm going to drop in to see Ima first."

"Not a word, right?" Avreimi reminded him.

"Oh, come on." Chezky was insulted. As if he had to be told *that*!

"Listen to me, young man." The old woman screeched so loudly that Chezky was forced to move the phone receiver away from his ear. "It's not *kibbutz* Tel-Chana anymore. Is this the number of the kibbutz office? Yes! Was I the kibbutz secretary? Correct! But there is no kibbutz today. The kibbutz was privatized. Today, it's a *moshav shitufi*—a cooperative settlement. Western imperialism has vanquished the last Communist fortress in Israel!"

Chezky was not all that interested in the settlement's legal status or the financial ramifications of kibbutz privatization, but this was a way to initiate a conversation with the woman. She mourned the death of idealism and the rise to dominance of the country's capitalists, who, in her opinion, had no values and no beliefs. They were just waiting for the older generation to die out because it was too expensive to provide them with care. They didn't remember that those old folks were the ones who had built the State with their own two hands, who'd drained out the swamps, paved the roads, and established settlements. But today? Everything was a quick fix, everything was disposable—a throwaway world. No respect for their elders…

"Actually, I'm looking for someone who was once on the kibbutz with you," Chezky cut in gently, when his patience had reached its limit.

"Well? I knew them all." The old *kibbutznik* rose to the challenge with glee. "I've been here since 1950—two years after the establishment of the State. I used to work in the turkey coops during the day and handle the administrative paperwork at night. Not like these days, when—"

"His name was Shlomo Kohlberg. He was a child when he came from an orphanage in Yerushalayim."

"Shlomo Kohlberg?" The all-knowing old woman was surprised. "Could you be talking about Momi Arzi?"

"No. Shlomo Kohlberg."

"The religious boy? Chareidi? Lived in Yerushalayim?"

"Yes."

"Who became a *ba'al teshuvah*?"

"Yes."

"The adopted son of Sonia and Mikush?"

"Uh… I don't know…"

"I've got everything in my head," the old woman boasted. "Who else remembers that Momi Arzi was once Shlomo Kohlberg? Only me! Once a kibbutz secretary—always a kibbutz secretary! Listen, young man. I'll give you Sonia Arzi's number. I'm sure she'll be able to give you Momi's number in Yerushalayim."

Kibbutz Tel-Chana, 5772 / 2011

"HERE ON THE KIBBUTZ, THEY USED TO HAVE A SAYING: 'G-d takes the good ones for Himself.'" A tight smile emerged on the deeply wrinkled face of Sonia Arzi.

She was sitting in an upholstered armchair in the living-room of her modest apartment in Tel-Chana's older section, her walker within arm's-reach. On the sofa facing her sat Avreimi and Chezky, and on the low table between them the Filipino aide had set down some refreshments: a bottle of cold soda, and pretzels and chocolate that she poured into bowls straight from the packages, which she opened in front of their eyes so that they would not suspect their kashrus. The bowls, like the cups she brought from the tiny kitchen, were plastic and disposable.

The two brothers shook their heads in sorrowful agreement. All souls return in the end to their source beneath the Throne of Glory, but Abba really had been among the best of the best.

The elderly *kibbutznik* waved a hand in dismissal as she realized that her two young guests had not grasped her full meaning.

"I meant that our best people became *ba'alei teshuvah* and turned religious," she clarified. "Your father was a wonderful boy. He could have gone far. We gave him the best education. We gave him love and warmth. I really don't know what went wrong. Why he had to betray us that way and become religious." She spat out the last word as if it were a curse.

When Chezky had first spoken to Sonia Arzi—on the previous day, immediately after he had received the number from the former kibbutz secretary—he had found it hard to believe that he was talking to a woman who was approaching the age of ninety. She was quick on the uptake and expressed her opinions with great clarity—especially those that clashed with the views of whomever she happened to be talking to.

Chezky had tried, in that telephone conversation, to discover whether or not she was already aware of his father's death. After all, Abba had been her adopted son. Within a few sentences, it became clear to him she had not yet heard the bitter news. And, within a few more, he realized that the news was not so bitter to her. Though she expressed surprise that a man not yet in his sixties had suddenly passed away, her murmured, "I share your sorrow," did not sound as though she shared this or any other sorrow.

"You can come over, to hear stories and look at pictures," she had agreed to his request. "But don't expect me to speak well of him. I am not so quick to forgive a child who turned his back on us with such ingratitude. He lacked for nothing here. We gave him everything. We treated him exactly like a son of the kibbutz. On army furloughs he would come home to us. He had a roof over his head here when the army gave leave for Shabbatot and holidays. We raised him with the values of cooperation, hard work and the brotherhood of man. He was a part of the great family of workers all over the world. But he decided to cross the line and choose religion. For that there is no forgiveness, even after his death."

"In short, it won't be pleasant," Chezky had warned Avreimi in advance of their visit. "She's a die-hard Communist and a sworn radical leftist. Before she started having problems with her legs, she told me, she would spend her weekends volunteering in Arab villages and helping the 'poor refugees' there. The only holiday she celebrates is the first of May—the workers' holiday. And Stalin, in her eyes, is the sun around which the world revolves to this day."

The trip from Jerusalem to Tel-Chana was filled with apprehension.

"He was one of their most promising youth group leaders." As he drove, Chezky recalled another tidbit that Sonia had dropped in their phone conversation. He explained to Avreimi that their father had been a group leader in the HaShomer HaTzair youth movement. "Everyone predicted great things for him in Israel's left-wing faction," he said. Avreimi heard the echo of Zalman Berkovitch's spine-chilling shouts: "Communists! Go to the KGB! Go back to Russia!"

The paths of Israel's first and only Communist kibbutz were as green and well-tended as they'd expected. What they hadn't expected was the sight of so many crocheted *kippot*. They saw a group of teenaged boys, two modestly-dressed women pushing babies in strollers, and an older man wearing a huge crocheted bowl of a skullcap from which wild *payos* flew as he drove a car that sported a big, orange flag.

"Ask someone," Avreimi urged. He had meant that Chezky should ask for directions to Sonia Arzi's house, but the answer they received solved, as well, the riddle of the many "national religious" figures in the settlement.

"Sonia Arzi? An old woman? Then she must be from the kibbutz," said a sunburned boy with a peeling nose and a large white "Na-Na-Nach" *kippah*. "This section is for those who were forced out. This is where we're staying temporarily until we go back to Gush."

Chezky recalled now another detail that he had noted in the course of his search, but which had seemed irrelevant at the time: Tel-Chana had been joined by a group of families from Gush Katif—a development that had aroused the ire of the last of the Communists on the kibbutz, who had long since seen their world collapse.

"How do we get to the kibbutz?" asked Chezky.

"It's down the road. You'll see: where the orange flags turn into red flags," the boy joked. But he didn't receive the expected chuckles in return. Neither Chezky nor Avreimi were in the mood for jokes just then.

"Come in, come in," Sonia Arzi called out from her place in the living room, when they knocked on the door of her home. Her vinegary voice was in stark contrast to the perpetual smile worn by the Filipino woman who opened the door for them.

"Shalom," Chezky and Avreimi greeted her as they walked hesitantly inside.

"Don't be afraid—we know the rules. No shaking hands, only kosher food, disposable dishes. Your father trained me already," Sonia Arzi reassured them, in a voice that was far from reassuring.

The Filipino, apparently inured to her employer's manner, motioned graciously for them to sit down.

"So you're Momi's sons." Sonia scrutinized them critically.

"We knew him as Shlomo Kohlberg," Avreimi said. "We heard the name Momi for the first time yesterday, from the kibbutz secretary."

"Drora Tzeiler?" The old Communist pursed her lips as if to indicate that she didn't have a very high opinion of *her*, either.

For a few minutes, silence filled the room.

"After the army, he simply disappeared," Sonia Arzi said suddenly. "We threw a party here for him and some other soldiers who'd finished their military service. There was also a nice ceremony in the local branch of HaShomer HaTzair. We thought he would join the kibbutz and realize his potential, but he cut off all contact. Disappeared. As though the earth had swallowed him up."

Chezky and Avreimi said nothing.

"And then, about four years ago, he suddenly appeared again. That was after Mikush died."

"Who?"

"Mikush. My husband. There was a nice funeral on the kibbutz. Members of the movement came from all over the country—Jews, Arabs, Knesset members. Mikush was the secretary of the Kfar Saba Maki branch. That's the Communist Party. And suddenly, who shows up? Momi! Religious, with a beard and those clothes... Everyone was stunned. In shock! For twenty years no one laid eyes on him, and suddenly he's back—and he's *dati*. The first thing he did was come over to greet me.

"I don't know how, exactly, but Mikush knew that Momi had become a *ba'al teshuvah*. He never told me. Mikush wasn't a big talker, but he knew enough to call Momi half a year before he died, to ask if he would say Kaddish at his funeral. Shall I tell you I liked that? No! All your life you're a passionate Communist who doesn't believe in anything, and suddenly, when you're about to die, you fold up? Well, if you'd known Mikush you would have understood. He never had much of a backbone.

"Anyway, the funeral was surreal. One minute, the last of the Communists are standing around the open grave, singing the "International" with all their hearts—do you know the "International"? It's the Communist hymn, the Soviet Union's anthem—and the next minute, a religious man is standing there with a hat and beard, saying prayers and reciting Kaddish, and suddenly all those atheists are covering their heads and answering 'amein.'

"Ever since then, he comes around once a year, on the anniversary of Mikush's death. He gathers a few people and goes to Mikush's grave to say Kaddish. It's easier now. There are all those religious folks around, so he doesn't have to work too hard to get his ten men..."

"But where was Abba for all those years?" Avreimi tried to turn the conversation into practical channels.

"I don't know," Sonia said, lifting her head slightly. "I didn't talk to him at the funeral and I didn't say much to him when he came around each year. I don't really know why I'm talking to you two. You're walking proof of his great betrayal. Momi's sons were supposed to be the next generation of the left in Israel, and the future of the kibbutz. If you two and some others had been here, we wouldn't have been forced to sell the kibbutz to... those extreme right-wingers who walk around here with their millions of children. We poured our hearts and souls into your father and his friends—and look at you. All dressed in black, and you probably aren't gainfully employed. It's good *you* don't serve in the army."

The Filipino served her mistress a cup of tea. Chezky opened the bottle of Coke and poured some for himself and Avreimi.

Sonia Arzi sipped slowly. When she next spoke, she did not look at the brothers but through the window at the vivid green outside.

"You should have seen him," she sighed. "Such a handsome boy—tall, talented. I remember him walking down these paths in his blue shirt with the white lacing, and the group of students surrounding him in admiration. How proud he was when he received his instructor's badge and stuck it in his lapel! Mikush went down to Kfar Saba and bought him new sandals, in honor of his becoming a youth-group leader. Mikush knew how to get along. He had friends in the city. But Momi, your father, refused to accept the gift. It was against the values of HaShomer. Do you know what he did? He went to one of the Arab villages, found a boy about his age who was walking barefoot, and gave him the sandals."

"There's something we still haven't figured out," Chezky said. "How did Abba actually come to the kibbutz? He was in an orphanage until he was five, and then he came here. What happened?"

"That's something you'll have to ask Drora." Sonia was dismissive of such trivialities. "She was the kibbutz secretary. She was the one in charge of bringing in the children."

Half an hour later, when they left their adoptive grandmother's house, they passed the home of Drora Tzeiler, who proved that it was possible to be an elderly, old-time Communist and at the same time full of laughter and humor.

"It was someone in Jerusalem by the name of Yechezkel Polowitz," she said, taking pleasure in memories of the past. "We did all our business with him."

On the drive home, Chezky phoned Yoni Schlusserman, administrator of the orphans' home.

"Hey, Kohlberg, what's up? Have you found something?"

"Almost nothing," Chezky said discreetly, employing a required skill for any good lawyer. "Tell me—do you happen to know someone by the name of Yechezkel Polowitz?"

"Yechezkel Polowitz? Why do you ask?"

"His name came up. The truth is, I'm sort of stuck here."

"Well, that's the old man—our previous administrator," Schlusserman said.

Chezky's fingers gripped the steering wheel forcefully. "The one who's... half-senile?"

"Yes. Do you know him?" Yoni Schlusserman laughed, forgetting that he was the one who'd called him that when speaking to Chezky.

"Not yet." Chezky tried to keep his voice light and even. "So, where does he live? And how can I meet him?"

Soviet Union, 5733 / 1973

THE TALL, EXPANSIVE BUILDING WAS COLD. THE SQUARE windows were always closed and no curtains had ever fluttered in the breeze. Its sealed, dusty exterior revealed nothing of the many activities that took place within its corridors, nor did its unimpressive appearance reflect the building's importance or the generous budget that the KGB's Department 19—R-19 for short—garnered every year.

The building was perched on the bank of the Dnieper River, which cut through Kiev, capital city of Ukraine. But the area was the most remote of all the city's suburbs. In this region one still saw a mixture of uniform, Soviet-style apartment blocks along with fields for agricultural crops. A little further downriver the residential homes disappeared, and fields of golden wheat spread to the horizon.

Despite the ornate style in which the structure had been built in the heyday of the Soviet empire, featuring sculptured columns and pointed gun turrets, time had coated the building with a layer of dust and soot that rendered it unremarkable.

The courtyard fronting the building was also devoid of any beauty. There were no trees or flower beds. Generally, it was covered with either grimy snow or piles of autumn leaves, tossed about by passing gusts of wind as easily as the KGB could sentence an ordinary Soviet citizen to ten years' hard labor in Siberia.

A high fence surrounded the courtyard. The central steel gate, fashioned with stylized openwork, was wrapped in chains and heavy padlocks that had rusted from lack of use. This gate was not meant to be opened. The entrance that the building's architect had designed had been sealed, as well, with a graceless layer of cement.

No one in the neighborhood knew what the building—which had once, in the distant past, served as a government school—was used for today. For a long time it had been abandoned, until one day it was suddenly reoccupied. In Kiev, as in all Soviet cities, people didn't ask too many questions. They were happy if they managed to obtain a loaf of bread or half a pail of potatoes, a warm coat for the winter or a pair of boots.

Nevertheless, rumors flew and speculation was rife. These ran the gamut from a mental asylum to an orphanage to an educational institution for children of anti-government individuals who had been sentenced to either a quick death by firing squad or the slower death of exile to Siberia. The building's heavy guard kept away the curious and the nosy. One child, it was whispered, had crossed the large beet field and approached the facility's fence, never to be heard from again. Though no one knew the alleged child and no parents stepped forward to confirm the story, it was enough to fend off people who had no wish to become more closely acquainted with members of the KGB and the militia.

In the past, the old-timers remembered, the building's front gate had stood wide open, and at day's end schoolchildren had burst happily through it. In the building's present incarnation, the gate was locked and all movement in or out of the building took place through the rear, out of sight, over a bridge that spanned the Dnieper. The bridge was new. It had been designed and erected within two short months, and without any budgetary restrictions, the moment the Politburo—the Soviet Union's highest governing body—decided to create R-19.

And over this bridge, which generally carried supply trucks, KGB vehicles and employee vans, there now moved a convoy of long, black cars headed by the presidential limousine. The limo's passenger was a man with the face of a sturdy farmer, thick black brows and a mane of slicked-back hair, who answered to the name Leonid Brezhnev.

The convoy passed a prominent sign at the entrance that read "University of Kiev" (no one ever admitted, either verbally or in writing, that R-19 actually existed) and continued on to the building's rear entrance, which had recently become the main entrance.

In a crowd outside this door stood a large welcoming committee, all of them excited and tense in anticipation of this visit. Every person standing there owed his status and success to the man in the limousine. He had personally undertaken the initiative that had created this department, which had all its needs met with a lavish hand, like the spoiled child of busy parents.

The difference was that the child need only remain quiet and not disturb his parents, while R-19 was required to produce results. It had to implement programs in return for the indulgence it received from its father, Brezhnev, and Mother Russia.

The goal was very clear; the problem was that the spoiled child was torn by two conflicting views as to how to achieve it. Representatives of both these views stood side by side now, in the welcoming committee. Both of them watched as the leader of the Soviet Union stepped out of his limousine and smoothed his hand over his suit jacket, whose lapels sagged beneath the weight of his gilded medals. He studied them through a pair of spectacles.

Soviet public libraries were full of books extolling Communism and blackening the decadent capitalistic West. Soviet readers were fed a steady diet consisting of one truth: every citizen worked joyfully on behalf of the state and its people, and received his needs on an equal basis with all his happy fellow citizens. Forging ahead in a personal business initiative with the goal of enriching oneself was considered a terrible sin against the People, a sin that weakened the collective and inevitably brought crime and corruption in its wake. The farmer and the laborer were the builders of the Revolution, and thus worthy of all praise.

But the libraries of the Kremlin, in Moscow—so said those in the know—contained Russian translations of every book of economics and business administration that appeared in the United States. These books were sealed off from the general public and could only be read with the permission of those on high. One of these enthusiastic readers was Leonid Brezhnev himself. There was no danger that these corrupt ideas would burrow into his brain and shatter his shining faith in the righteousness of Communism. On the contrary, he read them in order to understand why the West was such a failure, while the Soviet Union was flourishing so beautifully. He read in order to glean, from the trash heap of American thought, a few useful tips that could be translated for use in the Communist system and aid in the Revolution's success. Such as, for example, what he was doing in R-19.

He got the idea from a biography of one of America's foremost car manufacturing tycoons, who told how he had divided his company into two separate firms, encouraging competition between them and creating a lively rivalry between the two. The managers of both firms, previously friends, turned into bitter enemies. Their wives, who had once regularly shopped together, now loathed each other. Their children fought so much in school that it became necessary to separate them. But the industrial tycoon sat in his luxurious villa and counted the profits that rolled into his bank account from both of the rival companies.

"Accursed capitalist!" the Soviet leader spat at the picture of the American millionaire on the book's jacket. "Despicable opportunist, who thrives on humanity's weakness! Heartless egotist!" And then he wrote himself a note to make use of that tycoon's methods when necessary.

Professor Andrei Willotzky and Professor Andrei Kalinin were the Soviet version of the two competing C.E.O.s of the American car industry. Many believed that it was their shared first name, in a spurt of humor that amused only Brezhnev, that formed part of the reason for his decision to put them in charge of the department's two divisions. Between the two Andreis, of course, there was neither humor nor laughter, but only a deadly rivalry, fed by the knowledge that in Kiev—as opposed to Detroit, the car capital of the U.S.—the one who did not produce the goods would not find himself unemployed. On the contrary—he would have more labor than ever before. A very great deal more hard labor…

The leader of the Soviet Union shook hands warmly with Andrei Willotzky and Andrei Kalinin. They were both about his age, and the three shared a long history of meetings and more than a few secrets.

The president's entourage entered the building and moved toward the large conference room on the first floor, where they were to receive learned reports from the division heads regarding the progress of their programs, about past achievements and goals for the upcoming fiscal year.

"I'd like to introduce two outstanding employees in my division," Professor Willotzky said as they walked down the corridor. A handshake from the president, and a few personal remarks, were a worthy prize for a worker's effort and an encouragement for further dedication. These two, in the professor's opinion, were deserving candidates.

"Comrade Yevgeny Yompolsky," Willotzky told the president, "a psychiatric student in the University of Kiev. One of our shining stars."

Yompolsky, Brezhnev thought to himself as he extended a hand to the young man. *A Jew. How long will they dominate all of Russia*?!

He forced a smile to his face and uttered a few words of good wishes.

Yevgeny Yompolsky stepped back, and the professor motioned to a second young man, much less handsome, with a low forehead, deep-set eyes, and a powerful build. The young man stepped forward, and the president's heavy-lidded eyes opened slightly wider. This student looked no more than sixteen.

"Oleg Marinov," Professor Willotzky said. "Great leadership qualities. Does very unique work with our youth."

Leonid Brezhnev thumped the young man's shoulder in an extraordinary gesture of goodwill, and wished him well.

Jerusalem, 5772 / 2011

The orphanage's previous administrator lived in a spacious apartment that took up the entire top floor of a building in Bayit Vegan. From what Chezky had managed to learn, the apartment had been acquired in the good old days, when politicians and public figures were able to enjoy unrestricted benefits from "hidden gifts" without them being subject to the scrutiny of the pitiless media. In large, clear letters on an oversized mailbox, separated from the row of mailboxes belonging to the rest of the building's tenants, were the words, "Rabbi Yechezkel Polowitz."

"Looks like he has something to hide, no?" Chezky remarked as he and his brother finally managed to activate the elevator to Polowitz's apartment after a great deal of effort. The first line of defense had been in the lobby, in the form of a door with a sophisticated intercom system, complete with an electronic eye.

"Do you have an appointment?" asked a voice over the intercom that identified itself as belonging to the *rav's* secretary, after Avreimi and Chezky said that they'd like to speak with Rabbi Polowitz.

"No," the brothers admitted. "But it's urgent."

"He's unavailable right now," the intercom said. "He's resting. What is this about?"

"It's about someone who once lived in the orphanage," Chezky said.

"And what's so urgent about that?" the secretary asked from the top floor. "It's Erev Shabbos!"

"We traveled here specifically to meet him," Chezky said. He pleaded until the man relented and opened the door with a long buzz.

"Fifth floor in the elevator," he said, without mentioning an apartment number—perhaps because there was only one door on that floor, protected with a heavy lock and additional security cameras.

"Don't sound so hostile," Avreimi told Chezky. "We're talking about a man who's done a great deal for the community. You're not supposed to accept *lashon hara*, and with all respect, I'm still not sure we can trust that Communist *'tzaddeikes'*..."

Chezky weighed his brother's words and then nodded his head in partial agreement. There was truth in what Avreimi had said. It was important to have an open mind, with no preconceived notions.

"*Shalom aleichem.*" The door opened in front of them, interrupting their low-voiced conversation. The secretary was about fifty, with a short gray beard and an ink stain from a leaky pen decorating his shirt pocket.

He ushered them into the apartment's living room, which was filled with furniture but devoid of humanity.

"Just a few minutes," he said, and disappeared down a long hallway, leaving the brothers to form their impressions of the place. It was easy to see that the apartment had been built to a high standard and later improved upon. More recently, however, it had begun to age along with its owner. No one had bothered to remove the dust from the furniture or to reglue the peeling corners of once-costly wallpaper.

The enormous living-room windows offered a panoramic view of Jerusalem's western neighborhoods and, beyond, the hills that surround her. A crowded bookcase, protected by glass doors, lined half the living-room walls, while on the other half were numerous photographs of the apartment's owner shaking hands and posing with Torah luminaries and rabbis. Others showed him standing beside the prime minister, various city mayors, and generations of government ministers.

Five minutes later, the secretary returned with a vigorous step.

"You can go in now. But I must warn you that he cannot always answer. Sometimes he lacks the strength to speak. He's not a young man anymore."

The half-senile administrator, Chezky thought, remembering how Yoni Schlusserman had described his predecessor.

"We'll give it a try," Avreimi said, adding silently, *and may Hashem help us.*

The gray-bearded secretary led them down the long hallway. The smell of old age filled this portion of the house: a mixture of medications and disinfectants. Through the open door of one of the rooms, they glimpsed a hospital bed and a chest of drawers piled high with pill boxes and medical equipment.

The office was at the end of the hall.

Yechezkel Polowitz had a white beard which, in years past, had been majestic and flowing. Even now, when it had grown sparser, it still gave him a definitely rabbinical appearance. He sat in a wheelchair, which was nearly hidden from view behind the big, paper-strewn desk in front of him. Avreimi caught sight of a new-looking computer that looked like an alien transplant in the old-fashioned room.

Yechezkel Polowitz regarded his visitors in silence. One eye drooped slightly, while the other did not fully focus.

"Sit down, sit down," the secretary urged. He apparently served as the driver, waiter, aide, newspaper-reader, letter writer, and anything else that was needed.

"Rav Polowitz," the secretary said, raising his voice so that his employer would hear him. "Here are two brothers whose father was in the orphans' home. They would like to ask the *rav* if he remembers him."

The secretary turned to Avreimi and asked, "What is his name?" After hearing the answer, he leaned closer to the elderly former administrator.

"His name was Shlomo Kohlberg," he announced. "He was in the orphanage in the year 1956. He arrived from England at the age of four and stayed for less than a year."

The old man in the wheelchair did not move nor speak.

"He passed away not long ago, and they're looking for information about him," the secretary said.

There was another long moment of silence. Only then did the old man open his mouth and say, in a slow voice cracked with age, "There were many. I can't remember them all."

"Our father was sent to a secular kibbutz," Chezky said, trying to be forceful but retreating in the face of the old man's pitiful weakness. "Were there many children who were sent to secular kibbutzim in those days?"

Once again, there was a delay before the elderly administrator reacted, as though it took his mind time to digest the question and locate the answer. But when he spoke, he said nothing new. "I don't remember. You have to check in the office."

Chezky didn't bother waiting for the secretary to translate. "We went to the office, but someone cut our father's page out of the orphans' book," he said, leaning slightly closer to the old man and trying to appear firm. "We also searched the archive. All the documents pertaining to my father were missing. Someone removed them."

"In the office," repeated the old man, after the usual time lag.

"He's saying that all the details can be found in the office, and he doesn't remember, it was so many years ago, and there were so many orphans, always coming and going, and he was busy with many other things." The gray-bearded secretary offered a wealth of information embedded in those few words.

Frustration made Chezky more daring. "All we found was this," he said, placing the letter from the British rabbi, R' Shabsai HaKohen Gordonsky, on the desk with a little thump.

The old man's eyes moved very slowly down to the letter.

Chezky added his father's childhood passport picture to the display on the desk. Avreimi noted that his brother was angry and hastened to soften the atmosphere.

"That's all my brother found at the orphanage," he said respectfully. "Does the *rav*, perhaps, remember our father's face? It's very important to us to know what happened to him during those years."

Yechezkel Polowitz raised helpless eyes to his secretary.

"No, he doesn't remember," the secretary said, in a tone that said this meeting was about to be brought to a close.

"We traveled to Kibbutz Tel-Chana, where our father was transferred from the orphanage," Avreimi said. "And the kibbutz secretary gave us your name."

"She said, 'His name was Yechezkel Polowitz. We did all our business with him,'" Chezky added with an accusing look.

"Many people say many things," the secretary stated. "The *rav* is very tired. And, as you can see, he doesn't remember."

He escorted them to the door, singing Rabbi Polowitz's praises all the way. He talked about how busy the *rav* had been in those days, involved in community affairs from morning to night. Among his projects had been the orphans' home, which he had founded at the behest of Israel's Torah leaders in order to rescue orphaned children arriving from Holocaust-torn Europe as well as the children of new *olim*, and how his name was lauded by one and all to this very day…

He summoned the elevator for them and sent them on their way with great politeness. Then he checked the small screen beside the door, to make sure they'd passed through to the lobby at the bottom.

Only then did he permit himself to release an angry, pent-up breath and place a call to the orphanage office. He dialed the direct number, which bypassed the outer-office staff.

"Schlusserman," he said, not bothering to say hello. The secretary's voice resembled a snake's hiss. "They were here. Kohlberg's sons were here."

Yoni Schlusserman's answer did not come immediately. "So they came," he finally said.

The loathing between the two men was mutual.

"And they managed to get to the secretary of Kibbutz Tel-Chana," the secretary added frostily.

"So what? What do you want from me?"

The secretary uttered a silent, furious curse. "They also have a letter that they found in the archive. And a picture! Why did you let them go down to the archive?"

"If you don't mind," Yoni Schlusserman said in the same poisonous voice as the other man, "those were the old man's explicit instructions. That's what you said, right?"

"But I don't understand how that letter was still there!" the secretary said angrily.

"So next time, clean up better." Yoni Schlusserman was pleased to test his enemy. "If someone ended up with something, it was because of you."

"Oh, be quiet!"

"Don't dump your mistakes on me," Yoni Schlusserman said, speaking slowly but clearly. "You only cause harm, and that's because you think you know it all. They pay you to feed him and wipe his nose. Don't get involved in something you don't understand."

"Wise guy," the secretary muttered as his face turned gray. "You think you're so smart…"

Soviet Union, 5733 / 1973

"ANDREI SERGEYEVICH." THE LEADER OF THE SOVIET Union addressed Professor Andrei Kalinin in the time-honored Russian manner, which included his personal name as well as his father's. "Please render your report on the progress that's been made in your division."

President Leonid Brezhnev and the chiefs of R-19 were seated in an opulent and spacious conference room. In glaring contrast to the building's deliberately bland exterior, this room was expensively furnished. There were crystal chandeliers, heavy drapes, and huge, grim-faced portraits of the leaders of the Revolution, who seemed to gaze down from the walls at their spiritual heirs to make sure they did not stray from the proper path.

The table in the center of the room was enormous, its size underscored by the paucity of people seated around it. Only six individuals were present at the meeting. Leonid Brezhnev sat at the table's head. To his left, some distance away near the corner, sat his close aide, ready for any order. Four additional chairs, two on each side, held the two Andreis and their deputies. Their expressions were neutral and their gazes direct, but their churning insides reminded them that the next hour or two would determine fates. The remaining twenty chairs ranged around the table—which was covered by a red tablecloth, making it resemble a bloodstained battlefield stretching to the horizon—were empty.

In the natural course of things, such a limited forum would have generated an air of warmth and friendship. But between the heads of the two divisions lay a long-standing rivalry that had developed, with time, into a real hatred. And Brezhnev's imposing and fear-inducing presence did nothing to thaw the atmosphere.

Andrei Sergeyevich Kalinin cleared a suddenly dry throat. He straightened his back in his chair and lifted his head slightly.

"Comrade Leonid Illich Brezhnev, General Secretary of the Communist Party and President of the Supreme Soviet," he began, in a tone of voice normally used to address a packed auditorium. "In this last year, the division that the Party has appointed me to head has implemented your brilliant and inspired initiative: to renew the effective activity of the longstanding Union of Militant Atheists, which in years past operated in our blessed homeland in accordance with strictest Bolshevist principles. Our friends, the organization's members, are working with dedication to spread its message in the United States and Western Europe."

Kalinin's deputy took a book with a red binding from his briefcase and passed it to him. Bending slightly forward, the Professor set the book down before Brezhnev with a flourish.

"Over the course of the year," he continued, gesturing at the still-closed book, "we have established ten branches, six in America and the remaining four in Europe, of the 'League of Critical Thought'—a name which was chosen to camouflage its true purpose. An additional branch, in Canada, was forced to shut down after the authorities discovered its close link to the local Communist Party. They declared it illegal and arrested its staff. We were forced to bring in the…"

"Move on," Brezhnev ordered, furious over the reported failure.

"The detailed report," said Kalinin, who revived when he saw the president open the book and begin rifling through its pages, "describes all the activities that have been carried out by our various branches, with the goal of planting doubt in the people's minds about the truth of their religions—specifically Christianity, of course—and to undermine their faith. Our activity includes the publication of scientific books and manuscripts on the subject of atheism, anti-religious propaganda, and the dissemination of the idea that traditional customs are invalid and harmful to the modern man."

A brief, nostalgic smile lightened Brezhnev's face. "And the *Bezbozhnik*?" he asked. "Do you publish that over there as well?"

The newspaper *Bezbozhnik* ("Atheist" in Russian) had appeared in print in the Soviet Union in the period between the two World Wars, and was the mouthpiece of an organization that called itself the Union of Warrior Heretics, whose avowed goal was to undermine religious faith among its citizens and turn them into a great nation of unbelievers.

Kalinin weighed his answer carefully before he replied. "In America and Western Europe, we are unable to operate as efficiently as we do here, in our blessed motherland. We must be cautious so that our work may continue for an extended period. Only thus can we achieve our long-term goal: weakening the enemy and destroying him from within."

Professor Andrei Willotzky, the other Andrei on the opposite side of the table, let out a snort of derision, louder than he had intended.

The president of the Soviet Union turned slowly to look at him. "Comrade Andrei Pavelovich has some critique, I believe?"

"Destroying religion will not bring victory to the Revolution," Professor Willotzky declared. "Even if we publish article after article in opposition to the priests and monks, proving that they are degraded and deceitful, people will continue to believe. I don't think that's the way to weaken the enemy."

Brezhnev's glance traveled back to the other side of the table, waiting for a reaction.

Professor Kalinin waited a beat, rummaged through his thoughts, and said, "I would like to show Comrade Brezhnev a certain item."

Once again he signaled his aide, who took out a small, square box made of fine wood. Kalinin placed the box in the center of the table, near the red-bound book, but did not open it. He was enjoying the sight of his leader and his rival leaning slightly forward to see the box, trying to guess its contents.

His efficient aide already had another item in his hand—an office folder made of rigid cardboard. He passed this to Kalinin.

The Professor opened the folder and took out a number of official letters, each bearing the logo of some organization or institution.

Now he opened the lid of the wooden box and moved it closer to the head of the table. Inside, on a bed of velvet cloth, lay a fragment of ancient parchment, no larger than the palm of his hand. The Soviet president put on his glasses to study the parchment closely. On it were scrawled several lines in Arabic, though the letters were less rounded and more pointed than the familiar Arabic alphabet.

What is this? Brezhnev posed the question with his eyes.

Kalinin picked up the first of the pages in his hand. "This is a letter from the Division of Archeology and Anthropology of the Pushkin Museum in Moscow. It was sent to several institutes and important world experts, asking them to investigate a rare find that was discovered in an archeological dig."

He gestured at the wooden box and its velvet lining.

"The discovery is a piece of parchment, about 1,500 years old, which has been remarkably well-preserved. It is written in Kofi lettering, one of the ancient forms of Arabic writing. According to various other signs, it appears that the parchment is part of a document cataloguing the delivery of a herd of camels, issued by the authorities in the Higaz province to Abdullah ibn Abdul-Mattalib—who, according to tradition, was Mohammed's father."

"And...?" Brezhnev growled.

Kalinin set the rest of the pages on the table while reading out the names of the institutions from which they'd arrived: the National Archeology Museum in Athens, Greece; the Petrie Archeological Museum in London; the division for Near-Eastern Studies at Johns Hopkins University in the United States; and the Louvre, in Paris. "All of them," he said, "have first-class experts who have verified the authenticity of this rare discovery."

Kalinin paused a moment for dramatic effect. Brezhnev took advantage of the silence to complain, "We have plenty of fine laboratories and experts right here in the Soviet Union. We don't need the opinions of the Americans and the British."

With an effort, Kalinin managed to curb the smile that threatened to erupt on his face.

"The problem," he said, "is that this parchment is neither 1,500 years old, or even one year old. This 'antique artifact' was produced here, in this very building, by the experts of my division!"

The Supreme Leader's bushy eyebrows shot up in astonishment.

"In other words: we've succeeded in developing a method by which to create 'antiques' from every period, in such a way that no laboratory or expert in the world can detect the forgery even with the most modern methods."

Professor Willotzky—the second Andrei—drooped in his chair. His rival's performance had been impressive. "But what can this be used for?" He was unable to stop the question before it left his lips. It was exactly what Kalinin needed in order to continue his mesmerizing performance.

"A good question, Comrade Andrei Pavelovich." Kalinin sent him a smile dominated by predatory teeth, and glanced at the president. "I believe that Comrade Willotzky's wife comes from Turkmenistan, where Communism has been at work for many years trying to uproot the citizens' Islamic faith... not always successfully. Were you to show this piece of parchment to your mother-in-law, or perhaps to *her* mother, Comrade Willotzky, she would undoubtedly be moved to the depths of her being and kiss you with reverence. But when the news reaches the world's museums that a discovery was made in a dig somewhere in Saudi Arabia or Yemen, which proves that a writer from those times had plans to create an imaginary "prophet" who would disseminate words of meditation and contemplation, the entire world will be cast into turmoil. It will serve as incontrovertible proof that Islam is a fraud. That he was nothing more than the product of a creative writer's fertile imagination.

"What will that do to your mother-in-law's faith, Comrade

Willotzky? What will that do to the millions of Muslims throughout the world?

"And that's only the beginning. We can do the same thing to Christianity, to Judaism, and to any other religion. We will cut the ground out from beneath the feet of believers and show them that they are leaning on empty air. Imagine what would happen to the United States if, one day, millions of Christian believers learned that everything they've been taught since childhood is nothing but fiction, and that all the Church's values are based on lies."

A look of satisfaction settled over Brezhnev's face.

Jerusalem, 5772 / 2011

In silent accord, Avreimi and Chezky Kohlberg did not exchange a word on their way down from Yechezkel Polowitz's apartment. The silence continued as they exited the elevator and stepped into the lobby on the ground floor, crossed into the building's parking lot, and walked out into the street—as though the walls, columns, and bushes might have ears.

It was only when they were walking along the sidewalk toward the bus stop that Avreimi opened his mouth.

"I pity him," he said. "Poor fellow."

Chezky did not share his brother's compassion. "He deserves it," he said sternly, kicking a small stone with the tip of his shoe. "He's corrupt and repulsive."

"What a thing to say?!" Avreimi scolded.

"Why—because of his long beard? That doesn't impress me. What kind of business did he have with the kibbutzim, tell me that? What sort of 'merchandise' did he bring them, and what did he get in return? I wouldn't be surprised if he sold Abba for a nice price, exactly the way they sold Yemenite children when the State was founded."

"You can't accuse a person who's been involved with *chesed* and communal affairs his whole life, simply on the basis of someone who is unfit for testimony for every possible reason."

"You're naïve, Avreimi."

"Or maybe you've lost your innocence, Chezky, and think that the whole world is a liar."

"What 'whole world'? Did you see him? For all his senility, you can see the slyness in his eyes. And you know what? I don't even know if he's really senile. Maybe he's just pretending!"

"Now you're really exaggerating…"

For a few minutes, the brothers walked in silence, arguing without speaking.

"If we could only have asked Abba…" Chezky said suddenly, in a softer tone. Avreimi turned his head in surprise.

"Do you know how many times I find myself almost dialing his number?" Chezky went on, staring straight ahead. "Do you know how many times in these past days I've thought: *If only I could talk to him*? When he was alive, I thought that there were fathers and sons who were closer than we were. But now, suddenly, I feel how important he was in my life."

Avreimi said nothing, except, "Here's the bus stop."

"Especially now. Throughout this business, I've thought more than once: I wonder what Abba would have done in our place?" Chezky seemed almost to be talking to himself.

Avreimi hesitated a moment. Finally, he decided to speak. "If we could have asked Abba, I don't think we would have reached this point."

Chezky shot his brother an angry look.

"I also remember Abba all the time," Avreimi continued. "The things he used to say, the conversations we had. I think he's looking down at us and asking, *what in the world are they doing*? Do you know what he told me on the last night of his life? At the time, it didn't seem significant, but suddenly I see it in a new light. He spoke to me about the Gemara in *Chagigah* that says: *What is mysterious to you, do not explore, and what is hidden to you, do not investigate.*"

A shiver ran up Chezky's spine.

"D-do you think he knew that…?"

Avreimi shrugged.

"They say that forty days before a *neshamah* goes up to *Shamayim*, it senses that the end is near… But let's leave all that aside for now.

That was Abba's way of living. He hid all sorts of things—and now we're about to expose them all."

Chezky let out a long, frustrated sigh. He couldn't say that Avreimi was wrong, and yet…

"I know." Avreimi seemed to have read his thoughts. "I'm here, too, and I went along with you to the orphanage and Tel-Chana and Chacham Reuven. I'm also torn between both sides of the question."

"Do you think we ought to stop?"

"Absolutely," Avreimi said.

"Are you serious?"

"Very."

"You know that Abba grew up in an orphanage, was sent to a kibbutz, served in the army, somehow became a *ba'al teshuvah*, and that a poor lost soul goes into a panic when he sees Abba's picture—and you don't wonder what the story is?"

"I wonder, all right. But we shouldn't have started this in the first place."

"Listen," said Chezky. He took a page from his pocket. "It's not so simple. I've organized the information we have, and there's a problem."

Avreimi tightened his lips, but looked at the page. Chezky had created a neat chronological table, listing the years and the events that had taken place in them.

  1952 — Abba is born
  1956 — Abba arrives at the orphanage
  1957 — Abba is sent to a kibbutz
  1971 — Abba goes into the army

"By the way, I spoke to someone today," Chezky said quickly, before his brother could read the next line.

Avreimi lifted his questioning eyes.

"You remember Sonia Arzi, Abba's adoptive mother, telling us that his army superior was named Allon Koler? I spoke to him."

Avreimi emitted a bark of angry laughter.

"I just didn't have a chance to tell you yet…" Chezky felt the need to apologize.

"Well, what did he say?"

"He was completely stunned to learn that Abba had become a *ba'al teshuvah*. He told me that Abba had been an outstanding soldier, extraordinarily idealistic and principled. The salt of the earth, a true *kibbutznik*. He said that Abba was extremely leftist in his views—a stance that was not popular in those days. This was after the Six-Day War, when everyone was drunk with victory and wanted to annex the West Bank.

"What he actually said was that after the Yom Kippur War, Abba simply disappeared. No one saw him. He didn't appear when the reserves were called up, didn't come to meetings of his army unit or to memorials for his fallen friends. Allon Koler searched for Abba, he says. This was during the heyday of the *teshuvah* movement, when people were going back to their roots. It was the age of Ohr Someach, Arachim, Nesivos Olam—all the big names. 'Every month, we would hear about another member of our unit who had become a *ba'al teshuvah*,' he told me. Each time, another familiar face would appear in his yeshivah: a decorated pilot, a famous comedian…"

"In his *yeshivah*?"

"Ah!" Chezky smacked his forehead. "I forgot to mention that he, himself, became a *ba'al teshuvah*. Today, he's a Rosh Mesivta in Bnei Brak. He was very moved to hear that Abba had done the same, and of course was sad to hear that he had passed away. 'I saw an announcement in the newspaper about Shlomo Kohlberg, but I didn't imagine he was Momi Arzi,' he said."

"Momi Arzi," Avreimi sighed. "That name again…" He returned his gaze to the printed table in Chezky's hand.

>1973/4 — Abba is released from the army and disappears
>1979 — Abba marries Ima

"In short," Avreimi summarized, "we have a gap of five years, from 1974 till 1979, when we have no idea where Abba was or what he was doing. What we do know is that sometime during those five years he became a person who was *shomer Torah u'mitzvos*."

"Exactly."

"This disappearance of his—that's where everything is hidden." Avreimi's eyes were still riveted to the page. "I have a feeling that if we knew what Abba was doing during those five years, a lot of things would become clear."

"So you're going on with me?"

Avreimi looked at his brother and sighed.

Chezky leaned closer. "You're with me—if only to make sure I don't do anything stupid. Right?"

Avreimi looked at his brother, and sighed again.

"Maybe you'll laugh," he said after a moment, "but there's something that's been bothering me since we returned from that kibbutz. Sonia Arzi is angry to this day that Abba left her and… Mikush, or whatever you call him… after his army service. And I say: that doesn't fit Abba. It doesn't fit him today and it doesn't fit him then. I have a feeling that he didn't do it willingly. There's something else here. He was forced for some reason."

"Since you're talking along those lines," Chezky said slowly, "I also have a feeling, not so clear yet, that keeps getting stronger every day…" He hesitated.

"What kind of feeling?"

"The feeling that Abba may not have died of natural causes."

Avreimi's eyes widened in anger.

"The idea popped into my head in the orphanage archive, when I realized that someone had removed Abba's papers from there as well. But I thought that I was panicking needlessly, and calmed myself down. But from day to day, with everything we've discovered, I'm beginning to think there might be something to it."

"Don't talk nonsense! It seems to me you're influenced by the stuff you're learning about—all those violence crimes and court cases."

"There's something bigger here, Avreimi. The missing years, Zalman Berkovitch's terrified reaction to the picture—and don't forget the man who came to find Abba during the *shivah* and then ran away, the Russian who asked about archeology, and all the rest. Something's fishy here. Something doesn't add up. There's some big secret."

"You're imagining things," Avreimi said dismissively.

"What am I imagining?"

"Abba collapsed in the middle of Geulah, in broad daylight. What kind of nonsense are you suggesting—that someone shot him? Poisoned him? Assassinated him? What are you thinking?"

"Who told you that he collapsed in Geulah? Were you there?"

"Chezky, what's the *matter* with you?"

"They rushed us to the house, and we went from there to the funeral home. What do you know about what happened before? Did you check it out?"

Avreimi narrowed his eyes suspiciously. "Why? Do you have some other information? Is there something you know?"

"That's the whole point—we don't know anything. They told us that he collapsed and that they tried to revive him for an hour. And we believed them."

"What reason would anyone have for lying, Chezky?"

"That's exactly what I want to find out. Whether someone lied… and, if so, why."

Avreimi sighed in helpless frustration.

From his jacket pocket, Chezky removed another paper.

"Here's the name of one of the Hatzalah volunteers who treated Abba. I want to talk to him. Will you come with me, or should I go alone?"

"Where did you get that?" Avreimi's forehead wrinkled in surprise.

Chezky unfolded the page.

"There was a news item about Abba. The volunteer was interviewed."

"An article? Where?"

"Someplace—it doesn't matter where," Chezky said shortly.

"What's the volunteer's name?"

Chezky glanced down at the newspaper page. "Tzvika Rothman," he said. "He's a well-known volunteer. I don't think we'll have a problem tracking him down."

Avreimi looked at his watch. It was still four hours to Shabbos. His wife had doubtless already set off from Modiin Illit, and he had to be at the bus station to meet her and help with the luggage and stroller.

"I don't know," he said. "I have to think about it."

"You'll have all Shabbos to think. I have no classes on Sunday, so I'll be free."

"There'll be plenty of other things for me to do on Shabbos," Avreimi replied with a sad smile. This was the second Shabbos since the *shivah*. Last week they had all been at his mother's house, but this time Chezky would be going to his wife's parents, and Ari had elected to stay in yeshivah. That was a good thing. But it meant that it was up to him, Avreimi, to learn with his younger brothers, and generally stand guard to make sure the joyous Shabbos spirit was somehow preserved…

"You'll be coming to 'Mishnayos' on Motzaei Shabbos, right?" he asked Chezky. "We'll talk then and decide what to do."

"Okay, Avreimi. Good Shabbos, I'll see you."

Soviet Union, 5733 / 1973

PROFESSOR ANDREI KALININ APPEARED CONFIDENT OF success. The counterfeit parchment from the Mohammed era was perfect. His division would now formulate a systematic plan for undermining the religious belief systems of the citizens of the West. To that end, they would use theologians and experts in Christianity, who would prepare a series of archeological finds and ancient proofs, which would come to light gradually and arouse turmoil in the hearts of all believers. It would fragment Western society, lower national morale, and ultimately lead to triumph for the Communist Revolution.

The Soviet leader, with a glance, gave the floor to Kalinin's rival, Professor Andrei Willotzky.

"Comrade Chairman," Willotzky began, "as I have long contended, based on numerous studies, religious faith needs no proof. Therefore, destroying the factual basis for the existence of historical figures, or sowing doubt over the authenticity of holy texts, will not make people abandon their faith. Faith is an emotional matter.

It takes place within, in the heart, and cannot be fought with logic and intelligence."

He paused a moment, watching the Soviet leader to see if his argument had been absorbed in Brezhnev's plodding brain.

"*My* strategy, Comrade Chairman, is designed to dismantle the American and Western enemy emotionally. To melt away societal unity and turn America into a herd of individual sheep, leaderless and devoid of authority. I will turn them into egotistical people, self-indulgent and lacking in ideology.

"Unfortunately, it is not in my power to astonish you, Comrade Chairman, with an archeological item in a wooden box, as my colleague has done. In order to demonstrate my idea, I invite you to spend ten minutes watching a certain scene that is unfolding not far from this building, in one of the huts on this property."

Jerusalem, 5772 / 2011

There was no difficulty locating Tzvika Rothman. All of Jerusalem knew him. Chezky needed no more than a single phone call to learn where he was from morning to night: in his small printing firm on Rechov Yeshayahu. Unless, of course he had left to cover some gruesome accident with multiple casualties.

The brothers were still some distance away when they saw that they had come to the right place. A shiny motorcycle stood outside the printing house, poised to leap into action. On the back was a medical-supply box containing a wealth of life-saving equipment.

The proud owner of "Rothman Printing: The Center for Printing, Graphics, Publishing, and Document Copies, Black-and-White or Full Color, Single-Page, or Large Quantities" was a pleasant man of forty or so, rotund, jovial, and as energetic as a high-dose pep pill. He sat in the heart of the modest store in an executive swivel chair, behind a large desk piled high with a pyramid of papers, notepads and rubber stamps, invitation samples and ad drafts. He noticed Avreimi and Chezky standing in the doorway and invited them with a gesture to come in, although he did not immediately address them. He was busy with a phone conversation while simultaneously issuing instructions to a graphic artist sitting in her corner. Another call shrilled to announce its presence on his cell phone, while the beeper on his belt merrily joined the party with a stream of beeps and updates.

Five full minutes passed before the communications storm abated. The brothers hastened to take advantage of the lull.

"Are you Tzvika Rothman?"

"So they say." The man grinned proudly, as though he had just invented this inane quip.

"We are the sons of R' Shlomo Kohlberg."

"Remind me—what was it? A booklet? Advertisement?"

"What???"

"Did you order some work here?"

"No… You… treated him. He collapsed in the street…"

"Oh! Sorry." Rothberg did an immediate professional about-face. "When was this?"

"Three weeks ago."

"Where?"

"Not far from here, on Rechov Ashtorei HaParchi, corner of Reishis Chachmah."

"And what happened to him?"

"He died. They tried to revive him and then brought him to Bikkur Cholim Hospital…"

Tzvika Rothman remained impassive, like those members of the Chevra Kaddisha on whom death no longer makes an impression.

"How old was he?"

"Under sixty."

"Shlomo Kohlberg?" Rothman scratched his head with ink-stained fingers. "Ashtorei HaParchi and Reishis Chachmah? I don't remember such an incident… Just a minute—how did you even get to me? Who told you that I treated him?"

Chezky reached into his pocket and took out the copy of the article he had found on the computer. "Here. You were interviewed…"

Tzvika Rothman glanced at the paper and burst out laughing.

"This is nonsense from what's-his-name, the organization's

spokesman. He probably issued this press release in my name so that the reporters would call me."

"Even though you weren't there?"

Rothman chuckled good-naturedly. "Well, not everyone who knows how to perform resuscitation knows how to talk to the media. Understand, *yungerman*?"

Avreimi was finding it hard to grasp how this deceitful world operates.

"But..." he said in disbelief, looking at the copy of the article, "you say here that when you arrived on the scene you saw that there was nothing to be done, yet you 'worked' on our father in the street for an hour..."

"That's what we always say," the seasoned volunteer remarked, while punching another number into the phone. "But wait a second. I'll check to see who was really there."

Avreimi and Chezky were speechless with anticipation.

While he waited to connect, the printing-house owner went over to inspect the noisy copy machine, which was rhythmically spewing out pages—fresh message posters that would adorn the streets of Jerusalem by morning. His brow cleared as someone finally came on the line.

The conversation between the speaker and the Hatzalah volunteer began with several mutual joking barbs, an exchange of the latest news, and a number of friendly put-downs. "But listen," Rothman finally said. "Here's what I'm calling about. Do you remember Kohlberg, who died on Ashtorei HaParchi about three weeks ago? You threw the wolves my name—we still have to settle the score on that. But who really treated him?"

Avreimi and Chezky watched the play of expressions on Rothman's face as he listened to words they couldn't hear.

"No, no, no, there's no problem at all." Rothman calmed the person at the other end, who seemed to have become agitated, and glanced at the harmless visitors seated before him. "It's just that his sons have come to see me. They want to hear what happened and all that, you know..."

Another pause in the conversation.

"He's checking," Tzvika Rothman told the Kohlberg brothers. Several minutes passed as the proprietor moved around the room with the phone tucked between his ear and his shoulder.

The conclusion of the search at the other end concluded with a broad, understanding smile that spread over Rothman's face.

"It was Sotzkover, you say? Thanks a lot. *L'hitraot!*"

He turned to Avreimi and Chezky.

"Well, what did I tell you? There are people who may know how to resuscitate someone, but you simply cannot send them to the media." He repeated the joke, filled with pleasure at his own wit and completely forgetting that, in this particular incident, the resuscitation efforts had not helped…

R' Moshe Sotzkover was a gentle, quiet soul. It was easy to see that he had no hand in media matters. Three weeks earlier, on a Sunday afternoon, he had been learning in the small shul on the corner of the street, when someone who knew that he was versed in first aid ran in and urgently summoned him outside.

"So you're his sons…" he said, his face filling with empathetic pain. "He was young, wasn't he? There are still children at home, right?"

"The youngest is not yet ten," Avreimi averred.

"I was undecided about whether to talk to you," said Moshe Sotzkover. "I thought about going to the *shivah*, but I didn't have the courage. I also thought about calling, but afterward I decided that it wasn't my job. I'm not an investigator or a detective."

"Why?" Chezky asked, as a shiver began to creep up his spine.

"Look, there were a few strange things. The more time that passed, and the more I reviewed the events, the clearer it became that something wasn't right. I thought about talking to my stepfather-in-law—my mother-in-law's husband…"

"But what happened there?"

"Look, I've been at a number of such scenes, and I know what it's like in the field. It looked to me as if your father had not collapsed in the street. Someone—I have no idea who—brought him there, unconscious."

Avreimi and Chezky felt as if someone had whisked the ground from beneath their feet. The man's brief words had confirmed their worst suspicions.

"Maybe you really should talk to my father-in-law..." Moshe Sotzkover suggested.

"Who is he? How can he help?"

"He's a good man, a *ba'al teshuvah* and a really fine person. He married my mother-in-law a few years ago. He doesn't talk much, but he was a senior man in the Shin-Bet (Israel's bureau of internal security) or the Mossad or some such thing. I think he could help."

"What do you think?" Avreimi asked Chezky.

Chezky appeared to be in the grip of panic. They'd dug and dug—and suddenly the whole business had taken on a very sinister cast...

"Do we have a choice? What else should we do—go to the police? Press charges? I'd rather talk to 'one of ours.' "

"What's his name?" Avreimi asked Sotzkover.

"Itzik Peled."

Both brothers jerked upright in surprise.

"Itzik Peled? Who lives on Rechov Dovid Yellin?"

"Just a minute—are you Brachah's son-in-law?"

Now it was Moshe Sotzkover's turn to look surprised. "Yes. Do you know him?"

"What do you mean, 'know him'?" Chezky exclaimed. "Our father was the one who helped him do *teshuvah*! He came to see us during the *shivah* and couldn't stop crying. I even think my parents made his *shidduch*."

"So Itzik Peled was in the Shin-Bet?" Avreimi's eyes opened wide in astonishment. "I always thought he was some sort of private investigator or something. He ate at our house on Shabbos many times, but never talked about his work."

"Well, if you two know him, the whole thing will be a lot easier," Sotzkover said. "I'll call him and see if he can talk to you now."

Soviet Union, 5733 / 1973

EVERYONE ROSE FROM THEIR SEATS AND PREPARED TO LEAVE the conference room. Brezhnev's aide hastened to bring his fur hat and thick woolen coat. Like all good aides, he had known in advance what each of the "Andreis" had prepared. In order to view Professor Willotzky's little drama, it was necessary to leave the heated building and walk several dozen meters through the freezing Ukraine weather—and the leader's health must be safeguarded at all costs.

Waiting in the hallway outside the conference room were several additional aides and consultants, who joined the Soviet ruler and the division heads. Brezhnev's progress was heavy and slow, the result of several neurological strokes that had afflicted him in recent years, and which had been duly concealed from the nation in best Soviet tradition. However, his illness had not affected his stubbornness and intransigence in the slightest. He had never deviated from his ambition to weaken his greatest enemy—the United States—in every possible way.

The wooden hut they were heading toward was massive. The big front door was misleading. One might be forgiven for assuming that a spacious auditorium lay behind it, but when it was opened they saw only one small, dim room. There were no other doors leading from this room to any corridors. On the wall facing the door, side by side, were two long windows covered with drapes.

Professor Willotzky did not make them wait long. Striding to the windows, he pulled aside the drapes with a flourish, exposing the fact that the room was nothing more than a viewing chamber for what was taking place in the building's larger portion.

"We call this place the 'aquarium,'" he explained.

Behind the two windows were two large rooms, separated by a thick wall but resembling one another with astonishing accuracy, as though each was the mirror image of the other.

Each of the two rooms looked like a small paradise for children. Each featured a low table surrounded by colorful wooden chairs and piled with books and toys. In another corner stood an additional table with bottles of sweet drinks and plates of candies, chocolate bars and cookies. A corner of each room held a rabbit hutch in which three white bunnies munched on greens, while another corner was a repository for all sorts of dress-up clothes: adult suits and dresses, old hats, shoes and boots, scarves and costume jewelry.

For a moment, one might have been forgiven for wondering if the identical rooms were nothing but an optical illusion. Each of the rooms, however, had a different person inside, organizing the toys and checking to make sure that all was ready for the viewing. Brezhnev recognized them. These were the two outstanding students that Professor Willotzky had introduced to him earlier: the psychiatric student Yevgeny Yampolsky and youth counselor Oleg Marinov. To his astonishment, both young men continued what they were doing in their separate rooms, even after he positioned himself at the window. They made no sign at all of having seen him.

"This is a one-way mirror," Professor Willotzky said, as though divining his thoughts. "They can neither see nor hear us. Only *we* can watch *them*."

The leader nodded his understanding. He had read somewhere

about this clever American invention: to see without being seen. *Where was democracy?* he thought scornfully. *Where were equal rights? Hypocritical capitalists…*

Professor Willotzky removed the receiver from a telephone that was mounted on the wall, and dialed the number 9.

In the well-insulated viewing room, no sound was heard. They saw the student go to the phone, near the rabbit hutch, and pick up the receiver.

"You can bring them in," Professor Willotzky said.

Yevgeny Yompolsky glanced up at the honored viewers and gave them a brief odd nod. Only belatedly did Brezhnev realize that the student couldn't see them; he only knew that they were there.

Professor Willotzky dialed number 8. Now it was Oleg Marinov's turn to pick up the receiver in his room and receive the same order: "Bring them in."

Twenty seconds passed. Then the door of the right-hand room burst open and fourteen children, aged five or six, streamed in. The youngsters looked around for a moment, their shining eyes greedily taking in all the goodies waiting for them. Then they scattered and fell joyfully on the toys and sweets.

Professor Willotzky directed Brezhnev's attention to the left-hand room, which was still empty. After a few seconds, the door of this room also opened. But the people who entered were not children. They were adults who appeared to be in their twenties. Soon they, too, had scattered among the room's wonders.

"Note the behavior of each group," the professor urged. He crossed his arms across his chest and stood facing the pair of windows.

He knew that what the leader of the Soviet Union was about to see was no less stunning than the counterfeit parchment that his arch-rival, Professor Andrei Kalinin, had just presented in the conference room.

Jerusalem, 5772 / 2011

The neighborhood streets were very quiet on Sunday morning, momentarily calm after the din of Shabbos and gearing up for the busy week ahead. But Chezky and Avreimi, walking along the pavement, felt as though everything was roiling insanely around them. Huge waves seemed to roll off the rooftops in great, furious breakers, threatening to explode over their heads and drown them in their depths.

Two weeks earlier, at the conclusion of their week of mourning, they had put one cautious foot in the water. Back then, the current had still been weak and slow, and they had allowed themselves—Chezky to a greater degree than Avreimi—to go with the flow of their natural curiosity in uncovering secrets from the past. Gradually, however, the whirlpools had grown more rapid, more powerful, and more menacing, until suddenly it was impossible to break free.

Without warning, they found themselves turning wildly in the center of the whirlpool, growing dizzy, losing their breath, throwing out helpless arms on every side in an attempt to grasp onto something, but finding nothing. They were being sucked down to some unknowable place, to the endless deep…

Perhaps Itzik Peled was their rescuer, sent to them from on high to free them from these ominous straits…

"We're almost there." Chezky broke the tense silence as they turned into Rechov Dovid Yellin, passing Yaakov's grocery.

"Do you remember Shimshy Burstein?" Avreimi asked in a low voice a few dozen yards later.

Chezky didn't offer an answer. Nor did Avreimi wait for one. They both remembered Shimshy Burstein, *zichrono l'vrachah*. Who in the neighborhood didn't remember him—Brachah's husband and owner of the clothing store? That is, her *first* husband. Before Itzik Peled. Who in the neighborhood didn't remember Shimshy, so friendly and full of life, so happy to help everyone with his big, good-natured smile? Which of the neighborhood kids hadn't bought a new shirt for Yom Tov in his store, or a pair of pants for his big brother's bar mitzvah? And when any of the neighbors had a new baby, where did they go to buy a gift—a warm stretchie, a pair of quality bibs from America, or some tiny, adorable outfit—if not the Burstein clothing store on Rechov Yosef ben Matisyahu? And what a terrible shock had seized the neighborhood that stormy winter afternoon, when word began spreading from house to house that Shimshy had been killed in a car accident on the Jerusalem-Tel Aviv highway.

Avreimi and Chezky remembered themselves as boys, watching from the balcony of their home, frightened and alarmed, as the street slowly blackened with humanity. They remembered seeing the neighborhood women gather in the courtyards amid bitter weeping, and the eulogies of which they understood nothing but the wails and sighs. They remembered, too, how a number of *rabbanim* and community activists had gathered in the living room of their home a few days later. From the sounds that reached their bedroom through the closed door, they managed to grasp that money was being collected for the Burstein family.

As their father told those gathered there, "The shop always ran at a loss." And they remembered how, dating from that time, their mother made a point of always making her clothing purchases at Burstein's, even though the big store on Rechov Strauss had opened by then. And how they would enter the store apprehensively, and take whatever Mrs. Burstein offered, afraid to say that they didn't like it lest it distress the widow. Sometimes her children would come home from school to eat lunch in the small room behind the shop. The youngest of them had been the girl who was today the wife of Moshe Sotzkover, the paramedic who'd tended to Abba on Ashtorei HaParchi, corner Reishis Chachmah.

And now, Brachah Burstein was the wife of Itzik Peled.

She had remarried…

A second marriage…

Identical thoughts passed through the brothers' minds. The situation was a little different in their case. Brachah Burstein had already married off all of her children by the time she remarried, while their mother was younger and had children at home. But at some point she, too, would have to rebuild her life…

The thought was painful. Any attempt to banish it only strengthened it, as though their hearts were bent on feeling the pain. It was only Itzik Peled, in opening his door for them, who put a stop to this silent self-torture.

Avreimi and Chezky were taken aback. This was their first visit to Itzik Peled's apartment. The building's external appearance gave no hint of how handsome and well-cared-for the apartment was inside.

How long had they known him? Something like ten years. Where their father had picked him up they didn't know, but from the start he had stood out among the gallery of regular Shabbos guests. "He's a tough nut to crack," they remembered their father saying to their mother one Motzaei Shabbos. "Many layers. Many layers…"

Like all young boys, they'd been curious, but they'd been brought up not to upset the guests, many of whom carried around bundles of sorrow and buried secrets. They learned not to ask too many questions and to read between the lines. They deduced that Itzik Peled had been a yeshivah *bachur* in his distant past, and had even lived in the neighborhood—opposite what was once the Central Hotel. They understood that his childhood name had been Isaac Eisenfeld, and that he had studied in a yeshivah in Bnei Brak. While some of the other guests chattered away, charting the whole course of their lives—including some things that one would have preferred not to know—everything about Itzik was cloaked and mysterious. He never said more than he had to. For instance, until today they hadn't had a clue that he had worked for Israeli intelligence at all, let alone been a senior figure there.

In the beginning, he would talk about some sort of job that he had been forced to leave in deep disappointment. He had spoken about feeling betrayed, and Abba would quote, *"There is no fear of G-d in this place, and they will kill me."* Itzik had been single then, no longer a young man, bitter and disappointed. But from month to month he had changed—literally, before their eyes.

He transformed himself from a completely secular person to a mitzvah-observant one, imbued with fear of Heaven and setting aside times for learning Torah. He abandoned his clean-shaven look when Abba began urging him respectfully to think about marriage. Then he grew the silver beard that graced his face today, which, together with his frameless spectacles, gave him a neat and respectable appearance.

"Come in, come in," he invited them. Noting the tension in their faces, he made an attempt to thaw the atmosphere with a mild joke. "Brachah is in the shop, so please understand if the refreshments are nothing special."

It was a small but pleasant apartment that he had bought and fixed up before he married. There was a long table in the dining area, a bookcase, and a seating area. Through the large window the Kohlberg brothers could see a view of the city, strewn with the red roofs of the Machane Yehudah shuk and the Nachlaot neighborhood beyond.

"Come with me," Itzik said, and led the way to his den.

This room contained an office desk with a leather armchair on one side, and three facing metal chairs. The most noticeable thing about the room was the lack of any personal items, as though this was a sterile environment. "An interrogation room" was the comparison that rose to Chezky's mind. The desk was totally bare, as were the walls. The bookcase along one wall did not feature open shelves, but locked compartments. Only one small shelf near the desk held a single book, apparently well-used—*Michtav M'Eliyahu*, Vol. I.

Itzik sat down in his chair, and the two brothers took seats facing him. He immediately jumped up, as though he had forgotten something, left the room, and returned bearing a bottle of water and a plate of cookies that no one wanted. Chezky wondered if Avreimi had also noticed the fact that the room had no windows, or that the door was made of hermetically-sealed steel.

"We didn't know you worked for the Shin-Bet," Chezky remarked, after his host had resumed his seat.

"Who said I was with the Shin-Bet?" Itzik asked, opening the bottle.

Chezky was silent in the face of this denial.

"Never mind, it doesn't matter." Itzik released him from his confusion with a dismissive smile. "What is it that the newspapers like to say? 'There are things that it is still too soon to discuss.' Let's see how I can help you."

He opened a drawer and took out a pad of paper and a pen.

"But first," he told the two brothers, "do you have cell phones?"

"Yes."

"For greater security, let's shut them off. Give them to me."

"Why?"

"It's always best to be cautious. Cell phones can serve as excellent listening devices in the event that someone is interested in what you have to say."

Avreimi turned even paler than he had been before. "You think that somebody… is following us?"

"Actually, I don't think so," Itzik said, and smiled. "You two are not important enough. Still, it's best to be careful."

Avreimi and Chezky took out their phones and turned them off.

"Not good enough. Take out the batteries," Itzik instructed. "Cell devices continue to broadcast electronic signals even when they're turned off. Almost the only way to really turn them off is to remove the battery."

In stunned silence, Avreimi and Chezky did as they were told.

"Do you have a laptop computer or tablet?"

"I have one," Chezky said.

"Let's do the same thing," said Itzik Peled. A minute later, he had freed the battery from Chezky's laptop. "By the way, that's another advantage of 'kosher' phones. With I-phones and some other sophisticated models, it's sometimes hard to get the battery out. At secret army and intelligence meetings, they're not even allowed inside."

"Itzik, you're scaring us," Chezky said.

Itzik Peled gave him a calming smile. "Routine security measures. Nothing to get excited about."

He picked up the pen and lifted his eyes to look at them. "So," he began, "Moishy tells me that there are some things that are unclear to you about… your father."

Avreimi and Chezky exchanged a glance, and decided that Avreimi would be the spokesman.

"There were a few things even before," he said. "But what scares us the most is what he said—that Abba, *zichrono livrachah* didn't collapse in the place where he was found. Someone brought him there."

Itzik leaned toward them slightly over the desk. "Look, my dear friends. I love Moishy. He's a wonderful boy, a good husband, and a *talmid chacham*. But, with all due respect, he's not in the business of criminal investigation or pinpointing the cause of death. He can't decide these things."

"There were some other strange things that happened during the *shivah*," Avreimi continued. He began to list them: the English-speaking stranger who'd showed up at the house, the Russian who asked if Abba was still involved in archeology, R' Zerach's revelation that their father had been an orphan, the documents that had vanished in the orphanage's office and archive, Zalman Berkovitch's violent reaction to their father's picture, and their visits to Chacham Reuven, Sonia Arzi, and Yechezkel Polowitz. He concluded his recitation with Allon Koler's declaration that there was a black hole spanning five years in their father's life.

His story took over an hour to tell. Avreimi talked and Itzik Peled asked only the occasional clarifying question. Chezky studied Itzik's face the entire time. There was no sign of emotion—neither surprise nor anger nor sorrow. His face was a mask, revealing nothing of what was going on inside his brain.

"You know what? Let's go out into the field," Itzik suggested at the end. "Let's go to Geulah. It's not far. Let's see what we find there."

Tel Aviv, 5772 / 2011

H E SEEMED TO BE FLOATING INSIDE A DENSE CLOUD THAT enclosed him, white and opaque, on all sides. His mind was empty of thought, his body devoid of sensation. He simply—wasn't. He did not exist. Nothing.

And then, slowly and gently, something bore him upward, and he was suddenly above the cloud, able to see, trying to think, to be. And he knew that this state was very fragile, very temporary, and that he would almost immediately begin sinking downward again…

Moving his eyes was impossible. He mustered all his strength to the task of focusing on the point on which his eyes were already fixed. He managed to see: a pair of hands resting on a table, limp, inert, the fingers long and weakly splayed. His mind was working with nightmarish slowness, so it was a long time before he understood: *Those are my hands.*

Something at the edge of his field of vision seemed strange, odd, out of the ordinary. The sleeves… the color… But letting his gaze travel the length of his arm, from those limp palms up to the elbow, called for monumental strength. And he was so weak... He wanted nothing. His eyes saw but didn't see. They closed of their own accord, the lids so heavy...

Suddenly, a thunderbolt exploded in his ears. A voice was calling him. A thick, distorted sound, like a thousand meaningless sirens.

A storm exploded in his mind. Echoes of sound beat against the walls of his skull like balls of steel. Flashes of light darted past his eyes but did not form any clear picture. His head was tilted sideways, like a wilted stem; his neck muscles lacked the strength to hold it erect.

And again he was rising upward, and there was a slight clearing as a ray of sunlight managed to pierce the clouds. His sleeves were a pale-green hue, the fabric creased and indistinctly patterned. With a mighty effort, his eyes traveled up to his shoulder, then his chest. It was a nightshirt! On the pocket were some letters that he could not decipher. What did they say? What was that word? He tried to focus, but the strain brought pain, as if someone was drilling incessantly into his head.

Once again his eyes closed and his mind clouded over. For an eternity that lasted several minutes, he remained sunken in total nothingness. He had disappeared again, lost in non existence, detached from reality until the next wave came to lift him back into the world.

The pants he was wearing were of the same cloth: pale green, with the same dull pattern. And he was sitting on a plastic chair in front of a scarred wooden table.

Exhaustion weighed him down, but sudden fear lent him new strength. Slowly he lifted his head, directing his eyes to the left. He was in a room with light-colored walls. Some sort of abstract picture hung on the wall.

The moment of clarity passed quickly, leaving a series of questions in its wake. Where am I? Who brought me here? What am I wearing?

And again the thunderous noise, exploding at him from somewhere. Now the sound seemed more familiar, reminding him of something but still an unexplained mystery.

All too soon, however, he was again floating on a sea of nothingness, his open eyes transmitting nothing inward to his brain. Everything disappeared; everything around him died for another indefinite period of time that had no beginning and no end and was all emptiness.

And then again, the explosion of thunder, broken, unclear, yanking him from the depths and suddenly gaining meaning:

"Barak, do you hear me?"

It was a voice speaking to him. Someone was calling his name. Who was it?

His head was now hanging down so that his chin rested on his chest. His brain was transmitting an instruction: *Lift your head so you can see the man.* But between the order and its implementation yawned a turbulent sea of impossible effort.

Very slowly, centimeter by centimeter, he tried. *Don't let me get lost again. Don't let me disappear...* He succeeded in bringing his gaze to the shapeless flowerpot resting in the center of the table. Beyond it, further away, was something large and white that looked like a wad of cotton. And from the center of this wad came the voice: "Barak Altman, can you hear me?"

Barak closed his eyes, took a trembling breath, collected strength from every remote corner of his body, and slowly lifted his head a fraction more.

"Barak, how are you feeling?"

He opened his eyes. The figure on the other side of the table was a man. A man in a white coat. He was smiling. He was asking how he felt. He was waiting for an answer.

"I'm..."

He struggled to enunciate the syllables that did not want to emerge. With painful slowness, he got them out, one by one. "I'm... o... kay."

And again, abruptly, his head poked up above the waves, and for a moment his thoughts were clear and sharp: *I'm in a hospital! This man is a doctor! Where's my mother? How did I get here?*

He began sinking again into the thick down comforter that enveloped him in darkness.

The doctor's voice reached him from afar, accompanied by strange echoes so that it sounded distorted, unhuman: "Barak, you are in a hospital because you didn't feel well. My name is Dr. Yevgeny Yompolsky, an experienced psychiatrist. I am here to help you…"

Jerusalem, 5772 / 2011

The Avreimi and Chezky who left the Peled apartment bore no resemblance to the pale figures who had knocked on the door an hour and a quarter earlier. They felt revitalized and reenergized. Nothing had really changed. The situation was as complex as ever. But at least they were no longer on their own.

Chezky felt as though his shoulders were lighter and his step a bit freer. Avreimi's heart had eased as well, leaving him feeling better than he had in many days. Only now did they realize how heavy the burden had been. Only now, when they had someone to share their fears and apprehensions, when they had someone from whom to seek advice, did they grasp the confusion under which they'd been laboring.

A little surprisingly—to Chezky, at least—Itzik Peled, in their whole long conversation in his office, had avoided any mention of his service in the security network. The words "Mossad" and "Shin-Bet" did not pass his lips. Nevertheless, he radiated calm and competence. He knew what he was doing, and he was on their side. Had he been in the picture before this, they would have avoided a number of "beginner's" errors.

He was shocked, for example, by Chezky's suggestion that they lodge a complaint with the police. "Are you out of your mind?" he exclaimed. "Turn to the blue-coats? Do you want units of police officers and detectives to descend on this spot, two meters from Kikar Shabbat? Have you any idea what would happen? Within a day and a half, you wouldn't be able to step out into the street. And you—and your father, *zichrono livrachah*, of course—would be plastered across the front pages of every newspaper: 'Suspicion of Foul Play in Geulah…'"

"And don't forget Ima," Avreimi murmured, with a glance at Chezky. All she needed was for the whole world to start digging into the circumstances of her husband's death—and, no less painful, into the mysteries of his life, past and present. And what would all of it do to Ari, Miri, and all the younger children…?

"Couldn't we get an injunction against printing or publicizing anything?" Chezky asked.

Itzik Peled snorted. "An injunction… Ostensibly, they issue those based on the needs of the investigation, but they're actually based on the needs of public-relations and image. If some district police supervisor thinks this story would help him in his battle with the general supervisor, no injunction would help. He would find a way to get the story out."

The Kohlberg brothers exchanged a helpless glance.

"Look," Itzik said quietly as they descended the stairs in his building. "If we should ever feel a need to involve the police, we'll go to the top. I still know some people there. But we're getting ahead of ourselves. I still have no indication that this was not a natural death."

"If only…" Avreimi said. Long minutes later, he was still thinking about the strange significance of his words: a son hoping that his father had met his death in a natural way and not, for example, at the hands of a Jew-hater or some other agent. Or was it actually preferable for their father to have died *al kiddush Hashem*? The whole situation was insane…

The three men spoke little as they strode down Rechov Dovid Yellin and turned left to Rechov Pines. Avreimi and Chezky had known Itzik Peled for many years, but not well. There had been Shabbos guests who'd turned into family friends and whom the children had liked. Itzik had stopped coming to their house after he married Brachah Burstein, but even when he had visited frequently the children had always maintained a respectful distance, both because of his age and primarily because of the air of seriousness that enveloped him. "The solemnity of the *ba'al teshuvah*," their father used to call it.

As they passed the barbershop that they had patronized ever

since they could remember, Chezky unwittingly passed a hand over the unprecedented thatch of hair on his neck. When his father had died, he had already been in need of a good haircut. And his hair was not the only thing that had grown long. So had the list of things he had been neglecting. Life had come to a screeching halt at 2:50 p.m. on that Sunday three weeks earlier. He was not investing himself in his studies as he had done before. He had hardly been attending his classes at the Institute. Givat Shmuel had once been his home away from home. Since the *shivah*, he had attended several lectures by Attorney Safrid and had taken an exam that couldn't be pushed off. He had not yet received his grade, but this was the first time that he wasn't wondering how close he had come to one-hundred percent, but rather how close he had come to sixty…

He wasn't coping much better on the home front—not to mention the *Mishnayos* he had undertaken to learn before the *sheloshim*, now just one week away. And he wasn't managing to get any learning done, and not because of lack of time. While Avreimi seemed more successful at maintaining his routine, and had hardly missed any learning *seder* at the *kollel*, Chezky had to admit that he, himself, was coming apart at the seams…

"It was like that with me, too," a friend told him. The friend had lost his mother under similar circumstances several months before. "Take your time until the *sheloshim*—but after that, you need to get back to yourself. This is a natural process of working through grief."

How could Chezky explain to his friend that, in his case, the work of processing his grief had not yet even begun? Each day brought its new calamities and revelations, as their investigation yielded ever more questions.

They turned right, to Rechov Pri Chadash, passing between the noise of children in the Talmud Torah to their left and the sounds of prayer floating out of the Zichron Moshe shul to their right. Just one more quick left and then another right…

Avreimi grabbed Chezky's hand. "I haven't been here since the… you know." He sounded anguished.

Chezky bit his lower lip as his eyes filled with moisture.

Itzik Peled either didn't notice the brothers' emotion, or chose to ignore it. He slowed his energetic step and began advancing down the gentle incline of Ashtorei HaParchi. He walked slowly, like a tourist, casting curious looks in every direction. He peeked into courtyards, glancing occasionally over his shoulder and even lifting his head to study the upper stories of the buildings they passed.

A few more meters brought them to the intersection of Ashtorei HaParchi and Reishis Chachmah. Itzik stopped walking. With furrowed brow and compressed lips he regarded the narrow streets going off in all four directions.

"It was here," Avreimi whispered to Chezky, controlling himself with a visible effort.

Leaving them where they were standing, Itzik moved purposefully into the dead-end street to their right. He halted in front of one of the houses and looked at it with interest.

"Where, exactly, did he… collapse?" Chezky asked Avreimi, lowering his own voice.

"I don't know."

"May we can ask his son-in-law, Moshe Sotzkover," Chezky whispered.

"Maybe… but what difference does it really make?" Avreimi's face was long.

Chezky nodded his sorrowful agreement.

Avreimi roused himself. "Come on, let's join Itzik. Let's hear what he has to say."

Itzik Peled was already on his way back toward them, his face uplifted as his eyes traveled from point to point in the surrounding area.

"What are you looking for?" Chezky asked when Itzik was close enough to hear him.

"Someone who can tell me what took place here three weeks ago," Itzik said with a trace of a smile.

"Eye witnesses?" Chezky asked. Last semester, he had studied the laws pertaining to witnesses to a crime. In this case, there might be a good number of them: neighbors from the nearby buildings, shop workers, pedestrians, boys from the yeshivah on the corner.

"Just a minute," Avreimi began to protest. "That would—"

"That would arouse too much publicity—true," Itzik interrupted. "That's why we're not going around talking to people. What I'm looking for, to tell the truth, are cameras."

"*Cameras?*"

"Yes, cameras. Security cameras, inspection cameras, traffic cams. Everything is equipped with video surveillance nowadays: streets, banks, buses, offices. Whether you like it or not."

"Seriously?"

"Certainly. People have no idea of the extent to which their every step is being recorded. The world is crawling with cameras: visible ones as well as invisible, private cameras and those belonging to public entities such as the police, the municipality, or security bureaus."

"And all that recorded material is probably stored somewhere…"

"Of course! Traffic cams were designed for use in real time. If the control center sees that there's heavy traffic in a certain area, it changes the traffic lights to free up the cars. If a car is stuck in the middle of a tunnel, a barrier is lowered and traffic diverted to a different artery. Actually, though, even traffic videos are saved for one reason or another. The security bureaus, on the other hand, are obligated to store the footage that their cameras record. If there's a break-in at a shop, or if a hundred shekel goes missing from the cash register and you want to know if one of your cashiers helped himself to it, you have to rewind the footage and watch it, minute by minute."

"So you're looking for cameras that might have picked up… what happened here three weeks ago?"

"Yes. But it's not that simple. Too much time has passed. These systems have a limited memory. When the hard drive is full, older recordings are automatically erased. In general, ordinary systems save material for about two weeks."

"So we've missed it by a week."

"That is a bit of a problem."

"Just a second. I don't understand." Avreimi looked over at a nearby store. "You want us to go in and ask the shopkeeper to let us see his video footage? Why should he agree?"

"We won't go in, because the footage has already been erased," Chezky said irritably. "Didn't you hear what Itzik said?"

"Just a moment, friends," Itzik said, trying to calm the waters. "Look over there to the left, at the very end of the street. What do you see? A bank. Now, look to the right, and what do we have? A medical clinic, next to a kindergarten belonging to a large educational organization. Such places generally sign up with a security firm, where the videos are saved for a longer time. Besides, there's no need to ask permission to look at the footage. The link between the cameras and the security center is made via the Internet, and the security level is not high. There are entities that simply hack into these systems to get these videos—and save them."

"Who, for example?"

"For example, the Shin-Bet." For the first time, Itzik named the organization he had thus far failed to mention.

"Is that legal?"

Itzik paused before answering. "Was killing your father legal?"

Avreimi and Chezky stared at him in horror.

"So now you're agreeing that someone did kill our father?" Chezky asked. "You spoke differently before."

"*Suppose* someone killed him. If it *turns out* that someone killed him," Itzik hurriedly corrected himself. "I'm not deciding anything yet. Maybe, after we view the video footage, we'll know more."

Soviet Union, 5733 / 1973

FOR SEVERAL LONG SECONDS, SOVIET LEADER LEONID Brezhnev stood motionless. His eyes, wide with amazement, darted rapidly back and forth between the two windows and the two playrooms.

With each passing minute, the spectacle became more astounding. Involuntary gasps escaped Brezhnev's mouth as he leaned closer to the glass, the better to see. This was unbelievable! Simply unbelievable…

Professor Andrei Willotzky stood with arms folded across his chest, slightly behind Brezhnev's shoulder. He, too, was watching what was taking place in the two rooms, enjoying his leader's reaction and waiting for the right moment to begin his explanation.

To his delight, Brezhnev's curiosity got the better of him even earlier than anticipated. He turned to the division head and asked, with a half-smile curling a corner of his mouth: "Well, Comrade Willotzky? Perhaps you will tell us what you put in their food?"

Everyone in the viewing room made sure to smile.

The fourteen children in the right-hand room were behaving exactly as expected. They burst noisily into the room, surveying the plethora of toys and good things to eat with shining eyes. They quickly became absorbed in playing, reading, and eating. As expected, several groups had formed in the room: a few children were at the table, looking at picture books; others preferred to sit on the floor and play with blocks. Four youngsters clustered around the rabbit hutch, shrieking with pleasure and fear when one of the bunnies chomped on the carrot that they offered it through the cage's bars.

In the left-hand room, the same thing was happening. Everyone played, chatted, and munched on sweets. They behaved exactly as one would expect children to behave. There was just one problem: they were adults.

"How can this be?" Brezhnev burst out. "How did you turn grown people into... small children?"

Tel Aviv, 5772 / 2011

"Good job, Barak! Congratulations!" Svetlana called from the nurse's station, as the seventeen-year-old finished his slow walk along the length of the ward's wall.

This was Barak Altman's seventh day in the psychiatric hospital and he was beginning to break free—admittedly, very slowly—of the catatonic state in which he had been admitted to the ER a week earlier.

For four days, he had been in a state of complete detachment. Then he had begun opening his eyes, moving his hands and feet, and emitting choppy syllables. On the fifth day, Dr. Yompolsky made his first attempt to carry on a conversation with him. It was apparently too early.

"*Reacts slowly and belatedly to the sound of his name,*" the psychiatrist jotted on Barak's medical chart. "*His reaction includes a slight sharpening of affect, but hardly any verbal response. Will continue to follow up.*"

From that day, the pace of Barak's improvement had begun to

pick up, Svetlana noted happily. And today he had risen from his bed and taken his first, hesitant steps outside the room. He did not stray far from the wall, and from time to time was forced to stop and lean his shoulder against it. He did not make eye contact with any of the other patients, and he certainly didn't speak to them.

"Congratulations, Barak! Nice work!" the nurse called again.

The youth looked at her and then cast his eyes down again. He did not smile. The corners of his mouth did not make the slightest upward movement. He merely turned and began retracing his tiny, unsure steps back to his room.

Svetlana was insulted by the way he had ignored her. Dr. Yompolsky told her that he expected the boy's emotions to be remote and his reactions robot-like at the start of treatment. "Often, the body returns from paralysis before the psyche does," he explained, and asked her to inform him if there was any change.

That afternoon, Barak once again sat in a plastic chair beside the wooden table. The figure facing him did not look like a vague wad of cotton, and his voice did not sound distorted and strange. He looked and sounded like a very pleasant fellow.

"*Shalom*, Barak," the man said. "Do you know who I am?"

Barak shook his head, his dreamy eyes not meeting the doctor's.

"My name is Dr. Yevgeny Yompolsky. I am a doctor in this hospital. How do you feel, Barak?"

"O-o-okay."

The cadence of his speech was slow and his voice thick, but he could be understood.

"Barak, you didn't feel well a few days ago, and your mother brought you to us," Dr. Yompolsky explained. "What do you remember of the recent past?"

Barak spent a long moment trying to recall.

"Nothing," he said slowly.

"You collapsed. You spent several days more or less unconscious. Did anyone hurt you? Distress you? Do you know what caused this?"

There was another long silence before Barak mumbled, "Nothing."

"How do you feel now?"

"O-o-okay…"

"Good, Barak. I'm glad to hear that. I will come back tomorrow to see how you're doing. Perhaps I will give you some medicine, and I hope you'll be able to go home soon."

On his way out of the ward, Dr. Yompolsky passed the nurses' station. "Tomorrow, prepare the package for age six," he whispered to Svetlana, after making sure that none of the staff was within earshot.

Jerusalem, 5772 / 2011

Despite Itzik Peled's reassuring explanations, his words deeply unnerved the two brothers.

"Do you really think there's a possibility that someone killed our father?" Chezky asked in agitation.

"Guys, I didn't say anything official," Itzik said. "Be patient and let me get hold of the video recordings."

A sigh of sadness rose from the depths of Avreimi's heart.

"Let's just fix the timetable," Itzik went on. "The ambulance was called, I believe, at ten minutes to three?"

"Correct."

"And when was your father last seen alive?"

"At two-thirty, my father-in-law saw him on Rechov Malchei Yisrael," Avreimi said.

"That means that we have twenty minutes to reconstruct," Itzik concluded. "I'll get to work. With Hashem's help, we'll soon have a full picture."

"But… he didn't stay in one place for twenty minutes," Chezky protested.

"Naturally not," Itzik agreed. "We'll have to put together video clips from different sources. For example, if he took money out of the ATM machine and then got on the bus, or changed money at the Exchange, or passed an intersection that has a traffic camera—we'll use every source to put together a timetable of his actions. There are investigations that use videos from dozens of sources.

It's sometimes possible to track a person over a long period of time, even hours."

"And in our case?"

"Let me check it out. I'll see how much material I can get my hands on. I'll need to dust off a few old connections. We'll talk later."

"*L'hitraot.*"

"Just one thing..." Itzik said, stopping them. "You mustn't say a word on this subject over the telephone—not to each other, nor to me."

"Aren't you overreacting?" Chezky asked, hoping for some reassurance.

"I'm not overreacting," Itzik said. "Until we know what's going on, we need to follow some basic safety rules. Okay, you're free to go. I need to walk around here a bit more."

Avreimi and Chezky headed off in the direction of Malchei Yisrael, while Itzik entered the old shul whose plaque proclaimed that it had been built by good Jews from America. He sat down on one of the benches, among the mostly American young men who were in the *beis medrash*—perhaps the grandsons or great-grandsons of the founders—and opened a random volume. Not to learn. Who could learn now? He simply wished to blend into his surroundings, not stand out in any way.

The pleasant chant of learning lapped at him as troubled thoughts kicked and churned in his brain. What to do? What was his next step? The situation was not a simple one. He would have to find his way between the raindrops. The problem was, he was dealing with a downpour that had already created several very swampy puddles...

Once, things had been simple. Once, all he had to do was walk into the office of Giora Shagai, head of the technology division—a childhood friend from the days when they had walked these very streets, calling themselves Isaac Eisenfeld and Zelig Hackerman. But Giora had left Shin-Bet a long time ago and was now languishing in the prison system. Twenty-five years he had been sentenced to, a cheap price to pay for his costly betrayal and all the classified information he had passed to the enemy under the code name

"Alex." Twenty-five years, with no possibility of time off for good behavior. Yaron Kaspi, who'd headed up the Shin-Bet back then, had put all his weight behind seeing to it that the traitor's punishment was as severe as possible, and that the former department head would end his miserable life behind bars.

At first, Itzik Peled had participated in the outpouring of hatred and loathing that reigned in the upper echelons of the organization, all directed at Giora Shagai. After all, Giora had been planning to kill him in Rome and then claim that Itzik was "Alex." For many months, a faded picture of the traitor had hung in the organization's dining room, for use as a dartboard. But a year after the sentence was handed down—a sentence about which a complete media blackout had been scrupulously enforced—Itzik, too, disappeared from the corridors of the organization. At the same time, he began to be seen more and more frequently in other places. For example, the Kohlberg family's Shabbos table, in the Achva neighborhood, so close to the place where he had grown up with his father, Avreimel, and his mother, Ruchele...

And gradually, to everyone's surprise—none more so than himself—his anger at Giora had dissipated. The closer he drew in returning to his childhood roots, the more he recognized that Giora's corruption had not begun with his betrayal of his country or workplace, but rather with the great betrayal that they shared—the betrayal of their parents and teachers.

Together, they'd removed the *yarmulkes* from their heads and then, at eighteen, entered the army. Together they'd broken their poor parents' hearts; together they'd hardened themselves against all the tears and the pleading. "A person who would betray his family would betray his country," Shlomo Kohlberg once told him, at the start of their acquaintance. "Why have you been privileged to be different?"

And Itzik had immediately answered, "Apparently I have *zechus avos* or some other merit. I could easily have ended up in jail, like my friend."

His attitude toward Giora Shagai changed from anger to pity, and one day he even requested permission to visit him in prison.

He put his request form through the usual channels, through the head office in Tel Aviv, but an hour later received a furious call from Yaron Kaspi, who had already ended his tenure as head of the Shin-Bet and was now serving as a consultant to the prime minister on terror-related issues. "Peled, are you an idiot?" barked the man who did not recognize the existence of first names. "Drop this idea. Otherwise, you'll end up sharing the same cell as Shagai!"

Five years later, Yaron Kaspi had called him again.

"Peled, how are you?... I just wanted to let you know that this week, in a random car accident in Rome, someone by the name of Vittorio Lorencini was killed. Know him?"

Of course he knew him. The Saudi-born banker and son of the Italian Nazi criminal Joseph Lorencini—and the conduit through which "Alex" had passed all that security information into the enemy's hands. He wondered why it had taken them five years to catch up with him...

"By the way, Peled, I heard that you're about to get married," Yaron Kaspi had continued. "Better late than never, as they say. The main thing is that you should have *mazal tov*!"

And now, Itzik Peled thought as he leaned on the aged *shtender*, the time had come to jump into the water again. The problem was that the water was crawling with killer crocodiles, and the scent of blood was already in their nostrils.

26

ITZIK PELED STOOD UP WITH A SIGH. *SEDER* WAS OVER AND THE *beis medrash* was emptying. He left the yeshivah building and began walking up the hill in the direction of Zichron Moshe. He preferred a slower *davening*, but because of the Kohlberg brothers' visit he had missed his usual *minyan* and had to catch Minchah while there was still time.

The rays of the setting sun cast a morose tint over the neighborhood homes. Itzik found himself sinking into his own sad thoughts. The whole business had begun in 1993, about 18 years earlier. He was already serving in a senior position in the security organization. Less than three years later, shortly after November, 1995, he would be appointed a division head. One morning, he received a call from Daniella Zamir, the chief's indefatigable secretary:

"Peled, come up here right away," she ordered.

In Yaron Kaspi's office sat another man, unfamiliar to Itzik. He was British from head to foot: tailored jacket, elegant leather shoes, and a haircut that ensured that every hair remained in exactly the right place.

"Let me introduce you," the Shin-Bet chief said in English, "to Mr. Sean Mackenzie, of the British MI6."

Itzik Peled had shaken the visitor's hand, stealing a surprised look at the head of his bureau. MI6? What was he looking for here? Let him talk to the Mossad. After all, the British organization that paralleled the Israeli Shin-Bet was MI5.

"MI6," Yaron Kaspi confirmed. "Their Iranian desk, to be precise."

The Englishman offered a chilly smile.

"Listen, Peled," the chief began. "There's a port in southern Iran called Bandar-Abbas. Heard of it?"

Itzik nodded. He had definitely heard of it. For years, Bandar-Abbas had been a miserable assortment of dirty shacks and muddy huts. In the seventies, however, the Shah of Iran had decided to erect a large naval base in that location. To that end, he had decided to build two new cities right there, in the middle of the desert: Bandar-Abbas and Bandar-Bushar.

"This Bandar-Abbas," the chief continued, "sits smack in the middle of the Persian Gulf, in the Strait of Hormuz. The oil faucet of half the world. Our friends in London need to sniff around there for reasons of their own."

"O-kaaay…" Peled stretched the word out, as if to say, *What's our connection to all of this*?

"Who designed and built those two cities for His Majesty, Mohamad Reza Pahlavi?" the chief asked.

"Aha!" Itzik Peled began to comprehend. Naturally, the answer was: Israeli construction firms.

He laughed. "The *chevrah* had quite a party there, eh?"

"They sure had some kind of party…" the chief chuckled. And the Englishman, in his restrained manner, agreed.

The sixties and seventies, as all three of them knew, had been one long economic party for the Jewish state because of her varied links with the Shah. Israeli security firms provided weapons for his army behind the United States' back. The Shah paid a high price for these arms, and for much more. Israeli construction and engineering firms designed and implemented hundreds of military, commercial, and private projects throughout Iran. Not many people knew, for example, that the Hilton Hotel in Teheran was built by Israel's Solel-Boneh, or that the communications tower in the capital city was designed by Israeli engineers. The same was true of many factories, bridges, government buildings, and military installations. Israelis also designed and built many of the royal family's sumptuous palaces, as well as the luxury neighborhoods of Iran's elite. No one dreamed that it would all blow up in their faces one day, when Iran turned into a radical Islamic republic.

"She was a beautiful country," Yaron Kaspi said suddenly. "I was there several times, with the prime minster and security ministers. You know—unofficial visits... What wealth there was, what splendor. Unbelievable luxury: solid-gold faucets, walls papered with jewels, gardens with plants and flowers from all over the world. But what corruption... and what tyranny. He was truly paranoid, the Shah. His security people were undoubtedly among the cruelest in the world. As bad as that of the Revolutionary Guard today, do you think?" He threw a glance at the British agent, who tightened his lips and nodded in polite agreement.

"And that's what finally brought us the Muslims," Yaron Kaspi concluded. "The nation got sick of the corrupt Pahlavi regime—and accepted instead the insane regime of Khomeini and his heir, Ali Khameini."

Neither of the other two men responded. After a moment of silence, the Shin-Bet chief moved on: "Mr. Mackenzie, as we've said, is requesting our help to reach people and entities in Israel that can provide intelligence, plans, schematics, and everything connected to Bandar-Abbas. You can start with the architect, Ron Heyman—whose office basically designed the city—and go on from there."

Itzik wrinkled his brow suspiciously and addressed the Englishman in amused rebuke: "Couldn't you have simply broken into his office? You need *us* for this?"

The British agent tilted his head in embarrassment and looked over at the Shin-Bet chief.

"They tried, "Yaron Kaspi said. "Three guys broke into Heyman's office yesterday—but they were caught. What they didn't know was that Heyman also designed the reactor in Dimona, and a few other projects aimed at… promoting peace. So the boys in blue send them to us. Like true English fish, the three men gave away nothing under interrogation. The only thing they remembered was the phone number of the British Embassy. Well, you can figure out the rest: A call was placed from there to 10 Downing Street, and everything was settled in the blink of an eye. Within the hour, the three intruders were on their way back to London and we've received Mr. Mackenzie in their place. Belatedly, he's decided to work through proper channels."

"And what's my job?" Itzik asked.

"You are freed up from all other obligations. You will assist our guest."

"And what do we get in return?" Itzik addressed the question to Mackenzie, but Yaron Kaspi answered first: "Complete cooperation. Every assistance, in exchange for all the information."

"Right here and now?"

"Here and now."

"Then let's go…"

The Englishman cleared his throat, shifted slightly in his chair and began to prove that he could actually talk and not just smile.

"First of all, gentlemen, thank you in the name of Her Majesty's government and in the name of our Foreign Ministry for your good will. We're dealing with a shipping container making its way to Iran. We have learned from a reliable source that the upper echelons of the Iranian government—and I mean the very highest circles—have shown an interest in this container. Let's put it this way: the Supreme Leader, Ali Khomeini, has said that he wishes to see the contents of that container when it reaches its destination."

"What is the container's point of origin?" asked Yaron Kaspi.

The Englishman sighed, but a deal was a deal: all cards on the table. "We have a source known to us as 'the Clerk.' He works in an insignificant part of the building that holds the Supreme Leader's office. I recruited him three years ago, while serving as deputy economic attaché in our embassy in Teheran."

"And you, I gather, are an economist from birth…"

"I was, of course, an undercover agent," Mackenzie continued doggedly. "For three years, the Clerk supplied trustworthy intelligence, though of little value to us. Now he's brought us a real bombshell: While in the building's elevator, he overheard a conversation between two senior men in Khomeini's office, and grasped that there's excitement and anticipation there over the arrival of some sort of container from Ukraine. He even managed to catch a glimpse at the documents that the pair were holding, and memorized the container's serial number.

"We checked out the number, and learned that the container is 40 feet long and belongs to SRT, a well-known German shipping firm. It left Hamburg, via Kherson, for Bandar-Abbas. According to the shipping manifest, it contains toys, office supplies, and writing implements."

"Okay, I don't think Khomeini's office has run out of pens. What's really in the container?"

"That's exactly what we need to find out."

"And why did you wait until now?"

Once again, an uncomfortable expression crossed the Englishman's face. "Actually, we tried to check out the container while it was still in the port of Kherson. We sent two expert agents from London and activated a longtime local agent who'd worked for us back in the Soviet era. There was a problem. The container was situated near the port's mesh fence, and on the other side of that fence some Ukrainian workers spent the entire night repaving the road. We simply could not make a physical approach to the container for fear of being exposed."

"Innocent workers, or disguised security personnel?"

"I don't think they were that sophisticated. In any case, the only thing we managed to do was to mark the container with some white paint that one of our people found on the site. So we have the container's serial number as well as the identifying mark on its exterior."

"And now you want to find it in Bandar-Abbas."

"Precisely."

Over the course of the next two days, Itzik Peled and Sean

Mackenzie visited a number of architects and engineers, infrastructure contractors and foremen who, astonishingly—or perhaps not—all expressed nostalgia for those merry days in Iran. "Do you know what it's like to design a new city from scratch, and to see it going up in front of your eyes?" enthused architect Ron Heyman. "Unfortunately, I was unable to be present at the city's inauguration, because by that time the Shah had fallen and Khomeini, for some reason, didn't invite me." Itzik and Sean listened to many interesting stories and folklore, but they did not glean much information of any significance.

"I think we have no choice but to turn to the enemy," Yaron Kaspi told his secretary. A few minutes later, the phone on his desk rang. "The Mossad chief is on the line," the secretary said dryly.

Things began moving faster now. The Mossad had a file that contained all the material that the British required. Mackenzie understood how his hosts, the Shin-Bet felt. He, too, would have preferred to fall into the dirty water of the Thames wearing his most expensive suit, rather than lower himself to ask MI5 for help. He also had no idea what his bureau was giving up in exchange for Israel's generosity...

"There is a twenty-story building that looks right out onto the harbor. It's an office tower housing shipping companies, customs agencies, and the like. If you get hold of an office on an upper floor and a good pair of binoculars, you'll be able to see everything that comes in and goes out," said the Mossad man who had been ordered to help in any way he could. Help the British, of course. Not the Shin-Bet.

"I can give you the name and number of the building's owner," he told Sean Mackenzie. "He's a seasoned Farsi businessman who will doubtless demand a high price. We have an office in Muscat, the capital of Oman, on the other side of the strait; you can run your operation from there. We also have a list of students in Iran who oppose the regime and are prepared to work to help topple it. You can activate them."

Several days later, an innocent and unfortunate student by the name of Reza was installed in the shipping office in the tall building, peering out at the bustling harbor of Bandar-Abbas. The sophisticated binoculars with which he scanned the activity in the port had been graciously supplied by the Israeli Mossad.

Reza managed to report by telephone to his British handler in Muscat that he had seen the container taken off the giant ship, *Odessa*. But two hours later, he was screaming in a Revolutionary Guards torture chamber. For years afterward, Itzik wondered whether the British had deliberately betrayed Reza by giving him the binoculars with Hebrew lettering on it, in order to divert attention to Israel. His prime suspect was Sean Mackenzie, though he never found any proof.

Sunset was fast approaching. Itzik Peled entered the shul. All of that was ancient history, he thought. The big question was: Who else was going to suffer from that British-Israeli deal? Shlomo Kohlberg had already paid the price. He wasn't coming back. But his foolish sons were making some terrible mistakes. They were digging their graves with their own hands…

Givat Shmuel, 5772 / 2011

CHEZKY KOHLBERG SAT BEFORE HIS COOLING CUP OF coffee, distracted and troubled. Attorney Safrid's law lecture was due to begin in five minutes, but Chezky had neither the desire nor the will to attend. He had more important matters on his mind.

Since yesterday, he had not been able to stop thinking about the conversation that he and his brother had had with Itzik Peled. From time to time he glanced at his phone, checking to see if he had missed a call from the Shin-Bet man. Itzik had said that he would get hold of videos that had captured the final moments of their father's life, and Chezky was impatient to see them. Perhaps they would finally unravel the great mystery that was giving him no rest. Or maybe, he thought, those videos would only deepen the riddle and add another layer of mystery…

"Everything all right?" Dror, the cafeteria manager, asked with a smile. He was on friendly terms with all of the students.

"Perfectly all right," Chezky replied, in a far-from-convincing tone.

Many of the tables began to empty. Students began hastening toward various lecture halls, though not a few remained where they were. Say what you will about the Givat Shmuel Institute, its cafeteria was incomparable. Its clientele included not only the *chareidi* student body, but also workers from nearby office buildings. Those with *kippot* came because of the kosher certification; the bareheaded were drawn by the quality of the coffee.

Chezky didn't get up. Under normal circumstances, he could be found among those hurrying to class, but he couldn't seem to drag himself there now. A strange lassitude enveloped him. He gazed idly around at the other tables, trying to pass the time. At one of them sat three senior men from a local high-tech concern, arguing on some topic. In ordinary times, he would have eavesdropped on their conversation. These days, however, nothing but the riddle of his father's life and death held any interest for him.

At another table, in front of a new-looking laptop computer, sat a classmate of his. He was wearing cotton pants, a designer white shirt, a *kippah* much smaller than the one his parents had brought him up to wear and curly *payos* that he had not yet found the audacity to cut off. Nearby, at a different table, a solitary and unfamiliar man drew Chezky's attention. The fellow had a strange look: sturdy and muscled, with a bald pate and a low forehead. He sat and read a newspaper with what appeared to be great concentration—until he lifted his eyes and stared right at Chezky.

Chezky quickly lowered his own eyes, confused and surprised. From a man with that kind of physical prowess, he would have expected a rather dull and opaque expression, but the man's eyes held a disturbing acuity. Chezky had a feeling that he knew him from some place, but he couldn't put his finger on where. He must come here to the cafeteria from time to time, Chezky concluded.

Still holding his newspaper, the stranger took out a cell phone. He glanced briefly at the screen and accepted a call with a pressure of his thumb. For several seconds he listened, and then his forehead creased in anger and surprise. He stood up and began quickly making for the exit.

Chezky shrugged his shoulders and returned his attention to the croissant in front of him. He had bigger problems than some visiting coffee-drinker passing through the cafeteria.

He sat there a while longer, and then got up to leave. *Maybe I should call Itzik,* he mused. *Maybe he forgot. He must have other things on his mind. Or maybe he's just waiting for us to call him.* Actually, Chezky reminded himself, Itzik had warned them not to discuss the matter over the phone. So what, then? Were they supposed to travel to Jerusalem and go to his house?!

As he walked through the cafeteria, he passed the table where the man with the newspaper had been sitting. The paper was still on the table. Chezky glanced at the headlines, but he couldn't read a word. Perhaps that was because the newspaper was in Russian.

Rotem Cohen would not have survived until eleventh grade had his father not been a senior bureaucrat with the municipality—in the Ministry of Education, to be exact. By the time Rotem reached the ripe old age of 17, he had been suspended from high school three times. In the summer break before twelfth grade, all the interested parties—the student, his parents, and his teachers—agreed that his education was over. His father arranged a temporary job with the Department of Municipal Parking, to keep him occupied during the final year before his recruitment into the IDF Rotem was still roving the streets—but now, at least, he was on the job.

The pace at which he issued fines was not particularly impressive, and his pad of parking tickets was slow to empty. He always wondered about the truth of the rumor that, among the regulars, those who issued the most tickets received bonuses. As far as the temporary inspectors were concerned, no one had offered him anything extra. But he didn't need incentives. Issuing fines and slapping parking tickets on windshields afforded him many moments of satisfaction. The costlier and shinier the car, the happier he was. Sometimes he lingered in the area to catch a glimpse of the driver's enraged face when he spotted the pink slip waiting for him under the windshield wiper.

Arguments, of course, were useless. Rotem, like the other inspectors, was equipped with a digital camera that captured the parking violation for all time and left irate drivers with nothing to say in their own defense. He especially liked to ambush people whose parking meter had only a small amount of time left. He would dash off a ticket one minute after the time ran out. And if some driver remembered to dash outside and put another shekel in the meter, only to find that the parking inspector had beaten him by half a minute—Rotem was overjoyed. If they'd shelled out 150,000 shekel for a car, he thought with pleasure, a 250-shekel fine wouldn't hurt them.

But things did not always go as planned. He would have been happy, for example, to slap a ticket on the black Buick LaCrosse that had been parked on Rechov Einstein for the past hour. When he reached it, there were still five minutes remaining on the meter. He waited patiently. He even took a picture of the car, in case the driver arrived in a hurry.

A minute before the meter expired, he saw the driver approaching at a rapid clip. Disappointed, Rotem hissed a near-silent curse. A guy like that simply *deserved* a ticket! He looked like a member of a crime family, or possibly even its head. Or maybe he belonged to the Russian Mafia, he thought, basing the guess on the language the man was speaking into his phone.

The man opened his car door, and then glanced back at the gate through which he had just come. Rotem followed the fellow's gaze. Very interesting, he thought. What's a crook like that doing in the ultra-Orthodox Givat Shmuel Institute? What was he looking for in a *chareidi* university? Was he planning some daring assassination or bombing?

An idea popped into the young parking inspector's head. Using his work computer, he could easily find out who this car belonged to, based on its license plate. How thrilling, for example, if he discovered that the car was registered to a known figure from the criminal underworld!

Rotem Cohen saved the picture in his camera. After his shift, he would go over to municipal headquarters and check it out. But first, he had to finish his daily round. He had wasted ten minutes on that bozo, and hadn't even been able to slap him with a fine…

Rotem continued to pace the sidewalk, seeking prey. The black car drove into the parking lot of one of the buildings across the street, paused there briefly and then left again. The driver glanced right and left and then turned into the opposite street, toward the highway.

Rotem watched the Buick in surprise. Something was different about it. Something wasn't the way it had been before—but what?

The car picked up speed and passed Rotem. A moment before it disappeared around the corner, he suddenly realized what it was: the license plates! The yellow license plates were gone, replaced by white diplomatic ones that included the tag number along with the letters CD. The driver had not even stepped out of his car. It seemed he had switched the plates in some automatic fashion, probably with the push of a button inside the car.

Excitedly, Rotem looked at the picture he had snapped earlier. The plates in the photo were, indeed, ordinary yellow ones. No doubt about it. The man had simply switched plates—which made his visit here, Rotem realized, much more significant. A shiver of trepidation ran up the young parking inspector's spine. This was no longer an idle tale, but something much more serious. Perhaps he should leave his post and go straight back to the municipal building right now, to find out to whom the car belonged.

Even before Rotem reached the Givat Shmuel municipality, the black Buick arrived at Rechov Yirmiyahu, in the heart of Tel Aviv. The barrier of the underground parking lot rose before it, and before long the driver was on the building's third floor, in the office of the First Secretary to the Ukrainian Embassy in Israel. Near the desk waited an old friend—Dr. Yevgeny Yompolsky.

No one had witnessed the psychiatrist's entry into the embassy of his native country. Even if anyone had decided to follow his car from the hospital's parking lot, he would have discovered only that Dr. Yompolsky had driven to Ichilov Hospital, which many respectable doctors often do. There he had left his car and entered a van with tinted windows and diplomatic plates. The van had left Ichilov's parking lot and made its way along Arlozorov and Ben-Yehudah Streets to the embassy parking facility, which was protected from foreign eyes.

"What's happening, Oleg?" Dr. Yompolsky asked. He had been summoned here from his hospital with no explanation.

Oleg Marinov, the embassy's security officer, had no choice but to admit that he simply didn't know. He, too, had been summoned from Givat Shmuel, by a message from the First Secretary to return at once.

"*Dobro otra* (good morning)," said the diplomat, walking into the room. He sat down in his armchair and placed a photograph on the desk.

Both men leaned over to look at it. The photo featured three men, one older and two young.

"This was taken yesterday," the First Secretary said.

"Where?" Oleg asked.

"In Jerusalem. Corner of Ashtorei HaParchi and Reishis Chachmah."

Oleg stared at the diplomat, stunned. "Where did this come from? Who took the picture?" he asked.

"The important thing is who was photographed," the First Secretary answered in a voice like ice.

"All right, these are Shlomo Kohlberg's two sons," Oleg said. He placed the tip of his thick forefinger on the head of the third man in the photo. "But who is this?"

The First Secretary was surprisingly well-versed in the world of Israeli intelligence. "His name is Yizzik Pelet," he said, trying his best to pronounce the Israeli name. "He held a senior post in the Israeli Shin-Bet until about eight or nine years ago. One of the most senior men in the organization. To this day, people think he left for personal reasons."

"But the truth is a little different," the Ukrainian diplomat continued. "A short time before he left, Peled was suspected of misusing interrogation procedures and breach of trust. He underwent an internal disciplinary hearing, at which the three judges found him at fault and decreed that he be expelled from the service."

"What was he on trial for?" asked Oleg.

"Using national resources for his personal needs," said the First Secretary. "I don't know all the details, but I understand that he inherited a great deal of money from his father, and someone disputed the will. Peled arranged matters so that he got the money through endangering the lives of citizens and the interests of the State."

"So why was it only a disciplinary hearing?"

"Because he exposed a mole in the Shin-Bet—a division head who'd been passing secret material to the Saudis through some Italian banker. While the mole's trial was going on, they didn't touch Peled. But when the fellow was found guilty and sent to prison, the Shin-Bet director, Yaron Kaspi, insisted on a hearing for Peled as well. Personal integrity is very important to Kaspi, as anyone who knows him will tell you…"

"And…?"

"The Shin-Bet's disciplinary court is made up of former senior personnel. One of the judges began to exert pressure to acquit Peled and leave him in the service. During the time that that senior official was in the service, he hadn't liked Peled and had even blocked his promotion. Now he was turning the world over to try and keep him inside. It was head-to-head battle between the Shin-Bet chief and that former senior official. The chief threatened to resign, and the matter reached the prime minister's office. In the end, they reached a compromise: Peled would be acquitted in the disciplinary hearing, but he would resign from the service. Many suspect that all of this was just for show. He's still involved in Israeli security—if not in Shin-Bet then in some other secret service which, in our estimation, is handling the matter that we're involved in."

"That's just a guess, I understand," Oleg clarified.

"A guess, but a well-founded one," replied the First Secretary. "Shortly after Peled 'resigned,' he began to be close to Shlomo Kohlberg. He started gradually to lead an Orthodox lifestyle and even put on a *kippah* and grew a beard. He married a woman who's a friend of the Kohlberg family and has an apartment in the area."

Oleg looked at the picture again. Avreimi and Chezky Kohlberg, together with Itzik Peled, on the spot where their father had died.

"Who's the former senior official that was so concerned about him?" he asked.

The First Secretary tried to recall. "Arnoni, Marnoni... something like that."

"Could it be Armoni?" asked Oleg Marinov. "Shaul Armoni?"

"Yes, yes, that's it. Shaul Armoni."

The tension in the Ukrainian security officer's face cleared. "I will investigate the matter," he said, in a tone of undisguised relief.

Kibbutz Tel-Chana, 5730 / 1970

THE BI-WEEKLY MEMBERSHIP MEETING IN THE KIBBUTZ social hall was expected to be routine and boring, like most of the meetings in Tel-Chana. Only a few knew about the drama that Momi Arzi was about to bring about.

At the front of the room, near a simple table, sat the kibbutz secretary, its treasurer, and another member whose job it was to record the protocol. The three waited for their fellow members to free themselves from their jobs and come in. The meeting had been scheduled for eight p.m. and it was now a full twenty minutes later.

There were several items on the agenda: setting a vacation budget for the kibbutz members—the economic situation was difficult and it was impossible to waste money on spas when there was no cash for plants and seeds; accepting two new members into the kibbutz; a proposal for acquiring a new generator to replace their present dying one; and, once again, the vexing problem of "private property": one of their number, Moisha Poinsatta, had received an electric refrigerator from his Iranian aunt upon her move to an old-age home, and he insisted on keeping the refrigerator in his room instead of turning it over for the kibbutz's use.

"Look." Mishke, the treasurer, signaled to Drora, the secretary, gesturing with his head at Momi Arzi and two of his friends, who'd taken seats at the back of the social hall. It was not usual for eighteen-year-old youths to attend the kibbutz's routine meetings. They preferred spending the time with their friends or even, lately, debating the youths whose loosening morals and serious ideological atrophy were undermining their fundamental Socialist principles.

"And look at *them*," the secretary told the treasurer, gesturing discreetly at Mikush and Sonia Arzi. Momi's adoptive parents sat side by side, silent and tense, from time to time throwing distressed looks at Momi and his companions.

"What's the kid up to?" Mishke asked in an anxious whisper, his elbows resting on the table and his clenched fists hiding his mouth.

"What do you mean, 'up to'? Who's up to anything?" Drora whispered back. "He's a good boy. An idealist. One of our most successful young men. At the last HaShomer HaTzair meeting, he won a lot of praise even though he's a Communist from Tel-Chana..."

The treasurer was not reassured. "He didn't come here to see how we make decisions. Look at Mikush and Sonia. They're wound up like springs!"

The kibbutz members already present were enjoying glasses of pop and biscuits. The women chatted amongst themselves while vigorously knitting sweaters and scarves. At eight-thirty, one member, Efraim, came in straight from the field, boots caked with mud, without bothering to go to his room first to shower and change his clothes. He was well and truly furious. Two irrigation lines had been stolen from the fields, and he was certain that youths from Tul-Karem were responsible. "An Arab is an Arab," Efraim muttered behind his auburn mustache, eliciting angry looks from members who could not tolerate his heresy against the ideal of the holy brotherhood of man...

"They're not to blame." Miriam lifted her head from her knitting to defend their neighbors. "It's all because of Golda's government, which is perpetuating the oppression and won't give them the right to exist."

"So let them steal irrigation lines from Golda! What do they want from us?" Efraim shot back as he sank heavily into one of the chairs. "You're all naïve," he added mockingly. "Stalin died, Communism died... everything died." He pointed a scornful finger at the picture of the leader of the Soviet Union, Leonid Brezhnev, hanging on the wall of the social hall.

Everyone fell silent. The period between the Six-Day War and the Yom Kippur War was a difficult one for Israel's Communist Party. The Israeli left had been stunned when the Soviet Union broke off diplomatic ties with Israel and rumors about the Soviet rule of terror began filtering into the West. At a Shomer HaTzair meeting held the year before, an official resolution was passed wherein the youth organization confessed that it had been mistaken in its long years of support for the Soviet Union.

"Friends," Drora called out at last. "I am opening these proceedings, and ask again that you come on time and not be late. We all have work tomorrow morning. The first item on the agenda: the vacation budget. The floor goes to our treasurer. Mishke, please."

The debate over the vacation budget generated some emotion, but in the end the treasurer's proposal was adopted without demur: Sick members could not travel to spas, but would be treated within the kibbutz. Healthy members would receive no vacation stipend at all.

The debate over Moisha's traitorous deviation from ideology in desiring to hold onto his inherited refrigerator was stormier. How could he keep a refrigerator in his room? Everything belonged to the collective. There was no such thing as personal property. "The next thing we know, people will start having radios in their rooms... or maybe even own their own cars!" members said. "What will happen to the idea of the kibbutz?"

The only one who did not participate in the discussion was the accused member himself, who dozed right through it. Only when it came time to vote did he open one eye and state in his deep voice that, if his refrigerator was taken away, he would leave the kibbutz. No one wanted this. Moisha Poinsatta was the best dairy farmer in the entire kibbutz movement. His departure would mark the end of Tel-Chana's dairy.

"All right, we'll decide this in the office," Drora said quickly, and removed the item from the day's agenda.

"Are there any other topics that anyone wishes to raise?" Mishke, the treasurer, asked as a prelude to concluding the meeting.

At the back of the room, Momi Arzi stood up. "Yes," he said. "My two friends and I would like to ask permission to raise the subject of our recruitment to the army."

"What's the problem?"

"Tomer, Ro'i, and I have decided that we do not agree to serve in Israel's army of conquest. We request permission from the kibbutz to refuse."

"Are you out of your mind?" Mishke shouted, sending a fiery glance at Mikush and Sonia, who looked thoroughly miserable.

Amos, another member, rose to his feet. "There's a war going on, soldiers are being killed in the Canal, and you guys want to sit at home?" he yelled.

This was the War of Attrition. The Egyptians were shelling Israeli positions all along the Suez Canal in an effort to weaken her and force her to retreat from the Sinai Peninsula. Hundreds of soldiers had lost their lives in the bombardment and through incursions by Egyptian commando units. The citizens of Israel were suffering from the prolonged bloodletting, but the end of the war was not yet on the horizon.

Momi remained unruffled. He continued declaiming the speech he had prepared over the past few days: "This war is unnecessary," he declared. "The government has stubbornly chosen to remain in the conquered territories and to disinherit tens of thousands of Arab residents in the Gaza Strip. And all of this is for the sake of building settlements near Rafiach that will just serve to perpetuate the crime against the Palestinians. We are not prepared to play any part in this policy of oppression or in military action that goes against our conscience."

The kibbutz members were in turmoil. Only Mikush and Sonia, Momi's parents, sat quietly in their seats, hunched into themselves.

They had all heard about the group of courageous high-school seniors from Jerusalem who'd sent a letter to Prime Minister Golda Meir, saying that her obstinate refusal to pursue any peace initiative had made them wonder why they should be drafted into the army and perhaps sacrifice their lives. One of the signatories of the inflammatory letter had been the son of MK Victor Shem-Tov, a leading Mapam figure. And now, young people from within their own kibbutz were rebelling and refusing to be drafted.

Mishke, the treasurer, failed to subdue the shouting. His forehead was red and perspiring. "You don't know what you're doing!" he screamed. "The government is already choking our kibbutz. They are already hostile to us. Those spoiled brats in Jerusalem can write all the letters they want to Golda Meir. What will they do to them? Here, we're in their hands. They won't buy our produce and our apples will rot on the trees."

Momi stood where he was, calmly observing the tumult he had caused. He waited for the agitated voices to quiet down.

"Friends," he said, "since we were children, you've raised my friends and me to a life of labor based on the Communist ideal and the brotherhood of nations. My friends and I discussed it a great deal before we brought our proposal here to the kibbutz meeting. We are not prepared to become the oppressors of our Arab brothers. We are ready to pay the full price and spend three years in a military prison!"

Some people started clapping, but the applause quickly died under the burning glares of the treasurer and secretary.

The debate was rekindled, and this time more than a few voices expressed their support for the boys' initiative. "We also paid a price for our ideology," said Tzvika, and was rewarded by several nodding heads. "We were hungry for bread and shaking with cold, because we were faithful to Communism."

"These are different times," Noni blared.

"Not true!" shouted another member. "It's the same struggle. Once it was Ben-Gurion—now it's Golda."

"And what do your parents say?" the kibbutz secretary asked Momi.

All eyes turned toward the Arzis.

"Sonia has the floor," the secretary announced, seeing that Momi's mother had something to say.

"I support Momi's request," Sonia said after a brief hesitation. "We are educating our children to be guided by their conscience. We cannot stop them at the testing hour."

Her words encouraged another thunderous exchange of views in the large room. Finally, the kibbutz secretary decided that the debate had run its course. She put the matter to a vote.

"Who is for Momi Arzi's proposal?"

Hands lifted into the air, Sonia Arzi's among them. The secretary and treasurer counted the hands carefully.

"Who is opposed?"

Once again, hands were lifted and counted.

"Who abstains?"

This time, only a few hands appeared. One of them was Mikush Arzi's.

"Well, friends, we have a tie. Thirty-three for, thirty-three against. Is there anyone who wishes to change his or her vote?"

Silence filled the social hall. Quick glances were thrown around the room.

Very slowly, Mikush's hand inched up.

"Opposed," he said quietly, lowering his eyes.

The treasurer and secretary were visibly relieved. Momi's features sharpened, and then hardened in suppressed anger.

Drora, the kibbutz secretary, gaily announced the results of the vote: "This kibbutz meeting rejects Momi Arzi's proposal and forbids him, Ro'i Goldman, and Tomer Bar-Ezer from refusing the draft. We believe that our youth will know how to accept the movement's ruling and carry out the majority decision. This meeting is adjourned."

Modiin Illit, 5772 / 2011

"Chezky, this isn't appropriate," Avreimi groaned in visible distress. "To sit in a *kollel* and watch films…?"

The brothers were in the women's section of the *beis medrash* in which Avreimi learned every day. Chezky's laptop was open in front of them. From below, afternoon *seder* rose in tumultuous waves, but the Ezras Nashim was deserted.

"Stop worrying already," Chezky ordered. "We have to see this, don't we? We didn't come here for entertainment."

Avreimi was compelled to acquiesce. "Okay, but hurry," he begged.

Itzik Peled's messenger had reached Chezky in a white Toyota, a scant hour after the Ukrainian had left the Institute in such a hurry. The man had maintained his anonymity, calling on an unlisted number to ask Chezky to meet him outside the Institute gates. With a baseball cap on his head, a pair of large sunglasses, and the collar of his coat turned up despite the unusually warm weather, he was concealed almost from head to toe.

"Here are six video clips," the man said, handing Chezky a computer disk. "All of them are from the last hour of... you know. By the way, this is important for you to know: these videos cannot be copied onto a computer, and they will be deleted from the disk a quarter-hour after you first activate them."

Chezky grinned. He thought the guy was joking.

"I'm serious," the stranger said. "This is a basic security measure, to ensure that the files don't fall into the wrong hands."

Chezky looked at the disk. It seemed perfectly normal.

"There's not a lot of material here," the man said. "The footage doesn't cover all the relevant time, but it's what we've managed to get so far. When there's more, we'll make sure to get it to you. What you need to do is take a careful look and see if you notice anyone or anything suspicious, odd behavior, things like that."

"And then?"

"And then I'll be in touch. No phone conversations, of course—not between the two of you, or between you and the 'boss,' okay? Pay attention to the clock at the bottom of the screen. If you see anything of interest, mark down the minute and second. Afterward, you can discuss it with him."

Chezky wasted no time. He traveled immediately to Modiin Illit, in the grip of an intense excitement and curiosity. Avreimi was very surprised to find his brother standing in the doorway of his *kollel*—and even more surprised to hear why he had come. Chezky asked him where they could talk in private. The Ezras Nashim was the best place.

The last images of their father moved them to tears. The first clip had come from a camera attached to an ATM machine on Rechov Malchei Yisrael. It lasted only twenty seconds. Their father—at a strange angle because the camera had caught him from below—punched in his PIN number, withdrew 500 shekel, and put the money in his pocket.

"They found several hundred shekel in his wallet," Chezky said in a slightly choked voice.

"No one knows when his time will come," Avreimi said soberly. "A person takes some money out of the machine, and doesn't know that in just an hour he'll be in a world where there's no money or gold or precious gems…"

"I know," Chezky mumbled.

The next clip demanded closer attention. For the space of two minutes their father appeared standing at the southern rim of Malchei Yisrael, talking on his cell phone. Gauging by the angle of the video, it had apparently been taken by a camera situated in one of the stores between Rechov Yonah and Rechov HaYeshivah. Their father looked very calm. Several acquaintances passed by and greeted him, and he nodded back at them. No one suspicious appeared in the clip.

"Oh, there's my *shver*!" Avreimi called out in surprise, when the third clip began playing. On the screen appeared his father-in-law, R' Muttel Hershkowitz, chatting briefly with their father and then parting ways. The source of this video, according to the symbol on the screen, was a Jerusalem municipality traffic cam.

The next two clips had also been taken from different corners of Rechov Malchei Yisrael. The final clip was a little different. The images that appeared on the screen now came from Rechov Ezer Yoldot, a narrow street near Kikar Shabbat. At the end of the street stood a gleaming Chevrolet van, the lower half of which was black and the upper half beige. Its license plate was concealed by a parked car. Their father stood near the van's window, talking to someone inside. According to the clock at the bottom of the screen, the conversation had taken place ten minutes before he was found lying on the ground.

"Who's in the car?" Chezky asked.

"It's not the driver," Avreimi remarked. "Abba is talking to someone sitting next to the driver."

The clip was short, no more than ten seconds.

"Can you run that again for me?" Avreimi asked.

Chezky rewound the clip slightly.

"Who can that be?" Avreimi wondered aloud, moving closer and peering into the screen.

Chezky returned to the beginning of the clip.

"What do you think?" Avreimi asked. He glanced at his brother, and for the first time noticed how pale he had become.

"What's the matter?" Avreimi was alarmed.

Chezky's legs were trembling. "You don't recognize the car?"

"No." Avreimi stared at the screen again.

"You don't remember where we saw it?"

"I really don't."

With a sudden jab, Chezky slammed down the laptop's cover.

"We're going to Yerushalayim," he declared. "We have to talk to Itzik."

Tel Aviv, 5772 / 2011

"Yompolsky's gone back to the hospital," the First Secretary told Oleg Marinov. "What did you want to say that the doctor mustn't hear?"

The embassy's security officer smiled. "What I wanted to say"—he leaned toward the First Secretary, as though about to impart a secret—"is that Armoni is an old friend of ours."

"Really?" The Ukrainian diplomat's face lit up. Then, abruptly, he sobered. "All right, I didn't hear anything from you. We don't deal in such things."

Oleg Marinov twisted in his seat to get the phone from his jacket pocket. He leaned back and dialed a number.

"*Shalom*, Shaul," he said, when his call was answered.

The First Secretary wrinkled his brow in surprise. He hadn't known that Oleg, who'd been in Israel for just a few years, had managed to acquire such fluent Hebrew.

"*L'hitraot*, Shaul." Oleg concluded his call with Armoni in less than a minute.

"It's okay," Oleg announced. "Itzik Peled is on our side. He's working with Shaul Armoni. Everything's under control."

29

It was with mixed feelings that the members of Kibbutz Tel-Chana observed the military induction of Tomer Bar-Ezer, Ro'i Goldman and Momi Arzi. Their parents and friends worried about their welfare and hoped they would return home safely—while the anxious kibbutz administrators hoped that the three would not do anything foolish to make headlines, in the worst sense of the word. Tel-Chana already had dirt on her face. Everyone viewed the kibbutz as anti-Zionist, traitors, Soviet puppets, and spies. Even Israeli left-leaning organizations such as Mapai and Mapam kept their distance, regarding the kibbutz as a hotbed of radical extremists.

"To tell the truth, Tomer and Ro'i don't worry me," Mishke, the treasurer, said in a private administrators' meeting. "They're only being dragged after Momi. But *he* could make real trouble for us. That... young idealist will refuse to carry out some order, and that will be the end of us."

"I think you ought to have a talk with him," said Drora Tzeiler, the kibbutz secretary. "He's a smart boy. He'll understand."

The talk that took place between the treasurer and the young soldier-to-be was filled with flattering smiles and sly winks—all on the treasurer's part. Mishke tried to explain the facts of life to Momi: With all respect to exalted ideals such as the brotherhood of nations and the status of the world's workers, such things belonged in youth-group meetings, cultural-center lectures, and lofty ideological conferences. In real life, he said, one must get along, be flexible, smooth out the sharp edges. In the army, one had to forget everything and do what he was told.

"You don't always have to trumpet your opinions," he said. "You don't have to walk around with a copy of *Lenin's Complete Works* in your pocket."

It was five minutes before Mishke realized that Momi had no idea what he was talking about. He switched strategies.

"The most important thing, Momi, is the survival of this kibbutz. We're the last ones to keep the coals burning—the last stronghold of Communism in Israel. Everyone out there wants to eliminate us. Ben-Gurion, Golda, and the rest are part of the imperialistic conspiracy headed by America. We mustn't give them any excuse to harm the kibbutz."

Such talk about "the good of the movement" was something Momi understood well. The three years of his military service passed without incident. There were no refused orders or disturbances of the peace. More than once, he ground his teeth when forced to stand guard over war criminals who were building settlements on land the international community did not grant them. More than once he was near his breaking-point, such as when forced to take part in evicting an Arab family [although Momi did conveniently "forget" that four of its sons were murderous terrorists]. Each time, he reminded himself that he was working for the good of the Revolution. He was an agent inside the enemy's camp. He was serving in Israel's army of conquest for one purpose only: the spread of Communism.

Momi waited impatiently for the date of his release: October 7, 1973.

Two months before that date, his unit was transferred from the plain of Rafiach to the Sinai Peninsula, and posted in a bunker that was part of a line of military strongholds built on the bank of the Suez Canal. The bunkers were made of reinforced concrete, to protect the soldiers from enemy shelling. But it was boredom that threatened to do them all in. All around them were nothing but golden sand dunes, to the horizon. From time to time, the monotony was broken by pointless bullets from an Egyptian sniper, or a brief burst of shelling that caused no damage.

A few days before his release from the army, Momi approached his commanding officer, Allon Koler, and requested a furlough.

"Listen, Momi," the officer said. "I already gave two religious guys a furlough for the holiday. When they come back—you're free to go."

"And I don't get a holiday furlough?"

"Really, Momi. They're *datiim*. They fast all day. After Yom Kippur, you're released."

"Yom Kippur…" A smile rose to Momi's face.

"Stop being so anti-religious," Allon scolded. "That's their faith, and they believe in it no less than you believe in your Stalin and Lenin."

Actually, Momi hadn't been mocking them. He had been remembering a certain amusing episode that had taken place on Yom Kippur, eight or nine years earlier.

Even on irreligious Tel-Chana, Yom Kippur was a quiet day. People stayed at home and didn't go out to work. One day, a group of youths discovered that there were a number of kibbutz members—the elderly, mostly—who secretly went to pray in a shul at nearby Kfar Saba.

"Let's make a demonstration against them," one of the teenagers suggested.

"We can collect a pile of rocks to throw at them!" another added with ideological fervor. "An atheist should be an atheist, all the way through. Not go to *beit knesset* on Yom Kippur."

But when the youths hid in ambush near the road leading to the kibbutz from Kfar Saba, Momi was stunned to find that one of them was… Mikush, his adoptive father and secretary of their Communist Party branch.

Mikush approached him, pale and shaken, and made him swear not to tell Sonia, his wife, about what he had done. "I told her I was going on an outing with friends. If she finds out I went to *beit knesset*, she'll kill me."

Momi had kept his word and not told Sonia about it—but he had never understood how people can observe rituals that they don't even believe in.

"Okay," he told Allon Koler. "I'll stay here. But first thing Sunday morning, even before they get back—I'm out of here."

"Done," Allon said. He had no idea that, at the height of Yom Kippur itself, a fierce and painful war would break out. A war that would go on to exact a toll of more than 2,000 IDF soldiers' lives…

At 1:40 that afternoon, Egyptian forces began a deafening bombardment along the entire strip. Simultaneously, Syrian forces invaded the Golan Heights. The rise-and-fall wail of sirens alerted the populace of Israel. Men clad in white lifted their heads from their *machzorim* in fear. Jeeps began moving along the empty roads to pick up army reservists. Harsh news came from the front, instilling terror in every heart.

The row of fortifications along the Suez Canal, known as the "Bar-Lev Line" after former General Chaim Bar-Lev, consisted of 32 well-fortified bunkers along the Canal's east bank. Until that afternoon, they'd been considered virtually impenetrable. But such expectations were quickly crushed. The Egyptian Army surprised and overran Israeli territory, almost undeterred. The Line had let them down.

"They're crossing the Canal!" Allon Koler shouted into his radio. His eyes could not believe what they were seeing.

Only twenty of the strongholds were manned on that black day, and each held only several dozen soldiers. These men were helpless before the endless waves of infantry and armored lines that crossed the Suez Canal under cover of an artillery barrage of unprecedented power.

The despairing cries that flooded the IDF communications network very soon reflected the bitter reality:

"I see them rushing into our territory!"

"Command, this is 'Vision.' We're surrounded!"

"They're shooting at us from every direction!"

"Command, this is 'Milano.' We have five wounded and three dead. We're not going to make it!"

"Command, do something. They're on top of us!"

"Command, this is 'Walnut.' Are you sending help? Our situation is grave!"

"Command, Command, do you hear?"

"Command, they're in the trenches. They're throwing grenades."

"Command, this is 'Daisy.' We're…"

"*Shema Yisrael…*"

Modiin-Illit, 5772 / 2011

"Wait a second." Avreimi stopped Chezky. "Before we get to Itzik… Whose car is that?"

Chezky stood up in agitation, grabbing his head with both hands.

"What idiots we are! What idiots…"

"Chezky, what's the matter with you? Whose car is that?"

Chezky looked at his brother. "We saw it last Friday. In Bayit Vegan," he said quietly.

Avreimi's jaw dropped in shock.

"It belongs to…" He hesitated before guessing.

"Yechezkel Polowitz," Chezky said. "I remember noticing it in the parking lot under the building. It's an unusual vehicle, imported individually. There aren't many of them in this country—and certainly not in those colors, black and beige."

Avreimi gaped at his brother with stricken eyes. "He can't have driven it himself. That's why Abba spoke to him through the passenger window."

"Correct."

"What could they have been talking about? Did they know each other? Did you ever hear Abba mention the name Polowitz?"

Chezky looked at his brother in disbelief. "Are you kidding? Don't you get what's happening here? Polowitz is the villain of the story. You're forgetting that it was in his orphanage that Abba's papers disappeared."

Avreimi was stunned.

"You're not claiming that he murdered Abba, I hope," he said sarcastically.

"Why not?" Chezky was beside himself. "Why not?"

"Because he's a religious person, a *shomer Torah u'mitzvos*," Avreimi retorted.

"And sending children to an anti-religious kibbutz is okay? Turning Jewish children into Communists is okay? Don't you remember what the kibbutz secretary told us? 'We did all our business with him'!"

"But—to kill someone…!?"

"Yes, yes," Chezky said firmly. "Someone who is capable of killing a soul can also kill a body."

Avreimi was struck dumb. It was impossible to argue with his brother's logic.

"Believe me," Chezky said. "I didn't like him from the first minute, there in his ivory tower in Bayit Vegan. I don't believe he's 'half-senile, as that young administrator described him. He is very well aware of what's happening, but pretends to be confused in order to avoid difficult questions. You saw Abba talking to him through the window. That's not the way you talk to someone who's not clear in his mind."

Avreimi bit his lip, as though he had suddenly understood something.

"What?" Chezky demanded.

"If you're right," Avreimi said slowly, "if he's only putting on an act, then when we came to his house he knew exactly who we were."

Chezky felt a cold chill pass through his body.

"And if his driver is the same man who opened the door for us," he added, "then he also knew exactly who we were and what we'd come to talk about…"

"That secretary did look kind of sly," Avreimi admitted.

"So what do we do now?" Chezky was raring to go. "Should we go back to Polowitz and confront him with the facts? Or maybe we should go back to the orphanage? We can speak with Yoni Schlusserman, the present administrator."

"Chezky, Chezky, Chezky." Avreimi tried to calm his brother. "Slow down. The first thing we have to do is talk to Itzik Peled. After that, we'll see."

"Well, then, let's go."

Avreimi looked doubtfully up at the big clock on the wall of the Ezras Nashim. "Maybe we should see him tomorrow?"

"Why tomorrow?" Chezky exploded. "Let's go right now! I came here especially from Givat Shmuel."

"The *seder* lasts until seven," Avreimi said. "And I want to spend some time at home, too. Last night I came home late..."

Chezky thrust his laptop into its case. "I'm going now. If you want to come, then come. If not, not."

Fifteen minutes later, both brothers were seated side by side on a bus going to Jerusalem. Avreimi grumbled inwardly, but kept his feelings to himself. He understood that there are situations when you mustn't get in the way of a determined ox—especially when the ox in question is on a rampage.

Kibbutz Tel-Chana, 5737 / 1977

THE CURLY-HAIRED YOUTH RODE UP TO THE KIBBUTZ GATES on an impressively large motorcycle. His face was sunburned and he wore a leather jacket.

Near the guard booth, he braked and put one foot on the ground.

"Excuse me, where is the Arzi family?" he asked.

The guard studied the visitor, from the tip of his shoes to the top of his helmet. What did this odd stranger want with the "Arzi family"? he wondered. What business could this motorcycle rider have with Sonia and Mikush?

"Go straight on, and turn left after those trees. It's the sixth house," he replied.

The motorcyclist lifted his leg, restarted his engine, and roared off into the kibbutz. The guard watched him go. Only after a few seconds did he realize what had been so strange about the young man's appearance. While on the surface he had looked completely like "one of ours," from under his leather jacket some long, white strings had fluttered behind him as he drove. *Yet another ba'al teshuvah*, the guard thought with a grimace. Another victim caught in the trap that had already taken so many. And now, the bigger question: what in the world could a young *ba'al teshuvah* want with Sonia and Mikush Arzi?!

Lately, their numbers had been increasing daily, the guard continued his musing. Like cockroaches. Every day brought its tale of another person who'd joined that cult. And not just any people, but the best of them, the salt of the earth: senior officers, commando fighters, academics and bohemians. It was like an epidemic that was sweeping the country. This one went to a seminar, another had an encounter with a persuasive demagogue, and a third simply "saw the light." Even here in Tel-Chana, the epidemic had claimed at least one victim: Tomer Bar-Ezer, son of Moisha Poinsatta and Rocha and one of the most successful young men on the kibbutz. Something had gone wrong with his head and he had become a *ba'al teshuvah*.

It all started with that accursed war. The Yom Kippur War. The boy had returned a different person. Where was the pre-war Tomer, always joking, always merry, the life of the party? The post-war Tomer was quiet, sad, walking the kibbutz paths with bowed shoulders. The Bar-Ezers' neighbors said that he cried out in his sleep at night. Moisha and Rocha didn't know what to do with him. Instead of a young man ready to take his place as a member of the kibbutz, they'd received back from the army a full-grown infant who wept a great deal and could stare for hours at pictures of friends who'd been killed all around him on the banks of the Canal.

And then, just when it seemed that he was beginning to recover, a new woe had befallen them. No one knew where those soul-hunters had caught Tomer. All they knew was that he had been invited to a lecture by some rabbi in Tel Aviv, and afterward attended a seminar at which they stuffed whatever they wanted into his brain. From there, it was a short hop to a yeshivah for the newly-returned in Bnei Brak.

Tomer's parents fought for their son with all their might. They tracked down the yeshivah and traveled to Bnei Brak to liberate him and bring him home. But those rabbis and lecturers had done their job. They had brainwashed Tomer good and well. He had smiled as he told his parents that he had it better here than he had ever had it in his life, and that he was staying in yeshivah of his own free will and not by force. They tried in vain to explain that these rabbis were adept at taking advantage of a young man's shaky emotional state after the trauma of war. "We'll take you to the best psychologists," they pleaded. But he merely opened up a huge volume filled with crowded black lettering, and told them that this was the best psychologist in the world, and that the war had only made it clear to him that he had been living a lie and must search for the truth—even if meant sailing across the ocean or climbing clear up to the heavens…

Tomer's parents returned to the kibbutz, gray-faced and grieving. "They stole my child," Moisha told his friends. "But not only him. Do you know who else is in that yeshivah for *ba'alei teshuvah*? I nearly had a heart attack when I saw them, sitting there and swaying over their big books. Gal Gonen…"

"Gal? From Kibbutz Ha'Arba?"

"Yes. And Uriel Sarig, from Kibbutz Tidhar—General Sarig's son. And the actor Oz Malki, and that artist… what was his name? The one who lives in Tel Aviv, near the sea…"

The only thing Tomer's parents were able to extract from him was a promise that he would come back to the kibbutz for every other Shabbos. But that might have been a mistake. It simply broke their hearts to see how he had deteriorated. By his second Shabbos, he was already wearing a… *kippah*. They thought they'd explode on the spot. Rocha had cried—and Rocha knew how to cry! But her tears were useless.

Moisha screamed at his son until his face turned blue, and finally asked him to at least refrain from leaving the house all Shabbos, lest he embarrass them. In the dining room, however, they discovered that the whole kibbutz already knew. They all looked at Moisha and Rocha with open pity, and came over to hug and encourage them, exactly as they'd done to Ro'i Goldman's parents after he was killed in a direct hit by a mortar shell on the last day of the war.

Then came those white strings—the *tzitzis*, or whatever they were called. And after that Tomer started wearing a dark suit and hat even in the summer, at the height of the season's heat. Then he decided to take back his grandfather's original name, Helfman. "As though Bar-Ezer was a bad word," Moisha Poinsatta whispered in the dining room, insulted and not trying to hide it.

The kibbutz guard wondered again why a strange young man, wearing *tzitzis* and riding a motorcycle, was on his way to see Sonia and Mikush Arzi.

The motorcycle reached the small house with its surrounding garden, which appeared to have once been well-tended. The rider slowed down and braked beside the gate. He propped up his bike, took off his helmet, and shook out his hair. As the guard had suspected, beneath his helmet the youth wore a *kippah*, which clung to his curls with the help of two bobby pins.

The gate squeaked slightly as he entered the yard. The door of the house was open, but he knocked anyway. A woman in her fifties peered out from one of the rooms.

"Oh, hello," she said. She had been expecting him since their brief phone conversation—more eagerly than she was prepared to admit.

"Mrs. Arzi?"

"You can call me Sonia." With a gesture, she invited him to come inside.

"Thank you. I'm Allon Koler, Momi's commanding officer."

"Yes, I figured as much. Sit down, make yourself comfortable," Sonia said. "I'll bring you something to drink." She disappeared into the kitchen.

Allon Koler had encountered this "I'll bring you something to drink" from his other visits to parents of fallen soldiers. The real meaning was, "I'll go to the kitchen to try to master my tears."

He entered the house, which was actually a small apartment consisting of three small rooms and a kitchenette. Sonia Arzi favored woven furniture; judging by the way she had raised Momi, Allon surmised that she had bought the pieces in some Arab village. And she had probably insisted on paying more than they were worth, to compensate the poor villagers a tiny bit for the injustice perpetrated upon them by the Israeli government…

The bookcase, too, was made of some woven material. Allon stood in front of it, hands in his pockets, scanning the titles on the shelves: fine Hebrew literature, biographies of Stalin and Marx, a full set of the *Encyclopedia Ha'Ivrit*, along with—*l'havdil*—a one-volume Tanach crammed into the top shelf, as untouched as the day it had been printed. A cultured home, a good family.

Allon compressed his lips. He himself had grown up in an agricultural settlement. His parents had a failing chicken coop that mostly brought in losses. As a son of a moshav, he had always felt a sense of inferiority in relation to the kibbutzniks, who'd absorbed culture and values, literature and music…

"So are you also going to ask where Momi disappeared to, eh?"

Allon Koler turned. He hadn't noticed that Sonia had returned to the living room, bearing a tray with two glasses and a plate of cookies.

She sat on the sofa, waiting for him to speak. It was clear that she had noted the *kippah* on his head—and was deliberately not saying a word about it.

"Yes." He sat facing her on one of the armchairs. "First, he didn't show up for reserve duty. He doesn't attend our unit reunions. We haven't even seen him at memorials for friends who were killed. He's simply dropped out of sight."

Sonia Arzi was silent for a long moment.

"That's the same question I ask myself," she said at last. "He was here for a few months after the war. We thought he would join the kibbutz. But one day he walked into the house, packed a few things, and told Mikush and me that he was leaving. Since then, we simply haven't seen him."

"When was this?"

She closed her eyes to calculate. "In March or April of 1974. I remember that he was no longer here at the May 1st rally."

"Three years!"

"That's right. And since then—no contact. No calls, no letters, no regards. No one else has seen him, either. People knew that we were looking for him. They would have told us if they'd run into him somewhere. At first, Mikush and I made the rounds of the hospitals. We even searched for him in psychiatric wards. We thought that maybe he was suffering some kind of post-traumatic shock from the war and it had suddenly got the better of him. Many boys were that way after what they saw. We even checked to see if he had left the country. My husband has a role in the Party, and someone in the Interior Ministry investigated for him. But no, Momi didn't leave the country."

"How can a person disappear so abruptly?"

"That's my question, too. The truth is, I thought he was with you people. I said: Maybe he's become a *ba'al teshuvah* and is sitting in some yeshivah."

Allon Koler chuckled sadly. "That's something, Mrs. Arzi, that I can guarantee will never happen. Momi is the last person who'd ever become a *ba'al teshuvah*."

"How can you know that?"

"You gave him a good education." Allon's fingertips touched his *kippah*. "I'm sure you've noticed that the values I live by today are not the same values that you hold dear, but Momi was one of the most moral people I've ever met. He's a believing man, in his way, and his values have been tested in the harshest of ways."

"Ah." Sonia waved a dismissive hand. "He was ruined in the army. He became materialistic, a pursuer of money, like this whole country."

"Why do you say that?"

"In the months before he vanished, he worked for pay outside the kibbutz. Do you understand what that means? Among us Communists, that's the worst thing a person can do. Instead of joining the communal kibbutz, he chose to make financial profit outside."

"What sort of work did he do?"

"An archeological dig. At some ancient site."

"How did he come to do that?"

"I have no idea. He had never been interested in antiquities—but suddenly he was buying books and reading articles and working overtime at the dig. . . But what difference does it make? The boy is gone. One day, he just up and disappeared."

Jerusalem, 5772 / 2011

Itzik Peled's study had not changed in the 24 hours that Avreimi and Chezky had last been there. The walls were still bare, the shelves closed and locked. Only the desk bore an item that had not been present the day before: a laptop computer.

"So you received my *mishloach manos*," Itzik said with a smile. "And I understand that you saw something interesting." He booted up the computer as he spoke.

"It was in the last clip," Chezky said.

"Let's watch all the material together. Maybe there'll be something else that you didn't notice before."

The first video clip began playing on the monitor screen—the ATM camera. This time, as before, the brothers became emotional at the sight of their father in his last moments of life. But, again, they saw nothing unusual. The second clip showed their father talking on the phone. Here, too, a second viewing added nothing to their understanding.

"In the next clip, our father is talking to my *shver*," Avreimi said.

"Let's take a look." Itzik started the video.

Several seconds passed. Muttel Hershkowitz appeared, shaking their father's hand with a smile. Suddenly, Chezky jumped as though bitten by a snake. "Just a second! Look at *him*!" He pointed at a person passing in the street behind the two men.

Itzik Peled rewound the clip and ran it again, in slow-motion this time.

"There," said Chezky. Itzik paused the video.

"Do you remember him?" Chezky addressed his brother.

Avreimi looked at the screen. "Isn't that the Englishman who came to the *shivah*?"

"Yes!" Chezky turned to Itzik. "You remember, we told you that an English-speaking man came to the house during the *shivah*, looking for our father. When he heard that Abba had passed away, he simply ran off. And there he is. That's the man!"

"Just one thing is strange," said Avreimi. "He's walking right past Abba and acting as if he doesn't know him."

"Really strange," Chezky agreed.

Only now, when Itzik Peled was sure that his voice would not betray his shock, did he allow himself to ask, "Which day did you say he came to the house?"

"The Englishman? Certainly not in the first couple of days."

"When, then?"

"When? Let me see… I think it was… on the same day that Abba's Rosh Kollel came."

"That's right. And Yuri, Abba's supervisor at work, also came then, along with two co-workers. I remember that the Rosh Kollel and Yuri sat side by side, and I thought it was strange that they were there at the same time."

"So which day was it?"

"Wednesday, I think."

"This clip, of course, is from Sunday," Itzik said. "That means that the Englishman was in the area at the time that your father collapsed. Then, four days later, he arrived at your house and was stunned to hear that he had died."

"Exactly."

"Who can that man be?" Avreimi asked.

"We'll have to investigate," Itzik said, although he knew that was completely unnecessary. He knew the man well. He just hadn't known that he was in Israel.

Sean Mackenzie. That was the man. He was twenty years older, and must certainly have risen through the ranks in Britain's MI6. Back then, eighteen years earlier, he had been the head of the Iranian desk in the British intelligence service. What position did he hold today? That needed to be ascertained. But one thing was clear: the episode of the container in the Bandar-Abbas port continued to exact its price, even today. And not only that, but the same actors were continuing to play in the region.

On the computer screen, the next clip began, but Itzik's thoughts were somewhere else. He had always suspected that Sean Mackenzie, the seemingly perfect English gentleman, was a cruel and ruthless operator. He had long ago decided that Mackenzie was the one who had betrayed Reza—the Iranian student who'd run surveillance on the port—to the Revolutionary Guard…

"Here's the car." Chezky's words cut into Itzik's thoughts.

"Which car?" he asked, trying to focus.

"Yechezkel Polowitz's. The orphanage administrator."

Itzik looked at the monitor. The license plate was not visible in the video.

"Who told you that this is his car?" he asked Chezky.

"I know the model. It's custom-imported. There aren't many cars like these in Israel."

To Chezky's disappointment, Itzik Peled did not attach much significance to his revelation.

"I'll check to see how many cars like this are in the country," he said. "It may be nothing more than coincidence."

"You knew our father," Avreimi said. "Did he have any connection with Yechezkel Polowitz? Because all the documents about Abba in the orphanage disappeared, too…"

Itzik shrugged. "Documents are always going missing from all sorts of places. Who knows? Maybe your father asked for them at some point."

Chezky said, "Do you think it's a good idea for us to ask our mother?"

Avreimi rose up, cheeks flaming. "Never! It would only upset her. Do you want her to start crying again?"

Chezky beat a hasty retreat from an idea which he, himself, had not really thought all that great.

Itzik Peled ended the meeting by announcing that he would concentrate on investigating two points: the English-speaking visitor and Yechezkel Polowitz's car—if, indeed, it *was* his car.

"I'm planning to come in to see Ima tomorrow afternoon," Avreimi told Chezky after they'd left Itzik's house. "Maybe you should go visit her now?"

"I'm going to Ma'ariv right now, and then I'll stop in to see Ima," Chezky promised. "By the way, I'll be in Yerushalayim tomorrow, too. But I have a lot of errands to run."

"I think we did well in turning to Itzik Peled, no?" Avreimi remarked before they parted ways.

"Absolutely," Chezky agreed.

"Abba is probably happy with us," Avreimi said. "He always trusted Itzik."

Kibbutz Tel-Chana, 5737 / 1977

ALLON KOLER FELL SILENT. A THICK CLOUD OF DISCOMFORT filled Sonia Arzi's living room. Disappointment and bitterness seemed to float in the air like twisting coils of smoke, though Sonia's face remained hard and shuttered.

Allon felt sorry for her. He had visited more than a few homes of dead or missing soldiers, and had sensed the grief and loss. There was something more here. Sonia was not Momi's biological mother, and her reactions were different. She was insulted. She was angry. Sonia Arzi felt that Momi had shown base ingratitude in leaving. Apart from the pain and the longing, she felt hurt.

The silence stretched and thickened. Sonia sipped from her cup of tea, her mouth pursed in an expression of grievance.

Setting the cup on the table, she stood up. She faced the window, her back to her guest.

"It was something in the war," she said abruptly.

Allon lifted his eyes. Sonia heaved a long sigh.

"There was something in the war that changed him," she said, returning to the sofa. "He returned from there a different person."

Allon nodded his head slowly. "We all came back from the war different people," he whispered, half to himself.

When he looked back at Sonia, he was surprised to see her eyes glistening with tears. He knew that she wanted to know what it had been like there, during those terrible days, but she was too proud to ask.

"There were just thirty of us in the bunker," he began. "Some of them were Nachal, some were reservists, and there was one soldier who'd been sent by the military rabbinate to arrange prayers for anyone who wanted them. We had a bad feeling. We'd noticed activity among the Egyptians for several weeks, we'd seen that they were making preparations for crossing the Canal, but command headquarters was blind. Our division commander kept reassuring us. He said that we had nothing to worry about. They were all enraptured by a concept. What was it that Golda said just a few days before the war? 'Our situation has never been better.' The complacency was so great that they canceled the order for soldiers to sleep in their uniforms, to be ready for an attack.

"And then came Yom Kippur. The religious guys prayed, while the others continued doing their usual jobs: repairing the fortifications, standing watch over the Suez and Port Tawfik, bringing ammunition to the shooting positions. Routine.

"At 1:40, I received an order over the radio to prepare my men for an imminent attack. I shouted out the order, and all the soldiers started racing around. Just minutes later, we began to come under an artillery bombardment of unprecedented proportions. The Egyptians were shooting along the entire length of the strip like madmen. For three-quarters of an hour, no one could so much as stick a head out of the bunker. The entire perimeter was decimated: the direct hits brought down our communications channels as well as our shooting positions. Now the thirty of us were trapped inside the fortified bunker and couldn't get out. The stronghold positioned about ten kilometers to our rear had also absorbed a heavy bombardment and all our tanks had been destroyed.

"And all this time, we were hearing the Egyptian tanks and

armored personnel carriers outside. They were crossing the Canal and speeding into Sinai: armored lines, trucks bearing infantry corps, jeeps carrying cannons and who knew what else. Egypt's entire Third Army was invading Israel between our strongholds—and we were in the bunker, on the bank of the Canal, deep in enemy territory.

"It's impossible to describe our feelings at that moment. A deathly fear. As the hours passed, bands of Egyptians tried repeatedly to storm our bunker. We returned their fire and repelled the attacks, but we were still trapped and surrounded. We stayed there for four full days, while everything collapsed around us. The artillery barrage was continuous. We asked for help, for artillery cover, extraction, something. Command headquarters told us, 'Stand firm. Help is on the way.' But nothing happened.

"Over the radio, I could hear nearby bunkers surrendering or being destroyed. I heard the screams of the wounded and the officers' despair. And all the while, Egyptian commando units continued attacking and trying to storm our bunker. They went about it in a methodical way: one attack at first light and another at dusk. Meanwhile, we were managing to hang on, but we had three men dead and several wounded, among them the poor soldier from the military rabbinate.

"My men fought nonstop, until they had no more strength. Momi went from one person to the next, encouraging them. As their leader, I knew how desperate the situation was. Our food and water were running out, as was our ammunition. My medic was exhausted and our medical supplies diminishing by the minute. I looked at those soldiers and saw them deteriorating before my eyes. It was a terrible crisis: we knew that our army was strong and victorious—the Six-Day War and all that—and now, suddenly, we were like sitting ducks. Morale had hit rock-bottom. Without Momi, I don't know how it would have ended.

"Then I was wounded, too. Momi took over the command. On the fifth day of the war there were several attempts to free us. All of them failed. Israeli tanks tried to reach us, but it was impossible. The entire area had been seeded with mines, and there were ambushes with RPGs and missiles. On the seventh day, we started talking about letting ourselves be taken prisoner. A message came from headquarters, saying that the government higher-ups had decided we could be allowed to surrender, since they'd been unsuccessful in freeing us from the rear.

"Momi came to consult with me. He was agitated. He said that surrender was out of the question. We must fight to the last drop of blood! I said forget about national pride—I just wanted my men to get safely home. No one would benefit from another thirty casualties in this war. 'Look at that poor kid,' I told Momi, pointing at the soldier from the military rabbinate. 'He didn't even want to fight. He simply wandered into a war that was not his. What would it give anyone if he died here?'

"Momi let himself be persuaded. He told command headquarters that we would only surrender to the Red Cross or the U.N. Otherwise, the Egyptians would cut us down the minute we stepped out of our bunker. He was told that they would try to contact the U.N., but to prepare a white flag in the meantime. Momi took charge of the preparations for surrender. He burned documents, prepared a plan for destroying the little ammunition we had left, and delegated tasks to the other men: who would carry the wounded, who would take the dead…

"The next day, a boat approached us from the Egyptian side of the Canal, bearing the Red Cross. Using a megaphone, they asked for the commander. Momi went out, unarmed, carrying the white flag. He walked up to the bank and stepped onto the boat. There were apparently some U.N. representatives on board as well. By that point, I was half-dead. Most of the time I was only partially conscious."

Sonia Arzi was growing tenser by the minute.

"But you didn't surrender," she suddenly interrupted. "You were not taken prisoner. Momi always told us that he liberated the rest of you to the rear."

"True," Allon affirmed. "Momi returned in turmoil from his meeting with the Red Cross people. The Egyptians had not agreed to let us take our wounded and our dead, and that was unacceptable to us. He gathered together whoever could still walk and said that there was no choice but to try to free ourselves. He would not shoot his injured friends, nor would he leave our dead behind."

"And then…"

"And then he contacted military headquarters, and that night they managed to hook up with us and get us into Israel. Exactly what happened, I have no idea. I was released from the hospital four months after the war. Momi came to visit me once during my stay, but there were other people in the room and we couldn't speak freely. He didn't contact any of the others.

"And after that, as you know, he disappeared…"

Jerusalem, 5772 / 2011

"It's Chezky!" Miri called out to her oldest brother.

Avreimi—who, as usual, had come to his parents' home on Tuesday—seized the opportunity to help young Yoel study for his Chumash test the next day. He had left his phone set to vibrate, and someone had been calling again and again, making the cell phone dance on the buffet until he had finally asked his sister to find out who was trying to reach him.

"Chezky?" Avreimi repeated in surprise. "Give him to me."

"Avreimi, where are you?" Chezky asked in excitement.

"Ima's house."

"I have something that you have to see!"

"Is it a matter of life or death?"

"No—but it's really urgent."

"I'm learning with Yoel right now."

"So come down to me for a minute. I'm right outside."

Avreimi thought for a long moment. "No," he said at last. "I'm going to learn with him for another half-hour, and then I'll come down."

"Avreimi!" Chezky yelled.

But all he heard was, *"L'hitraot"*—and then the dial tone, as his brother hung up.

Over the course of the next thirty minutes, Chezky calmed down somewhat, and even forgave Avreimi for not obeying his order at once.

"Listen," he told his brother. "I think I might have mentioned this to you… Ever since Abba was *niftar*, I couldn't get close to the area of Ashtorei HaParchi and Reishis Chachmah without breaking into a sweat and feeling my heart start pounding like crazy. Last week, for instance, my wife asked me to buy her a book. Ever since I've been a kid I've been buying books at Weill, but I just couldn't bear to be that close to the place where it happened. I ended up going to another store.

"After we were there with Itzik Peled, day before yesterday, those symptoms simply went away. An hour ago, I passed by there and felt fine. I even went in to say hello to Mr. Weill. He said that he had felt terrible when he heard about the tragedy, and he also told me something interesting: From time to time, Abba used to buy basic Jewish books from him and send them to people who'd recently become *ba'alei teshuvah*… But that's not why I called you here. After chatting for a few minutes, Weill told me that he had something for me—and pointed to the security camera outside his store.

"'I don't usually review the videos,' he told me, 'but yesterday I needed to look at the film from the day your father died, and I suddenly saw him passing the store. It was early afternoon, presumably not long before he collapsed. I didn't have the heart to erase it. I thought you might want to see it, so my employee copied that part onto a disk.'"

As he spoke, Chezky opened his laptop and inserted the disk in its drive. It took a few seconds for the program to be activated and the clip to start running.

"Ashtorei HaParchi," Chezky said, as if there was any need to point out the place.

On the screen, people passed to and fro down the street. Two students from a nearby yeshivah seemed to be hotly debating some point in their learning; groups of young girls passed, chattering cheerfully; an elderly couple paced slowly, pushing a child's stroller filled with their purchases.

"Abba passes by during the sixth minute," Chezky whispered.

He fast-forwarded the video until it reached the end of the fifth minute.

"There's Abba," Avreimi said, his brows coming together as he brought his face closer to the screen. "Look how he's walking—almost running!"

"Isn't it strange?" said Chezky. "I'm not used to seeing him that way."

"Looks like he's running away from something."

"Yes, it does…"

"Does Abba appear again?"

"Keep watching," Chezky said.

Once again, they saw people moving along the narrow street. Three minutes had passed on the monitor's clock, when they sudden spotted a familiar figure.

"*What*???" Avreimi's eyes opened wide in fear.

Chezky looked at him, nodding his head with tightened lips.

"I don't believe it!" Avreimi put a hand over his heart. "He's following Abba. He was there when it happened!"

Chezky didn't say a word.

"So what… Why…" Avreimi was beside himself. "Are you sure it's him?"

Chezky rewound the video. The image reappeared, clear and staggering.

"What a mistake I made," Avreimi mumbled to himself.

"Mistake? What mistake?" Chezky asked. But Avreimi didn't seem to hear the question.

Chezky rewound the picture again, and enlarged the image.

There was no room for error. It was Itzik Peled.

So not only the mysterious Englishman had been present when their father had returned his soul to his Creator; not only Yechezkel Polowitz had been in the area of the crime; but also their father's good friend Itzik Peled himself…

Kibbutz Tel-Chana, 5737 / 1977

"WHERE COULD HE HAVE DISAPPEARED TO?" ASKED Sonia Arzi. Her voice was filled with a bottomless pain. "Momi was always a responsible boy."

Allon nodded his head in empathy, passing a hand through his curls and adjusting the *kippah* on his head. The squeak of the gate sounded from outside, and then footsteps on the path leading to the house.

"Mikush, my husband," Sonia sighed.

Allon Koler stood up to greet him.

"This is Allon Koler, Momi's commander in the army," Sonia explained.

Mikush Arzi's handshake was limp and lacked strength. Languidly, he studied his guest. Allon saw the way the kibbutznik's eyes lingered on the *tzitzis* and the *kippah* perched on his head.

Mikush turned an inquiring glance on his wife.

"He came here to *ask* about Momi," Sonia said. Allon could see the spark of hope extinguish in the adoptive father's eyes.

"He went through the war with Momi," Sonia continued. "He told me about those days in the bunker, at the Suez Canal."

"And did you hear anything new?" Mikush asked, sitting tiredly on the sofa.

"No. The same thing. He was unconscious for the last two days." She gestured at their visitor.

Suddenly, Allon realized that he hadn't told her anything she hadn't known before. He had thought that he was telling her about Momi's great moments, and lifting her spirits, but apparently she had already been aware of it all. It was *she* who'd been trying to extract from him some new information regarding those eventful days.

Mikush got up and went quietly toward the kitchen.

Abruptly, he turned.

"We don't believe all the news about Momi," he said.

"What news?" asked Allon. He regretted the words even before they were out of his mouth.

"Don't play the innocent." Sonia lifted herself slightly in anger. "We're not stupid. We know exactly who sent you here."

Mikush stood in the kitchen doorway, shoulders dropping, letting his wife conduct the battle.

"Now they send *ba'alei teshuvah*—a new tactic," Sonia sniped. "Or is that also a disguise?!"

Allon's expression was sincere. "No one sent me," he said. "I came because I haven't seen Momi for a long time."

Momi's adoptive father took one step into the living room. His lower lips trembled. "They say that Momi was a traitor. That he sold secrets to Egypt in order to save himself. They say that he left battle maps and plans of the line of strongholds in the bunker when he left."

Allon wrinkled his brow, trying to remember. "I recall that they said some such nonsense after the war," he said in surprise. "But no one took it seriously."

"They say that none of the strongholds, all along the Canal, managed to liberate itself to the rear so easily," Mikush said. "The Egyptians stopped their shelling for two hours and let the Israeli tanks approach without hindrance. They're saying that when

Momi went out to that Red Cross boat, he made a dirty deal with the Egyptians: He would give them classified information, and they would give him a window of time, free of shelling, so that he could get out. From the boat, they claim, he returned to the bunker and put on a show. He said that the Egyptians had not agreed to terms for their surrender, and that they would have to get themselves out despite the danger. That's how they got away so cleanly. The Egyptians simply let him go, and that's how he and his men were able to reach command headquarters unharmed."

Allon Koler looked at Sonia Arzi. Her face was drawn in anguish.

"He was no traitor," she said, but her voice lacked the firmness it had held a just a moment before. "Momi did not betray his country."

Mikush heaved a trembling sigh.

"But... even if it were true," Allon said, "Momi didn't only save himself. He saved thirty men from certain death. Egypt was wiping us out, one by one, in cold blood. Everyone knows what took place at the Canal. I would have been dead within 48 hours if I hadn't reached a hospital."

"Go tell that to the Shin-Bet," Sonia whispered, staring out the window.

"And besides," Allon Koler added, "at that point in the war, on the seventh day, the maps and plans would not have helped the Egyptians at all. The line of strongholds was already seen as a burst balloon."

Sonia and Mikush exchanged a pain-filled glance.

"A week ago, a bereaved couple came here," Sonia said, eyes downcast and fingers playing with the fringe of the tablecloth. "Their son had been killed on the ninth day of the war. They screamed and cursed and blamed us. 'It's because of you that our son is in the grave,' they said. 'Because of your traitorous son...' They came from Ramat Gan to the kibbutz to see with their own eyes the parents who had raised a Communist traitor in their home. That's what they said..."

"I think the Shin-Bet sent them," said Mikush, shaking his head in sorrow and taking a sip of tea that had gone completely cold.

"We've searched for Momi in every jail, civil and military. We went to the most senior people in the country, begging them for a sign that he was alive. We didn't ask for the right to visit. We didn't ask that he be freed. We didn't ask for anything—just the knowledge that he's alive and breathing somewhere. But there's no one to talk to. We know that he's not in any official prison, but we've been told that the Shin-Bet has secret jails, above the law. That they can bury people forever and no one would know."

Sonia Arzi took out a handkerchief and wiped her eyes.

Allon sat in his armchair, elbows on his knees with his fists supporting his chin. From outdoors came the whisper of the wind in the trees.

"Momi is no traitor," he said confidently.

Sonia and Mikush stared at him.

"Momi is no traitor. I know that with certainty," Momi's commander repeated.

Jerusalem, 5772 / 2011

"Let's not be in a hurry to assign blame," Avreimi told Chezky, after taking a few moments to recover his wits. "It could simply be an unfortunate coincidence. Itzik never told us that he was or wasn't there. We haven't caught him in a lie."

"You are so naïve," Chezky said. "Itzik Peled was following Abba just minutes before he died—and you think that's a coincidence?"

"Why don't we ask him?"

Chezky nearly jumped out of his seat. "*Ask* him? Are you crazy? Don't you realize that he's part of the plot?"

"What plot?"

"We still have to find that out. But Itzik, in my opinion, is our prime suspect."

"And how, exactly, will we find out?"

Angrily, Chezky slammed down the lid of his laptop. He had no better answer. "How do I know? We can go to the police."

"Really? You heard what Itzik said about the police."

Chezky burst into bitter laughter. "'What Itzik said'?" he mocked. "I see you still believe him…"

"I don't *dis*believe him," Avreimi corrected. "Don't forget that Abba admired and trusted him—and Abba was not mistaken in people. He had a good eye."

"Anyone can make a mistake. Even Abba. It would be madness to show him this clip."

Avreimi's mouth twisted in frustration. He tilted his head from side to side as though weighing something.

"What?" Chezky asked.

Avreimi couldn't muster the courage to say what was on his mind.

"Well?" Chezky pressed.

"Itzik has this disk," Avreimi admitted in a low voice.

"Really? Where from?"

"From me." Avreimi couldn't meet his brother's eyes.

"*What???*"

"Weill gave me the disk as well, but I had no way of looking at it. So I gave it to Itzik."

Chezky looked like he wanted to murder someone. "When?" he barked.

"Lunchtime," Avreimi said, clearly regretting it with all his heart.

For a very long moment, there was silence between the brothers. Avreimi was inwardly scolding himself for his hasty action.

"Tell me," Chezky said at last. "By Jewish law, is one permitted to punch his older brother if he's a total idiot? What's your legal opinion?"

It took Avreimi a minute to realize that his brother was joking. He looked at Chezky.

"I don't know if I would have done any differently," Chezky said ruefully. "Well, what do we do now? What do you think?"

Avreimi had still not recovered from the enormity of his gaffe.

"We could go to him innocently and say that we have some more video clips. See how he reacts," Chezky suggested.

"That's an idea."

"Where is this from?" Itzik took the disk from Chezky after ushering the brothers into his office.

"A bookstore on Ashtorei HaParchi. Weill's. Do you know it?"

Itzik narrowed his eyes suspiciously and looked at both brothers in rapid succession. "Is this the same disk that you brought me?" he asked Avreimi.

Avreimi nodded, his heart skipping a beat.

"Actually, I haven't had a chance to view it yet," Itzik said. "Let's see what we have here."

In no time at all, the disk was playing in the computer.

For five minutes and a bit, not a sound was heard in the room.

"There's your father," Itzik said in the sixth minute.

"Yes. Let's watch a little longer." Chezky's voice was slightly unsteady.

Three pairs of eyes remained fixed on the monitor until Itzik Peled's image appeared, walking down the street.

Chezky sent a surreptitious look at his prime suspect's face, but it was a mask that revealed no feeling or internal process at all. Itzik Peled gazed at the screen without a tremor. Only his lips tightened a bit.

The silence in the room did not end when the clip did.

"What do you say?" Avreimi asked.

Itzik appeared preoccupied, his eyes still on the screen and his forehead creased in thought.

"Amateurs," he said finally.

The brothers looked at him in surprise.

"Amateurs?" Chezky echoed.

"Not you," Itzik hastened to explain.

"Who, then?"

Itzik did not reply. He seemed to be thinking about something else.

"What were you actually doing there, behind our father?" Chezky asked.

Itzik Peled gave him a troubled glance, and suddenly smiled.

"I sensed that you were on the warpath from the minute you walked in," he remarked.

"Congratulations!" Chezky's lip curled. "You sure know how to read people. Were you able to read our father, too?"

Avreimi bit back a rebuke at his brother. But Itzik smiled forgivingly.

"I can understand what you must be feeling," he told Chezky. "Let's go together to Weill's bookstore. I want to investigate something."

The walk was uncomfortable in the extreme. Itzik Peled and the two brothers strode rapidly, without exchanging a word. Avreimi was in the grip of his distress, but Chezky strengthened himself with his thoughts: Itzik was a professional manipulator; it was impossible to believe a word he said; he hadn't expected to be caught, so he was under pressure; he would do anything now to save his skin…

The small bookstore was bustling. Two boys were looking at the newest comic books, devouring them from cover to cover; a mother and her two daughters came in with a list of schoolbooks as long as summer vacation; a Chassidic youth asked for a *Kiddushin Oz V'Hadar,* and a new author came with her husband to see if her books still held pride of place on the central shelf, or had already been sent to the rear of the store. R' Moshe Weill and his wife, behind a small table littered with post-it notes, somehow managed to give each customer what they wanted—with a smile.

"Hello, Avreimi and Chezky. Hello, R' Yitzchak," Mr. Weill said upon seeing the tense trio step inside. "How are you?"

"Baruch Hashem. R' Moshe," Chezky said, "we wanted to ask you a few questions about the video clip you gave us."

"Ah. Please."

"Is there any place where we can talk privately?" Itzik asked, glancing around at the busy store.

"Let's go upstairs," the shopkeeper suggested, already moving toward the staircase leading up to the gallery. Here were crowded shelves of books as well as a tiny office that barely held the four of them.

"I don't want to take too much of your time," Itzik Peled began. "Avreimi and Chezky showed me the clip—congratulations on preserving it. Just tell me this: why did you review the videos? Was there a robbery here? A break-in?"

R' Moshe Weill chuckled. "Someone simply asked for my help, and I suddenly saw their father."

"What do you mean, 'someone asked for your help'?"

The shopkeeper's face grew long and worried. "Why? Is there some kind of problem?"

"No, no. Everything's all right," Avreimi quickly reassured him. "We just wanted to check something."

"So you're suddenly detectives?"

Although the question had been addressed to the brothers, it was Itzik Peled who answered: "I am a private investigator. A kind of private investigator… There is something suspicious here that I was asked to look into."

"Here's what happened," said R' Moshe Weill. "A fellow came into my store and said that 500 dollars had fallen out of his pocket a few days before. He had come out of the *gemach* up on Rechov Chagiz, and when he reached Malchei Yisrael he realized that the money was gone. As he passed my store he saw that I had a camera, and asked to see if it had caught the money falling out of his pocket, or whether anybody had picked it up."

"So you showed him the video, and suddenly saw Shlomo Kohlberg."

"Actually, I didn't look at the screen. I let him review the video by himself. I was sitting at my desk doing some paperwork. Suddenly, he said to me, 'Look, there's Shlomo Kohlberg.'"

"How did he know our father?" Chezky asked.

"I have no idea. Lots of people knew him…"

"And then he must have said that his sons would probably be happy to see the clip," Itzik speculated.

"Maybe. I don't recall exactly."

"What did he look like?"

"Actually, it was a little strange. He wasn't a classic *chareidi*. I was even surprised that he had received a loan from the *gemach*, but there on Rechov Chagiz they really give to everyone without discrimination. I didn't check his antecedents. A Jew needs help—why not?"

"Certainly, certainly," Itzik agreed. "Well, did he find the money?"

"I have no idea," R' Moshe Weill admitted. "He didn't see himself in the video at all, and finally remembered that he had actually gone down Rechov Yaakov Meir and not on Ashtorei HaParchi. I wonder if he found it…"

Chezky appeared stunned, but he was smart enough not to say a word until they'd left the store after thanking its owner.

"Do you get it?" Itzik asked.

"Not really," Avreimi said.

Chezky did get it. "Who *is* that man? Maybe we should check the cameras from the day he reached the store with that tale of a missing 500 dollars?"

Itzik laughed. "I can guarantee that you won't see him. Those people know their job well. They know how not to get caught on camera."

"So how come *you* weren't careful?" Chezky heard himself ask.

Itzik gave him a level look. "Who says I was even there?"

"We saw you."

"Oh, really?" There was mockery in Itzik's voice. "The fact that you saw me on the video doesn't mean that I was there. It's possible to edit and splice every video in such a way that even professionals would have a hard time detecting the forgery. One thing is certain: someone made sure that you and your brother received the *impression* that I was there. Someone wanted that clip to reach you—and it did."

Kibbutz Tel-Chana 5737 / 1977

"How do you know he's not a traitor?" Sonia and Mikush Arzi asked. Their voices were tinged with hope.

"I knew him well," Momi's commander said. "He had a backbone. A person like him would not betray his country."

Why do you say that? their eyes asked.

"Let me tell you something about Momi," Allon said. "Today, as a believing Jew, it seems like the kind of inflexibility that comes from arrogance—but it testifies as to Momi's character.

"It was three hours after the outbreak of hostilities, near the end of the fast. It was time for *Ne'ilah*, and all of us in the besieged bunker, with the shelling going on outside, felt as if this were the great and terrible Judgment Day. It was clear to us that we were about to die. People were waiting for the fast to be over so that they could write farewell letters to their families. I told you earlier that we had one soldier with us who'd been sent by the military rabbinate. Zalman Berkovitch was his name. In short, on Yom Kippur night and morning, he organized prayer services in one of the bunker's side rooms. The religious men naturally attended, and some of the secular ones joined as well. There were two or three guys who were 'anti-religious' and made fun, trying to disrupt the proceedings. Momi, by the way, did not go near the room.

"But at *Ne'ilah*, every single man was present. Even those who'd laughed and disrupted before. They held *machzorim*, they cried and screamed and pleaded with the Almighty to save their lives, to let them escape from this nightmare unharmed. You know how it is: When a sword is resting on a person's neck, even the biggest heretic will reveal the spark of faith that's hidden inside.

"Only one man stood aside and didn't pray. Momi.

"He was pale. He was as terrified as the rest of us. He could hear the nonstop noise of the artillery barrage, as the Egyptian forces swarmed over the area and surrounded us. But he didn't join the prayer.

"I come from a traditional home. I grew up on a working moshav. I told him, 'Momi, take a *machzor* and I'll show you what we're up to.' I thought he might be embarrassed, that maybe he needed someone to break the ice. Do you know what he answered? 'No, Allon. I won't pray. It's no trick to be a heretic when it's convenient, and to remember G-d when you suddenly need Him. I won't pray today. Maybe one day I'll look into this question of faith to its depths. But to do *teshuvah* under pressure? Not me! Not Momi Arzi.'"

Allon Koler was feeling emotional. He took a sip from his cup of tea.

Sonia and Mikush waited silently for him to continue.

"Listen, I'm not here to criticize the way you brought him up, heaven forbid. Today I know with absolute certainty that G-d sometimes puts a person into difficult situations in order to wake him up. Momi, in his arrogance, rejected the sign that G-d had sent him. But one thing I'm sure about: Momi had solid principles. He would not sell them in order to save himself. Betrayal was simply not in his lexicon.

"They say he had a window of opportunity to escape? That doesn't bother me. Not after the war. I'm telling you: we saw miracles and wonders during those days. That war brought terrible tragedies—but we also saw open miracles, with our own eyes.

"I passed the command over to Momi on the fifth day of the war, after I was wounded. We had many conversations. The situation was still very bad, but we realized that we'd already survived a few days so we also had hope. Among other things, I talked to him about what had happened during *Ne'ilah*. He teased me: 'See, Allon? I didn't pray—and I'm still alive.'

"I answered him: 'Idiot, that's because I prayed for both of us!'

"That struck something in him. I think that was the first and last time I saw tears in his eyes... At the time, I was not doing well. I was burning up with fever and kept fading in and out of consciousness. It looked like I was going to join the pile of bodies in the bunker's last room. Momi took my shaking hand and held it with both of his.

"After a moment, he recovered. He smiled his bashful smile and said, 'Listen, Allon. I hope that heaven accepted your prayers for yourself as well. Not just for me.'

"Not much later, I became unconscious. What happened afterward, I just don't know."

Jerusalem, 5772 / 2011

Avreimi and Chezky stood outside Weill's Bookstore with long faces. Itzik Peled had hurried home, leaving them to stew in their feelings of guilt.

"'A person who suspects the innocent will be afflicted physically,'" Avreimi quoted. "We jumped to conclusions and convicted him."

Chezky recovered with impressive speed. "I'm still not so sure he's innocent. He put up a good show, but it doesn't tell us a thing."

Avreimi decided not to argue with his brother.

"What interests me more," Chezky said, sounding less friendly, "is why you didn't tell me that Weill had given you a disk."

Avreimi shrugged. He couldn't tell the true reason...

"And even more," Chezky continued the attack, "what changed

for you so suddenly? At first you were against any investigation at all—and suddenly you go with me to Itzik Peled and are interested in every detail."

"Well, which do you want?" Avreimi asked defensively. "If I go with you, that's also not good?"

"Avreimi, I've known you for a long time. I have a feeling that you went to the Rosh Yeshivah and asked him what to do. And he said that in order to keep an eye on your wayward little brother, you have to go along with him to make sure he doesn't do any damage. Am I right?"

Avreimi was at a loss.

"And what if I did ask the Rosh Yeshivah?" he asked after a beat.

"I'm sick and tired of all your... stuff!" Chezky was mad. "Well, why are you afraid to answer? Did you go, or didn't you?"

A mischievous smile appeared on Avreimi's lips. "That's called a paradox," he told his brother. "If I asked, I'd certainly tell you that I didn't. So even if I say I didn't go, you can't really believe me…"

Chezky snorted. "Sometimes you really get on my nerves, you know that? I'm going home. 'Bye."

A light rap sounded on the door of the Peled home. Itzik finished *bentching* as Brachah, his wife, got up to answer.

A moment later, she returned to the kitchen. "It's Kohlberg's son," she whispered.

"The son?"

"The oldest one—Avreimi."

Nothing in Itzik's face betrayed the broad smile that spread in his heart.

"Show him to my study. I'll be right there," he said.

"Good evening," Itzik said as he entered the room. His visitor was already seated. "Where's Chezky?" A quarter-hour earlier, Itzik had called Avreimi on a secure line and asked him and his brother to come over.

"He… had to go home."

Avreimi had supplied the answer that Itzik had expected. So, a rift had arisen between the two brothers, he mused. A most positive development... He made a last check: "Have you two quarreled?" he asked with a smile.

He didn't need a verbal answer. Avreimi's face told him everything he wanted to know.

"All right," Itzik said. "I wanted him to be here, too, but you can tell him everything afterward. Let's get down to business."

Brachah walked in, served some refreshments, and asked Avreimi how his mother was. Then she left, closing the door behind her.

"I want to prepare you up front," Itzik said gently. "What you're about to hear about your father this evening won't be easy. What you've discovered up till now, you and Chezky, is only the beginning."

Avreimi filled his lungs with air as though readying himself to dive into deep waters.

"Perhaps it's a good thing that you're here alone," Itzik continued. "I don't know how mature or responsible Chezky is. He suspects that I'm working against you, and I have no desire to convince him otherwise. He's a child. He'll grow up..."

Despite the turmoil of emotion inside, Avreimi felt flattered. Itzik noticed this with satisfaction.

"Well, then," said Itzik Peled. "I'll tell you this right from the start, without hiding and without evading: The widespread belief in the security services of the State of Israel is that your father, *z"l*, was a traitor to his dying day."

Avreimi recoiled in his chair, total shock written across his face.

Itzik went on: "I know that it will be very hard for you to hear this, but many people don't believe that he became a genuine *ba'al teshuvah*. They claim it was camouflage."

Now Avreimi shot forward, his trembling fingers gripping the edge of the table. "What are you saying?" he burst out. "How can you talk that way about my father?"

Itzik didn't budge. "I'm telling you what they *say*. I mentioned that that's the widespread belief."

"And what do *you* say?"

Itzik Peled didn't answer.

"*What do you say?*" Avreimi pressed, his voice shaking with suppressed anger.

Still Itzik was silent.

"My father was not a traitor!" Avreimi shouted. "How can you say such things about him? He helped you all your life. He hosted you for Shabbos meals. He married you off..."

He collapsed back in his chair, tears in his eyes.

"You're so upset," Itzik said calmly, "that you haven't asked the necessary question: If everyone thinks that your father committed a crime deserving of a prison sentence—how is it that he was able to walk around freely?"

Avreimi gaped at Itzik.

"I will answer the question," said Itzik. "But it's a long story."

He opened a drawer in his desk and took out his laptop. After pressing a few buttons and moving his mouse, he turned it around to face Avreimi. On the screen was an old photograph featuring three men: an older one of about 45, flanked by two younger men in their twenties. The three were sitting on a bench in some hilly clearing. Behind them was a sign in Hebrew. The picture, then, had been taken in Israel.

Itzik pointed to the young man seated on the right.

"That's your father, at the age of 21," he told Avreimi. "After he finished his army service."

Avreimi's breath stopped. This was the first time he had seen his father as a young, secular Jew. As... Momi Arzi. The face looked the same, though he was clean-shaven.

"This young man," Itzik pointed to the second figure, "is someone you met last week."

The man was religious. He was wearing a *kippah* and had a beard.

"Who is he?"

"Zalman Berkovitch."

"No-o-o-o..."

"Yes," said Itzik. "We were all young and handsome once."

"And who is this?" Avreimi asked, pointing to the older man seated in the middle of the bench.

"That's the big riddle," Itzik said. "In order to solve it, the intelligence services of Israel and Britain toiled for long years."

"But who took the picture? And where was it taken?"

"The photograph was taken secretly by a Shin-Bet agent in the year 1974, after the Yom Kippur War, just a few months after your father was released from the army and went back to civilian life.

"You already know that your father was an ardent Communist in his youth. After the army, he planned to return to the kibbutz. But then he traveled to Haifa, to a gathering of the Israeli Communist Party. His reputation had preceded him as one of the most successful members of the Communist youth movement. Everyone spoke excitedly about how he had put his kibbutz to the vote over his desire to refuse the draft on ideological grounds. Even more, they admired his ability to accept the kibbutz's verdict, to allow himself to be inducted and to serve fully and without demur.

"The Party conference was attended by honored guests from the Soviet Union and its satellites: East Germany, Romania, Poland, and the like. The man who appears in the center of the photo had come from the Soviet Union on a flight that had stopped in Europe. He brought with him a letter of greeting from the president of the Soviet Union, Leonid Brezhnev, delivered a speech at the conference, and held meetings with Israeli Communist activists. That was how he became acquainted with the young Momi Arzi—not knowing that, in doing so, he would seal his fate."

Israel, 5734 / 1974

The old, smoky minibus making its way from Tel-Chana to Haifa was filled with cheerful teenagers, at least in the rear section.

Near the front sat some of the older members, sated with meetings and conferences, who had received a day off from their work routine to represent the kibbutz at the 18th Party Convention. In the rear, the enthusiastic young people were throwing admiring looks at Momi Arzi, the mystical group leader. They were drinking in his words. All of them, of course, wore their youth-movement shirts: a white button-down with a red triangle above the tie. They also sported the movement's symbol: a red star enclosing a hammer and sickle, to show their identification with the Soviet Union.

Momi was excited as well. This was the first Communist Party convention in Israel in several years. He had missed the previous one because he had been serving in the IDF and had been prohibited from participating in political activity; when the one before that had taken place, he had been too young to appreciate it. He remembered how he and his parents had traveled to Nazareth, where the convention was held. Mikush Arzi was allotted a local hotel room for the three days of the convention, because he served as secretary of the Party branch in Kfar Saba. "I finally feel as if I'm with like-minded people," Sonia Arzi told her husband. "I'm so tired of being among people who give you accusing looks and view you as a Soviet agent or a Communist spy."

Momi didn't recall much about that gathering except large halls draped in red, speeches filled with pathos, and fiery ideological arguments into the small hours of the night. He also remembered the many policemen who constantly patrolled the convention hall, ostensibly to provide protection from right-wing hoodlums, but actually—as his parents explained to him—in order to mark down and follow up on everyone who entered the Party hall. To this day, he remembered the warning whispers that circulated among the grown-ups: "Don't talk to Jacoby. He's a Shin-Bet plant."

"Momi," one of the youths said, "do you think we'll meet people from the Soviet Union at the convention?" They already met monthly with Arab youth groups for joint activities, but meeting actual Soviet youths was, so far, an unattainable dream.

"I very much hope so," Momi said. "You know it's not easy for them to come here. At the airport, the Shin-Bet stops anyone who looks as if he's heading for the convention. The thing that scares Israel's Bolshevik authorities is the fear that we'll meet, face-to-face, with the happy citizens of the Soviet Union, our motherland. People who get up in the morning with a song on their lips, who go out to work each day as laborers or farmers and receive everything they need from the government, share and share alike."

"But why?" another boy asked.

"Very simple," explained Momi. "That's how the corrupt governments of the West continue to oppress the workers. They tell the masses that the Soviet Union is run by a dictatorship. They spread wicked anti-Soviet propaganda. And all in order for the wealthy to become wealthier and the poor to become poorer—and the capitalists to continue on their merry way."

The young people fell sadly silent in the face of the injustice that rules the world. "Listen closely to the speeches," Momi advised. "Even if you don't grasp all the concepts, you'll be able to ask questions afterward. And remember: the Revolution will triumph! The future is ours!"

The minibus had reached the outskirts of Haifa and begun to wind along the narrow streets toward the Wadi-Ninas neighborhood where the convention was to be held.

"Who's that?" one of the boys asked Momi, pointing at the stranger who'd joined them back at the kibbutz and had taken a seat near the driver. He was tall, gaunt, and dressed in a gray suit—and had been silent throughout the trip.

Momi didn't know, nor did he ask. If the fellow was in the minibus, it meant that he belonged there.

The minibus traveled along Rechov Chaviri, the main street of lower Haifa. In the distance, the convention hall could already be seen, red flags waving out front and a large placard, in Hebrew and Arabic, announcing: "Welcome to the 18th Israeli Communist Party Convention."

The excited youths climbed the stairs, their eyes devouring all the sights. Representatives and Party members from all over the country met and mingled in the lobby in a medley of languages. The United Communist Youth band from Nazareth played lively march tunes. Communist Knesset members walked around with a self-conscious air of importance, drawing eyes wherever they went.

To Momi's great surprise, the quiet stranger who'd ridden on the minibus with them turned out to be one of the movement's leaders. He shook hands and conversed with the representatives, moving with impressive ease from English to Arabic to Russian. Who was he?

Momi soon had his answer. The man sat in the center of the dais, and the emcee raised his voice in excitement: "I have the honor of introducing Comrade Professor Andrei Kalinin, from the University of Kiev—a special guest who has come from our beloved motherland to convey the greetings of Party Chairman and president of the Soviet Union, Leonid Brezhnev!"

Thunderous applause shook the auditorium. The professor then delivered a speech, to rapt attention.

Momi sat riveted throughout. Near the end of the speech, Adnan, an MK's aide, approached Momi and motioned for him to leave his seat. "Come outside for a moment," he said. The two passed into the lobby.

"How are you, Momi?" Adnan asked. "I saw your parents, Sonia and Mikush, in the auditorium. How are they doing?"

"Everyone's all right," Momi answered. "But that's not why you called me out here."

"Listen, Momi—I need your help. Actually, not me—the Party. One of our guests from the Soviet Union has asked for a tour of the country. I got you a car and I'm asking you to be at his disposal over the next two days."

Momi stared at his friend in astonishment. Adnan was young, but well-connected at the apex of the Party. He would not have asked such a thing on his own cognizance.

The young Arab understood the reason for Momi's silence. "This is not my request. It comes from on high. Very high. The highest you can imagine."

Momi shifted his weight from foot to foot, considering this. He had come here to listen to speeches, to participate in debates and get to know people—not to serve as a tour guide.

"The request comes from abroad," Adnan whispered. Momi nodded his head in understanding.

Adnan looked around, and then surreptitiously slipped a car key from his pocket. "A white Peugeot 404. It's waiting on Rechov Al-Asfahani, right behind this building."

Momi accepted the key.

"Drive to Rechov Hassan Shokri. There's a small hotel on the corner called 'Al-Motaran.' Go to Room 6 on the second floor. He'll be waiting for you there."

With a shrug, Momi turned to go.

"By the way, the guest is an archeologist. He wants to visit the sites of several digs in the country. Do you have any knowledge of the subject?"

"Archeology? What do I have to do with archeology?"

"Okay, okay. He'll explain it to you when you see him. You'd better go."

The Peugeot was waiting for Momi, as promised, on Rechov Al-Asfahani. The drive to Rechov Hassan Shokri took no longer than five minutes, and the Al-Motaran hotel turned out to be a small place run by an Arab family. Momi climbed a worn staircase to the second floor. Room 6 was at the very end of the corridor. He knocked on the door and someone inside roared for him to come in.

Momi pushed the door open, and was astounded to see Professor Andrei Kalinin himself—the man who'd driven in the minibus with them, and who had just been on the dais, addressing the Party convention.

But… how had he managed to get here so quickly? What was going on?

The man gave him no time to ask questions. He handed Momi a note that read, "Drive to Dan Panorama Hotel, Room 817."

Momi couldn't believe what his eyes were seeing. He read the note a second time, looking from the paper to the man and back again. The man took out a book of matches, extracted one match and lit it. He gave Momi a last few seconds to memorize the note's contents, and then touched the burning match to it. It caught fire instantly.

The Dan Panorama Hotel was handsomer and more opulent than its predecessor. Momi wasted no time reaching the eighth floor. The door to Room 817 was slightly ajar. He pushed it open gently and peered.

A stranger sat there. If the man in the previous room had resembled an ascetic Soviet professor, this fellow looked more like a learned Frenchman of lavish tastes. He sported a fine suit, a good tie, a modish haircut, and a pair of thick, horn-rimmed spectacles. He sat facing the mirror, inspecting his reflection. Suddenly, in the mirror, he caught sight of Momi standing in the doorway. He turned with a scowl.

"Who are you?" he asked in English.

"Uh, excuse me…" Momi retreated.

"What do you mean, 'excuse me'? Why are you barging into people's rooms?" He stood up and walked menacingly toward Momi.

Momi was not afraid of him. He knew he was strong enough to subdue the man in seconds. But this was not the time to get embroiled in a fight. Not when he had an important mission to carry out for the Party.

"I apologize from the bottom of my heart," he said, taking another step back.

"Just a minute." Suddenly, the man smiled. "Do you recognize me?"

Completely taken aback, Momi gazed into the man's face.

"I am Andrei Kalinin!" The man burst out laughing. "This is simply a disguise. If *you* don't recognize me, then no one will."

Momi gaped at him in disbelief.

"Fifteen minutes ago, I finished my speech at the conference, and they brought me here," Andrei Kalinin explained. "The man you met in the Arab hotel is my double. I understand that, by coincidence, he traveled to Haifa in the same minibus as you. He will walk around in the neighborhood of the Arab hotel; he will sit and smoke and read books in Russian. Your Shin-Bet will be sure that I am in Haifa—while you drive me to several archeological sites."

Momi was still in shock. Andrei Kalinin had already left the room, closing the door behind him. He summoned the elevator to take them down to the parking lot. It wasn't until they were seated in the Peugeot that Momi found his tongue.

"The first place I want to visit is Masada," Professor Kalinin said. "By the way, how conversant are you with Jewish tradition and the commandments of the faith?"

Momi grinned. There was nothing further from him than Jewish religious customs.

The car exited the parking lot and continued down the slope of the Carmel toward the Haifa-Tel Aviv Highway.

"Do you know anyone who is more knowledgeable about Judaism?" the professor asked. "Money is no problem. I will require some explanations on religious topics."

One name popped immediately into Momi Arzi's head. The

only religious Jew he knew: the soldier from the military rabbinate who'd been in the Suez Canal bunker with him during the war.

"I know someone," he said, thinking out loud. "But I don't know if he'll agree to come. His name is Zalman Berkovitch."

THE PEUGEOT'S WHEELS SWALLOWED UP THE COASTAL highway at a nice clip. Momi's grip on the large steering wheel was confident. This was the largest and shiniest vehicle he had ever driven. The few cars on the kibbutz were old and worn, acquired at fourth- or fifth-hand, and in the army he had mostly driven command cars and armored personnel carriers.

Momi felt a certain sense of guilt. It was very, very un-Communist-like to drive a comfortable and costly French-made car. And, worst of all—it was fun.

Near Hadera, Momi finally managed to quiet his conscience. He placed an arm on the windowsill, letting the wind blow into his face and ruffle his hair.

If he had expected to while away the time listening to tales of life in the Soviet motherland, Momi was in for a disappointment. Professor Kalinin preferred to grill him about life in Israel and on the kibbutz. The few answers he did supply were not particularly encouraging.

"I must admit that life is not easy for us," the professor confessed.

"Do not forget, Comrade Momi, that the entire world is waging an ideological war against us. The U.S. and Britain—with their mighty armies and thriving economies—are doing everything in their power to hurt us and bring about our collapse. The millions of hired workers who toil for minimum wage in the West serve as cannon-fodder. Those wretched laborers work from morning to night in exchange for a few pennies, while enriching the wealthy.

"The authorities have convinced the working public that democracy and freedom will bring them happiness, and that the Communists only wish to harm them. But *I* tell you, Momi: This style of leadership will end by destroying the world. How is it possible for some illiterate man from North Carolina to decide who pushes the nuclear button? How can a drunken, unemployed American determine who will serve as president of the United States—and have his vote considered equal to that of a Ph.D. in nuclear engineering in some New York university?

"Democracy appears enlightened, but it is a system that places the most fateful decisions in the hands of empty-headed people. A nation must have a leader—and it is the leader's job to lead!"

Momi continued driving, while lending an attentive ear. He had reached the outskirts of Tel Aviv and was wondering how to get onto the highway to Jerusalem.

"I am not saying that our own situation is completely rosy," Professor Kalinin continued. "America and Europe disseminate corrupt, anti-Soviet propaganda. They tell of long lines in front of bread shops and the lack of basic products. And you know something, Momi? I won't deny it! There *are* certain shortages. But who created them? Who caused them? The Americans, with their sanctions, which they impose to starve our nation! They aim nuclear warheads at our cities and force us to divert all of our resources toward defense. And then they have the nerve to blame *our* behavior..."

"They, of course, will say that *our* leaders are corrupt," Momi remarked, clearly disagreeing with such an unfounded claim.

"What else?" Kalinin chuckled. "They don't know any other reality. Over there, all leaders are rotten from the bottom up. And how could they not be? When a president owes his election to flocks of voters and must constantly appease them—how can he *not* become corrupt? In our own system, the Party appoints a leader on the basis of his talents and abilities. The country calls on its most elite citizens to take their places at the helm of government. And that is why our leaders walk a straight path, are incorruptible and modest, and serve as outstanding examples to the nation!"

"How I'd love to live in the Soviet Union," Momi said.

"Who knows? Maybe one day your dream will come true." After a moment, the professor added, "And perhaps the day will come sooner than you think…"

The Peugeot was approaching Sha'ar Hagai. "Another half an hour, and we'll be in Jerusalem," Momi remarked.

"How the governments of the West rule the masses—that is the question that troubles our leadership," said Professor Kalinin. "How they create an obvious dictatorship with all the appearance of a democracy, so that millions of people willingly accept a corrupt and despicable leadership."

Momi didn't answer. He sensed that his guest had not finished speaking. There was more to come.

"I argue that religion is the primary tool that Western governments use in order to rule," Professor Kalinin continued. "The United States is a very religious nation. It has tens of thousands of churches, priests, and preachers. These men of faith drag the masses after them. Let's say you are unemployed, your life is in the dumps, you have nothing to eat and are considered a failure. But on Sundays you come to church and the priest showers you with hope and comfort. People have to believe in something. That's a deep emotional need. To survive their miserable lives, they need a feeling of connection. Give them an inspirational talk, a few hymns and rituals—and you own them. I told Brezhnev: 'Let me undermine their faith, and you will see them collapse like a tower of cards.'"

"But here in Israel," Momi pointed out, "as I'm sure you know, we are dealing with Judaism."

"Judaism is a tough problem," Professor Kalinin acknowledged. "Judaism is a much harder nut to crack. But never mind—Judaism is in its sunset years. Look around. How many religious Jews are there?

Not many... and they will naturally diminish with time. The problem with Christianity is that you don't have to do much in order to feel like a believer. The religion demands a minimum of obligations. You may be a despicable criminal, but you can go to church, confess your sins, donate some money, and come away feeling cleansed and pure... until the next crime. Christianity allows people to feel comforted at a wonderfully cheap cost—while satisfying that deep emotional need. Take that away, and you've destroyed them."

The Peugeot drove into Jerusalem. Momi began to feel nervous about involving Zalman Berkovitch.

"I hope that he'll agree to come with us," he told the professor.

"We'll persuade him," Kalinin said with a laugh. "There's one language that everyone understands." He took a bundle out of his pocket, held together with a rubber band. Momi gaped. The bundle contained a great deal of most un-Communist money. American dollars.

Momi pulled up beside a group of people. "Pardon me, how do I get to Meah Shearim?" He received precise instructions. A short drive brought them to Rechov Malchei Yisrael, where they crossed Kikar Shabbat and continued into the winding maze of Meah Shearim.

Professor Kalinin roused himself from his thoughts to peer out the window. He seemed stunned. The human landscape presented to his view was different from anything he had seen thus far in Israel since he had landed 24 hours earlier.

"What is this?" he demanded. "What is this place called?"

"This is Meah Shearim. A religious neighborhood," Momi explained, amused by his guest's astonishment. "Ultra-Orthodox, to be exact."

Profressor Kalinin gazed around him. "And how many such people are there in Israel? What does this group number?"

Momi shrugged. "I don't know." Apart from a few anti-*chareidi* demonstrations that the youth movement had organized, he had never been especially interested.

"And this... friend of yours that you're taking us to. Is he like these people?" The professor sounded a little worried.

"Not exactly. He went to the army. He's a little more open."

"What does that mean? These people don't serve in the army?"

Momi laughed as though he had just heard a good joke. "In my opinion, these are shirkers, parasites, people who take from the State but don't give anything back."

Kalinin's expression relaxed a bit. "Then what is their standing in the State?"

"I think there are many people who hate them even more than they hate the Arabs."

Professor Kalinin listened to this answer with a certain satisfaction.

Momi got slightly lost in the narrow streets, and was forced to ask a passerby for further directions. He leaned across to call through the passenger window, "How do I get to Rechov Baharan?"

"These types are the most problematic of all," the professor told Momi when they were moving again. "I work in Kiev. Well, you're intelligent enough to understand that the University of Kiev is not exactly my place of work… On occasion, I visit KGB headquarters and come across these types. They constitute a difficult problem in the Soviet Union today. They smuggle in religious books, organize secret Jewish-studies classes, find ways to eat kosher, and try to bring Jewish citizens back into the chains of religion." He heaved a long and frustrated sigh. "They are problematic indeed. If you catch one—two more pop up. If you invade an apartment where illegal religious activities are taking place, the next day you'll have three such apartments.

"One day, we entered a home where a supposedly loyal citizen had been reported for conducting religious activities. We went from room to room, but didn't find a thing. Suddenly, in the bathroom, we discovered a large hole that had been dug in the floor. 'What's this?' we asked. The man who lived there said that they had a crippled son who needed a large bathtub. Okay, what can you do? We returned to headquarters and summoned the loyal citizen who'd reported his neighbor. We asked him for an explanation. And he told us: 'That hole in the bathroom—that's the religious activity. It's something they call a 'mikveh.'

"Of course, by the time we returned to the house, there was no one left at home..."

Momi finally found the street he was looking for, which featured several small workshops along its length. On one of them was displayed a shaky sign: "Carpentry Shop." He parked the car and they got out.

The sounds of sawing and hammering floated out to them from the workshop. Outside the door sat an elderly Yemenite Jew, his curly sidelocks sprinkled with sawdust. His eyes were fixed on a small book in his hand and his lips moved rapidly.

Momi approached him. "Pardon me. I'm looking for Zalman. Zalman Berkovitch."

The Yemenite lifted his eyes from his book of *Tehillim* and studied Momi, from sandaled feet to bare head.

"You need Zalman?" he asked in his distinctive Yemenite accent. "What for? He's working now."

"I'm a friend of his. From the army."

"Friend? From the army? Didn't they cause him enough trouble? Come in the afternoon."

At that moment, the sound of the saw stopped and, to his employer's dismay, Zalman himself poked his head through the shop door to see what was going on.

"Momi, Momi! What are you doing here?" he cried in surprise. "How are you?"

Momi shot a triumphant look at the Yemenite, and then turned to Zalman. "How do you guys say it? *Baruch Hashem*." He grinned and thumped Zalman's shoulder.

"Reb Yechi, I'm taking a five-minute break," Zalman told his boss.

The Yemenite made an indeterminate gesture with his hand and returned to his *Tehillim*.

Zalman took off the gray smock that had been protecting his clothes. "So what's happening?" he asked Momi. "I haven't seen you since we got out of the army. What are you up to these days? Have you found a job?"

"You could say that," Momi murmured, and pointed at the car.

Zalman whistled. "You've moved on in life, Momi." Then he chuckled. "So where's Momi the Communist? Has he disappeared?"

When they were out of earshot of the carpentry shop, Momi said, "Zalman, I need you to do a job for a day or two."

Zalman glanced back at Reb Yechi. "I have a job." He was puzzled.

"How much do you make here a month?" Momi whispered.

"320 *lirot*."

"With me, you'll make 50 dollars in two days. Do you know how much each dollar is worth? Four *lirot* and 20 *agurot*. That comes to at least 200 *lirot*."

Zalman suddenly noticed that there was someone sitting in Momi's handsome car. "And who's that?" he asked.

"Some archeologist. He wants a tour from someone who knows something about Judaism. He pays well. Come on, Zalman—take a day off and come on a little trip with us."

Jerusalem, 5734 / 1974

IT WAS VERY EASY TO PERSUADE ZALMAN TO TAKE A COUPLE of days off from work. The fifty-dollar bill that Momi pulled out of his wallet did the job quickly and efficiently. But the old Yemenite turned out to be a tough nut to crack. He refused to release Zalman from his job. Money made no impression on him at all.

"Yechi doesn't need money," he said, referring to himself in the third person. "What would Yechi do with two hundred dollars? This dresser needs to be finished today and taken over to Mr. Ratzabi's house. After that, Zalman can go wherever he likes."

Professor Kalinin listened to Momi's translation of these words, and motioned for him to double the incentive for the fish that was close to the net.

Zalman's eyes turned very round as he stared at the second fifty-dollar bill that Momi pulled out of his wallet. "Take a two-month salary. Leave him and come with me."

"I quit," announced Zalman Berkovitch.

"No problem," the Yemenite answered tranquilly. "Finish Mr. Ratzabi's dresser and you can go."

But Momi had already thrown his arm around Zalman's shoulders and was leading him toward the car.

The Yemenite was left where he sat, gazing at the retreating Peugeot and shaking his head sorrowfully. "*Aveirah goreres aveirah,*" he mumbled to himself. "First he went to the Zionist army, and now he's spending his time with bad people…"

The Peugeot climbed toward Rechov Yafo.

"You did the right thing," Momi encouraged his friend. "Do you want to spend your whole life as a carpenter's assistant?"

For some reason, Zalman Berkovitch did not appear especially heartened. He sat in the car's back seat in silence, watching the Jerusalem streets pass quickly by and knowing that what was done was done.

"Where are we going?" Momi asked the Professor.

"Masada."

Momi glanced at Zalman in the rear-view mirror. "Have you ever been to Masada, Zalman?"

Zalman roused himself from his thoughts. "Uh, sure. For our eighth-grade class trip."

"Me, too," Momi laughed.

He parked near a bookstore, bought a map, and studied it. The way to Masada was a lot simpler today, Momi thought. You went down toward the Dead Sea and then turned right onto Highway 90. The route did wind through occupied territories, but there was no denying that it shorted the trip wonderfully. When he had taken the trip with the other kibbutz children, it had been before the Six-Day War and the occupation of the West Bank. The northern portion of the Dead Sea had been Jordanian territory, and they'd been forced to make a wide detour to arrive at the southern portion of the Dead Sea via Be'er Sheva and Arad.

"We're on our way," Momi announced.

Within a few minutes of their starting out, the urban landscape changed to dry desert. The narrow road wound among cliffs and wadis. Here and there were Bedouin tents and flocks of sheep led by children. Professor Kalinin was quiet, and Momi followed suit. From time to time he threw a look at Zalman, hoping with all his heart that he would deliver the goods.

They hadn't seen each other in a long time. Since leaving the army, they had met in the street once or twice. The last time they had been in each other's company had been during the war, on that daring journey along the bank of the Suez Canal from the besieged bunker to IDF headquarters. Three hours of walking in total darkness, in deathly fear, their lives hanging by a thread. They walked in a long, exhausted line, carrying the corpses of their fallen comrades in silence, and trying to soothe the wounded as they groaned with pain. Fear crawled through every cell of their bodies: Every dune might conceal an Egyptian ambush; invisible enemies on every hill could suddenly start firing on them and finish them off.

Momi had been driving for over an hour. The Dead Sea stretched to his left and the road seemed endless. As they passed near a crossroads sign directing them toward Masada, Professor Kalinin began to grow excited.

"Do you know what it is to touch 2,000-year-old relics?" he asked Momi. "Do you know what it is to feel history with your bare hands? There's work and research going on in Europe as well, but for an archeologist there is nothing like the Middle East—and especially Israel. Here is where the prophets walked, and kings and judges. It was here that all the events described in the Bible occurred. Do you read the Bible, Momi?"

The question surprised Momi.

"To be honest—not so much," he said with an embarrassed chuckle. "It's not the most recommended reading on the kibbutz."

"Read it," the professor urged. "Read the Bible. You live here, in the Holy Land. With all respect to the written works of Lenin and Marx…"

Because Momi did not know how to react, he chose silence. He parked the car near the site's visitor center and they all got out and stretched.

"Buy three tickets. I will wait here," said the professor.

Momi walked toward the ticket booth, Zalman Berkovitch hurrying along in his wake. He appeared agitated.

"Three tickets for the site and the cable-car?" asked the clerk.

"Momi... Momi..." Zalman tugged at his friend's sleeve. "I'm not going up in... that."

Momi stared at Zalman in astonishment. His friend's bulging eyes were fixed on the cable car, which was making its slow way toward the summit.

"Why not?" asked Momi.

Zalman couldn't answer. He was frozen in fear.

"Why not?"

Tears began to sparkle in Zalman's eyes.

"Zalman, there's no choice. You're coming up with us," Momi declared. "You said you were here as a kid. So what happened?"

"Back then... *that* wasn't there yet..." Zalman said, shaking so hard that he could hardly get the words out. "We... climbed up... on foot. On the... snake path..."

"What's your problem?" Momi huffed. Tickets in hand, he strode toward the cable car's point of embarkation. "It's strong. These are thick cables. We'll be up there in a minute."

Zalman dragged after him with faltering steps. "I can't... I just can't..." he kept mumbling.

"What are you afraid of—getting stuck? Worst case scenario, we'll wait a bit until someone comes to get us out," Momi said. "Stop whimpering like a baby. Grow up."

The cable car came and the doors slid open. Zalman remained rooted to the spot.

"Going up?" an employee asked the trio.

Professor Kalinin stepped into the car. Momi paused a moment. When he saw that Zalman was still hanging back, he hauled him inside by force.

Zalman buried his face in his hands, immobile as a statue.

The moment the door snapped shut, everything fell apart.

He burst into wails, his entire body trembling uncontrollably and his face as pale as death. After a moment, he collapsed onto the floor of the cable car and covered his head with his hands as though protecting himself from some invisible threat.

"Zalman, Zalman, what's the matter with you?" Momi asked.

He stooped to embrace his friend, but he couldn't hear the sounds of war shrieking through Zalman's head. The Egyptian artillery, the cries of the wounded...

"*Command, Command, I see them racing into our territory!*"

"*Command, we're surrounded!*"

"*I repeat: they're shooting at us from all directions!*"

Mortar shells fell on every side, each salvo shaking the ground, grenades exploding in the bunker's doorway, planes passing overhead and dropping their bombs with a terrible crash.

"*Command, this is 'Milano.' I have three dead. We're not holding out!*"

"*Command, do something. They're almost on top of us! They'll slaughter us all!*"

"*Command, this is 'Sunflower.' Are you sending help? Our situation is desperate!*"

"*Command, Command, do you hear? The Egyptians are in the trenches. I see them.*"

"*Command, this is 'Sugar.' I'm the last one left alive...*"

"*Shema Yisrael...*"

"*Tell my parents that...*"

"*Shema Yisrael, Hashem Elokeinu...*"

With a slight thump, the cable car reached its destination.

"Zalman, we're here. Come on," Momi said.

Zalman hurled himself at the doors, pushed them wide open, and fell onto the ground outside, weeping desperately.

"Come on, Zalman. Sit up," Momi begged his friend. He opened his canteen and held it out. Zalman couldn't hold it, so Momi slowly fed him sips of water.

"Okay, can we start the tour?" Professor Kalinin was impatient.

Momi threw him an angry glance. Even back in the cable car, his Soviet guest had stood with folded hands, in complete calm, devoid of emotion.

"Give him a chance to calm down," Momi said, stroking Zalman's head as if he were a small child. "I think he's afraid of enclosed spaces. We were together in the war..."

The professor checked his watch. "Let him calm down—but quickly," he ordered in a cold voice. "I want to see the Jerusalem digs today as well, and tomorrow we have the north."

Momi clenched his teeth, experiencing a strong desire to punch the professor's face.

"It's okay," he whispered to Zalman. "It's okay. Try to get up. You'll be all right."

The tour itself was fascinating. An on-site guide recited all the standard tourist information by rote, and it quickly became clear how important it had been to bring Zalman Berkovitch with them. Professor Kalinin asked many questions that arose about *terumos* and *ma'asros*, gifts of *Kehunah*, Shabbos observance, and immersion in the *mikveh*. The guide did not have all the answers, and it was Zalman—who had recovered his equilibrium—who provided them fluently, with Momi translating for the professor.

Four hours later, the professor thanked the exhausted guide warmly.

"Let's go down," he said, and started for the cable car

Momi halted. "Zalman and I are going down on the snake path."

The professor's face darkened. "Don't be silly. I have no time for hikes now."

"You can take the cable car. I'm going down with Zalman on foot."

Over the course of the next few minutes, Momi learned that the pleasant-mannered professor also knew how to bellow with all his might. But it didn't help.

"Comrade Kalinin," Momi said, pale but determined, "I do not abandon my friends, neither in the trenches nor on Masada. We'll meet at the bottom in half an hour."

Momi and Zalman descended the narrow dust trail at a rapid clip. The view of the Dead Sea at sunset was stunning, but they did not pause to enjoy it for even a moment.

"We were here on our eighth-grade class trip," Momi reminisced. "But, with our Communist upbringing, they showed the events that took place here in a negative light. They told us that Masada is a Zionist myth aimed at arousing nationalist feeling; that they raise the banner of those suicides in order to encourage young people to die in the Israeli Army; that the people who were here clung to a value system that was outdated and moldy... I'm sure they told you other things."

"Of course," said Zalman. "I was also here in eighth grade. It was my last year in the orphanage. I remember that we climbed the snake path, with the administrator, Yechezkel Polowitz, leading the way. Do you remember him?"

"Polowitz?" Momi shook his head. "I barely remember the orphanage at all. I moved to the kibbutz when I was only five."

"You were only five?" Zalman asked. As though to himself, he murmured, "At five years old, they sold you to the kibbutz."

Momi laughed heartily. "Sold me? Who sold me?"

"Who? Yechezkel Polowitz, who else?" Zalman said. "You were fine merchandise. Orphaned of both parents, the son of a Partisan hero, and no relatives in Israel. You must have fetched a nice price..."

Momi punched Zalman affectionately in the ribs. "Look, even if Polowitz, or whatever his name was, made a few *lirot* off me, I owe him a bouquet of flowers. Look at the wonderful life he gave me: two great parents, a kibbutz that's like one big family, a fine education. I did my military service and am successful in life."

Zalman didn't answer. They had reached the foot of the mountain, where an angry Professor Kalinin waited impatiently.

Israel, 5734 / 1974

MOMI BIT HIS NAILS ALL THE WAY TO HAIFA. THE BUS WAS AN ancient relic, with hard wooden seats, but that wasn't what bothered him. His mind could not stop seeking an explanation for the strange and inexplicable summons he had received the day before.

It had been Adnan, the Knesset member's aide, who had called to inform Momi that he had an appointment at precisely twelve noon at the Party house in Haifa. Adnan had not specified whom the meeting was with—nor had Momi asked.

At the Party house, he faced a long, chilly corridor. There was no trace of the festivities that had taken place here just one month earlier. Momi advanced in accordance with the instructions Adnan had given him: third floor, Room 309, a brown door with a sign reading, "Do Not Disturb."

Momi knocked on the door. Adnan opened it with an expressionless face, ushered him in, and left.

The room was not large. It was a bit dim, with the curtains tightly drawn over the windows. Behind a simple table sat three men with stern faces. Momi had glimpsed two of them at various Party functions. The man in the middle was a stranger to him. He sat with head held high and his hands clasped before him on the table.

The man on the right spoke first.

"Comrade Momi Arzi, you are standing before a Party tribunal. On the agenda: your eviction from the Party register. What do you have to say in your defense?"

Momi was stunned.

"Eviction?" he managed to say, with difficulty. "Why? What have I done?"

The two men at either end of the table smiled at one another behind the middle one's back. "'Why,' he asks!" one of them quipped with a grimace, before whispering something in Russian into the ear of the man seated beside him.

The man in the middle nodded once, and then lifted his head to stare directly at Momi. He spoke slowly, in a rich Russian.

"We are all soldiers of the Revolution," he said. "We bow our wills and our individual desires to the good of the great concept: the advancement of Communism in the world. We are at war, in a struggle against an entire hostile world. There is no room among us for weakness of character. There is no place in our ranks for the soft of heart. The Revolution does not tolerate members who do not accept authority and thereby sabotage the Party's activities."

"But…" Momi tried to frame a question, but was immediately silenced by a sharp gesture.

"If you were in our motherland now, in the Soviet Union, you might be sentenced to years of hard labor, as we treat all those who oppose the regime. To your good fortune, you are in a foreign territory, and the most we can do within the framework of our obligation to the Party is to evict you from its ranks—as a deterrent to others."

It took all of Momi's self-control to keep his mouth closed.

The voice of the head judge rose slightly. "Professor Andrei Kalinin arrived in Israel about a month ago from the Soviet Union, at great risk to himself, in order to encourage the Party comrades so dear to the hearts of the Soviet leadership. The Party tasked you, Momi Arzi, with an honored mission: to guide Comrade Kalinin in his travels, so vital to the Revolution's future. But because of your weakness, because of your intellectual softness, because of your disgraceful lack of judgment, you wasted Comrade Kalinin's valuable time and sabotaged the success of his mission."

Momi was beginning to understand why he was on trial.

"Friendship is an exalted value, and loyalty to those with whom you served on the battlefield is a lofty concept. But you are a soldier of the Revolution and totally subjugated to those above you. Therefore, your verdict is eviction from the ranks of the Party. Had your friend cried a bit on the way down from the mountain of Masada, no one would have rebuked you for holding his hand and wiping away his tears. But to disobey the order of a senior KGB officer—that is unforgivable.

"We are on a battlefield, and there is no room for mercy. If your friend is not strong enough, it was a mistake to recruit him for the job. Is it clear to you, Momi Arzi, that the day is coming when a person will be called upon to betray his closest friends for the good of the exalted idea? Is it clear to you, Momi Arzi, that another person's life and emotional well-being are as nothing when compared to the Revolution's ultimate triumph?"

The judge stopped speaking and resumed his former silence.

Momi, too, said nothing.

"What do you have to say?" asked the man on the right.

"I need to think," Momi replied.

"To think?" The man exploded. He stood up—but quickly resumed his seat after a look from the central judge.

"How much time do you need to think?" he asked Momi in Russian.

"Five minutes."

A smile touched the corners of the Russian's eyes. "You have five minutes. Do you wish to do your thinking here, or outside?"

"I'll go out," said Momi.

Adnan was waiting in the corridor, nervously smoking. He offered the pack of cigarettes to Momi.

"You're not normal," he said, his face wreathed in smoke. "You ought to be on your knees, begging and pleading for them not to evict you. You don't know who you're dealing with!"

"Who's the man in the middle?" Momi asked.

"He's from the Soviet Union. KGB or some such thing."

"He came for me?"

Adnan shrugged. "How should I know?"

Momi turned to look Adnan in the eye. "Do they seem trustworthy to you?" he suddenly asked.

Adnan was astonished. "What a question!"

"Because this whole thing is not that simple," Momi said, as though thinking out loud. "I could get myself in even more deeply."

"Listen," Adnan said. "The two Israelis are only window-dressing. The important one is the Russian."

"I want to talk to him," Momi said. "Alone."

Adnan grimaced. "They won't like it…" He went into the room.

A moment later, the door opened. The two Israeli Party workers left, throwing annoyed glances at Momi.

"Be my guest," Adnan said. "You can go in now."

The Russian looked slightly more human now. He moved one of his colleague's chairs to the other side of the table and gestured for Momi to sit.

"My name is Andrei Willotzky," he said. "Professor Andrei Willotzky. You asked to speak to me privately. That is not usual, but I have decided to deviate from the rules."

Momi filled his lungs with air and then leveled a look at Professor Willotzky.

"I suspect Professor Kalinin of being disloyal to the regime," he blurted.

Professor Willotzky's brows shot up.

"My friend and I spent three days with Professor Kalinin," Momi explained. "He visited archeological sites and asked questions about Judaism. He wrote a great many notes. On the last day, he asked us to take him to several Jewish bookstores in Meah Shearim, where he bought books from a list he had. I don't remember what they were called, but my friend said that they were fundamental works on Judaism.

"At each store, Professor Kalinin asked for the smallest and most lightweight books. He checked the thickness of the pages and the size of the print, and then pulled off the covers so that he could hide them in the walls of his suitcase.

"I wouldn't have suspected a thing, but my friend is a religious person, and he began to get excited. He told me that we were helping to spread Judaism beyond the Iron Curtain. He told me that there are people who smuggle Jewish books into the Soviet Union, and that our guest was apparently one of them.

"For a long time, I've been searching for the right way to transmit my suspicions to the authorities. And now that I've been invited to this tribunal, I thought it fitting to tell the story. The interest in archeology is only a cover for Professor Kalinin's true activity—which is going behind the regime's back to introduce anti-Revolutionary reading material into the Soviet Union."

Ten minutes later, the three members of the tribunal were seated in their places. Momi stood before them with bowed head.

"I have had a long conversation with the accused," said the leader. "He has expressed sincere and profound regret for his actions. I have taken into consideration his clean record and his willingness to make every effort to repair his actions. Momi Arzi will remain a member of the Party, and I anticipate a shining future for him."

As Professor Willotzky had ordered, Momi continued to carry out the instructions that Professor Kalinin had left before he had departed Israel. He looked for work on archeological sites and dug up the land from top to bottom. From time to time he offered a job to Zalman Berkovitch, who remained unemployed after the carpentry-shop owner refused to take him back.

Three months passed.

One day, Momi returned to the kibbutz to find Adnan waiting for him by the gate.

"Professor Kalinin has another job to be done. He needs you and your companion—the religious kid."

"A job? For how long?" Momi asked.

"It's a long-term thing, he says. You and your friend need to be at the Yafo port at eight p.m. tomorrow night. Look for a fishing boat named Telilah. The captain's name is Sammy. He'll take you from there."

Zalman Berkovitch did not like the fact that Sammy was a young Arab. Apart from that, however, he enjoyed every minute he spent on the fishing boat. He lay on the upper deck, hands beneath his head, gazing up at the dark sky strewn with clouds and taking pleasure in the endless horizons.

Momi was less happy. "Where are we going?" he asked Sammy.

Sammy smiled under his mustache, but did not answer.

An hour passed before the boat began to slow. "Almost there," Sammy said.

Zalman sat up in sudden anxiety. His sharp senses had begun to smell danger.

"Almost where?" Momi demanded.

Sammy pointed across the black water. Small waves began to foam up as a strange sound reached them from the depths of the sea. A moment later, a black submarine rose noisily out of the waves.

"Momi!" Zalman shrieked from the deck. "I'm not getting into that thing."

Momi's breath caught in his chest. "You may have to help me control my friend," he whispered to Sammy. "He's afraid of enclosed spaces."

"Momi, they're Arabs!" came another cry from the deck.

When the fishing boat was alongside the sub's nose, a door opened on the bridge. Two soldiers stepped out. They wore clean white uniforms, but it was impossible to mistake them for anything but what they were: Egyptian soldiers.

"Momi, they're Egyptians! They're Egyptians!" Zalman wailed. "I want to go back!"

"You can swim back," Sammy laughed, already on his way to seize Zalman.

It took three Egyptian soldiers to subdue the screaming, kicking Zalman and take him into the submarine. Momi watched the spectacle without expression. This had to be done. There was no other choice.

Only after Zalman was safely tucked into the belly of the submarine did Momi follow him inside.

When he reached the foot of the ladder, he heard a voice from behind. Someone said in Russian, "Welcome to my humble abode."

Momi whirled sharply around. He was standing face to face with Professor Andrei Kalinin.

Soviet Union, 5734 / 1974

PROFESSOR KALININ'S OFFICE WAS SPACIOUS AND OPULENT. A soft rug covered the floor, heavy drapes concealed the windows, and a most un-Soviet crystal chandelier illuminated the room. The wooden desk behind which he sat was carved and polished, its upper surface gleaming like a mirror.

"Sit, Comrade Momi," the Professor said, motioning at a velvet-upholstered chair, the likes of which the kibbutz-raised youth had never seen in his life.

Momi sat down in silence, still stunned by the events of the past fifteen hours.

The professor's face was stern. He waited a moment, and then bent slightly forward, his large hands resting on his desktop as he directed a cold stare at Momi.

"I could have given your friend a tranquilizer," he said. "He could have spent the trip peacefully asleep. He would never have known that he was on a submarine and would not have suffered an attack of claustrophobia. He would have woken up to find himself here, in the Soviet Union. That would have been the easy way—but it would have been a mistake. You must learn to overcome, to be strong, to cope with challenges and make difficult decisions. The day will come when you will thank me for this."

Momi nodded obediently.

The half-hour that he had spent aboard the submarine with Zalman had shaken him to the depths of his soul. Zalman had lost all semblance of humanity and had behaved like a wounded beast. He had thrashed about and screamed until he was hoarse. Foam had bubbled from his mouth, his eyes had protruded from their sockets, and all his muscles had involuntarily stiffened. It had not been words that emerged from his mouth, but incomprehensible shrieks and fearsome, animal-like cries.

At first, Momi had tried to calm him down, but Zalman beat him with his clenched fists, displaying a strength that Momi would not have believed he possessed. Finally, there had been no choice but to lock him in a small room at one end of the submarine, designated for prisoners and rebellious seamen.

After half an hour, the sub had begun rising to the surface. Professor Kalinin had warmly thanked the Egyptian captain. The three passengers had climbed up to the bridge and from there onto the deck of a Soviet merchant vessel that was cruising in the area.

"The Egyptians?" the professor explained to Momi. "They're nothing but a water taxi. We had to take you out in a hurry and had no available submarine, so we asked our friends for a small favor."

Why all the urgency? Momi had wondered to himself, as he stood at the railing watching the Egyptian submarine sink back into the depths.

He had no way of knowing that, at that moment, the Shin-Bet was investigating Kibbutz Tel-Chana, confiscating documents, combing every centimeter of his parents' house, and whisking them both away to a secret structure outside Tel-Aviv.

"I haven't seen him since this morning," Sonia told the investigators, when she was through accusing them of political persecution.

"Momi went to work at the Megiddo archeological dig, like he does every day," Mikush said, more frightened than his wife and far less strong.

Slowly, the news spread through the kibbutz: Sonia and Mikush's Momi was suspected of treason during wartime, and of passing information to the enemy.

On the ship, Zalman suffered from no fear. The wide expanse of the sea did not affect him the way small spaces did. Still, he was filled with trepidation over the future, and repeatedly heaped the blame on Momi.

"You said this would be a long-term job," he shouted. "You didn't say they'd kidnap us and take us to Russia!"

"You're a trickster!"

"I should have listened to R' Yechi. He warned me about you."

"I should never have come with you. Even in the army you were a Communist spy!"

Before the ship reached the port of Odessa, Professor Kalinin took Momi aside for a talk.

"If you don't bring your friend in line, we'll simply have to get rid of him," he said without fanfare. "And do not fool yourself with illusions: The one who will be required to shoot him will be you. No one will do the job for you. We have not come here for a picnic. Fateful matters are hanging in the balance."

By the time the ship reached port and the three passengers debarked and stepped into the official car that awaited them, the professor was able to declare that Momi had carried out his mission. Zalman was silent the entire time, withdrawn into himself.

The drive to Kiev took several hours. Kalinin sat in front. Momi and Zalman were in the back, trying vainly to sleep. Near nightfall, they arrived. The car crossed a bridge that spanned a river and reached a large site containing a three-story building. A sign welcomed them to the University of Kiev, making Momi smile to himself. He recalled how, at the Communist Party's convention in Haifa, Professor Kalinin had been introduced to the audience as a lecturer and researcher at the University of Kiev.

The official-looking car slowed near the guard booth at the entrance. Two armed soldiers peered into the car. After a moment, they stepped back and motioned to the guard to open the heavy steel gate. The car drove in and made its way directly to the entrance of the central building.

"Oleg!" the professor called to a short, sturdy youth who was waiting to meet the car. "Say hello to our two guests."

Oleg—Oleg Marinov, as he introduced himself—maintained a hostile silence as he led the newcomers to their room. Only later would Momi learn that the place contained two warring divisions, each headed by its own Andrei.

Oleg was a favorite of Andrei Willotzky, as was another young student by the name of Yevgeny Yompolsky, a slightly friendlier personality. Momi and Zalman "belonged" to Professor Andrei Kalinin. Momi very soon became all too familiar with his superior's office, which bore more of a resemblance to the Tsar's palace than anything else.

"Welcome to the KGB's Directorate 19," said the professor. He explained to Momi that the KGB consisted of 18 Directorates, each dealing with a certain area: collecting intelligence information, safeguarding the nation's security, and so on. Directorate 19 had been established to carry out special operations. It was so secret that not even all members of the Soviet Union's political elite were aware of its existence.

"And now, to work," he said.

He opened a drawer in his desk and took out several books that Momi recognized at once. They were the books that he and Zalman had purchased with the professor on his visit to Israel.

"I appreciate your courage in tattling on me," the professor said with a smile—much to Momi's discomfiture.

Andrei Kalinin turned the books to face Momi. "Do you know how to read what it says here?"

Momi looked at the small letters. They were written in the Hebrew alphabet, but the words were incomprehensible to him. Try as he might, he was unable to form them into meaningful sentences.

"Read, read," urged the professor. Momi tried with all his might: *"Rav u'Shmuel chad tani idihen u'chad tani idihen ne'an datani..."* He raised his eyes in despair. "What *is* this book?"

The Russian laughed uproariously. "*You're* asking *me*? Shame on you! This is a book called *Avodah Zarah*, one of a set of books known as the Talmud Bavli."

Momi shrugged. "Where I come from, we don't read those books. Maybe Zalman knows them better."

"That is precisely the reason we dragged him here," said the professor. "He is religious, and he is familiar with this literature: 'talmud,' 'midrash,' 'mishnah' and all the rest. He will teach you how to read them. It won't take much time, Momi. Your grasp is quick. You have a Jewish head, don't you?"

"Zalman, Zalman," Momi whispered in his roommate's ear, shaking his shoulder gently.

Zalman shuddered as he lay sprawled in his bed, hands covering his face.

"Zalman, I have to talk to you," Momi pleaded. "It's important."

Zalman's back stiffened in rebuke. Suddenly, Momi was talking nicely. Suddenly, he remembered him. He must be in some sort of trouble himself. But he, Zalman, would not forget what had happened to him this past week since he had been brought to this place. The nightmare journey in the submarine had only been a prelude to what awaited him in this prison. All at once, Momi had changed colors. He had acted as if he hardly knew Zalman, and had taken an active role in the tortures that Zalman had suffered.

First he and Oleg Marinov, the short, cruel Ukrainian, had thrown Zalman into a bathtub full of freezing water. Momi had also stood watching from the riverbank when Professor Kalinin had threatened to end Zalman's life in the Dnieper if he refused to cooperate. Momi had not been ashamed to look straight at Zalman and translate the threats from Russian to Hebrew.

Zalman had not been intimidated by the threats. On the contrary, the best thing he could have wished for was death. He spread his arms in the water like a man waiting for a bullet, stared at Momi with open loathing, and hissed through his teeth: "*A man who kidnaps a person and sells him... he shall surely die.*"

"What is he saying?" the professor asked Momi. "What is he saying?"

Momi did not answer. He focused his eyes on Zalman, teeth clenched, chest rising and falling in agitation. Then he lunged toward him and kicked him with all his might. "Don't curse me!" he yelled. "Don't you *dare* curse me!"

Professor Kalinin had roared with laughter. This was the first time he had seen Momi lose himself. He replaced his gun in its holster and left the two Jews grappling on the riverbank while he walked jauntily back to the central building.

Three days had passed since then, and to Zalman's surprise they had left him alone. For three days he had been lying in bed, crying. He had no mother or father, he was orphaned and alone, without family or friends. He had placed his trust in one person in the world—but he, too, had betrayed his trust. He had brought him here by trickery, to the land behind the Iron Curtain, and here he had shown his true face: Momi Arzi, a traitor to his people and his country, a secret agent of the evil Soviet empire, uprooter of faith and destroyer of Judaism.

He should have been distrustful of Momi. He should have questioned the purity of his motives. All the signs had been right there in front of him. Even back then, in their besieged bunker on the Suez Canal, he should have known.

During Kol Nidrei and Shacharis, there had been other soldiers who'd refrained from participating. But when the shelling began, when they realized that the Egyptians were surrounding the bunker, everyone had joined in the prayers. No one had stood apart—except for one person, heartless, completely sealed off, a heretic to his last breath. Momi Arzi was the only one who had refused to participate in the communal prayer. It was all so clear now. Watching Momi move around among the Russians, speaking their language, eating their food, laughing and joking with them—there were no more questions.

But now, suddenly, there was a new note in his voice.

"Zalman, I have to talk to you. Get up," Momi begged.

Zalman raised his head ever so slightly. There was a new

expression on Momi's face, one he had never seen before.

Momi pointed to the bathroom adjoining their room. He placed a silencing finger to his lips and motioned to Zalman: *Come with me.*

Zalman considered for a moment, and then stood up and followed Momi.

Momi locked the bathroom door from the inside, turned on the taps in the sink and the shower, and put his mouth to Zalman's ear: "They have microphones everywhere. This way, they can't hear. The noise of the water interferes."

Zalman stared at Momi in total astonishment.

"They listen to us all the time," Momi continued quickly. "In the rooms, in the hallways, even in the open areas among the trees. We don't have much time... I owe you a huge apology. I simply had no idea what I was getting you into. I didn't know myself. No one asked me. Anyway, the only way for us to get out of here safely is to cooperate with them—at least, outwardly."

Zalman nodded, swallowing the tears that threatened to burst out again.

"From what I understood from Kalinin," Momi whispered, "they wanted to get rid of you after his visit to Israel. You were a big danger: you'd seen a senior KGB officer in Israel. You saw him show an interest in archeology and smuggle Jewish books into the Soviet Union. From their perspective, that would be reason enough to shut your mouth forever. But then they had the idea—I don't know why—to bring you here."

The last sentence was not exactly accurate. Momi knew at least one other reason why the Russians wanted Zalman. Professor Kalinin had laid out the facts several days earlier: "If we had harmed him, Momi, we'd have harmed our chances of recruiting you—and I'm not saying that in your praise, but the opposite. You are ideologically weak. Your convictions are not firm and crystallized. You allow emotions to lead you. The kibbutz educated you to the best of their ability, but you were also influenced by your surroundings. You grew up in a capitalistic and imperialistic country. For three years, you served in the army and your commanders imbued you with false ideas. If we had enough time, we would send you to a concentrated intellectual seminar for several weeks, to be taught by the best Communist ideologues and philosophers we have."

Momi turned the taps so that the water flowed even more strongly. "Zalman, this is our life insurance, yours and mine. Teach me to read those books—or they're going to kill us both. Trust me. I did not abandon you at the Suez Canal, I didn't abandon you on Masada, and I won't leave you here, either. Only by working together will we manage to get away from them."

The workroom assigned to Momi was situated at the end of the second-floor corridor.

He sat at the table, head supported on his fists, lost in thought. Ten minutes later, he heard the door open. He lifted his eyes and smiled. "Now, *that's* the Zalman Berkovitch I know!"

Zalman had showered and freshened up in their room. A folded stack of new clothes had been waiting on the chair beside his bed, courtesy of Oleg Marinov.

Momi grasped both his hands, signaling without words: *It'll be okay! We'll get through this*!

"Okay. As you see, we have plenty of books," Momi told Zalman. On the table was the stack of books that Professor Kalinin had brought from Jerusalem. They had the thinnest pages and the smallest print that he had been able to find. Someone had rebound the books, and each cover now sported the book's name in Cyrillic letters.

"This place has a copying machine that they imported from the United States. They can enlarge each page that we need to use," Momi explained.

There were several additional books on a nearby shelf. Opening them, Zalman noted the stamps that testified to their having been confiscated from synagogues in Moscow or Kiev. One set of volumes, in particular, caught his attention. He picked up one of them—it was a *Bereishis*, one of a set of five *Chumashim*—and gazed at it in surprise. He had seen many *Chumashim* in his life, but this one was strange. In place of the usual Rashi, it contained an unfamiliar commentary.

"What is this?" he asked Momi.

"What's the problem?"

"I've never seen a *Chumash* like this before," Zalman said. He pulled out the *Shemos* and looked at it as well.

Suddenly, from the door, someone spoke a sentence in Russian. Professor Kalinin stood there, leaning casually against the doorframe.

"He says it came from the Karaites," Momi translated. "Here, in Kiev, there's a Karaite community, and they printed this *Chumash*."

Zalman let the book fall from his hands—much to the professor's amusement.

"What are Karaites?" Momi asked.

Before Zalman could answer, the professor spoke again. He said a few words and left the room.

"He wished you luck, and said that he's glad you made the right decision," Momi translated for Zalman.

Zalman and Momi exchanged a quick look, filled with meaning— a look that was not recorded by any hidden, sensitive microphones.

"Okay, where shall we start?" Momi asked.

"We'll start with the Torah and learn the Mishnah alongside. We can go on from there," Zalman said.

With expert fingers he browsed through the *sefarim* that Professor Kalinin had smuggled in, and then sent Momi off to copy the first pages of *Chumash Bereishis* with Rashi and the first *perek* of *Maseches Berachos*.

"You know what I just thought of?" Zalman whispered, after Momi returned with the pages and sat down beside him. "Hashem had to bring you all the way here, just so you'd learn a little Torah."

Momi threw an arm around Zalman and thumped his shoulder affectionately.

"Come on. Let's learn," he said.

The sun was sinking toward sunset when Momi entered Professor Kalinin's office. In a rare occurrence, Professor Willotzky, the Directorate's psychologist and Kalinin's rival, was seated beside him.

"Well? How's it going?" they both asked in suspense.

Momi Arzi burst into rollicking laughter. "He bought the story— hook, line and sinker," he announced, very pleased with himself. "He's in my hands. All I have to do is always remember what my mission is."

Soviet Union, 5737 / 1977

MOMI ARZI STOOD IN HIS APARTMENT DOORWAY, BREATHING heavily. He had been in the Soviet Union a mere three years, and already it was impossible to see in him the superbly fit soldier he had been in Israel. Russian food and long work hours had left their mark. He hardly stirred these days. The government flat he had been assigned, in a new suburb of Kiev on the southern bank of the river, was located on the eighth floor. His building was one of the few in the area whose elevator worked and was properly maintained, in honor of the KGB personnel and government employees that lived there. Momi had also stopped walking much since he had been allotted a budget for a car and acquired a small, beat-up, Soviet "Moskovitz 412."

It was a pity that today of all days, when his new flatmate had arrived and Momi had volunteered to help him bring up his suitcases, the elevator had chosen to break down. They'd been forced to climb all eight flights of stairs.

Momi did not like Kalinin's decision to introduce another KGB employee into the place Momi had been occupying these past two years—but he had no choice in the matter. He knew that he had been fortunate. There were few young people in the Soviet Union who had their own flat. The economic situation and the appalling shortage of living space had given rise to the phenomenon of the "communalism," in which several families were crowded into a single apartment and shared the kitchen and facilities.

He also had no complaints regarding the food. The long lines in front of bakeries and groceries were things he observed only from afar. He was able to buy what he needed from the "Broyzeka" store, designated for foreigners, tourists, and diplomats—and for privileged individuals such as KGB employees.

The new tenant was Ali, a young Iranian with a doctoral degree in Arab culture and Islamic writings. He had arrived at R-19 two months previously, but he and Momi had not had a chance to chat until now.

"How do you come to speak Russian so well?" Momi gasped as they climbed the narrow, winding stairs.

"The Soviet Embassy in Teheran offered a course in Russian," Ali replied with a grin. "Only a year later did I realize that the teacher who had come from Russia was not only a teacher, but a KGB agent."

Momi did not ask Ali if it had been that same teacher who had recruited him for his present mission. If he wanted to, he would share the information on his own. Rule Number One: Ask no unnecessary questions.

"You'll like the flat," Momi promised. "It's a really nice place, with a river view. I think we'll get along fine together."

Ali was slightly taken aback. He sensed that he was invading his colleague's privacy.

"Relax," Momi said. "Everyone knows that there's a shortage of government flats in Kiev, and the demand keeps on growing. There are two bedrooms here, and we can split the expenses."

He pulled a key from his pocket and turned it in the lock in the door.

"*Dobro pozalovat* (welcome)," he said as they walked inside.

Momi, breathing hard, made a silent vow to start visiting the exercise room.

The young man's eyes darted around, studying the kitchen and living room.

"Nice and clean," he observed with obvious relief. With a chuckle, he added, "Not so typical for a bachelor."

"I was well brought up," Momi replied. He directed Ali toward a low-ceilinged hallway. "Let me show you your room. It has a bed and a wardrobe, and a window that looks out over Marinsky Park. At this time of year, the chestnuts are in bloom. It's a stunning view."

All this while, Momi had been wondering whether his new flatmate was aware of their tail and had simply chosen to ignore it—or if he was still too naïve to have noticed that they were being followed.

A black KGB car had been trailing them all the way here, from their departure from R-19 to this building. As he showed Ali the view of the park from his window, Momi sneaked a downward look and saw the car and its two occupants parked in front.

Momi went to the kitchen, opened the refrigerator, and removed a bottle of vodka. It was one of a row of them, the price of which would have supported an average Soviet family respectably for several months.

He poured the drink into two glasses, handed one to Ali and lifted up the second.

"*Nazdarovya*," he toasted his new flatmate. "To our health!"

The two clinked glasses. As Ali downed the contents of his glass, an expression of genuine appreciation crossed his face. "Really fine quality," he said, and held out his glass for a refill.

Momi poured more vodka for Ali. "I don't know what they drink over there in Iran," he remarked. "But there's nothing like Stolichnaya vodka!"

Ali agreed wholeheartedly.

"And now, my friend," Momi announced theatrically, "Kiev awaits us!"

It had been Professor Kalinin who'd asked Momi to take Ali on a tour of Kiev and to point out its wonders. For this purpose, he had sent Momi home from work early today, and even reserved a table for them in an upscale government restaurant on Karshatztik Street—a place known for its fine Ukrainian cuisine and unlimited vodka.

Ali glanced at his watch. "I'll shower and change," he said. "We can leave in half an hour."

"All right, then. Half an hour," Momi echoed—just in case the KGB's secret listeners had not picked up the words clearly enough the first time. While he was out with Ali, the organization's technicians would enter the apartment and set up the required bugging equipment in Ali's room. In their kind of work, which dealt with highly classified state secrets, no one could be trusted.

These were essential security measures. They might feel annoying and even oppressive at first. In the early weeks, one constantly checked over his shoulder to see if he was being followed. But a person who had nothing to hide had nothing to fear. An individual who led a proper Soviet life, with no ideological straying, was meant to actually be happy that the State and the Party, through its security arms, were able to serve as a kind of inner conscience that kept him on the straight and narrow path.

The restaurant was fairly empty that evening. Momi and Ali sat at a side table, which was laden with plates of herring in onion sauce, hot deep-burgundy borscht and a generous quantity of *vareniki*—dough pockets filled with meat or fruit, and all manner of good things.

"The last time I ate here," Momi told Ali between bites, "the Russian Minister of Culture was seated at the next table with a famous French author—I forget his name—who'd come for a visit with his family. There was also an ambassador from some South American country, who got so drunk that they had to drag him outside…"

On second thought, Momi was glad that the restaurant's usual diners were absent tonight. He didn't want Ali, still in his first flush of innocence, to ask too many questions. In a Soviet Union that was hungry for bread, upscale restaurants fell into the category of luxuries that the average Soviet citizen could only gaze at from afar.

For the working-class citizen, the government had established public cafeterias—*stolovaya*—which served basic foods and cheap alcohol at reasonable prices. The few restaurants worthy of the name were officially designated for tourists and foreign diplomats, though in actuality an underground culture of bribery and payoffs had sprung up around them, as they had around most Soviet institutions. The "privileged" were able to dine regularly in these restaurants and to use them for parties. The managers of government industries, for example, though officially paid the modest salary of any public employee, were in reality outstandingly wealthy and so influential that the police were afraid to touch them. There were also members of the professions and the arts, who knew how to make connections with the right people in the corridors of power, and who also lived like kings as the country deteriorated around them. On an ordinary night, the sight of this restaurant might have sown doubts in the heart of even the most ardent Communist.

"When was that?" asked Ali, tearing off a chunk of fresh bread and dunking it in a bowl of sour cream. "When did you eat here?"

Momi sat back, at his ease. "When? Oh, about three years ago," he said—without mentioning with whom he had dined. Rule Number Two: never volunteer information.

In any case, that dining experience three years earlier had been a complete failure. It was back when Professor Kalinin had still held out hope for Zalman Berkovitch. He had ordered Momi to take him out for some fun in the city and to handle him with kid gloves.

It had taken Zalman no more than a few days to realize that Momi had no intention of becoming a *ba'al teshuvah*, and that his soul did not yearn for Torah. When he grasped that their joint learning was intended to fulfill an operational purpose of the Directorate, he refused to cooperate. He hurled every one of the Torah's curses at Momi, and declared that he would never believe another word Momi told him. Kalinin considered it worth their while to try and soften his opposition in other ways.

They went to Kiev's world-renowned opera-house; they sailed on the river and went sight-seeing in the city. His removal from the constant stresses of the Directorate was beneficial for Zalman, and his mood improved. But when they'd arrived here, at this government restaurant, the atmosphere had turned sour. Zalman sat in front of all the tempting dishes and refused to eat a bite.

"*Rasha* (wicked one)!" he scolded Momi. "You and that Russian administrator want to feed me *treife* food. Well, it won't work!"

Even when he took Zalman to the Pecherska Lavra—the popular tourist attraction considered one of the seven wonders of Ukraine—Zalman refused to enjoy himself. The spectacle was undeniably stunning: a collection of beautiful mansions built on the banks of the Dnieper, with gilded outbuildings and bell towers interspersed with rolling lawns and flower beds. But Zalman had decided that they were monasteries and churches, and refused to even look at them. "It's idol worship," he hissed, closing his eyes tightly. "An abomination!" And he spat on the ground.

"You don't understand," Momi tried coaxing him. "*Once* there were churches here, but today they're all museums and government buildings. You know that all religious activity is forbidden in the Soviet Union. There haven't been any priests or monks here for a long time." But Zalman wasn't convinced.

It was at this stage that Zalman was sent to a psychiatric hospital—and it was there, according to the doctors, that he calmed down. His room held a large collection of works on various scientific topics such as astronomy and physics, which he constantly read in tandem. Kalinin realized that, by supplying Zalman with the books he craved, he would achieve a peace that would bear practical fruit. He issued the order to buy him any book he wanted.

Momi and Ali finished their meal and left the restaurant, weaving slightly as a result of all the alcohol they'd consumed.

Momi was more talkative than usual. Though the meal with Ali had taken place within the framework of his job, he had enjoyed every minute. Ali had a personal magnetism, and Momi found that they had more in common than he had with any of his other Directorate colleagues. *If we'd met in Tel Aviv or Haifa, we would have been friends*, he reflected. Perhaps it was Ali's Middle Eastern background and natural warmth that had dazzled him, after three years among cold, stern, suspicious Ukrainians.

Momi's car was parked on Lenin Boulevard. They strolled up the narrow street that led there. The night was cold, but both of them were warmly dressed.

Suddenly, Momi froze.

"What's wrong?" Ali glanced at him. Momi looked as though he had seen a ghost.

"What's the matter?" Now Ali was becoming alarmed as well.

Momi didn't answer. But the man who was walking along the boulevard sidewalk was the last person he would have expected to see in the heart of Kiev.

Momi recovered and bent his head slightly, so that the man wouldn't recognize him. After a moment, he remembered that his face was largely concealed behind a scarf and fur hat in any case.

But what was *he* doing here? What was he doing in Kiev, behind what the West called the Iron Curtain?!

"ARE YOU ALL RIGHT?" ALI PLACED A SUPPORTING HAND on Momi's shoulder.

"Yes... Excuse me... It's just..."

Momi was completely befuddled.

"It's just that... I suddenly saw someone... from the past. Someone from... another place."

Ali followed the direction of Momi's stunned gaze.

"The guy in the long coat?"

"Yes." Momi shook his head to make sure he wasn't dreaming. How had that man entered the Soviet Union? And what, in heaven's name, was he looking for here?

"Who is he?" asked Ali.

Momi had no intention of answering the question. "Someone. Doesn't matter," he said.

The man continued along the pavement, moving away from them. He was already several dozen yards away.

Ali seemed to be in a jolly mood. "Want to follow him?"

Momi stared at him in shock. Of course he wanted to follow the man, but not in Ali's company...

"Come on! Let's think of it as a continuation of the adventure," Ali laughed. He began walking rapidly, closing the gap between himself and the man.

Momi studied his colleague suspiciously. Ali had apparently drunk too much. He quickly caught up with Ali, who was energetically trailing the man they'd seen. Momi understood the danger in what he was doing. He was placing his trust in someone he barely knew—someone about whose character he had no clue.

Was Ali trying to incriminate him? Would Professor Kalinin receive a report tonight about this deviation from acceptable behavior? Three years in the Soviet Union had taught him that a façade of innocence and friendliness could conceal a cruel and dangerous enemy. Momi pushed aside these thoughts and focused on keeping the man in the long, black coat in his sight. After all, it had been Ali who'd suggested that they follow the stranger. Momi was only coming along for the ride…

"He's going down to the subway," Ali reported. "Shall we go after him?"

Momi shrugged.

A short staircase led from street level to a large area lined with ticket booths. The stranger stood in line. Ali threw a grin at Momi, and stood right behind him in line. The man purchased a single subway token; Ali bought two. They went to the gate leading to the underground tracks, dropped in their tokens, and entered.

A long escalator took the passengers through a dimly lit tunnel carved deep into the ground. The man whom they were following was about twenty steps ahead of them. The descent was slow and it seemed as if it would never end. Momi found himself thinking about Zalman Berkovitch, who lived in terror of enclosed places. He would never be able to survive a trip like this, he thought to himself. He would scream with fear in such a dark and narrow tunnel.

Momi's main concern was not to lose sight of the man. Ali, oblivious to his companion's tension, chuckled with pleasure. "Do you know that this is the deepest metro station in the world?" he said. "Deeper than in London, New York, or any other city. It goes down 105 meters, no less!"

At long last, the descent ended and they found themselves in a spacious station. Ali gazed around, enchanted. "How beautiful!" he cried. "It looks like a palace."

The station was indeed opulent. The floor was made of shining white marble with mosaic stripes, the walls were wood-paneled, and from the decorated ceilings hung huge crystal chandeliers that cast a brilliant light. One of the walls featured a gigantic mural, depicting workers and farmers toiling with pleasure and thanking the good fortune that had enabled them to be born in such a beloved and thriving motherland.

Momi and Ali waited on the platform among the many travelers, from time to time peering over at the man who stood some distance away. After several minutes, they heard a loud roar that kept increasing in volume. Soon a long train appeared in the mouth of the dark tunnel, gradually slowing until it stopped and slid open its doors. The man boarded the train, and they followed suit.

Ten minutes and three stations later, the man got out. Momi and Ali did likewise. He walked toward the exit; they followed. Another escalator took them back to street level. The man walked a bit further and then turned into a small street named Mikelob Street. He entered a yard and disappeared into the lobby of Building 7, which was a large apartment house.

Momi and Ali paused near the gate and looked at one another.

"Go after him," Momi urged. "See which flat he goes into."

Ali was happy to rise to the challenge. Outside, Momi walked partway up the street and then slowly back again.

As he approached the gate of Building 7, Ali emerged wearing a smile. "Fifth floor, Apartment 6," he whispered to Momi, as though someone might overhear them.

Momi glanced up. What to do now? Wait to see if the man came out? Go up after him? Or perhaps contact the local KGB office and let them know the location?

A militia vehicle—belonging to the Soviet civilian police—was moving slowly down the street. Momi decided that he had run enough risks for one day.

"Let's go home," he told Ali. "I'm tired."

They had to find their way back to the car, which they'd left near the restaurant at the start of the evening. Once again they returned to the train station, where they bought tokens and then rode the subway back the way they'd come.

By the time they reached the car, Momi was exhausted. Tension and fear had drained the last of his energy.

"Can you drive?" he asked Ali, handing him the keys.

"My pleasure," Ali replied.

Momi sat silently in the passenger seat throughout the drive, head back, gazing out the window. He was lost in thought.

It was only as they stepped out of the car in their building's parking lot and walked toward the lobby that Ali spoke for the first time.

"Nothing happened today, right?" He winked at Momi. "It's certainly not something we'll want to discuss in the flat…"

Momi looked at Ali, seeing him suddenly in a different light. So he wasn't as innocent as he looked. He knew that the flat was filled with hidden microphones that recorded every word. That was also why he hadn't spoken in the car.

"Yes. Thanks," Momi mumbled.

"By the way," Ali said, "you still haven't told me who the man was."

And Momi, without thinking, in an unguarded moment, replied, "It's the administrator of the orphanage where I grew up."

I have to go see Zalman, Momi thought, as he had already thought who-knew-how-many times that week. Maybe *he* knew what Yechezkel Polowitz, administrator of a Jerusalem orphan's home, was looking for in the heart of the Soviet Union.

The idea of speaking with Zalman had occurred to him within minutes of returning home, but he had put it off repeatedly, each time for a different reason. For one thing, he knew that it would not be a pleasant meeting. He had betrayed Zalman's trust time and again, and there was no reason for Zalman to agree to talk to him at all.

The last time Momi had visited him at the psychiatric facility had been the previous year. He had felt some guilt over his friend's bitter fate, and had tried to stay in touch. The doctors had been the ones who'd urged him to curtail his efforts, as each visit only exacerbated the patient's condition and disturbed their peace. Each time Zalman saw Momi, he would tremble with fear, dash over to a corner of the room and start screaming, "*Yemach shemoinik! Yemach shemoinik!*"

Finally, Momi gathered his courage. He would do this, no matter what. He had never run from a challenge.

Before going home at the end of the day, he stopped at Professor Kalinin's office to let him know that he would be coming in late the next day. "I'm going to visit a friend," he said.

Kalinin raised a brow. "Which friend?"

"Zalman Berkovitch. I haven't been to see him in a while."

The professor gave him an odd look.

"It would be a good idea to ask Comrade Willotzky first," he advised.

Momi thought he hadn't heard correctly.

"Professor Willotzky?" he repeated in astonishment. "What does he have to do with Zalman?"

Kalinin twisted his mouth into a smile. "He drafted him into his division."

Momi almost ran over to Professor Willotzky's office. "What's going on with Zalman?" he asked with no preamble.

Professor Willotzky lifted his eyes to the agitated Momi. "He's in a good place. There's nothing to worry about."

But Momi most certainly *was* worried. "Where is he?" he demanded.

"They transferred him." Willotzky spoke patiently, but with the first signs of anger.

Momi speared him with his eyes. "Where to?" His eyes rose upward. "Heaven?"

Professor Willotzky laughed dryly. "Comrade Arzi, do not allow emotion to intrude on your work. Your friend had a job to do here. His job was finished and he was moved to a different place. More than that I will not tell you."

"What do you mean?" Momi almost shouted.

Professor Willotzky stood up to his full height and leaned toward Momi.

"You forget yourself," he said in a bloodcurdling voice. "You are forgetting where you are, and the difference between our ranks. You are addressing a KGB general!"

Momi collected his wits. He had, indeed, spoken out of turn. "Pardon me, Comrade Professor," he said.

A smile transformed the professor's face as quickly as the previous fury. "It's all right, Comrade Arzi." Playfully, he slapped Momi's cheek. "It is perfectly all right."

"I apologize for my outburst."

"No, no. It pleases me that you are concerned for your friends," Willotzky said. He paused to consider the matter. "It will be in order," he said at last. "I guarantee that you will still be permitted to see him."

Momi gave the division head a questioning look, but the professor added no explanations. "Go back to work," he said with another smile. "We are very pleased with your progress."

Jerusalem, 5772 / 2011

"And they did meet again," Avreimi Kohlberg said slowly. "Here, in Yerushalayim."

Itzik Peled nodded his head sadly.

"That's why Zalman Berkovitch reacted so violently when he saw my father's picture," Avreimi realized.

Itzik spread his hands in resignation. Yes, that was the reason.

"And now I understand his curses. '*Yemach shemoinik*,' 'Go to the KGB,' 'Go to Russia'…"

Avreimi had been sitting in Itzik's study all evening, listening to the true story of his father's life. As Itzik had warned him, it wasn't easy. His father appeared at times as cruel and hard-hearted, and Itzik had made no attempt to sugar-coat his descriptions. But as long as the candle is burning, Avreimi reflected, one can make repairs. His father had merited doing full *teshuvah*. He had left this world as a pious, good Jew. It was a fact that he had taken care of

Zalman Berkovitch and instructed Yaakov the grocer to provide all his needs.

After a moment, however, Avreimi felt his heart sink. He suddenly remembered the words with which Itzik had begun their conversation:

Your father was a traitor to his dying day.
He did not really do teshuvah.
It was only camouflage.

Soviet Union, 5737 / 1977

ANDREI WILLOTZKY'S ENIGMATIC WORDS GAVE MOMI NO peace. All day long, he thought about them and tried to understand what they meant.

On the one hand, the professor had said that Zalman Berkovitch had been transferred to another mission—as though that emotionally ill individual could succeed at *any* mission. And, on the other, he had promised that they would meet again. Was there a link between what he had said and Yechezkel Polowitz's unexpected appearance in Kiev?

The mystery of Polowitz, of course, also robbed him of his peace. From the way he was dressed, Momi thought, the orphanage administrator ought to be considered an enemy of the nation and the Party. His religiosity constituted an unforgivable crime. On the other hand, it was because of that man that he, Momi, was here. Polowitz had been the one who'd rescued him from a life of misery and orphanhood. This was the man who, in Zalman's view, had "sold him to the kibbutz"—thereby giving him a life of meaning and ideals. There was no doubt that Polowitz's ultra-religious garb was merely a disguise. Underneath those black clothes and that white beard beat the sensitive heart of a loyal servant of the Communist Revolution and the workers of the world.

Just one thing troubled Momi. He hated people who were afraid to stand behind their actions and who fled from responsibility. After his return from Masada with Zalman, he had felt the need to clarify the details: Why had he been transferred to the kibbutz? What was the meaning of the words, "you were sold"? And who, in fact, were his real parents? He had made the trip to Jerusalem, located the orphans' home, and asked to meet with the administrator.

Yechezkel Polowitz had not consented to let him into his office—not even for a brief meeting. His secretary had claimed that he wasn't there, but Momi glimpsed Polowitz slipping out the back door. There were apparently people who were always careful to show you their back, Momi thought—both in Jerusalem and in Kiev…

It was an era of change at R-19. The rivalry between Kalinin and Willotzky had diminished somewhat, apparently because they were working together on some new initiative. Yevgeny Yompolsky, the psychiatric student and Willotzky's protégé, had been transferred to another position in the KGB, after swearing faithfully not to say a word about R-19 or the projects in which he had taken part.

Ali, the Iranian expert on Islamic culture and Momi's flatmate and friend, announced one day that he would be returning to Iran, where he had another job waiting. Momi drove to the airport to see him off, and when he returned to his empty apartment he felt lonelier and more alone than usual. He had loved to drink with the friendly, intelligent Iranian, to play chess with him and talk about every topic under the sun. Now there were fewer mouths in the house—but the vodka, for some reason, was being consumed at a much faster rate…

Suddenly, he began to feel homesick. For the kibbutz, for his parents, for his army friends. He was no longer a child. Soon he would be celebrating his 25th birthday. Celebrating? Not exactly. Who was he supposed to celebrate with here? With Oleg Marinov, the cold-hearted Ukrainian? With Kalinin? Willotzky?

Momi stood at the window of his apartment, looking out and smoking. His mood was lower than it had been at any time since his arrival in the Soviet Union. Winter was nearly over. The snow, which had covered the world with a spectacular blanket, had stopped falling. The late-afternoon sun poured a sickly light over the crowded buildings, highlighting their gray misery.

What was happening back at the kibbutz? How were his adoptive parents? What did Sonia and Mikush think about the boy they'd reared with devotion for sixteen years, and who had one day simply disappeared? Were they angry at him? Worried about him? Perhaps they guessed that he had not merely fallen off the grid, but was working on behalf of the Party and the ideology in which they'd raised him.

Distant images flooded his memory. Here he was at 18, during a kibbutz meeting, standing up and demanding permission to refuse the draft into the corrupt, imperialist Israeli Army. Beside him stood two youths: Tomer Bar-Ezer, who'd returned from the war three years later a broken man. But at least Tomer was still alive—unlike their friend, Ro'i Goldman, who'd sustained a direct hit from an Egyptian shell on the last day of the war, and who'd returned to the kibbutz in a casket.

And here was Drora Tzeiler, the eternal kibbutz secretary, and Mishke, the stern treasurer with a pencil clenched between his teeth… And what about Allon Koler, his dedicated commander, who'd been grievously wounded during the war? And his former classmates at school? And his pupils in the youth movement, whom he had guided toward a life of work and cooperation? Whom he had taught to memorize Marx and Engels' *Communist Manifesto*?

Did they know where their admired leader, Momi Arzi, had disappeared to? Did they believe the rumors that he'd had dealings with the Egyptians: maps and plans in exchange for his life? And did they have any idea who was behind those rumors?

No, it had not been the Shin-Bet that had spread them, as so many probably thought. That had been the KGB's handiwork. The KGB, which had desired to burn all the bridges behind him, to ensure that he would have no good reason to return to Israel.

"Momi? Where are you?" called Oleg Marinov. "Professor Willotzky is looking for you."

Momi had spent the morning in Dr. Galina's laboratory. Dr. Galina was the Directorate's top restorer, and her lab was on the building's third floor. They'd been scrutinizing a piece of "ancient" pottery that she had been working for the past two weeks to create. The pottery shard was to be sent by special agent to an archeological site in Saudi Arabia where a British delegation had established a "dig." The agent was to find a way to secretly hide the vessel so that it would be discovered by the diggers. When the writing on the pottery was translated and publicized, it would pose a stunning contradiction to Islamic tradition—another step in eradicating religion from the world.

"Momi, where are you?" Oleg called again.

When Momi stepped into the corridor, Oleg urged, "Quick, go downstairs. The professor is waiting for you outside."

Momi took the stairs two at a time until he reached the exit. Professor Willotzky was seated in his car, a black Volga bearing tags that proclaimed that it belonged to the KGB's vehicle fleet.

"I want to show you something," the professor said after Momi got into the car. He started driving.

The Volga left R-19's precincts and crossed the bridge over the Dnieper. But it did not turn toward downtown Kiev. Instead, it veered south, toward the forest.

Momi was gripped by sudden fear. Willotzky, concentrating on his driving, didn't say a word, and the silence did not auger well. Momi had heard of executions in the forests, of citizens whose burial places were not known. Had Willotzky decided to get rid of him?!

As though to heighten his apprehension, the professor slowed the car. He took a long strip of cloth from the glove compartment and ordered Momi to cover his eyes. Momi did as he was told, ironically feeling a little calmer. This type of execution had been prevalent in Stalin's time, during the dark fifties. The enlightened and progressive Soviet Union had left such terror tactics behind. Still, despite these convincing arguments, his heart beat rapidly and a cold sweat covered his body.

Since he could not see what was happening, Momi's hearing was sharper and he was tuned into what was happening around him. He heard the sound of a gate opening with a squeak, and a guard's mumbled greeting. The car continued for a few more yards and then stopped.

"You can open your eyes now," Willotzky said.

Momi pulled the strip of cloth off—and his eyes opened wide in shock. "What is this? Where are we?" he asked in disbelief.

He was in the heart of Tel Aviv.

The Volga was parked at a curb on Rechov Allenby—as testified by a street sign written, of course, in Hebrew.

Momi's head swiveled around as his eyes absorbed the sights. There was the Mashbir department store, and there a *makolet* bearing an Osem sign. Here was a "Dan" bus stop, and a post office with the familiar logo of a deer…

"What is this? What's going on here?" Momi stared at the professor, who merely smiled.

"Can I get out?" Momi asked. The professor assented.

He opened the car door and stepped out hesitantly, as though unsure of the ground beneath his feet. It was a ghost street. Though no living being could be seen, it was authentic down to the last detail.

Momi walked into the grocery store, whose door stood open. He couldn't believe what he was seeing. On the shelves were Tnuva products, and Elite, and other Israeli companies. He picked up a bottle of Tempo and shook it. It was a real bottle, and the drink fizzed inside the glass. From another shelf he picked up a package of biscuits and opened it. The biscuits were tasty and fresh. Other shelves contained canned goods, bottles of oil, and bags of flour and salt, just like in Israel. Even the scale on the counter had been made by "Ma'oznei Ha'aretz," so well-remembered from his childhood.

Like a dream walker, Momi left the *makolet* and went over to the kiosk at the street corner. Familiar newspapers hung outside: *Davar, Al Hamishmar, Ma'ariv, Hatzofeh*. The newspapers, by their dates, were one month old. Their headlines spoke of Prime Minister Menachem Begin and of Egyptian president Anwar Sadat's upcoming visit to Israel.

A music store across the street attracted his attention. Hurrying over to it, Momi found himself surrounded by all the singers and bands he had grown up with on the kibbutz. On the shelves were Israeli records and tapes of all kinds. Large posters of music icons hung on the walls, but there was no one standing behind the counter to sell the merchandise.

The front of a nearby building featured a large Magen David. Momi went inside. He saw a large room filled with benches, siddurim, and a Holy Ark covered with a curtain of embroidered velvet. It certainly looked like a shul, Momi decided, despite the fact that he had never in his life set foot in one.

Professor Willotzky walked in, a broad smile on his face.

"Well? What do you say about all of this?" he asked.

Momi was effusive. It was amazing, stunning, unbelievable. But what was it for? Could it be a backdrop, built for filming a movie that took place in Israel? Because, if so, he thought privately, there was plenty of room for improvement. The logo of the "Atta" company, in the department store's window display, was backward. And the kitchen that he had seen in one of the buildings had amused him greatly. If that was meant to be an Israeli kitchen, it definitely should not boast a Russian samovar for making tea, but rather a Sipholux for preparing cold seltzer...

Or maybe, the uncomfortable thought crossed Momi's mind, the professor had some way to read his mind. He knew how much Momi missed Israel, and had had something built to remind him of home...

Professor Willotzky sat down on one of the benches in the "shul." Momi took a seat facing him.

"You are doubtless asking yourself," he began, "why we built this site.

"About half a year ago, one of our senior agents began to operate in Israel. A most successful agent. He came with a bogus identity as a new immigrant who'd arrived in Israel several years before. He found work as an engineer in a security enterprise in a small city called Yokna'am. He rented a flat and made friends. For a period of time he was a sleeper, doing nothing except assimilate into his surroundings. Half a year ago, as I said, we 'defrosted' him and he began to operate, sending us high-quality material."

Professor Willotzky rummaged through his briefcase and took out a picture. It showed a man being led away in handcuffs by a number of men in civilian clothes.

"Three months ago," the professor continued, "the man was caught by the Israeli Shin-Bet. Do you know how they caught onto him? Do you know what first aroused their suspicion? You won't believe it: He didn't know what a Crembo was! You surely are familiar with that sweet snack? Every Israeli knows it. Our agent received rigorous training; he studied Hebrew, Judaism, and Israeli history. There was just one thing that our trainers hadn't known to tell him: that in the summer Israelis eat *'artikim'* and in the winter they eat Crembo. Our man is sitting in jail today, and we'll have to pay a high price to free him."

"So you want me to teach Russians what Israelis eat?"

"What they eat, how they think, what they dislike, what makes them angry."

"People who will then be sent to Israel."

"Not only to Israel. But there, too."

Momi weighed the idea in his mind.

"There's just one problem," he said, gesturing at the *Aron Kodesh* with his hand. "I'm no expert on Judaism. We never went to synagogue or observed Jewish laws and customs."

Professor Willotzky smiled.

"I thought of that, too," he said. "I know that you grew up on a kibbutz and are not conversant with Jewish tradition. You will not be able to teach our people how to behave during a Sabbath meal or on the various festivals. Therefore, we have another teacher who will work with you. She is a good Communist, but also very well-versed in all Jewish customs."

Momi accepted the order in silence.

"Another thing," the professor continued. "To be appointed an instructor, you will require a higher clearance than you now hold. You certainly deserve it. You will shortly be promoted to the level of *starshina*."

Momi was surprised. A promotion in rank would upgrade both his salary and his circumstances. This was certainly good news. And it would correct a minor injustice: in the IDF, he had been a mere staff-sergeant. For political reasons, he had been prevented from attending an officers' course and becoming a sergeant-major, the Israeli equivalent of the Soviet *starshina*. It was symbolic that here, in the Soviet Union, he would finally be granted the rank that had been denied him in Israel…

"There's just one thing that Human Resources insists on. Despite the fact that you have proven your loyalty above and beyond the call of duty, you are not a citizen of the Soviet Union. In addition, you are a bachelor. In order to receive a promotion in rank and become an instructor in the KGB school, all you have to do is get married.

"My proposal is very simple: Marry the woman who will be serving as an instructor alongside you. As far as I am concerned, the marriage may be a fiction, on paper only. Just to cover the administrative side of things. The instructor is a veteran, accomplished agent, professional and pleasant. I think that the two of you will get on fine together. By the way, she is Jewish by birth, in case that's important to you. Here are her documents. Take the day off tomorrow, go to the municipal office, and make all the arrangements."

"Who is she?" Momi asked with interest. "Do I know her?"

"I don't think so, though she has worked for us in the past," replied Willotzky. "Her name is Anna Aranowich."

Avreimi shot up from his seat. "My father was married in Russia?"

"Yes," said Itzik Peled.

Avreimi could not believe what he was hearing. "Does my mother know about this?" he asked.

"You don't understand..." Itzik tried to explain, but an agitated Avreimi cut him off.

"Do you mean to tell me that my father was married twice? Why should I believe you? Why am I even sitting here and listening to this? I—"

Itzik slammed his hand down on the table. "Enough!" he shouted. "Maybe you can hear me out patiently to the end?"

Avreimi sank back in his chair and gave Itzik a doleful look. Itzik lowered his voice again.

"What do you know about your mother?" he asked Avreimi. "Where is she from? Where was she born?"

Avreimi narrowed his eyes in suspicion. "Chezky and I were saying, just recently, that we know hardly anything at all. Only that there's family in America who are hardly in touch."

"And have you ever met any of these relatives?"

"Actually... no."

"Have you ever seen pictures? Does she tell you stories from her childhood? Stories about the city she grew up in in America?"

"Not really." Avreimi was impatient. "What are you trying to say?"

"Don't go fainting on me," Itzik said. "I told you at the start that you were going to hear things today that would not be easy. Anyway, your mother was born in Kiev, in Ukraine, and was given the name Anna Aranowich. She had a strict Soviet education, despite the fact that she was a Jew. By the way, she's worked very hard to erase any trace of a Russian accent from her speech."

Avreimi felt on the verge of collapsing. The blows had come at a dizzying pace: his father, under suspicion of spying, his mother, born in Russia. What else would be revealed?

A second passed before the next blow came.

"As you must realize," Itzik said, "your mother was an outstanding KGB agent. She held the rank of *starshina*, like your father."

"And... is she also suspected of espionage?" Avreimi asked, not bothering to hide the tremor in his voice.

"Unfortunately, my dear Avreimi, the answer to that is— 'yes,'" Itzik answered.

Soviet Union, 5737 / 1977

Momi finished his workday in a particularly foul mood. Professor Willotzky's new project did not appeal to him. He had enjoyed working in the antique-creation unit. It posed an intellectual challenge, a mind game on a global scale. He was shaping reality and bringing about change in the consciousness of millions of people. And, in addition, he was acquiring invaluable professional knowledge in a field he might pursue one day. Would he glean the same measure of satisfaction from turning people into pseudo-Israelis? A loyal soldier does as he is told, and he would present himself at his new post tomorrow. But was he happy about it? Definitely not.

And apart from that, did he have nothing better to do with his life than to get married by executive order? Anna Aranowich... what kind of name was that? Why did an outstanding KGB agent go around with such an openly Jewish name? And how did she come to know all the intricacies of the Jewish religion and its customs?

He left R-19, intending to go home. Instead, he found himself driving aimlessly through the streets of Kiev. His hands gripped the steering wheel and his eyes watched the road, but his thoughts were far away. Without realizing it, he drove onto one of the bridges that spanned the western Dnieper, toward the old city and its ancient neighborhoods. He crossed the Podil Quarter and passed the green hills with their mansions. His car seemed to drive itself along a broad boulevard; he merely sat and let himself be drawn into the stream of traffic.

The blare of a horn roused him abruptly. He braked, hard. Lost in his thoughts, he had nearly gone through a red light and crashed into a streetcar that was crossing the intersection.

Momi shook his head, trying to return to reality. *Where am I?* he wondered. He looked out, seized by a sudden panic. All his senses tensed. The fog that had clouded his mind seemed to lift in an instant, exposing the reality that had been hidden from him until now.

He was on Lenin Boulevard. The street to his right was Mikelob. That was it! That was the source of his guilt feelings. This was where it had all begun: the emotional turmoil, the memories that kept dragging him off to different places and times, the criticalness that he suddenly felt toward the system…

This was where he and Ali, his Iranian friend, had followed Yechezkel Polowitz, administrator of the orphans' home. How simple—and how clear, Momi thought. That episode must be gnawing at his conscience. As an upright Communist, and moreover as an employee of the KGB, he should have reported it to the proper authorities. He hadn't done so, and that was undermining his peace. For several days now, a murky distress had been making him inexplicably irritable. Why had he begun to feel so apprehensive lately? What was he afraid of? After all, he had done nothing wrong. The feelings themselves worried him. What was he hiding? What was he hiding from *himself*? What was it that his KGB instructor had once said? "If you feel guilty, you apparently *are* guilty. All that remains is to discover the reason…"

What a fool he was! Why hadn't he done it at the right time? Why had he not reported the sighting on the very next morning? That had been stupidity of the highest caliber. At the time, he had been afraid that Ali would give him away. When days had passed without that happening, he had calmed down. But he had not been sufficiently assiduous in protecting himself. He should have gone to Professor Willotzky's office and told him all about it.

Momi parked his car under Building 7, the one that the orphanage administrator had entered that night, and considered the situation. Now that he was about to be promoted to the rank of *starshina*, he would have to undergo a security investigation. He must solve this problem before that happened. If he had ignored it until now, that was no longer possible. The matter would be exposed and would arouse serious suspicions.

The question would be asked at once, dragging further questions after it: Where have you been until now? Why did you delay? What was the reason for your failure to report this? What do you have to hide? Are you still in contact with foreign agent Yechezkel Polowitz? How many times have you met since then? Did he give you anything? Did *you* give him anything? Is he the only foreign agent with whom you have had contact since your arrival in the Soviet Union? Please present a list of all the people that you have met these past three years. Why did you hide this from the authorities? Have you passed any information on to Israel? Who are your contacts? It is in your interest to answer. You'd better spill everything you know. We have special methods for people like you. What a pity. You have a nice face…

Momi was filled with pure terror. The kind of terror that weakens the knees, melts the insides, and sends an icy chill up the spine. For the first time, he understood the kind of deathly fear that people who'd escaped the Soviet bloc talked about. Until now, he had believed these accounts to be nothing but a cheap Western libel. Now he felt fear invading every cell of his body, taking possession of his entire being.

A militia vehicle passed in the street, yanking him out of his uneasy thoughts. He would get up and do something, he decided. He would go to Professor Willotzky on his own initiative and tell him the whole story. Maybe he would say that it took him some time to realize the significance of what he had seen. Or that he had been negligent in not reporting it at once, but was now stepping forward to fulfill his patriotic duty to his country and his Party, ready to supply his testimony complete with names and details.

Once again, Momi heard Ali's gleeful whisper after following Polowitz inside: "Fifth floor, Apartment 6." Perhaps it would be a good idea to go up there and see the place for himself, he thought. That way, he could testify more faithfully, and maybe even be able to avoid mentioning the fact that Ali had been with him.

Without thinking twice, Momi got out of his car, pushed open the gate, and walked into the lobby.

It had once been a handsome building, but that had been many years earlier. Now it had disintegrated from lack of proper maintenance, and its message was one of neglect. Momi began climbing the stairs while scanning the names on the doors: typical Russian family names. From behind the doors came sounds of life: children crying, people talking or shouting, cooking aromas, and the whirr of a washing machine. Some of the doors were open, in an attempt to ease the crowded conditions inside the flats just a little.

Momi reached the fifth floor. The door of Apartment 6 was closed; it bore no name or insignia. He hesitated. Should he knock? And if someone opened the door, what would he say? What was he searching for here? Whom had he come for?

He looked around, etching the details in his memory, and then began descending the stairs. When he reached the third floor, he heard voices rising up toward him. He slowed down, the better to hear and see them.

They were two young men with overgrown hair and cheap clothing. For some reason, he thought that they were students. Something about them seemed familiar, but he didn't know what it was. They passed him, absorbed in animated conversation. Momi continued his descent at a snail's pace, listening to the pair and trying to figure out where they were headed.

He heard them climb one floor and then another. They opened a door and entered an apartment. Judging by the time it had taken them to get there, he thought it probable that they had gone into Apartment 6.

A moment before they closed the door behind them, he caught a single word in the flow of conversation. It was Hebrew. One of them said, "*moreh.*"

Momi stood transfixed in shock. Were they Israelis? Or Soviet citizens acting in opposition to the regime, agitating to leave their motherland and immigrate to Israel? If so, they were to be considered provocateurs and incendiaries, counter-Revolutionary criminals intent on spreading anti-Soviet propaganda. And had Yechezkel Polowitz given them books and printed material for dissemination among enemies of the State and the Party?

Momi continued his descent slowly, sunk in thought. He left the building, crossed the yard, and went out into the street. He continued on down the sidewalk toward his car, still lost in his musings— which was why he did not notice the black car that had turned the corner into this street and braked beside him.

From the car burst two KGB men. They jumped him, grabbed his arms, and threw him roughly into the car. Someone put a blindfold over his eyes, someone else snapped on a pair of handcuffs, and the car shot forward.

No one spoke. Momi knew that there were at least three KGB men in the car with him: the two who had captured him, and the driver. By the rules, he knew, a KGB vehicle was never left in the street with its engine running, minus a driver. That was something he had learned in the basic course he had taken in his first days at R-19. He also knew that the three were not silent due to a lack of topics of conversation, but in order to frighten him and make him panic.

He could also envision what was coming. The drive would take a long time. Even if the arrest had taken place a mere two minutes from local headquarters, they always drove out of town, traveling several kilometers before turning back into the city. That would make their captive think he was being taken to some remote location, far from his friends and family. He might spend several months no more than a few blocks from his own home, but he would feel like he was on his way to Siberia.

For the same reason, Momi knew, when they reached their destination they would take away his watch and his wallet, confiscate his belt and shoelaces, cut off his buttons and remove any personal tokens. In one fell swoop, a person was transformed from a proud citizen with full rights to a nameless prisoner at the mercy of the system.

The blindfold was removed only when the car halted after a thirty-minute drive. He was taken into a gloomy building, led down dim corridors, passed through steel doors, and finally brought to an interrogation room.

Opposite him sat a stocky interrogator with a genial face. The man wore the uniform of a KGB officer, heavily decorated with medals.

"Do you wish to confess?" he asked.

Momi would have laughed, had he not felt so much like crying. "Confess to what?" he asked. "What have I done? Why was I arrested?"

The interrogator smiled, revealing a crooked gold tooth. "Everything in its own time," he said in what was meant to be a soothing tone. "Everything in its time. Believe me, Comrade Momi: you will not leave here without knowing what you stand accused of. Let us first sign a confession, and then we can proceed."

Momi studied the man's face. To his surprise and apprehension, the fellow wasn't joking.

"I have committed no crime, so I have nothing to confess. But I can tell you about myself."

"Please do," the interrogator invited with a gracious smile.

For three years, Momi had rehearsed the details of the identity that had been cobbled together for him in case of need. The words emerged naturally and fluently.

"My name is Momi Arzi. I was born here in Kiev to my parents, who are no longer alive: Boris and Ludmilla Arzi."

"What is 'Arzi'?" the Russian asked. It was not Arzov, Arzeyev, Atozovsky, or Arzishvili.

"Our name was Arzin. My parents were Jewish," Momi admitted in a low voice, as though caught out in a flaw. "They changed our family name because we planned to immigrate to Israel. After they were killed, I kept the name, Arzi, out of respect to their memories."

"When were they killed?"

"Six years ago. They are buried in the old cemetery in Kiev."

Had the interrogator taken the trouble to visit the old cemetery, he would indeed have found the graves of Boris and Ludmilla Arzi, who had lost their lives in an unfortunate traffic accident in the year 1972. The KGB excelled at fabricating fine cover stories for its agents.

"I understand the respect you feel for your parents," the interrogator said. "But they were, in fact, traitors to their country. There are plenty of Soviet citizens here of Jewish extraction who have detached themselves from international Zionism, which works hand in glove with corrupt Western capitalism."

Momi touched his chest with outspread fingers. "One of them is sitting before you right now," he declared. "I may be a member of the Jewish race, but I am also a loyal and devoted citizen of our motherland. I have no thought whatsoever of immigrating to any other country. I was born in the Soviet Union and I am prepared to serve my country in every way possible!"

The interrogator, Momi quickly realized, was well versed in his fictitious personal history. "I understand that you were a member of the Komsomol (the Soviet youth movement), and they were satisfied with your political consciousness."

Momi nodded his head in grateful modesty.

"And what do you do today?"

"I am a student. Here, in the University of Kiev."

This detail, too, should the interrogator wish to investigate, would prove completely accurate—although his fellow students would have said that their friend Momi seldom put in an appearance at the university.

The interrogator continued talking as he looked through the file in front of him. "You live alone in a flat, you are unmarried, you have a car. You enjoy a good lifestyle, compared to the average Soviet citizen."

Momi shrugged. He could not supply the true reason. He must not acknowledge that he worked for the KGB Such a declaration would also be pointless. If he told this interrogator that he served in R-19, the man would either burst out laughing or start yelling, depending on his mood. Everyone knew that the KGB had only 18 Directorates, no more. *You claim that there is an additional Directorate, Number 19, and that you work there?! For that fabrication alone you can be judged guilty of disseminating false propaganda and spreading fear and despair through the civilian population...*

In an instant, the Russian's face changed and was filled with fury.

"Look, Momi, at how much our country has given you." He slammed his heavy hand down on the table. "And you are ungrateful, spreading anti-Soviet propaganda—just like your traitorous parents!"

Despite the extensive mental preparation he had undergone, Momi was alarmed by the interrogator's forcefulness.

"What... what are you talking about?" he asked, surprised to find that his voice was shaking.

The Russian fixed him with an accusing stare. "For your own good, it would be preferable for *you* to tell *me* what I am talking about. That will save you several years of hard labor."

"I... I can't tell you about things that I haven't done."

The interrogator leaned forward, as though about to impart a secret. "Listen, young man. Don't think that you know everything. Sign the confession, and you can be home tomorrow. But if you don't sign, tomorrow you'll be on the train to Siberia."

Momi's fear was laced with incomprehension. He grasped the nature of the threat very well, but what he didn't understand was the other man's meaning when he had said that Momi could be home tomorrow. Which home was he referring to? And how, exactly, could he return there?

"I will not sign anything," Momi said. "I am innocent of any wrongdoing."

The Russian clasped his hands and gazed at Momi in distress. His whole manner indicated, *Don't say I didn't try to help you...*

A moment later, Momi felt two strong hands grip him from behind and pull him to his feet. A black hood was pulled down over his face and tied around his neck.

"Perhaps we will help you remember," said the interrogator, and left the room.

43

THE MOMENT THE DOOR CLOSED BEHIND THE INTERROGATOR, a hail of blows, kicks, punches, and slaps began to rain down on Momi.

He couldn't see who was beating him. He had no idea how many people were doing the hitting. He only knew that they were acting in silence, devoid of feeling, with no cries of anger or grunts of fury. They were simply doing their job, coldly and with calculation. Momi knew a thing or two about administering blows: He had received his training in the same place that these men had received theirs. It was clear that they had been instructed to inflict as much pain as possible without causing irreversible damage.

He absorbed the blows in relative silence as well. He knew why he had to undergo this torture. He was suffering for the Revolution, for the Party, for the world's workers. His torturers were unaware that he was not only an ardent Communist and a loyal Soviet citizen, but also their colleague, their brother, flesh of their flesh, serving in the same organization as they were and striving toward the same goal. Had they known who and what he was, they would have regretted every blow. It was he who could not tell them the truth. He was obligated to maintain complete silence, even unto death.

His orders had been crystal-clear: "If you are ever arrested for interrogation, whether by the militia or the KGB, you must wait patiently until your absence is noted in the Directorate and a search is instituted. You must never reveal the existence of R-19—even at the cost of your life and the lives of those you love."

That was why he was not kicking and screaming. That was why he did not resist the beating. He clenched his jaw hard and reminded himself over and over that he was suffering for an exalted goal. This was an inextricable part of his mission. He was a KGB man, an officer candidate, a senior member of the Party that had been appointed by the political leadership to defend the beloved motherland. Every blow was wreathed in honor; every kick like a scar from a daring battle; every punch a shining medal pinned to his chest.

The beating lasted, by Momi's estimation, about a quarter of an hour. Then it stopped. He heard the squeak of the door as his unseen assailants slipped out. Then there was nothing but silence.

Not a sound apart from his ragged breathing and shaky sighs. The hood was still over his head and his hands were tightly cuffed. Either he was sitting in a huge, deserted building, he thought, or this room was hermetically sealed from the outside.

Time crawled at an agonizing pace. How long had he been tied up in here? Two hours? Six? He'd completely lost his sense of time. It looked as though he had been forgotten here, condemned to die of starvation and thirst. What did they want from him? What great crime did they want him to confess to? What had he done?

An enormous thirst engulfed him. His mouth was dry, tinged with the coppery taste of blood.

"Is anybody there?" Momi called. But all he heard was his own echo.

His voice rose in near-hysteria. "Is anyone there? Can anybody hear me?"

No answer came. No one heard him. He felt his heart pound in a fear that swept through his entire body.

He tried to calm himself. All he had to do was wait a bit, until someone realized that he was gone. Patience... That's all he needed. A little patience.

Then the blood froze in his veins: He had left the building in the afternoon, so it was probably early evening by now. He lived alone and no one would notice that he was missing. Worst of all, Professor Willotzky had given him the day off to arrange his marriage to Anna Aranowich. He could end up rotting here endlessly. At least a day and a half would pass before anyone missed him. The interrogator had said that he could go home tomorrow, or else board a train to Siberia. Such words usually carried some weight. The interrogator had not made the remark at random. By the time they realized in the Directorate that he was gone, it might be too late...

Momi had never been so happy to hear anything as he was at the sound of the jingle of keys in the interrogation-room door. Anything, including another beating, was preferable to this horrific isolation...

He lifted his head even though he could not see inside the black hood. The heavy footfalls told him that it was his old friend, the interrogator. A wave of relief washed over him. He had prepared for this moment. He must convince the man of his complete innocence. He *could* convince him. After all, the interrogator was seeking justice, and would undoubtedly be persuaded by what Momi had to tell him. When he took the hood off his head, Momi would look straight into his eyes, one Communist to another, one KGB man to another—though he couldn't tell him that—and talk to him honestly and sincerely. The interrogator would believe him.

"Well, Momi," the Russian said before he sat down. "Have you managed to remember what you did?"

"I am a loyal Soviet citizen," Momi said, bracing for the blow that was sure to come. "I've done nothing."

The interrogator pulled the hood from Momi's head. Then he unlocked the handcuffs and rang a bell that rested on his desk. A middle-aged woman came in and set down a plate of food and a flask of water. "You're probably hungry," the interrogator said. "Go ahead—eat something."

Momi looked at him with a sense of relief. At last, they'd found out who he was, he thought. But he still must not say a word about R-19. Maybe they hadn't sent an order from on high to release him. They'd probably confirmed that he was a state employee and that his hands were clean. Now he must be doubly vigilant. He was hungry and thirsty, and fell on the food with an appetite.

"Satisfied?" the Russian asked, when Momi had finished his meal. "Good. Now we need to take a little trip together."

They left the room and walked down a long, narrow corridor that led to an inner courtyard. A Zil truck was waiting for them, its engine droning and belching out smoke. Momi was lifted into the rear compartment and restrained again. The interrogator joined the driver in the front seat.

After a jerky and winding drive that lasted fifteen minutes, the truck stopped. The driver shifted into reverse, drove another short distance, and then halted again. Momi heard the interrogator step out and walk to the rear of the truck. He issued an order, and the canvas curtain was taken down.

Momi squinted as floodlights washed over him. He was in the heart of Kiev's old cemetery. A sea of marble monuments stretched before him, and near the truck yawned two gaping holes. He recognized the place at once. These were the "graves" of his two "parents," Boris and Ludmilla Arzi, who'd been "killed" in a traffic accident six years earlier...

He tried to keep his expression neutral, but his sudden paleness could not be concealed. It looked as though his big lie had been exposed.

"I don't have to explain to you what's happening here, do I?" The interrogator came closer, climbing over the mounds of excavated earth. "Boris and Ludmilla Arzi, or Arzin, were not buried in this pair of graves, because before one can die he must first be born..."

Momi didn't answer. His stunned stare was fixed on the two gaping holes. Someone had dug a very deep grave here, he reflected. Why had they created such a problematic cover story? Why hadn't they provided him with a cleaner, smoother image?

With the help of one of his men, the interrogator climbed back up into the truck. He looked at Momi, eyes narrowed like a boxer in an arena, sizing up his opponent before the match begins.

"It would be interesting to hear what your real parents had to say about this," he remarked. "Sonia and Mikush Arzi, from Kibbutz Tel-Chana... Did I pronounce those names correctly?"

Momi held himself rigid in an attempt to cover his trembling. How had they discovered that he was Israeli? That he had parents on the kibbutz?

"What is your rank in the IDF? Staff sergeant, is it not?" The Russian smiled at Momi's confusion. "What position did you occupy during the Yom Kippur War?"

He sat on the metal bench beside Momi.

"Listen, young man," he said in an affectionate tone. "I could convict you of spying on behalf of Israel—or how about on behalf of the U.S.? That would earn you 20 or 30 years of hard labor. But I know that you're just a small fish. They threw you here from Israel to be the contact person for Aliyah activists, to teach them Hebrew, to spread Zionism. We saw you at Mikelob 7 twice—the headquarters of all those criminals here in Kiev."

Momi hoped the interrogator could not see the shock on his face.

"I like you. You're a good kid, and I want to help you. Sign a confession for me, and I'll take care of you. Tomorrow you can be home again. On my word as a KGB man. It's a shame. Why are you being so stubborn?"

Momi decided to continue being stubborn. In response, the interrogator decided to do the same. The truck returned to the prison, where soldiers roughly manhandled Momi off the vehicle.

"Take him to the holding cell," the interrogator ordered a pair of jailers. "When does the prison transport leave?"

One of the jailers glanced at the wall clock. "Seven a.m."

The interrogator looked at Momi. "You'll have all night to think," he said, with a broad smile.

Momi and his jailers walked down long, deserted corridors. Only the sound of their footsteps and the rattle of the chains on his feet disturbed the deathly quiet. His legs ached from sitting cramped on the truck for so long, but he didn't say a word. He just gritted his teeth hard.

After a trek that took 15 minutes, he found himself in a large, low-ceilinged room. It held several prisoners, all of them frightening-looking. A jailer unlocked Momi's chains, thrust him inside, and locked the door behind him.

"We leave at seven in the morning," the jailer informed the other prisoners. "Pack your things."

The prisoners roared and shook their fists, but the jailer had already vanished into the gloom of the corridor.

Momi stood near the cell door, in total shock. How had he come to this? He could be sent who-knew-where, buried in some labor camp for the rest of his life. He needed to think. He had to find a solution. There must be some way to extricate himself from this mess.

His body was battered from the events of the past few hours; his emotions were anguished and in turmoil. He sat down on a nearby straw pallet—and was promptly kicked violently aside.

"Nobody sits on my pallet!" bellowed a gigantic prisoner with an Asian cast to his features and long, powerful arms.

Unfortunately for Momi, he landed on another inmate's bag of clothing.

"Get off my stuff!" the prisoner yelled. This one had tattoos all over his body. He grasped Momi the way one picks up a slaughtered chicken and flung him to the other side of the cell. There, of course, a third inmate waited, eager to join in the fun.

Momi lay on the ground, downtrodden and humiliated. He was shaking uncontrollably. As his feelings overpowered him, he buried his face in his hands and burst into bitter tears. This was the end. No one was coming to rescue him. If these guys didn't finish him off overnight, they would do so over the course of the journey to Siberia.

He tried to pull himself together, to impose calmness on his stormy emotions. Instead of crying like a baby, he would be far better off using the time for thinking: What did they want from him? What was he supposed to confess to? What were they actually accusing him of? He had committed no crime. He knew that it was connected to Yechezkel Polowitz and the apartment at 7 Mikelob. It was also linked to the two Hebrew-speaking youths he had seen going up there. But what was *his* connection to them? And how did the KGB know about his past?

His fellow inmates did not allow the new prisoner to lose himself in his thoughts. They shouted at Momi and chased him from place to place. Wherever he sat down, he quickly found out that it belonged to one of them. A fellow with a bad eye and Caucasian features kicked him from time to time, trying to goad him into a fight.

Between blows, one thought kept returning to gnaw at him: why wasn't the KGB torturing him as they well knew how? Why not fracture his hand or smash his jaw? It wasn't that he especially wanted to have his bones broken—but the fact that they were being careful to leave him whole both surprised and troubled him. What were they plotting? What did they have in mind? What was he missing here, in the strange story of his arrest and imprisonment?

Suddenly, he understood. From the corner of his eye he caught the look of frustration that passed between two of the inmates. How had he not thought of this before? They were not prisoners, and this was not a prison. He could not be worked on with the usual KGB methods because of the simple fact that he already knew those from the inside. He must not let himself be dragged into a fight or any sort of violence. He must maintain absolute calm.

He sat down near the cell door, arms folded, and smiled at the furious inmates.

Ten minutes later, the jailer returned. Momi was taken back to the fatherly-looking interrogator. To his astonishment, the man appeared amused.

"Listen, Momi," he said. "I see that you're a hard nut to crack, so I'll lay out my cards for you. Right now, a spy-exchange deal is being brokered between the Soviet Union and the United States. Your own country, Israel, has also stuck her nose in, as usual. They want us to free 100 Aliyah activists and Hebrew teachers. I'd like to include you—but only if you sign a detailed confession for me now. The flight is being prepared even as we speak, and I can still get you in on the deal. In exchange for one small signature, you can find yourself on a plane back home, to Tel-Chana and your beloved parents and all your friends. What do you say?"

If Momi had been afraid before, now he was consumed with terror. Especially when he heard the interrogator's next sentence:

"We've already given your name to Israel through the French middleman. I hope to receive a positive answer regarding you. Tomorrow you could be welcomed as a national hero at Ben-Gurion Airport."

44

MOMI CLOSED HIS EYES AND PRESSED HIS FINGERS TO HIS temples. The interrogator had gone to fetch them both glasses of tea, leaving him alone. Now he really had something to think about.

If he did return to Israel within the framework of a spy-exchange deal, he would immediately be taken into custody for questioning. Then he could expect one of two scenarios to take place, each worse than the other: Either he would turn, overnight, into a famous spy—a Communist officer from Tel Chana who'd served as an agent for the Soviet Union. That would, of course, set in motion a fresh wave of persecution against the kibbutz, against his parents and their friends, and against the entire Israeli left.

The second possibility was no less heartwarming: The Israeli authorities would not publicize his name, and he would be incarcerated forever in one of the Shin-Bet's secret prisons he was assured existed — though no one actually knew about them.

Despair overtook him. Everything had suddenly become clear—and thus, doubly terrifying. Now he understood the inexplicable feeling he had had since his arrest: a secret hope that this whole thing was just a test of his loyalty in advance of his promotion. In his innermost heart, he had believed that the interrogator was working hand in hand with Professor Willotzky, trying to see if he could withstand interrogation without betraying any secrets. That was the reason they'd been handling him with kid gloves all along—relatively speaking, of course. He had not undergone genuine torture, and even the blows he had sustained were not the sort that leave any marks.

But now, suddenly, everything could be seen in a different light. The interrogator was not working with anyone, the arrest had not been staged, and this was no test of loyalty. The interrogator—who, judging by his actions, seemed to hold a very senior position—truly suspected him and was hoping to squeeze a confession out of him that would serve as an additional card in the spy-exchange deal now in the works. That was why they'd been treating him gently. They believed that in just a day or two he would be in the West, and must be sent home in reasonable condition...

A frisson of pure fear shuddered through him. The situation was complicated. Should he hint something to the interrogator anyway? He'd never betray any secrets, of course. He would not say anything explicit—just drop a clever hint. If his questioner really was a senior KGB man, perhaps he already knew about R-19...

No, Momi told himself. *No! You mustn't say or hint at anything. Those were your orders. There's nothing to be done except wait for them to come and free you.*

"I'm not signing anything," he told the interrogator, when the latter returned with the steaming tea half an hour later. "I am a loyal Soviet citizen, and I cannot be false to myself by declaring that I've broken the law."

The interrogator took his seat, sipped his tea, and encouraged Momi to do the same.

"No? A pity," he said in a coaxing tone. "You could miss the train. It's not every day that there's an exchange of spies. You're a smart boy, so I can tell you the inside story. The Americans have caught a big fish of ours: one of our agents who managed to land a position in the office of the Secretary of Defense in Washington. By the way, all the details have already been aired in the American newspapers; you can read all about it when you reach Israel. She started out as a simple stenographer, and worked her way gradually up to the position of executive secretary to the Secretary's chief adviser. She passed us wonderful material from the conference rooms of the American government. But, in the end, she was caught, interrogated, and forced to confess."

Momi took a sip of tea. He certainly needed it.

"Our Foreign Minister—who also happens to be my brother-in-law—has been handling the negotiations personally. The Americans will fetch a good price for our agent, and this is your chance. If you don't grab it now, I don't know when you'll ever have an opportunity to go home. All you have to do is sign the confession and answer a few questions regarding other members of your network."

Momi thought he would explode. It was unbelievable how ignorant the right hand was of what the left hand was doing! Although this fellow was indeed related to the Foreign Minister, it was reasonable to assume that he was unaware of R-19—which served directly under President Leonid Brezhnev and answered only to him.

"No one in Israel will welcome me as a hero," he told the other man. "I am neither a spy nor a secret agent."

The smile on the Russian's face resembled that of a cat that had just swallowed a whole pot of cream.

"You underestimate yourself, Momi," he said in the friendliest fashion. "You don't appreciate yourself enough. The Israelis are eagerly awaiting you. Your name was sent through the usual channels, and your friends over there are waiting impatiently."

Momi turned pale.

"I must admit," the interrogator continued, "that at first, the Israelis tried to deny your existence. They told the broker that they didn't know any Momi Arzi. At that stage, apparently, they did not believe that we would catch you. But now, I've received word that they've changed their minds. Apparently, your operators here attempted to contact you and realized that you'd been arrested. Now they are very eager to welcome you back. It's very important to them that you arrive home safely—so do not undervalue yourself. They have agreed to reduce their demands to twenty Aliyah *refuseniks*, as long as *you* are released as well. You are worth 80 activists to them! That's a good feeling, isn't it, Momi?"

It took every ounce of Momi's willpower not to curse out loud. This stupid Russian had exposed him. Until today, no one in Israel had known where he was. He'd left Israel, together with Zalman Berkovitch, in an Egyptian submarine at sea. He'd disappeared without leaving a trace. And now, this KGB man had handed the Israelis his name on a silver platter...

What complete madness! Even if Willotzky managed to stop the deal from going through in time, even if he succeeded in getting to him and taking him off the train speeding toward oblivion, this interrogator had destroyed him. It was impossible for him to ever return to Israel now. And who knew what price Sonia, Mikush, and the others at the kibbutz would have to pay? Even now, the Shin-Bet might be crawling all over the place and issuing arrest warrants...

"I am not an Israeli. I am not an Aliyah activist, and I will not sign any false confession," Momi stated.

The interrogator pressed a bell, and a jailer appeared. "Take him back to the cell," came the angry order.

The holding cell, amazingly, was empty now. However, this did not improve Momi's mood.

The hours passed with agonizing slowness. At each distant sound, Momi imagined that Willotzky or some other Directorate figure had come to have him released. Each time, his hopes were dashed.

At four p.m., the interrogator came to his cell. One of the jailers carried in a table and two chairs. The Russian pulled out a bottle of vodka and two glasses, and poured for both of them.

"Momi, this is the last minute," he said. "The plane lifts off this evening. Sign the confession, and we'll leave for the airport at five."

Momi did not drink the vodka. Nor, he said, would he sign a confession.

"You know what?" the interrogator said. "I don't need a confession. Just answer one question for me: Who was the dark-skinned young man who was with you the first time you came to 7 Mikelob?"

Momi needed a minute to grasp who the man was referring to. It had been Ali, his Iranian colleague, who had been with him and had dragged him into their bizarre pursuit of Polowitz through the streets and subways of Kiev.

"I have no idea what you're talking about," he said.

The interrogator smiled, exposing the crooked gold tooth. Then he leaned into his case and pulled out a photograph. In it, Momi and Ali could be seen outside the building into which Polowitz had entered.

"We know that he's one of yours," the Russian said, pointing at Ali. "We know that he's a Jew; you can't fool us. We had him in our sights because he had been in contact with anti-regime rabble, and then he suddenly disappeared. Tell me everything you know about him—and you can get on that plane."

Momi stared wide-eyed at the interrogator. Ali—a Jew? The Iranian had been in contact with those who opposed the regime? Was it possible that a hostile agent had managed to burrow his way into the KGB's most secret enclave? Impossible! This fellow must be up to something.

"I don't know what you're talking about," he repeated, when he could speak again. "I have not broken any laws. I do not oppose the regime. I am a loyal and honest Soviet citizen."

Furious, the interrogator stood up and left the cell.

Momi heaved a sigh of relief.

But his relief did not last long. Thirty minutes later, one of the jailers entered the cell. He placed fresh, clean clothes on the bed and ordered Momi to wash and shave. Momi wrinkled his brow in surprise. A moment later, the interrogator stuck his head inside the door.

"Momi, you're going home," he announced. "Aren't you happy?"

Momi was not happy. Not at all. But he was too stunned to say a word.

He changed his clothes and got ready. An idea popped into his head, providing a measure of calm. This was undoubtedly a test of his loyalty. He would now meet some of his colleagues from the Directorate, who would applaud him and praise him for his unyielding stance.

When Momi was ready, the interrogator studied him with satisfaction.

"In five or six hours, you will be home," he told Momi.

Momi gave him a questioning look.

"Israel has sent a special plane to fetch you," the Russian explained. "Along with you, there will be twenty other Jews who have been authorized to leave within the framework of the exchange. But you will undoubtedly be the star.

"In a minute, a doctor will be coming in here," he continued. "To tell the truth, I salute you. You did not sign a confession, nor did you give away any member of your network. We may be on different sides of the fence, but I admire men of principle."

Momi said nothing. Half an hour later, the familiar truck took him to the airport.

On the runway, which he could glimpse in the distance, two planes were already in place. One was El-Al and the other a French military aircraft. Twenty Russian Jews, deeply excited, were clustered at the foot of the gangway, surrounded by a circle of Russian policemen. Another truck waited nearby. After a time, an official car arrived bearing the Russian Foreign Minister, who had come to personally oversee the complex barter that he had devised.

This was no charade, Momi realized with cruel clarity. They were really about to extradite him to Israel.

An excruciating half-hour crawled by.

"We are waiting for our agent to be transferred via the French broker," the interrogator explained to Momi. "Then you and the other Jews will board your plane, and the Americans will board the French one."

Ten minutes later, the Foreign Minister approached the interrogator and another senior official, and whispered something to them. An order was shouted. The group of Israeli *refuseniks* began climbing the gangway leading up to the plane.

The second truck drove up to the French aircraft, and a group of ten people climbed out and began boarding that plane.

"Let's go," the interrogator told Momi. "You are a free man. I will now accompany you to the plane, and at the door I will hand you over to the Israelis."

Momi got out of the truck on buckling legs and began to climb the gangway, stair by stair.

Three steps before he reached the plane's entrance, Momi stopped. Slowly, he turned and looked behind him. If he still harbored a faint hope that something would happen at the last minute—that maybe this was just a test of loyalty, or that someone from R-19 would finally notice his absence—this hope was dashed, too. The Russian interrogator with the genial face waved good-bye from the foot of the gangway, as though parting from an old friend. The Foreign Minister was sitting at his ease in his official vehicle, talking on his car phone and looking very pleased with himself. The rest of the entourage, soldiers and KGB men, waited for the foreign planes to lift off for their destinations so they could return to their own daily routines.

For a long moment Momi lingered on the stair, taking in a panoramic farewell view of the city in which he had spent the last three years. He was acutely aware that these were his last moments of freedom. More than anything, he felt a bitter disappointment. The state he had believed in, and for which he had sacrificed his younger years, was handing him to his persecutors on a silver platter. The Party for which he had given up his home and his country was returning him to a place where he was considered a traitor and an enemy spy. To a harsh and vengeful Shin-Bet that would do anything in its power—anything!—to extract from him everything he knew…

Over the last few hours, he'd had plenty of time to think. His conclusions, in conjunction with a few tidbits that the interrogator had dropped, told Momi that he was about to become a very famous person. "Israel's new prime minister, Menachem Begin, is not prepared to give you up," the interrogator had remarked in one of their talks, as though to underscore to Momi how concerned his native land was on his behalf, and how eager she was to see him released within the framework of the exchange deal.

The Russian, of course, had no idea of the true motives behind this eagerness. Momi read newspapers and listened to the news, and he was aware of the political upheaval that had taken place in Israel in the previous year. Three decades of Socialist rule—Mapai, followed by the Ma'arach—were over, and members of the nationalistic right, headed by Menachem Begin, were in power. A *kibbutznik* spy? A Soviet agent? That was exactly what they needed right now. Begin, a fiery demagogue and inciter of the masses, would make mincemeat out of him. This would not only be a judgment of Momi Arzi, but of the entire kibbutz movement.

And this, he reflected sadly, was apparently the historic mission that the Communist Revolution had imposed on him. He could stop all of this with a single sentence. He could descend the stairs, go over to the interrogator, and tell him to please call Professor Andrei Willotzky at such-and-such a telephone number. But he would not do so. He'd sworn by all that was precious and holy to safeguard the secrecy of the KGB's Directorate R-19, even at the price of his life and his freedom. R-19 had a mission that was more important than the life of any one individual. Wars, too, demand that many people sacrifice their lives; that does not make them any less just.

At the plane's entrance, two young men about his age, in civilian clothing, stood waiting. There was no need to hear the Hebrew on their lips to know that they were Israeli. Momi guessed that they were Shin-Bet men. One of them extended his hand and smiled. "Welcome, Momi Arzi."

Momi shook his hand, wondering at this unexpected friendliness. The next moment, he was considerably more surprised to hear a wave of applause and cries of joy from inside the aircraft. The twenty *refuseniks* who had boarded before him were seated in the plane's rear seats. They all stood up now, in elation and excitement, and greeted him with deafening cheers.

One of them, an elderly Jew with a white beard reaching to his chest, could not contain his emotion. He stepped up to Momi, embraced him, and began to weep on his shoulder.

With the help of one of the stewards, the young Shin-Bet man gently detached the old man and returned him to his seat.

"Come with us," the second Shin-Bet agent told Momi.

At the front of the plane, in the area designated for the crew, stood a narrow metal table attached to the wall, with two benches on either side. Momi was pushed into one of the benches, and the Shin-Bet man sat beside him so that Momi was imprisoned.

The first agent closed a curtain that hid them from the Russian *refuseniks*. The smile abruptly left his face.

"Staff Sergeant Momi Arzi, I.D. number 228604," he said, "from this moment you are under arrest on suspicion of treason and spying on behalf of a foreign power. Everything that you say may be used against you in your upcoming trial. You are entitled to a defense, and an attorney will be at your service as soon as we arrive in Israel."

45

"Hold out your hand," said the Shin-Bet man, in a tone that did nothing to disguise the contempt he felt toward Momi. He clasped one half of a pair of handcuffs on Momi's hand with a snap, and then leaned forward to attach the other half to a metal ring fixed in the metal bench.

"For your personal security," added the Shin-Bet man. "And also for the State's security—if you care at all about that—I told the people here that you are an Israeli who has to return home. We gave them to understand that you're a Mossad agent who needed to be extricated in a hurry. That's why they gave you that round of applause, in case you were wondering. I'd like you to go along with us in this. Try not to let anyone notice that you're handcuffed, and of course don't say anything unnecessary to anyone."

Momi was silent. He had no intention of speaking either to the Shin-Bet or to the twenty passengers whom he despised with all his heart: Soviet citizens who had received everything from their motherland, but had chosen to turn their backs and immigrate to a land not their own.

The Shin-Bet men left him alone. To keep him occupied, one of them tossed him some Israeli newspapers and two books.

From the sounds that reached him, Momi realized that airport personnel were pulling the gangway from the aircraft and closing the passenger door. The pilot received the green light from the control tower and began warming up the engines with a mighty roar.

The pilot's voice came through the intercom system: "Welcome to this special El-Al flight from Kiev to Lod Airport. El Al is proud to host you, freedom fighters and activists for unrestricted Aliyah. We wish you a pleasant flight and a speedy assimilation in our country. Please fasten your seat belts."

With his free hand, Momi tugged at his seat belt and clicked it shut.

The plane began moving slowly down the runway.

At that moment, from the back of the plane, came a loud singing. It was started by the long-bearded Jew with the large *kippah*. Within a minute, all the *refuseniks* had joined in. Momi didn't recognize the tune, and at first he also had a hard time identifying the words, which were pronounced in an Ashkenazic, Diaspora Hebrew:

Mi-Mitzrayim gialtanu,
Mi-beis avadim p'disanu,
Mi-Mitzrayim gialtanu,
Mi-beis avadim p'disanu,
Mi-Mitzrayim.
Mi-Mitzrayim.

Momi closed his eyes in bitter despair. Tears prickled in his eyes and gathered on his lashes. *They* were leaving Egypt, getting free of what they considered a *"beis avadim."* But he was exchanging freedom and liberty for a prison from which he would never leave in his lifetime. And all because of an unfortunate mistake, because of bad timing, because of bad luck.

The plane slowed down near the end of the runway, and executed a wide horseshoe turn. The engines began thundering even more loudly, and then the plane burst into high speed as it taxied in preparation for liftoff.

Momi's eyes gazed fixedly out the window. He saw his

interrogator and the Foreign Minister as the plane passed them. Though only a fleeting glimpse, it was enough to make him smash his fist into the metal table.

Suddenly, the peacefulness that had reigned over the scene just a moment ago was shattered. There was a great deal of scurrying around on the ground. The interrogator ran as though seized with panic. The Foreign Minister stood by his car, perspiring and red-faced, screaming into his phone. Several of the soldiers and crewmen ran onto the runway, as though trying to stop the plane. But it passed them in a blur.

A sense of missed opportunities squeezed Momi's heart until he thought it would break in half. Someone had finally realized the mistake. At long last, someone from the Directorate had reached the interrogator or the Foreign Minister. Willotzky or Kalinin had sent word—just a few minutes too late.

And the song from the back of the plane grew even louder:
Mi-Mitzrayim gialtanu,
Mi-beis avadim p'disanu,
Mi-Mitzrayim gialtanu,
Mi-beis avadim p'disanu,
Mi-Mitzrayim.
Mi-Mitzrayim.

The plane's speed increased. Then its wheels lifted from the tarmac as the aircraft rose higher and higher.

The ecstatic passengers unbuckled their seat belts, seized one another's hands, and started dancing. In vain did the stewards beg everyone to return to their seats; the joy was uncontrollable. People who for long years had been imprisoned behind the Iron Curtain had suddenly merited salvation. What business did they have with safety belts? They'd left the chains behind and were on their way to freedom.

Momi was in a state of shock. His whole body felt frozen in pain and sorrow. If only he had been delayed just a few more minutes… If he had pretended to faint or suffer an epileptic fit. He could have drawn out the time. Why hadn't he thought of that?

The tears that he had held back until now burst forth suddenly, without restraint. He lowered his head into his arms and sobbed. Had he waited just another moment… had he delayed just a few extra minutes… What a waste. What a loss…

So absorbed was he in himself that he did not notice when the passengers' song suddenly faltered. They were looking fearfully out of the plane's windows.

He also didn't notice the four Soviet warplanes that surrounded their aircraft on every side.

Nor did he know that the Israeli pilot had received an explicit order from the Soviet control tower to turn around immediately and return to the airport at Kiev.

The first glimmering he had that something had happened was when he heard an alarmed call from the Shin-Bet man who had arrested him.

"How much time do we have?" asked the man.

Momi lifted his head. Something in the atmosphere had changed.

The door to the pilots' cabin was standing wide open. The group of Jews at the rear of the plane looked pale and stunned. The Shin-Bet man stood not far from Momi, holding the receiver of a strange telephone attached to a cumbersome-looking, khaki-colored case.

"Three minutes," came the answer from the pilot's cabin.

At that moment, he heard the thunder of gunfire.

The Shin-Bet man gripped the receiver and raised his voice. "Mr. Prime Minister, they've fired a warning salvo. If we don't turn around, they will take down the aircraft."

The young man waited for an answer.

A moment later, he motioned to the pilots. The gesture was unmistakable: *turn around*.

Momi's heart leaped with joy.

The pilot spoke over the intercom. This time, his voice sounded far less exuberant. "My dear passengers, we are forced to turn around and land back in Kiev. We hope that this is only a misunderstanding that will be speedily resolved, and that we will then be able to continue on our way to Israel."

Angrily, the Shin-Bet man slammed his phone into its holder. His colleague opened a cabinet near the pilots' cabin and removed several submachine guns and pistols. He distributed the weapons to the pilots and stewards, who, apparently, were expert in areas other than food and drink service...

The Shin-Bet man gazed long and hard at the group of downcast *refuseniks*. Then he turned to look at Momi with open loathing.

"You're going to pay for this," he hissed between his teeth.

The weather in West Berlin was particularly raw that day. A steady rain had soaked the branches of the bare trees and the earth beneath them. Frigid winds blew shrieking past the soldiers of the special military unit, sending waves of cold through their wet uniforms and mud-filled shoes. Conversations and orders in both English and German mixed and mingled, but did not clarify the situation.

Matters had been unduly prolonged. The German fighters were professional and possessed an extremely high level of endurance, but even they had begun to complain. They'd been summoned that morning from their base on the outskirts of Bonn, to provide security for an exchange of spies between East and West. They were told that one man, a KGB agent who'd been caught in the act, was supposed to be transferred to East Germany, where the Soviets ruled. As with many other such deals, the exchange was to take place on the Glienicke Bridge that spanned the Havel River, which connected Berlin and Potsdam.

At the last moment, however, a frantic phone call had halted the process. Since then, everyone had been freezing in their places for long, agonizing hours.

At five p.m., the sun began to go down. Hans Gerhardt, captain of the special unit, approached General Sam Rosewald, commander of the American base near Stuttgart and the most senior officer on the ground.

"What is the outlook on the exchange being carried out?" the West German asked.

The tall American removed his beret and scratched his head. He was not required to supply explanations to the West German officer. This was a government-to-government matter, not a military one. But it was preferable to provide the young officer with a few scraps of information, if only to calm his impatience and his men's muttered protests over the unprecedented delay.

"The Israelis are furious, and justifiably so," explained the veteran American general. "The exchange was cobbled together from two separate deals: the Soviet Union and the U.S., and the Soviet Union and Israel. Our deal with the Russians was satisfactorily concluded: They received three spies that we caught, and sent us the equivalent. But the Russian-Israeli deal was suddenly broken off. The Israelis were meant to set free the spy in exchange for an Israeli agent who was caught in Kiev, plus twenty Jewish Aliyah *refuseniks*. The plane had already lifted off, but just before it left Soviet airspace the plane was intercepted and forced to return to Kiev. They want to cancel the deal and demand that all the people on board the aircraft, now on the ground in Kiev, deplane. The Israelis, naturally, are opposed. The telephone lines between Jerusalem, Washington, London, and Moscow are burning up, and diplomatic pressures are mounting. Until further notice, here we stay."

The German captain nodded his head in understanding, but could not refrain from entertaining the thought that so many people were suffering on account of one individual. The Russian spy—whom the Israelis, for some reason, had dubbed "Mr. Crembo"—had arrived on a special flight from Israel to Germany, escorted by ten guards and Shin-Bet agents. A single-story, concrete structure on the bridge's western side had been placed at the Israelis' disposal. From there, the spy was supposed to leave on foot and cross the bridge to the eastern side.

The Israelis had a roof over their heads. His own men surrounding the structure, on the other hand, were cold and wet. And in the secondary security circle were hundreds of American troops who were doubtless also incurring cases of pneumonia this afternoon…

He lifted his binoculars and scanned the long, empty bridge spanning the river. To date, he had supervised several such exchanges over this bridge, which had served since the end of the Second World War as the border between the American zone and the Soviet one, and which had been accordingly nicknamed the "Spy Bridge."

Drops of rain danced on the black asphalt, the steel girders dripped with water, and the stone sculptures on either side of the bridge glistened damply.

On the other side, in the distance, he could clearly see the East German military posts. Among the officers were several senior Russians who were not enjoying the weather much either.

As usual, the German thought, the Israelis were causing problems, and everyone except them was suffering…

Some 1,400 kilometers away, near the edge of the Kiev airport, more and more military and police personnel streamed onto the site. They surrounded the Israeli plane and the 30 or so people on board.

Here, too, the hours had passed at a torturously slow pace. Tension and fear had left their mark on most of the faces. The twenty *refuseniks* were afraid and disappointed. They had been looking at freedom from up close. Immediately after lift-off, the plane's stewards had given each of them a travel visa that turned them into Israeli citizens. Their Soviet citizenship had been revoked by their great crime of wishing to move to the land of their forefathers… And then, suddenly, just a moment before their dream was about to come true, they'd been returned to Egypt, to the house of slavery, to the prison of the Soviet Union…

The Shin-Bet contingent—the two open agents, plus four others who had traveled under the guise of the aircraft's crew—ran from side to side, sub-machine guns on their shoulders, their expressions tense and grim.

Momi still sat in his corner, handcuffed. He maintained his silence, though his heart swelled with happiness and pride. His mood had improved wondrously. The Soviet Union had not betrayed him. The Party had not turned its back. It had all been an unfortunate mistake that had luckily been discovered in the nick of time. They were doing everything in their power to rescue him. Planes had been launched, soldiers summoned, and leaders of the State were personally dealing with his case.

Though an attempt was being made to keep from him what was happening outside, he overheard snatches of conversation. In charge of the plane at the moment was the Shin-Bet man who'd been in constant contact with Jerusalem via his cumbersome communications device. Though he spoke in codes and hints, Momi gleaned a very clear picture of what was taking place:

The first deal between Israel and the Soviet Union had been for the spy, "Mr. Crembo," in exchange for 100 longtime *refuseniks*. Negotiations had been moving at a snail's pace—until Momi's name entered the picture. From that moment, the pace picked up. The "price" went down to just twenty Jews in addition to him, and the Israelis even hastened to send "Mr. Crembo" to Germany, there to wait the deal's final authorization. The Russians understood that Israel was very eager to get their man back—and only later realized that Momi Arzi was not an Israeli agent, but the opposite...

And now, the Soviet government wished to cancel the entire deal. They wanted to have the passengers debark and to send the plane back to Israel with only the aircraft crew. The government of Israel, on the other hand, was digging in its heels and demanding that the exchange go through.

"There are 21 Israeli citizens on that plane. The plane itself is Israeli territory. It was intercepted in contravention of international law, and must be allowed to return to Israel," declared the Israeli prime minister to his British counterpart. "If the Russians try to break in by force, our people will not hesitate to defend themselves, and an international incident will be precipitated."

Time dragged. For brief periods, Momi dozed. He was unable to stand up and stretch. At a certain point, he noticed a ripple of excitement running through the plane, and roused himself.

He looked out the window. A gangway mounted on an airport vehicle was slowly approaching the plane. He tensed. Were they going to break in? Had the negotiations fallen through? Or had Israel finally yielded and agreed to cancel the deal?

He watched his fellow passengers. The *refuseniks* were as confused as he. No one had either the time or the patience to provide updates. The Shin-Bet men appeared extremely tense. Two of them stood with drawn weapons near the door the mobile gangway was approaching, while three others were dispatched to the four corners of the aircraft, where they instructed the *refuseniks* to bend over in their seats and cover their heads with their hands.

Only the commander still stood beside his strange communications device, speaking heatedly into the receiver with a hand over his mouth.

There was a light thump as the gangway met the body of the airplane.

To Momi's surprise, one of the guards near the exit turned the handle and cracked open the door.

The Shin-Bet commander was still busy with his animated conversation on the phone, and throwing strange glances at Momi.

From one of the Soviet vehicles stepped an officer, holding a communications device in his hand. The Russian officer walked toward the plane, the device snaking along behind him. He began climbing the gangway, holding the device up as though to prove that it was all he was holding.

The officer climbed up to the last step and thrust his device into the plane. One of the guards took it from him and pulled him inside.

At the same moment, the gangway was removed from the aircraft door.

The plane's commander was still on his phone, but he waved a hand toward Momi, as though to tell him something.

The other Shin-Bet man placed the phone on the narrow table in front of Momi. "Someone wants to talk to you," he said.

Momi lifted the heavy receiver.

"Comrade Momi. This is Professor Andrei Willotzky," said a familiar voice over the phone. It sounded slightly excited.

Momi suppressed the urge to cry. He steadied his voice. "Yes, Comrade Willotzky."

"Momi, I will ask you a few important questions."

"Please."

"Are you safe? Have any of the Israelis threatened you?"

At that instant, the Israeli commander rushed toward Momi Arzi. Momi waved him off with a gesture, and the Shin-Bet man halted a few yards away from him.

"There's no one near me."

The Shin-Bet man seized a sheet of paper and began scribbling a few words on it.

"Momi, do they have weapons in there?"

"Yes. Plenty of them."

The Shin-Bet lifted the page, rose on tiptoe, and placed it on the table before Momi.

Momi didn't even glance at it. He crumpled the page and threw it back toward the Shin-Bet man.

"Listen, Momi," said Willotzky. "We have an opportunity to get you off the plane and release the rest of the Jews. It all depends on one thing. Tell me honestly: have the Jews seen you? Did they see your face? We can't send twenty people to Israel who would recognize your face."

Once again, the Shin-Bet commander waved a new sheet of paper in front of Momi, trying to get his attention.

Momi didn't look at this one, either. His gaze went to the twenty pairs of eyes that were fixed on him from the rear section of the plane.

"Momi, what is your answer?" Willotzky asked impatiently. "We must reach a decision."

Jerusalem, 5737 / 1977

THE PRIME MINISTER'S RESIDENCE IN JERUSALEM'S TALBIYEH neighborhood was not unfamiliar to the two Shin-Bet men—the younger of whom was 30 and the older over 50—but this was the first time they had been here since the new tenant had moved in. They left their weapons with the guard at the entrance and walked up the familiar stone path toward the brown door.

The General Security vehicle, escorted by a police patrol car, sirens blaring and lights flashing, bore them rapidly from the airport to the Prime Minister's house. Despite the late hour, the P.M. had requested a detailed update. To the agents' surprise, the man himself opened the door for them and ushered them into his living room.

"I've known your commanding officer for many years," the Prime Minister told the younger man. "And now I'm pleased to meet you, too."

Shaul Armoni, the older of the pair, raised his thick brows in surprise. The P.M. had known him for years? From where, exactly?

"We were neighbors, Mr. Armoni. Don't you remember?" The Prime Minster looked at him with the ghost of a smile. "Our buildings were next door to one another."

If Shaul Armoni recognized the sting, he hid it well. His expression continued to be one of complete incomprehension.

"That apartment at 40 Rechov King George in Tel Aviv," the P.M. said, taking his seat. "You certainly remember it, Mr. Armoni. Don't you?"

Not a muscle moved in Armoni's face, but now his young companion understood very well. 38 King George was the address of the Likud stronghold—the Prime Minister's party. Until a year ago, before the political upheaval, the man had been considered a corrupt outcast. Rumor had it that the Shin-Bet had an apartment in the adjoining building, from which they listened in secretly to the Cheirut party, by order of the leaders of Mapai and Ma'arach, who had control in Israel then.

"For the past decade, there has been no secret bugging of opposition parties in Israel," Armoni said, leveling a direct look at the new P.M. "And those who were engaged in such things at the time did so on the orders of their superiors."

"Certainly, certainly." The P.M. smiled like a person who'd had his say and wished to close the subject. "I only hope that we didn't bore you too much…"

The Prime Minister's wife walked into the room. She placed a bowl of fruit and a bottle of cold water on the table for the guests, along with a cup of tea and a lump of sugar for her husband.

"Well, then, gentlemen…" The P.M.'s face sobered. "I'd like to hear a full, detailed report about our plane in Kiev."

The Shin-Bet men straightened in their seats. Shaul Armoni took a sheet of paper from his pocket and spread it out in front of him.

"At 17:50," he began, "a messenger brought this document, signed by the legal adviser and the president of the High Court in Tel Aviv. I immediately contacted the commander of the plane on the ground, and transmitted its contents to him."

The floor then passed to the younger man, who had just returned from Kiev:

"I received the call at 17:55, after several hours inside the aircraft. Unfortunately, by that time it was impossible to approach Momi Arzi. The Russians had brought a telephone to the plane, and he spoke with his KGB handler. Each time I tried to approach him, he waved me away. I was afraid that if the Russians sensed I was trying to communicate with him while he was on the phone, things would spiral out of control."

"It was a sensitive situation," agreed the Prime Minister. Hundreds of heavily-armed Russians surrounding the plane, awaiting the signal to invade it.

"Therefore," the plane's commanding officer continued, "I wrote it down on a paper. At first I tried to give it to him to read, but he wouldn't look at it. He just crumpled the page and threw it back at me.

"I quickly improvised a sort of paper sign, and waved it at him from a distance, but he was busy talking with his KGB handler and didn't look my way."

"What did the sign say?"

"'The State of Israel guarantees you amnesty if you allow the Jews to leave Russia.'"

"But he didn't see the sign," Shaul Armoni broke in.

The Prime Minister gave him only a brief look, and then turned his attention back to the younger man. "Did you get the conversation between him and his handler?"

"Yes. We attached a device that we'd brought with us to the cable that the Russian sent into the plane's door, and we heard the whole thing. He was talking with someone named Professor Willotzky. Willotzky asked Arzi if we had weapons inside the plane, and when he received a positive reply he said that they, the Russians, were prepared to release the Jews—but only if none of them had seen Arzi's face and would not be able to identify him in the future."

"Indeed," said the P.M. "We were prepared to pay a very high price just to let our brave brothers, the Soviet *refuseniks*, come to grace our land."

The two Shin-Bet men exchanged a quick look. They were very familiar with the Prime Minister's flowery oratory, but found it incredible that he spoke that way even at home...

"At that point," the plane's commander continued, "Momi Arzi paused for a long moment, and scanned the plane and the Jewish passengers. I tried to attract his attention to the page in my hand, but he didn't look at me. After a long pause, he looked down at the table and told Willotzky: 'No one, except for one Shin-Bet man, saw me. I'm locked in a small cabin at the rear of the plane.'"

"That's what he said?"

"In those words," affirmed the Shin-Bet man. "Willotzky instructed him to make sure to conceal his face when he left the plane. Ten minutes later, Arzi did leave. And ten minutes after that, we lifted off for Israel."

"We don't know what his motives are," the P.M. said in a slow, thoughtful voice.

"Our analysts," Armoni said swiftly, "believe that the Russian handler hinted to him somehow that he was being asked to lie and say that no one had seen him, even if this was not the case. That was in order to solve the international standoff."

"In any case, Momi Arzi doesn't know about the amnesty that was promised him," the commanding officer said. "He didn't see the document promising that he would not stand trial for treason and spying. He didn't even see my sign."

The Prime Minister placed a sugar cube in his mouth and took a sip of tea.

"Your analysts are incorrect," he told Armoni. "I know the KGB I was interrogated by the NKVD, its predecessor. A Russian handler or commander will never hint to his subordinate to lie to him. That's not the way they work."

"The reason doesn't matter," Shaul Armoni said impatiently. "Momi Arzi doesn't know about the pardon, and therefore it is open to being canceled."

"Why doesn't the reason matter?" the P.M. asked, fixing his eyes on Armoni behind his big glasses.

"That Communist *kibbutznik* is a clever lad," Armoni said. "I don't know what he tried to get with that lie, but he certainly profited in some way."

"If you ask me," the P.M. said, "we should not dismiss the possibility that the Jewish spark flickered to life in that 'Communist *kibbutznik's*' heart. He knew that if he would say that the new immigrants had seen him, there would be a bloodbath on that plane. Perhaps the enthusiasm and dedication of those Jews touched him, and he wanted to give them the chance to go to Israel. Perhaps he chose to endanger himself in order to save twenty Jews from spending the rest of their lives in a Soviet prison cell."

"Our analysts think otherwise," Shaul Armoni insisted. "And the legal people don't think that the pardon is valid. That... traitor doesn't deserve the benefit of the doubt."

A stern expression descended on the P.M.'s face. He raised a warning finger. "Be careful, Mr. Armoni, before you slap the label 'traitor' on one of our boys."

The Prime Minister stood up, indicating that the meeting was over.

"Mr. Arzi's pardon remains in force," he stated. "If he comes to Israel one of these days, he will not stand trial for his actions. Is that clear, Mr. Armoni?"

"As always, I obey orders, Mr. Prime Minister."

"I'd be happy if there were a way to let him know about this, over there in the Soviet Union. But I'm afraid it won't be easy," the P.M. added.

"It will be a bit difficult," Shaul Armoni agreed. "We'll see what we can do."

"Very good. Well, good night to you, gentlemen."

The car that had been meant to take them back to Tel Aviv had been diverted to a different mission. The two Shin-Bet men retrieved their weapons from the guard and walked toward Rechov Keren Hayesod HaYerushalmi, where another vehicle would be along to collect them.

Armoni was silent for a long time. The street was quiet at this late hour of the night. They sat down on a bench at a bus stop.

"This would never have happened with our former prime ministers," Armoni finally declared.

His younger colleague didn't know what to say.

Armoni thought about it for another long minute, and then waved a hand. "Let those Likudniks run the country. What does he think this is—Etzel? We haven't heard the last of that Momi Arzi. You'll see."

"What can we do? He's the Prime Minister." The younger man shrugged.

"That's exactly it." As though to himself, Armoni added, "Today he's the P.M.—and tomorrow, the opposition leader. The next elections will bring another political turnaround, you'll see. And then we'll have responsible people at the helm to steer the State. But *we* will always be around."

"What's that supposed to mean?"

"It means that only you and I know that Momi Arzi was granted amnesty. But we don't have to make any special effort to let *him* know that."

"And what happens if he turns up in Israel one day?"

Armoni's eyes were determined. "Not every account is settled in a courtroom," he said, touching his gun without realizing it. "There are other ways to bring traitors to justice."

Jerusalem, 5772 / 2011

Avreimi Kohlberg sat at the edge of his seat, hands and feet twitching nervously as he listened to Itzik Peled's story. He still clung to the heartfelt hope that this was just a fairy tale, and that, in the end, it would all turn out in some wondrous way to have been nothing but a figment of someone's imagination.

He had two normal parents who'd grown up in religious homes, married the way everyone did, and raised a beautiful family. One of them had died too young, as sadly sometimes happens in even the best of families…

Maybe it's all a dream, he thought, and pinched himself the way books are always having their heroes do. It was very late at night by now, a time when people were asleep in their beds. He'd phoned his wife earlier to let her know that he was busy with something important and would get home sometime during the night, but

Chezky had undoubtedly been trying to reach him for hours.

"My father told you all of this?" Avreimi asked Itzik Peled.

"He told me a great deal of it. There are some parts that I know from other sources, and there are some events that I participated in myself," Itzik said.

"Like what?"

"I had the honor of being the commanding officer on that plane," Itzik said. "It was many years ago. I was in the Shin-Bet then, and was ordered to be on that flight."

This came as a surprise to Avreimi—but also as a source of hope.

"Then you saw my father when the Jewish spark flared up in his heart?" he asked. For Avreimi, the most painful question of all was whether or not his father had left this world as a G-d-fearing person, a true believer, an observer of Torah and mitzvos—or, heaven forbid, as Itzik said some people were claiming, it had all been a disguise, a camouflage, and Abba had been... Well, it was better not to finish that sentence.

A pained expression crossed Itzik's face.

"On that topic," he told Avreimi, "I don't have good news."

Avreimi's breath froze.

"One of my jobs was to report on your parents every year."

Avreimi broke in: "To report to that man... Shaul Armoni?"

Itzik responded with an indeterminate movement of his head.

"Anyway, one of the questions was about their lifestyle," he continued.

"Well?" Avreimi was burning with suspense.

Itzik paused a moment before he went on. "For the past ten years, since I came to know your father, I've been reporting each year that, in my best judgment, he and his wife—your mother—were not people of genuine religious faith, but rather a pair of excellent actors who were carrying out their mission perfectly."

Soviet Union, 5737 / 1977

THE SHABBAT TABLE STOOD REVEALED BEFORE THE COUPLE in all its splendor: The table was spread with a white cloth, glowing flames flickered in the silver candlesticks, a pair of challahs, covered with an embroidered cloth, gave off a fragrant aroma, and a silver goblet rested beside a bottle of wine. Around the table stood eight chairs, each of which had a place setting in front of it.

"Shabbat Shalom," Momi Arzi said heartily.

"Shabbat Shalom," replied Anna Aranowich.

Momi adjusted the *kippah* on his head and stepped up to his place at the head of the table.

"Where did you come from just now?" Anna asked, her usually pleasant tone of voice turning didactic.

"I was in the *beit knesset*," Momi answered.

"And what did you do there?"

Momi lifted his eyes, as though trying to recall. "We said Minchah," he said. "And then Kabbalat Shabbat. The *rav* gave a short speech, and then we said Ma'ariv."

"How long did all of that take?"

Momi was silent, pressing his lips together in chagrin like someone who'd been caught out.

Anna looked at her watch. "The Friday-night services take about an hour and a half," she lectured. "You went to *beit knesset* when Shabbat began. And what did I do then?"

Momi narrowed his eyes in an effort to remember. "Remind me," he finally said.

"I lit candles," she said in a tone of mild rebuke, a teacher faced with a student's lack of familiarity with the material.

"Actually, why did you light the candles all the way back then?"

"Very simple. On Shabbat, lighting a fire is forbidden," Anna explained. "The woman lights candles before sunset on Friday, before Shabbat begins—and immediately after that, the husband and boys go to *beit knesset*."

Momi smacked his forehead in frustration. "I have to remember all the differences. They lit candles on the kibbutz, too, only they did it just before the meal."

"That's why I'm here." Anna smiled. "By the time we're done, you'll leave this place an upstanding Jew. Come on, let's continue."

Momi reached for the bottle of wine that stood on the table.

"Just a minute," Anna stopped him. "First you sing 'Shalom Aleichem' and 'Eishet Chayil.' Only then do you make Kiddush. What's going to become of you, Momi? You keep getting mixed-up!"

Only two weeks had passed since Momi was rescued from extradition to Israel by the skin of his teeth. Had the extradition taken place, it would undoubtedly have gone down in history as one of the stupidest steps ever taken by an intelligence agency. In the best-case scenario, there would have been consequences not directly related to his future: The unfortunate Russian interrogator would have lost his job, the Foreign Minister's position at the apex of Soviet leadership would have gone downhill, and long, tedious discussions would have been held in a variety of offices.

Momi had required several days to recover from the nightmarish experience he had undergone. Body and soul, he had been subject to a severe ordeal, and he spent most of the next few days asleep.

A great weakness had overcome him, to the point where Professor Willotzky sent a special KGB doctor to examine him and see to it that he made a speedy recovery. Even the professor himself came to visit him.

"You must recover quickly," he had told Momi. "Anna has already submitted an official request to the Department of Marriage Registration in the municipality. Conclude this matter, and you will receive a promotion to the level of *moyor* and return to work."

The wedding ceremony was brief, as befit a marriage of convenience, and the promotion ceremony even less festive. From now on, Momi would be able to serve as an instructor in the KGB school along with Anna Aranowich. In their first getting-acquainted conversation, he learned that she had already served for some time in the "School for Foreign Cultures," as the project had been dubbed. He discovered that the "campus" included not only the mocked-up version of Rechov Allenby, with its department store, *makolet*, and newspaper kiosk, but also a complete school in Hebrew, including a large library containing the best of Israeli literature and newspapers from recent years.

On one of the shelves he found something that caused his heart to skip a beat: a box containing all the holy books that Professor Kalinin had once brought to the Soviet Union for counterfeit purposes.

"We'll start by learning about the holidays," Anna had said in the course of that first meeting. "I'll have to provide some initial concepts so that you don't embarrass me. When we're confident enough, I'll take you home with me. You'll be surprised to know that there are still people in the Soviet Union like my father: stubborn as a mule and gripped by a 2,000-year-old faith. He will not give up a single custom or Jewish ritual. The old man's been arrested more than once, but at least he's learned that there's no use turning to me. I'm not prepared to help him. He is repeatedly fired from jobs because he won't work on Shabbat, or he says that there's some holiday or fast day he has to observe. I don't lift a finger for him. I told him explicitly that I do not intend to risk my career in the KGB over his nonsense."

"But what will you tell him? Who am I?" Momi felt as if the waters were closing over his head.

"What's the problem?" Anna laughed. "We'll tell him the truth—that we're married. He'll be very happy, you'll see. His greatest fear in life is that I'll bring home some non-Jewish spouse..."

Momi was confused. The strange marriage that Professor Willotzky had arranged for him was becoming more serious by the minute. He didn't know who Anna was. All he had been told was that she was a good Communist and a fine professional.

"If... if he's a religious Jew," Momi tried, "then our marriage won't be acceptable to him. It's a civil marriage."

Anna laughed as if she had heard a good joke. "You know what? Let's make the act perfect. My father will suggest that we get married by the rules of Jewish law—and we'll do him a favor and agree! What do you say? He has some rabbi who learns with him in the *beit knesset*, another old parasite who performs no useful service for society but only encourages leeches like my father to suckle from the State. He'd be glad to make us a Jewish wedding. Actually, we should have thought of that before. That way, my father wouldn't suspect anything."

"But who am I? Where did I come from? What's my story?" Momi was thoroughly bewildered now. "I can't say that I'm a former Israeli, and I also can't say that I'm a KGB officer."

"You continue using the cover story you were given," Anna said. "You're the son of Boris and Ludmilla Arzi, *refuseniks* who were killed in a road accident a few years back. Exactly what you told that idiot interrogator when you were arrested."

"So we're simply going to get married for real?"

"What one won't do for the Communist Revolution..." Anna said with a chuckle.

"Tell me, please, Sergei, what you remember about the holiday of Succot?"

Sergei Radinov stretched out in his chair with a nostalgic smile. "Succot..." he said dreamily. "Succot was the holiday I loved most of all when I was a boy."

"Did you celebrate it at home?"

Sergei was sitting alone at a small table in the center of a long, narrow room that was nearly empty of furniture or other amenities. At the far end of the room stood another, larger table, behind which sat three figures who studied him with interest.

"Did you celebrate Succot at home?" the question was asked again.

"My father, of course, didn't believe in all of that," Sergei said. "But my grandfather would start preparations several days before the holiday began. We had a small shed in our yard where the gardening tools were kept, and sacks of potatoes and various other things. Each year, as October approached, he would start complaining to the neighbors that the roof of the shed was leaking because the shingles were cracked and must be repaired before winter set in. Because of the economic situation, he would say, it was impossible to buy new shingles. Therefore, he would paint them and coat them with a special treatment that he would concoct. One day, he would take all the shingles off and lay them out in the yard. In the meantime, to prevent the work tools and food from spoiling in the sun, he would spread branches over the shed, which he brought from the woods behind our house. That was how he prepared a succah for himself that corresponded to the requirements of Jewish law, without any of the neighbors being the wiser.

"For eight days he would paint the shingles and examine them, one by one. During this period, as he made sure everyone knew, he would sleep in the shed so that thieves would not come in through the open roof. My mother would send him his meals there, and sometimes we, the grandchildren, would eat there with him. My father would get mad and say that Grandfather was endangering the family. But we children loved those days. We didn't understand how the family could be in danger from painting roof shingles. It was only when I began looking into Jewish sources that I understood what my grandfather had been doing all those years..."

Sergei finished his answer and looked expectantly at the three testers.

The trio conferred for a moment, and then the instructor

addressed him. All he knew about her was that her name was Anna. Her voice was cold.

"Very good, Sergei. The story is interesting and creative, but you are a certified liar. That was a fabrication from beginning to end."

Sergei narrowed his eyes, looking offended. "How can you say that? My grandfather paid for his faith with his life! He was arrested by KGB agents and died in prison. How can you say that I'm lying?"

"Very moving. Very moving…" she retorted with open cynicism.

Sergei Radinov closed his eyes and collected his thoughts. If Anna didn't "buy" the story, then he had a problem. He was a talented and ambitious KGB officer, about thirty years old, and his entire future depended on this test. He'd been born in a small city in Uzbekistan, not far from Tashkent, the capital, where he attended an engineering high school. A Party worker had noticed the talented youth and advised him to enlist in the Soviet navy. He was sent to the military university to pursue his academic studies, and quickly caught the eye of a KGB man, who offered him a place in the organization. Sergei had performed a variety of tasks within the KGB and had proved loyal and very clever. Professor Willotzky had pinpointed him along with a few other bright young people, and Sergei soon began his training at the "School for Foreign Cultures."

For six months he had undergone intensive training under Anna Aranowich and Momi Arzi and learned everything they could teach him about Judaism and Israeli culture. In their opinion, he was ready to be thrown into the water. Sergei was not going to be placed in Israel but rather in the United States, where he would be absorbed in the large community of Soviet Jewish immigrants. The story that had been constructed for him included a Jewish mother, and a grandfather who'd observed the mitzvot to a certain degree. He, of course, was meant to present himself as a person just beginning to be interested in Judaism and Zionism, someone who'd requested permission to move to Israel but decided somewhere along the way to immigrate instead to the land of unlimited possibilities.

Three sets of eyes were fixed on him in tension and hope. Sergei was the most promising of the present group of students, and this was the deciding test. Hanging in the balance was not only his personal success, but also the degree of professionalism that Anna and Momi brought to preparing the perfect spy.

Sergei nodded his head slowly, as though he had just remembered something. "Now that you say that," he told Anna, "I remember. I was just a little boy, and everything was unclear. Actually, my grandfather didn't paint the shingles every day. At the start of the holiday, for instance, there were a couple of days when he let the shingles dry. Then he went back to painting them for a few days, and at the end of the holiday let them dry for a couple more days."

Anna Aranowich smiled with relief. "That sounds more believable," she said. "At the start of the holiday and at the end, there are two days in which the Jews behave as they do on Shabbat. On those days, of course, your grandfather would not have painted shingles, because that is an action forbidden on the Sabbath."

She nodded at Momi Arzi, giving him the floor.

"What does the name Naftali Hertz Imber mean to you?" Momi asked.

"He composed 'Hatikvah,' Israel's national anthem."

"And David Ben-Gurion?"

"Israel's first Prime Minister."

"I'm going to show you two pictures and you will tell me, please, who is who."

Momi pulled out two photographs and showed them to Sergei.

"The one with the bald spot"—Sergei pointed at one of the photos—"is Ben-Gurion. The second may be Imber, but I'm not sure."

"You don't know what the composer of the national anthem looks like?" Momi asked in surprise.

"No. His picture has never appeared in the newspapers we get from Israel."

"He's right," Momi whispered to Professor Willotzky, the third member of the current "tribunal." "The average Jew will always recognize a picture of Ben-Gurion, but not Imber."

"I will now give you a list of names." Momi addressed himself again to Sergei. "I'd like you to tell me which one is not a Jewish novelist: Shalom Aleichem, Mendele Mocher Sefarim, Bialik, Alterman…"

Sergei broke in. "Alterman. He's a poet."

"Good. Tell me, please, what you know about Alterman."

Sergei Radinov promptly spewed forth an impressive litany of information about the well-known Israeli poet, including the fact that he was a drunkard who'd written many of his poems while under the influence of alcohol.

Momi returned the floor to his wife.

"Tell me, please, what your grandfather ate on Tishah B'Av. Do you remember that holiday?"

"First of all, it's a fast day, not a holiday," Sergei said with a hidden smile. "But if you're referring to the meal before the fast, he used to eat a hard-boiled egg dipped in some ashes."

The comprehensive test lasted several more hours. Sergei Radinov displayed a wide-ranging knowledge of different areas of Judaism. He did not know Jewish law and could not serve as a rabbi, but with respect to anything touching on Jewish folklore and custom, he looked exactly like a man who'd grown up with a mitzvah-observant Jewish grandfather.

Although Momi did not become an instant favorite with Anna's father, he was accepted without great opposition. The "Jewish education" that Anna had given him allowed him to present himself as the son of Jewishly-conscious parents, and if Anna's father suspected that things weren't exactly what they seemed, life in the Soviet Union had taught him that it was best to keep his thoughts to himself. He was surprised to find his daughter prepared to have a Jewish wedding ceremony, apart from the civil marriage procedure, but he kept his surprise to himself as well. More than once, Anna and Momi invited her father to visit them in their flat—the same one that Momi had previously shared with Ali, the Iranian—but her father, without offering a reason, refused to come.

A full year would pass, a year of work and the successful training of approximately twenty agents, before Professor Willotzky would drop a bombshell on the couple's heads.

T HE YEAR 1978 WAS A STORMY ONE IN ISRAEL. IN THE COURSE of his work, Momi found himself following the news: On the coastal highway, a terrorist attack took the lives of 35 people; Anatoly Natan Sharansky, the famous *refusenik*, was sentenced by the Soviet Union to 13 years in prison; the Nobel Peace Prize was awarded to Menachem Begin, Anwar Sadat, and Jimmy Carter, and in Tel Aviv a new museum was erected, known as "Beit HaTefutzot."

One day, Professor Willotzky asked Momi and Anna to come to his office at the end of their workday.

"Good evening to the young couple," the professor greeted them when they walked in. "Believe me, if they ever kick me out of the KGB, I could become a first-class matchmaker. I see that you're both very pleased with my match, aren't you?"

Anna blushed slightly, while Momi said with a smile, "Comrade Willotzky, as in every project you undertake, you have racked up another dizzying success."

"Sit down, sit down," Professor Willotzky said. His expression grew sober, a signal that the small talk was over and it was time to turn to work.

"What do you think of Number 6?" he asked.

Agent Number 6 was Alexander Kittin.

"Number 6?" Momi said. "He's the best of the lot. A very talented boy with wonderful intuition, a stunning grasp and a personal charisma that I've never seen paralleled. He'll do a good job—I have no doubt of that."

Professor Willotzky tilted his head and compressed his lips in concern.

Alexander Kittin was the sixth in the most recent round of agents that Momi and Anna had trained. In contrast to all the rest, he was a genuine Jew and brought with him a bit of knowledge from his grandfather's home. Willotzky had demanded that his training be faultless. After his stint in the "School for Foreign Cultures," he would be called upon to become absorbed into the Jewish community in Kiev and to make sure he became known as a *refusenik* who participated in anti-government demonstrations. Only afterward would he be sent to Israel, to serve his true motherland—the Soviet Union—from there.

"I've worked with him less," said Anna, "but I share Momi's excitement about him. He's one of a kind."

Alexander Kittin had needed less of Anna's instruction. From a professional standpoint it was preferable to leave him with his partial knowledge of Judaism, so typical of young Jews in Russia. It looked more natural. Momi, on the other hand, had worked hard with him on the Israeli part.

Alexander Kittin and his five fellow agents had arrived at the "School for Foreign Cultures" six months earlier.

Professor Willotzky had introduced them to Anna and Momi. Then, when the six had left the room, he had remarked, "Who knows? Perhaps you'll be neighbors with one of them one day."

Anna's senses went on high alert. This remark of Willotzky's had not been idle.

"Neighbors? Where?" she asked cautiously.

Willotzky smiled with pleasure. That Anna Aranowich was sharp as a razor...

"In... Israel, for example," he replied.

Momi's heart froze in his chest.

"In Israel?" Anna asked.

"We want to send you two to Israel," the professor explained.

"Me? To Israel?" Momi managed the words with visible difficulty. Not long before, he had been rescued from imprisonment in his native country. Professor Willotzky himself had saved him at the last moment, and returned the plane to Kiev at the cost of a highly unpleasant international incident. And now he was proposing to send him back there?

"I am not talking about a long-term stay. Just two or three years," the professor said.

"Me? To Israel?" Momi repeated, still in shock.

"I am aware of the great risks," said Professor Willotzky, "but we need you in Israel. You will have to carry out a mission there that cannot be accomplished from the Soviet Union. Discussions about this have been held in the highest circles. You will not be surprised if I tell you that additional tests of your loyalty have been conducted, and both of you passed them with flying colors. Therefore, I propose the task."

"Propose?" Anna asked.

"Yes. This is a proposal, not an order. You, Anna, would not be taking an especially great risk—but you, Momi, would be walking into danger. Therefore, you must be the one to make the decision. People know you in Israel: your friends from the kibbutz, soldiers from the army, people acquainted with your adoptive parents. You would have to change your appearance in some way."

Momi looked at Anna, and then at Professor Willotzky. "Two or three years, you said?"

"Perhaps less. There will be a project for you to complete, and then you can return."

"And my father will certainly remain here," Anna said.

Professor Willotzky nodded his head in feigned sorrow. "Both of you know the usual arrangements. This is nothing personal against you."

Momi and Anna did know the usual arrangements. Every agent who went out into the West had to have a sufficiently compelling reason to return to the Soviet Union. People with a wavering ideological backbone could always succumb to the lures of the West and decide to stay. The KGB wanted to spare them the ambivalence.

"Your father will also get a 'candy,'" Willotzky added. "When you return here, he will receive permission to immigrate to Israel."

"I'm not sure I want to give him that gift," Anna said coolly.

"You, too," the professor told Momi, "will have a small whip to constantly remind you who you are working for. I refer to your old friend—I'm sure you remember him—Zalman Berkovitch, who served in the army with you and also served us faithfully for a period of time."

Momi's eyes widened again. "Zalman Berkovitch is in Israel?"

"Yes, indeed. Unfortunately, he is not enjoying good emotional health. We were not able to restore him to precisely the condition in which we took him. But he is sane enough to point you out on the street. Another reason for you to change your appearance."

Nothing about this boded good to Momi, but he forced himself to smile. "I salute you, Professor Willotzky, on your long-range vision."

The professor nodded his thanks. "This is a project that I've worked on for a long time, and I'm glad that the two of you are cooperating. When can you give me an answer?"

"A positive answer will be given tomorrow," Anna said. Professor Willotzky smiled again.

"Of course, I'm not talking about an immediate departure. This is something that must be constructed carefully," he told them. "I hope that all six candidates will prove themselves. The plan is that, six months from now, you will be settled in Israel."

"I'm not going back there. Let that be clear!" Momi shouted at Anna. "If *you* want to—go ahead. I'll wait for you here. Tomorrow, I'm planning to give Willotzky a definitely *negative* answer."

"Don't shout." Anna peeked through the kitchen door, her eye glancing warningly at the connecting wall. Their next-door neighbors always pricked up their ears to hear their conversation.

Momi and Anna were in their eighth-floor flat with its view of Marinsky Park. She was fixing supper, while he paced the living room, angry and upset. All the way home from work they'd argued and debated the issue, pro and con, with Anna clearly on the side of giving Willotzky a positive answer while Momi wavered between an absolute negative and a partial retreat.

"Do you think I could be *there* without visiting the kibbutz?" Momi asked. "Without seeing my parents? It's simply inhuman to ask such a thing."

Anna chuckled dismissively. "You haven't seen them for four years now. So you won't see them for another two."

"It's not the same thing, and you know it!"

Anna cracked open two eggs and poured them into the pan.

"And I'm not even talking about the danger that I'll be discovered. There are thousands of people in Israel who know me: friends, soldiers from the past... People know me from all kinds of places. Why does it have to be me? Doesn't Willotzky have enough other people to send?"

"If he had enough people, he would send them."

"And don't forget that Shin-Bet man from the plane," Momi continued. "He saw me, and maybe even took a picture of me."

"Don't worry, you won't be discovered. No one will recognize you. Didn't you hear what Willotzky suggested?"

Momi grimaced. "Plastic surgery? I'm not having an operation."

"Why not? I know several agents who had that kind of surgery, and it went fine. They lift the cheekbones, make the jaw a bit more square, change the chin—and you're a different person."

"I'm not having an operation!"

"What are you afraid of?" Anna asked.

"I'm not afraid of anything!" Momi looked at his reflection in the mirror that hung in the hall. "I like my face and have no desire to go around for the rest of my life with a strange one."

"Afterward, you can have another operation, to restore your original face," Anna said. "I can introduce you to someone who did that. You can hardly tell."

"*Hardly* tell," Momi snapped. "Thank you very much. I'll pass. He'll have to find some other candidate."

Silence fell in the apartment. Momi stood at the window gazing down at the street below. Snow covered the sidewalks. The trees stood bare and shivering in the cold. A woman wrapped in a thick coat walked past, dragging two tired and well-bundled children by their hands. In Israel right now, the sun was shining and cheerful. In Israel, children were playing in the streets and the sound of their merriment filled the air.

Anna opened the refrigerator, removed a bottle of milk, and examined it. The amount that remained would barely be enough for two cups of coffee. For several days now, the shops had been out of milk—even the shops for the privileged. Vegetables and other food products were also in shorter supply than usual. In Israel, she had heard from Momi, one could enjoy a plethora of fresh produce and comfortable living conditions—all in the cause of furthering the Revolution and serving the Party.

They ate in silence, each of them lost in thought.

"I have an idea," Anna said suddenly. "What if you simply grow a beard?"

Momi stared at her in astonishment.

"A beard? Me?"

"Yes, why not? A beard can conceal the lines of your face and change your look completely. Don't forget, Momi, that you've also gained some weight since you came here. People over there remember you with a narrower face."

Momi looked at himself in the mirror and stroked his chin.

"Grow a beard…" he murmured, as though to himself.

"Try," Anna urged. "Let's see what it does for you. It's possible that even with a beard you'd have to fix your nose or the eyes, but those are small things. The main parts, like the jaw, lips, and cheeks, would be covered up."

"Who goes around with a beard these days?" Momi protested. "That itself attracts attention. A young person growing a wild beard…"

"Why? Look at my father."

"Your father? He's old."

"My father didn't grow his beard because he's old, but because he's religious."

Momi was quiet for a long moment.

"Are you suggesting that…" he asked hesitantly.

"Yes. Absolutely," Anna said with emphasis.

"You're suggesting that we live in Israel with religious people?"

"Why not? We'll live in a religious neighborhood and lead a religious lifestyle. We both know how to do that. You couldn't ask for any better camouflage than that."

Momi leaned back, neglecting his meal. Slowly, he said, "We may look religious to secular people, but in a group of religious people we'd be exposed right away."

"So we'll present ourselves as *ba'alei teshuvah*. You know that there's a big wave of *ba'alei teshuvah* in Israel these days. That way, we can acclimate ourselves gradually into the religious lifestyle, without arousing suspicion."

"*Ba'alei teshuvah* from the Soviet Union?"

"No," Anna decided. "That's too complicated. You don't have a Russian cultural background, and the first genuine Russian you meet might see through you. We'll present ourselves as Israelis, or… We'll think of something. But I, in any case, will have to get rid of my Russian accent."

"Can you do that?"

Anna smiled craftily. "Is there anything I *can't* do, Momi?"

Momi pretended to ponder the question. "Nothing that I can think of at the moment," he admitted.

"Okay. Tomorrow, stop shaving. Look at what you'll be saving! Ten precious minutes every morning…"

Professor Willotzky liked the idea. "Hiding in an ultra-Orthodox community is brilliant," he said. Momi's beard would grow enough in the next six months to change his appearance, and when he put on a *kippah* and a pair of glasses, not even his own mother would recognize him. They would also have to change their name to suit their surroundings. He would be called Shlomo Kohlberg, and she would change "Anna" to "Chana."

It would be a few months before they could acquire an apartment, Anna/Chana told Momi/Shlomo, because they would have to start like newcomers. Each one would join a separate group that catered to the newly observant. In time, they would make sure to be introduced by some matchmaker, as was the accepted practice in ultra-Orthodox circles. They would go the whole route: an engagement, a wedding, and *sheva berachos*, after which they'd begin living like a married couple again.

None of their neighbors or acquaintances would suspect that the pleasant, newly religious couple was actually an active Soviet spy cell, operating secretly in the heart of the State of Israel.

Modiin Illit, 5772 / 2011

AVREIMI KOHLBERG WAS SURPRISED TO SEE HIS BROTHER waiting for him in front of his building when he set out for Shacharis at dawn.

"Where were you?" Chezky demanded angrily.

"Sorry, sorry, sorry," Avreimi said with genuine distress. "I came home late last night and didn't turn on my phone."

"I thought something happened to you!" Chezky shouted, still recovering from his worry. "I thought that he killed you, too!"

"Who?"

"Itzik Peled. Who else?"

"Tell me, are you sane?" Avreimi snapped.

"I'm perfectly sane. *I'm* not going to be friendly to someone who betrayed my father, or hang around him for hours and hours."

Avreimi tucked his tallis-tefillin bag under his arm in marked reproof, and began striding in the direction of shul.

"Why weren't you available on the phone?" Chezky asked, following him. "When did you get back from Yerushalayim? What did he try to 'sell' you there?"

Avreimi responded to the questions in order. "You know that he always turns off phones in his office. I got back on the last bus. And I'll tell you what he 'sold' me—in detail—right after *davening*."

"Avreimi, you're so gullible! Gullible! Gullible!" Chezky yelled, when his brother finished relating what Itzik Peled had told him the previous evening.

They were standing in the shul's rear courtyard. Both of them were late for their respective studies, but they had no sense of the passage of time.

"Look how he turned your head," Chezky said. He began to enumerate on his fingers: "First: Abba was a spy, a KGB officer, and as cruel as some Russian Cossack. Two: Ima was also an officer in the KGB, a sly and clever operator. Three: Even poor old Zalman Berkovitch was a Soviet tool whose purpose was to make sure Abba didn't turn traitor. Four: Abba and Ima ran a daring spy cell consisting of six spies. Only Itzik Peled comes out smelling sweeter than roses—a fine, upstanding Jew. Truly one of the righteous pillars of the world!"

Avreimi smiled slightly. It was good to see Chezky holding onto his sense of humor even in these trying times.

"So maybe you can explain to me, my dear brother," Chezky continued, "what Itzik Peled was doing there, on Ashtorei HaParchi, a minute before Abba died?"

Avreimi had an answer. Itzik had proved that someone had made sure they'd see the video clip from Weill's camera, and had also explained that it was possible to edit any video to show whatever one wanted.

Chezky listened to his brother with suspicious patience.

"In that case," he asked, "how was it that coincidentally, with astounding *Hashgachah Pratis*, out of all the people in the world, it was Itzik's son-in-law Moshe Sotzkover who was the first one to treat Abba? Treatment that, of course, didn't succeed—since, as you know, our father is now lying in Har HaMenuchos!"

Avreimi felt as if someone had shoved a powerful fist into his solar plexus. He turned completely pale and turned speechless. *Moshe Sotzkover… Why didn't I think of that?* What was he doing there? And it was Moshe who'd directed them to Itzik when they came to him…

"We have to ask Itzik," he managed to say.

Chezky had to forcibly restrain himself from attacking his brother. He gritted his teeth and adjured himself to calm down so that the words would emerge in a rational fashion.

"I'm through with Itzik," he told his brother. "I already decided that yesterday. I'm going to see Polowitz now. If you want to come—come."

Avreimi thought for a long moment.

"I just want to stop off at home, to put back my tefillin and eat something."

Irritably Chezky looked at his watch. "I'm catching the nine o'clock bus," he hissed between his teeth. "If you're not there, I'm not waiting."

On the bus, Avreimi lowered his voice so that his fellow passengers wouldn't hear him.

"I'll tell you what Itzik told me about Polowitz," he said to Chezky. "You can decide whether or not to believe it."

"I can tell you right now that I *don't* believe it. But let's hear." Chezky leaned back in his seat.

"So, it's like this. He's nearly 90, but Itzik claims that he's really pretending and is not senile at all. He was born in England and has been living here all this time as a tourist, not a resident of Israel. Back in Britain, he was a longtime member of the local Communist Party—there is such a thing—and despite his beard and his rabbinic look, he went to the Soviet Union even during the times when it was sealed off to citizens of the West."

"In other words, Itzik Peled claims that Polowitz is a spy?" Chezky asked. "A *Russian* spy?"

"This is what he said about him: 'He's not a spy. He's the spies' *rabbi.*'"

From the station at Bar-Ilan they took a taxi. Chezky announced that he would pay. They got out on Rechov Bayit Vegan, a few dozen yards from Yechezkel Polowitz's house.

"We have to be careful," Avreimi warned. Chezky nodded his agreement.

The brothers did not exchange a word, but their hearts pounded with strong emotion as they came to within one building of the address they wanted.

"Let's peek in from the adjoining yard," Avreimi suggested.

The two entered the yard of the neighboring building and approached the bushes that separated the two yards. In one spot the foliage was thinner, and they could peer through unseen.

The expensive, shiny car was parked in all its glory in the parking area beneath the building.

"You see?" Chezky hissed. "That's the car!"

Avreimi looked at the vehicle and tried to compare it to the one they'd seen in the video clip. It was a Chevrolet, though a model that was not so well-known, and painted two colors: the bottom portion was black while the top was beige. On the car's roof were two short antennae.

"Maybe we should take a picture of the car," Chezky said, and took out his phone.

"Just don't let anyone see the flash."

"It's the middle of the day. Who's going to see a flash?"

A second later, neither of them was thinking about pictures or about the car.

The lobby door opened and a figure emerged. The parking lot, between the concrete columns, was relatively dim compared to the sunlit yard in which they stood. At first, they were unable to identify the figure. But then it stepped out into the light, and the brothers' hearts froze.

"It's Ima," Chezky whispered, grabbing Avreimi's sleeve.

Avreimi was incapable of saying a word. His mouth hung open and his hand covered it, as though to prevent a scream from bursting out.

"What is she doing here?" he finally managed to ask.

Chezky didn't answer. He saw now that their mother was crying. She paused for a moment and wiped her eyes with a tissue. Then she straightened and continued walking along the path leading from the lobby to the front gate.

"Where is she going?" Chezky whispered.

He had his answer at once. On the street, right at the gate, waited a high, black commercial vehicle with a nearly-silent engine. The moment their mother came near, a sliding door opened.

A man sitting inside stuck out a hand to help her in, but their mother rejected the help.

"*Nyet, spasiba* (no, thank you)," she said in Russian, while still standing on the sidewalk.

The man spoke a few words, also in Russian.

Their mother replied, a quick Russian sentence, and then climbed inside.

The sliding door closed behind her, and the black car drove quickly away.

"Did you hear? Did you hear? She spoke Russian!" Avreimi told Chezky. But his brother was no longer beside him. He'd shot out of his place and raced like a madman to the gate.

Avreimi hurried after him. "Chezky, where are you going? What are you doing?" he cried.

Chezky was still holding his phone in front of him, poised to take a picture. He leaped over a low stone wall and then the three steps leading to the street, pressing the camera button the entire time.

The black commercial vehicle disappeared around a bend in the street. Its taillights flickered red for a few more seconds and then vanished from view—along with their mother.

Avreimi, too, watched it from the gate, breathing hard. He found Chezky standing on the pavement, reviewing the pictures he had managed to take.

"It's a Mercedes Vito, the new model," he muttered to himself while enlarging one of the photos on the screen and studying it closely. "But you can't see the number."

Both brothers stood on the pavement, just a few yards from Yechezkel Polowitz's house. "Let's go back to the yard," Avreimi said. "We don't want him to see us."

Chezky followed his brother, still flipping through his photos.

"We have to go back to Itzik Peled," Avreimi announced.

Chezky continued to focus on the pictures. "Ah—here! This one's a little bigger." He showed Avreimi his phone screen. "Look at the color of that number."

The license tag was not the customary yellow, but white.

"What's a white tag?" Chezky asked. "I think it means a diplomatic vehicle or foreign resident. We can find out…"

"We have to talk to Itzik Peled," Avreimi repeated.

Chezky walked without speaking toward the lobby of the adjoining building.

"Do you hear what I'm saying?" Avreimi raised his voice slightly. "We have to talk to Itzik!"

Chezky turned to him.

"Why?" he asked innocently.

"*Why?*" Avreimi burst out. "You're asking why? They kidnaped Ima, she's talking Russian—what more do you need?"

Chezky was not ready to give in so fast. "So he was right about one thing. So what?" he said. Then, after consideration, he added, "Actually, do you accept Itzik's view that Abba and Ima were spies? It's not that clear to me. Maybe she was just born in Russia? Anyway, who said they kidnaped Ima? Maybe she went of her own free will."

Avreimi thought he would explode in the face of his brother's obstinacy. "I don't know anything," he snapped. "But he's the only one who can help!"

"Help?" Chezky repeated bitterly. "The way he 'helped' Abba? There are some people I don't want any help from."

"So what do we do? Go to the police?"

"I trust the average policeman," Chezky retorted, "more than I trust Itzik Peled."

"Really, Chezky…"

"Really. Really."

Avreimi wondered who could help them.

"Listen," he said, trying a different tack. "I came here with you— so you come to Itzik with me."

Chezky winked mockingly at his brother. "Avreimi, you didn't come *with* me. You came to keep an eye on me."

Avreimi's help came from an unexpected source. His phone

rang. He glanced at the screen—and was stunned.

"It's Ima," he said hoarsely

"Put it on speakerphone," Chezky urged.

Avreimi answered the call and pressed the speaker button. "Ima?"

It wasn't his mother, but Miri, their seventeen-year-old sister. She sounded close to tears.

"Avreimi, where are you?" she asked.

"Why are you calling from Ima's phone?" Avreimi countered with a question of his own. "Are you with Ima?"

"No," Miri said. "She left her phone here and went out."

"And what happened?"

"Someone came to the house looking for her. He said it was urgent."

"Where are you?"

"I couldn't call from home. The phone is in the living room and he's sitting there."

"Who is he? What does he look like?"

"I don't know. He only speaks English." Miri sounded like she was falling apart. "He said it's critical that he speak to Ima."

"Speak to her? About what?"

"I don't know! Can you talk to him? Where is Ima? Can you come here? Where are you? I'm scared…"

"Did he threaten you? Does he look dangerous?" Avreimi pressed.

"No, he's polite. But, I don't know… the children are here and Ima disappeared…"

"Wait a minute." Avreimi exchanged a quick look with Chezky.

"Give it to me," Chezky said, and took the phone from his brother.

"Miri, this is Chezky. I'm here with Avreimi, it doesn't matter why. Put the man on the phone."

After three sentences in English, Chezky nodded at Avreimi. Yes, it was the same English-speaker who'd come to the house during their *shivah* week, and who'd escaped as fast as he could when he heard that their father was dead. So he had finally gathered the courage to return for another visit…

MIRI GREETED AVREIMI AND CHEZKY AT THE DOOR, SLIGHTLY calmer than she had been on the phone. She had sent the younger children to their neighbor, Mrs. Fink, and left the front door open while she remained alone with their unknown visitor. At first he tried to strike up a conversation, but she had made it clear that she was not prepared to say one word until her brothers were there. She kept herself busy in the kitchen—demonstrating that she was present, but careful not to make eye contact.

"*Shalom*," Avreimi and Chezky called, walking in.

The stranger stood up to greet them. Chezky shook his hand and looked him over. Yes, this was the man with whom he had spoken during the *shivah*. He was dressed from head to toe in the pinnacle of British elegance and exuded the air of a businessman or foreign diplomat.

They all sat down at the table. Chezky explained to the stranger that his brother did not speak English, and he would therefore have to pause from time to time in their talk to translate.

"I can translate," Miri said from the doorway.

The brothers looked at each other. They hadn't taken into account their sister's presence. What to do with her? She was already here; it was impossible to simply send her away... Actually, this wasn't so bad. She was no longer a child. She was a young woman of seventeen, and the past three weeks had matured her even more.

"Come sit down," Chezky told her in Hebrew. He lowered his voice. "There are a few new things that we've learned over the past few days. We'll explain later."

Unexpectedly, Miri did not appear surprised.

"I've discovered some strange things, too." She lowered her eyes. "I really meant to talk to you two."

"Like what, for instance?" Chezky asked in a whisper.

"Let's do this later, okay?" Avreimi broke in. "Let's first hear what our guest has to say."

The three Kohlberg siblings turned to look at the British gentleman sitting with hands folded on the table, waiting patiently.

He cleared his throat. "I've come here because your mother is in danger," he said, and waited for Miri to translate his words for Avreimi.

"Not only is *she* in danger, but so are you," the man continued. "You are dealing with people who care very little for human life. They are trying to gain time by making you go around in circles. Every hour that passes increases the danger, but no one has bothered to tell you that. Three-and-a-half weeks have passed since your father's death—and tomorrow it may all blow up."

"What happens tomorrow? What may 'blow up'?" Chezky and Miri asked in one voice.

The Englishman stroked his chin in thought.

"Perhaps I should introduce myself first," he said. "My name is Sean Mackenzie. I am an official representative of MI6, Britain's secret intelligence service. My area of interest is Iran. In the past, I served in the British Embassy at Teheran, and in recent years I've been following events from London..."

"Just a minute," Chezky interrupted. "Leave the history. What blowup are you talking about? What's going to happen tomorrow?"

Mackenzie seemed slightly taken aback by this example of Israeli chutzpah.

"What do you know about your father?" he asked carefully.

Chezky tried to say something, but Avreimi—after hearing the question translated by Miri—quickly cut him off. "Sir, you have come to our home and we welcome you. We'd be happy to hear what *you* have to say." Miri translated for Mackenzie.

Chezky bit his lip, kicking himself for his impulsivity.

"You said that we have one day. What do you mean?" Avreimi asked, with Miri's assistance.

"Your father was an exceptionally clever man," Sean Mackenzie replied. "And he didn't rely on anyone else in the world. You are aware that he... once worked in the Soviet Union?"

"We heard something like that," Chezky said evasively, sending a quick glance at Miri to make sure she didn't fall off her chair.

"Then you must surely know that your mother worked with him."

Chezky was careful to avoid Avreimi's eyes.

"Well, dating from that period, your parents were in possession of highly classified information. Information that governments and various intelligence bureaus would give a great deal to get their hands on."

"Like what, for example?"

Sean Mackenzie chuckled. "You don't really expect me to tell you that," he told Chezky. "In any case, a number of countries are mixed up in this business: Britain—through the MI6 that I represent—the Ukrainian SBU that inherited the former Soviet KGB, and the Israeli Shin-Bet."

He waited for Miri to translate his answer for Avreimi, and then continued. "Your father set up a clever web of deterrents. Each of the three intelligence services knew that should Shlomo Kohlberg be harmed, that service could expect a reprisal within a month, at most."

"How?"

"He established a 'coiled spring' mechanism. You must know that your father was a very talented computer programmer. He created a small program, encrypted and protected, that was primed to send an electronic message on a certain future date. When that date arrived, the message would be sent out unless it was canceled beforehand. The only one who knew the password was your father. Therefore, all those involved in this matter had an overriding interest in keeping him alive."

"Why? What was in that message?"

"Your father had prepared a separate threat for each intelligence service. He could threaten the Ukrainians, for instance, by saying that he would expose their agents planted in the United States, and so on. The emails were addressed to the Prime Minister's office, as well as the Foreign Minister and the intelligence services. That way, your father created a three-sided balance of fear: Ukraine, Britain and Israel all had an interest in keeping him alive and well. Anyone who harmed him would seal his own fate, because at the appointed time for the 'coiled spring' to be activated, there would be no one to stop it—and the messages would make their way to their destinations."

The three Kohlbergs heard what Sean Mackenzie was telling them, but their minds refused to believe it. They knew their father as a man who worked hard to earn a living and set aside times for learning Torah. A man who sat at the head of the Shabbos table, sang *zemiros,* and spoke words of Torah… not some sort of secret agent who might pop up from the pages of a thriller…

Sean Mackenzie went on with his story. "The last time your father 'sprung the coil' was a few days before his death, on Tuesday night. He died on Sunday, and since then there's been no one to stop the messages from being sent out. Twenty-nine days have passed since then. The thirty days will end at noon tomorrow—and then several fateful emails will go out to several addresses."

"So what will happen?" asked Miri. "Will World War Three break out?"

Sean Mackenzie smiled briefly, and then shook his head like a person distressed in advance over what he was about to say.

"What will happen is that a government or two in the world may fall, and several people will be arrested and thrown into jail.

But that doesn't have to interest you. From your perspective, just one thing will happen: The whole world will know that Shlomo Kohlberg, your father, was a KGB officer and spied for the Soviet Union along with his wife. You can certainly imagine the implications of such publicity."

"Nonsense!" Avreimi said. "Who would believe such a thing?" But his bold words fooled no one—including himself.

"If you say that our father… created a three-way balance of fear, as you put it," said Miri, "that would mean that… no one harmed him. Right?"

A pained expression rose to Sean Mackenzie's face. "It's not pleasant to have to say this, but the most reasonable explanation is that they *did* harm him."

"Who?"

"The prime suspect is Ukraine. But Israel was a partner in the crime."

The three young people stared at him in confusion.

"Israel?"

"Israel," affirmed Sean Mackenzie. "Very simply, your father's deterrent with regard to Israel lost some of its power recently, so Israel no longer had any reason to protect him. For the same reason, incidentally, the Shin-Bet has a reason to try to drag out the time until tomorrow. They want those emails to be sent out and to damage the other parties—Britain and Ukraine. You must know that your own interests run counter to those of the Shin-Bet. They'd like to lull you to sleep."

"What about Ukraine? Why would she want to hurt herself?"

"Are you familiar with the expression, 'Let me die together with the Philistines'? The Ukrainians are prepared to absorb a certain amount of damage, as long as they can cause Britain a greater one."

Avreimi, Chezky, and Miri gaped at the man seated at the head of the table, in their father's usual place, who had just dropped a megaton bomb on them without the slightest warning.

"So… what can we do?" Avreimi finally asked.

Sean Mackenzie tightened his lips sadly. "The only entity that could save the situation is your mother. But she is not prepared to talk to us. It's a pity she's decided to cooperate with the Ukrainians…"

"She didn't *decide* to cooperate with them," Avreimi said, more in hope than in knowledge. "They kidnaped her…"

Once again, he heard the Russian sentences that his mother had spoken to the man in the black car. If he tried hard, he could somehow interpret events so that she had been forced to get into the car…

The next sounds were not imaginary, but all too real: a rapid thumping on the front door. The three Kohlbergs exchanged alarmed looks, but the thumpers did not wait for an invitation. The door flew open. In the doorway stood Itzik Peled, accompanied by two muscular security guards.

All eyes were fixed in surprise and confusion on the unexpected guests.

All eyes? Not exactly. Avreimi Kohlberg took the time to send a fleeting glance at Sean Mackenzie, at the head of the table. The secret agent's face was as calm and expressionless as before. Not a muscle twitched. It was Itzik Peled who seemed taken aback by what he saw in the apartment.

His two companions remained on either side of the front door, like sentinels at a gate. Itzik Peled advanced a few steps until he was face to face with the Englishman, with the table between them.

"Nice to meet you," he said in a frigid voice.

Chezky watched the spectacle in astonishment, and then turned to throw a look of rebuke at Avreimi. *You see?* He said without words. *Itzik* knows *Mackenzie! What a liar he is!* When they'd shown him Mackenzie on the video clip, passing behind their father on Rechov Malchei Yisrael, Itzik had given no indication that he recognized the man.

Avreimi did not understand what Mackenzie answered in English, but he certainly registered the fact that this was not the first time the two had met—or that they were not exactly pleased to see one another. They both looked tense, and there was no trace of a smile on either face.

An uneasy silence stretched for a moment, and then Itzik pulled out one of the empty chairs. "Mind if I join the conversation?" Without waiting for an answer, he sat down at the foot of the table, facing the Englishman.

"Continue, please," he said mockingly to Mackenzie. "Don't let me interrupt."

Another minute passed, and then, with a forced smile, Sean Mackenzie stood up.

"I believe I've already said most of what I came here to say," he told Avreimi, Chezky and Miri.

He took a business card from the pocket of his suit jacket and placed it in the center of the table. "If you need my help, you can call this number at any time."

Itzik's hand shot out and seized the card. He studied it with a smile.

"Same unit, eh?" he smiled cynically at the Englishman. "The Iranian desk… But you've been promoted, I see."

Mackenzie replied with a furious grimace in the guise of a smile.

He shook Avreimi and Chezky's hands, nodded to Miri, and walked to the door.

The two sentinels stirred, as though to stop him, but a quick gesture from Itzik made them step aside and allow him to pass.

"I would have been happy to detain him," Itzik explained to the three Kohlbergs, "but he is an official British representative and free to move around the country without restraint."

"He said some very serious things," Avreimi told Itzik. "He blames the Shin-Bet in… my father's death. He says that Israel had an interest in harming him."

Itzik motioned for the two bodyguards to leave. "Wait for me downstairs," he ordered.

Head bowed, he devoted a long moment to thought. Only then did Chezky and Avreimi realize that their sister was weeping. She was still shaken from the last sentence that had been spoken before the newcomers burst in.

"Who kidnaped Ima?" she asked Avreimi, in tears.

Itzik's head snapped up. "What do you mean, 'kidnaped Ima'?" he asked sharply.

"She went off with some Russian," Avreimi said quietly.

Itzik jumped to his feet. "What are you talking about?"

"We... went to Yechezkel Polowitz's house," Avreimi began.

"Yechezkel Polowitz! Why did you go there? What were you looking for?"

"He was... the administrator of the orphanage..."

"I *know* who Polowitz is!" Itzik interrupted. "But why did you go see him? What business do you have with him?"

Avreimi gestured weakly toward his brother.

"*I* wanted to go," Chezky announced.

"And why, if I may ask?"

"Why difference is it to you?"

Itzik narrowed one eye and gazed at Chezky with open menace.

"Anyway," Avreimi said, after a long moment, "she got into a black car and talked to someone inside. In Russian."

"They were Ukrainians," Miri added with a whimper.

"Ukrainians? Who told you that?"

"The British man said that Israel is working with the Ukrainians," Avreimi replied in his sister's place. He found it surreal to hear such words emerging from his mouth.

Itzik snorted. "I see he shared all the details with you. And how did that stranger manage to earn so much of your trust?"

The brothers answered with silence.

"After all, you know that he was also there, in Geulah, when your father died," Itzik continued relentlessly. "You saw him on the video clip. What makes him less suspect than me?"

Itzik gave the two brothers time to stew a bit in their own juices, and then went on: "Mackenzie is talking nonsense. He also has interests. And besides, anyone can lease a black car with a Russian driver."

Once again, the silence was thick with tension. No one volunteered to break it.

"Look." Itzik Peled softened his tone. "Your mother is a big girl. She knows what she's doing. Maybe she prefers to cooperate with the Ukrainians. Maybe she made some sort of a deal with them. How are the Ukrainians any worse than the British?"

Avreimi looked at Itzik, woebegone.

"That's comforting," he said bitterly. "That's really good news. She wasn't kidnaped. She went with them of her own free will…"

ITZIK PELED HAD NOTHING COMFORTING TO TELL THE THREE Kohlbergs. They sat before him looking the way they had on the first day of their week of mourning. Anything he might say would only upset them more.

A telephone vibrated in his pocket. He took it out, checked the screen—and an astonished expression crossed his face.

"Urgent call," he apologized, and stepped out to the balcony.

At first, no one broke the silence. They watched Itzik speaking on the phone and making decisive gestures, from time to time glancing at them through the glass that divided the living room from the balcony.

"You can't talk that way to Itzik," Avreimi scolded Chezky.

"I can talk however I want," Chezky retorted. "Don't tell me what to do."

Avreimi face darkened.

"But who is Yechezkel Polowitz?" Miri asked.

"We'll explain later," Avreimi told her.

The brothers continued watching Itzik as the latter conversed on the balcony. A few minutes later, he returned the phone to his pocket and stepped inside.

"Did your mother say anything to you before she left?" Itzik asked Miri, as though picking up their talk where they'd left it.

"She was upset today," Miri said, her tears finally drying. "She told me that she had to go out and didn't know when she would be back. Then she suddenly hugged me, in a way that's not so usual for her."

"That means she knew something," Avreimi said thoughtfully.

Miri's face suddenly crumpled. "I just remembered something else. She told me, 'Take good care of the children.' Now I understand those words in a different way…"

Her brothers were very worried. Itzik, on the other hand, appeared satisfied.

"I'd be interested in checking if she took her passport with her," he said.

Three pairs of eyes stared at him in shock.

"Our mother doesn't have a passport," Avreimi said for them all. "Our parents never left the country."

Itzik gave him an apologetic look.

"Maybe Chana Kohlberg had no passport—but Anna Aranowich certainly did," he said. "A Ukrainian passport, to be precise."

Chezky leaped up from his chair in anger. "Enough! Enough! I've had enough of this!" he yelled at Itzik. "Stop all these stories. Ukrainian passports, spy cells—what will you come up with next?"

Itzik leaned back and fixed Chezky with a penetrating look.

"You know what?" Chezky flared suddenly. "I want you to leave this house right now. You burst in without an invitation, and you're sitting here telling us old-wives' tales…"

Avreimi stood up and placed a soothing hand on his brother's shoulder. "Chezky, Itzik's not going. You're not chasing anyone out of here."

Chezky refused to be calmed. He shook off Avreimi's hand and began walking around the table. When he reached Itzik's chair, he grasped the back as though to toss him out.

"Good-bye. It's been a pleasure," he said, pointing at the door.

"Chezky, what are you doing?" Miri cried.

Chezky ignored her.

"Please go," he insisted, with a thump on Itzik's back in encouragement.

"*Chezky!*" Miri and Avreimi screamed.

Itzik slowly rose from his chair and stood at his full height, facing Chezky.

"Itzik, Itzik," Avreimi said in a placating tone. "You can stay."

Itzik paid no attention to him. His face was devoid of expression. He gazed directly into Chezky's furious eyes, and then raised his hand swiftly and gave Chezky's cheek a ringing slap.

Avreimi and Miri recoiled in alarm.

Stunned, Chezky touched his burning cheek.

Itzik's voice was cold and hard as steel. "Sit down!" he ordered Chezky, pointing at his chair.

Chezky tried for another moment to hold onto the shreds of his dignity. Itzik spoke again—a sharp command. "*Sit down*, I said!"

Chezky seemed to retreat into himself. He turned and walked obediently back to his seat.

For the first time, a flicker of emotion appeared on Itzik's face. He sat back down, a muscle in his jaw twitching. His efforts to control the tremor only made it more pronounced.

For a long moment, no one said a word. Chezky sat with a sullen face, tears sparkling in his eyes. Avreimi was quiet and solemn. Miri waited a beat and then stood up, went to the kitchen, and brought Chezky a glass of water.

When Itzik spoke, his voice was low.

"Do you have a ladder?" he asked.

"Yes, but Memelstein borrowed it," Miri said. "Our downstairs neighbors."

"Ask them to give it back," Itzik instructed.

Miri went to the door.

"What's the ladder for?" Avreimi asked—not so much because he wanted an answer, as in an effort to break the tension in the room.

"You'll see soon," Itzik said shortly.

Miri quickly returned and went to the utility porch off the kitchen. "They said they returned the ladder at lunchtime," she said in surprise. "Ima came and asked for it."

A minute later, her voice came back to them from the porch: "But it's not here!"

Itzik stood up. "Come with me," he said, and started for the master bedroom.

Avreimi and Miri followed him. Chezky straggled after them and stood waiting in the doorway.

"Here it is!" Miri exclaimed.

The ladder was leaning against the wall cupboard. On the bed was a pile of clothes and bed linens, as though a diligent housewife had been busy taking them down or putting them away. Itzik knew that this was intended to mislead them.

He moved one of the beds slightly, planted the ladder in the center of the room and climbed a few rungs. "Nice light fixture," he remarked.

Avreimi and Miri exchanged startled looks. The large fixture in their parents' room *was* unusual—not to mention odd. It had a round base fixed in the ceiling, its diameter about the size of a *shtreimel* box and its height about half that size. From the circle extended six short metal arms, each ending in a light bulb. When they'd been children, the Kohlbergs used to call the light fixture "the sun."

Itzik lifted his hand to one of the bulbs, and then paused and lowered his eyes as though he had decided to tell them what he was doing.

"This fixture was your parent's 'safe.'" He lightly turned one of the metal arms until a faint click was heard. Then he went to the opposite arm and turned it twice until two clicks were heard.

"There's a secret code here," he explained, as though there was a need for explanations.

Avreimi and Miri stood with dropped jaws, staring up at Itzik and trying to believe what was happening in front of their eyes. Chezky was surprised, too—but by something else: the door. The door of his parents' room, on which he was leaning, was different from the other doors in the house. How had he never noticed that before? It was heavy and solid—exactly like the door of Itzik's study. Had it always been this way, or had someone switched it at some point?

Itzik continued pursuing the code through the means of the fixture's arms. Avreimi tried to memorize the order, but became confused after the sixth turning.

"That's it," Itzik said after a few more seconds.

He placed his open palm under the fixture, and before their astonished eyes it split into two separate pieces: the narrow hoop from which the bulbs emerged remained fixed to the ceiling, while the circular box detached and landed gently in his outstretched hand.

Itzik Peled descended carefully, carrying the round safe. Avreimi and Miri, curious, moved closer, and even Chezky abandoned his post by the door. The safe resembled a round cookie tin, except that the walls were at least a centimeter thick.

Chezky hesitated, and then decided to risk another slap. "How do you know the secret code?" he asked.

Itzik was busy with the box. As he turned the screw-top lid a number of times, he countered with a rhetorical question of his own: "How do I know about the safe?"

All three Kohlbergs craned their necks when the lid was finally removed. Inside the round box lay a small booklet. Itzik picked it up and opened it.

"Your father's passport," he said, and handed it to Avreimi. "It was issued in Ukraine."

Avreimi opened the passport. Their father looked about twenty years younger in the photo. The pages were completely devoid of any stamps.

"What does this mean?" he asked, when he had finished flipping the pages.

"There was a second passport here—your mother's," Itzik said. "Earlier, I received a call from someone who explained the situation to me. Your mother had an airline ticket, made out to Anna Aranowich, of course. The flight was to Kiev, and it's due to lift off in a quarter of an hour."

The Kohlbergs stared at one another in shock.

"Then she went from Polowitz's house straight to the airport," Avreimi said. "It really *is* the Ukrainians—and they kidnaped her!"

Miri sat down on one of the beds, eyes bulging and both hands covering her mouth. What was happening here was beyond her capacity to handle.

"Can't you stop them?" she asked Itzik in a faint voice.

"I'm not sure you'll be happy to hear the answer," Itzik sighed. "But it seems to me that she's going of her own free will."

"Then can't you stop *her*?" The question burst from Chezky.

Itzik fingered the box for a few seconds as he thought.

"No," he said at last. "I can't stop her. I didn't mention this earlier, but your mother has worked for the Ukrainian Embassy in Israel for years."

"What?" Miri lifted tear-filled eyes. "She works in a school! She's a secretary there!"

"She's not really an embassy employee," Itzik explained. "She's most likely never even set foot there. This was simply an escape hatch that the Ukrainians gave your parents, in the event that the noose tightened around their necks."

"It already tightened around our father's," Chezky said.

Itzik nodded sorrowfully. "Anyway," he continued, "if I stop a foreign diplomat at the airport, it would cause an international incident. I'd need authorization from on high—the Foreign Minister, or even the Prime Minister himself."

A heavy silence descended on the room.

Itzik Peled climbed the ladder and replaced the cover of the fixture. The room again looked the way it always had.

"We're done here," he said. He turned toward the door.

"Just a minute," Chezky said behind his back. "How did you know to come here? How did you that the Englishman was here?"

"I knew," Itzik said curtly, and returned to the living room. The siblings lingered an extra moment in their parents' room.

"What nerve," Chezky said, his face suffused with anger. "To give me a slap like that, in our own house."

Miri silenced him with a pleading look.

"Not now," Avreimi said, when he saw that Chezky was still simmering. "We'll talk later."

Chezky bit his lip and swallowed the tears that threatened to spill from his eyes.

"Just one thing," he whispered quickly, trying to overcome the storm of emotion raging inside. "Did you see those bodyguards of his? Did you recognize the one on the left?"

"What are you talking about?" Avreimi asked.

"You remember when Yuri, Abba's manager at work, came during our *shivah*?"

"I remember vaguely."

"He came with two employees," Chezky said. "One of them is Itzik Peled's bodyguard.

"Really?"

"I'm positive."

"What does that mean?" Avreimi asked. "That Abba worked for… the Shin-Bet?"

Chezky shrugged. He didn't know anything anymore.

"One of the men in Abba's department, you say," Avreimi repeated slowly, as though trying to make sense of things. "He's one of Itzik's two bodyguards?"

Chezky nodded.

"Then either Abba worked for the Shin-Bet," Avreimi continued, working it out, "or Itzik is not a Shin-Bet agent, but works for whoever Abba worked for."

Miri's expression showed that she had something to add. But Itzik called them. He was ready to leave.

"We'll be in touch," he said before he went. Then he lifted a warning finger to Chezky. "And you—be careful around me. Clear?"

"You managed to get him angry," Avreimi admonished Chezky after Itzik Peled had gone.

Chezky rubbed his still-red cheek. "If a person kills a father, why shouldn't he smack the son?" he asked bitterly.

"Don't talk nonsense."

From the living room came the ring-tone of a cell phone.

"Hey, that's mine," Chezky said. "Do me a favor, Avreimi. Bring me the phone."

Avreimi did as he had been asked.

Chezky conducted a brief conversation on the phone. He didn't look happy.

"I have no strength for them," he sighed when he had disconnected. "That was from my school. They want to murder me. Since Abba, I've been absent a lot."

"Me, too," Avreimi said. "Especially in the last week."

"Do you really think that Itzik hurt Abba?" Miri asked.

"He was certainly part of the plot," Chezky answered unhesitatingly.

"Whose plot?"

Chezky wasn't all that clear on the subject, so he decided to diffuse the situation with a quip. "What do you want from me? I'm not only an orphan, I'm also an abused child. A little pity!"

Avreimi chuckled. He leaned closer to his brother and studied his face with feigned concern. The right cheek still bore the mark of the slap. "It's not so symmetrical," he said with mock-seriousness. "Want a smack on the other side, to even things up?"

Chezky smiled, too. The atmosphere thawed slightly, despite the complex and dismaying situation in which they found themselves.

"Is there anything to eat?" Avreimi asked, trying to warm things up even more. Miri went to the kitchen.

She opened the refrigerator. Suddenly, she cried, "Avreimi! Chezky!"

The two men ran to the kitchen. The freezer compartment stood open. Their sister gaped at them, stunned.

"What happened?" Chezky asked.

"Look. Ima prepared frozen meals for a week!"

The brother came closer to see. "She doesn't usually do that?" Avreimi asked.

"Of course not. Ima never freezes food ahead of time."

Avreimi stared into the freezer in shock. His mother, it seemed, had prepared well for her "kidnaping"...

He slumped down on one of the kitchen chairs. "Enough. I can't handle this." He gripped his head with his hands. "I'm starting to go crazy."

"Just starting?" Chezky put up water for coffee, got down a few cups, and found some cookies.

Soon the three were seated around the kitchen table, just as if they were the children of a happy family whose father had not died and whose mother had not taken part in some covert Ukrainian operation that seemed to be working hand in glove with the Shin-Bet...

"Tell me, Miri. What was it you started to say earlier?" Chezky asked. "What did you want to tell us?"

Miri finished her coffee. "Did you ever see Abba's office?"

"No. Never."

"I was there a few times. You know that Abba didn't like to eat outside the house—and certainly not pizza, falafel, and things like that. Sometimes Ima sent me over with food, when he forgot to bring some. He worked on Har HaChotzvim, Rechov Hertus 17, fifth floor."

"I'm guessing you saw Itzik Peled there," Chezky ventured.

"Actually, no," Miri said. "I didn't see him or anyone else. I would go into a kind of reception area where a secretary sat, and she would call Abba out."

"And?"

"A few days after the *shivah*, I went to Har HaChotzvim with a friend after school. She needed to bring her sister's portfolio to some advertising agency where her sister wanted to work. I didn't know the address ahead of time, and I suddenly realized that I was walking into the building where Abba used to work. My friend saw that I was emotional, but she didn't understand why. We took the elevator to the sixth floor, where she needed to go. When it was time to go back down, I asked if we could take the stairs. When we reached the fifth floor, I was shocked to see that Abba's workplace had disappeared!"

"Disappeared? What do you mean?"

"The door had a sign that said, 'For Rent,' and through the glass I saw that there was nothing inside."

Avreimi and Chezky had reached the point where nothing surprised them anymore.

"I don't know what I was thinking," Miri continued. "But when I saw a phone number on the sign, I jotted it down."

"Why?"

"No reason. . ."

"Well?"

"For a few days, I didn't do anything with it."

"Did you tell Ima?" Chezky asked.

Miri stopped to think.

"Actually…" she remembered, "I asked Ima something, but she didn't really pay attention."

"In short, you kept the number," Avreimi prompted.

"Yes. And a few days later I decided to call. I don't know why... Just an impulse, I guess. On the way home from school, I stopped at a public phone on Rechov Bar Ilan and dialed the number."

"Just like that?"

"I pretended that I wanted to rent the place."

"Nice," said Chezky. He couldn't stop himself from adding, "Ima would have been proud of you."

Avreimi threw him an angry look. Miri continued her story.

"A pleasant-sounding man answered. He said that he was with an office that rents apartments and offices. I tried to get some details from him: who'd had that office before, when did they leave, and exactly what they did there. He must have been bored, because he was ready to stay on the phone just to while away the time. He asked what I wanted to use the office for, and I made up some story about a graphics and advertising agency I was planning to open. I just wanted to get him into a conversation so he would give me some information. I asked, for example, if the previous renter had left behind any furniture or equipment, and who the building's other tenants were. I asked all kinds of questions.

"We spoke for about ten minutes, and then I suddenly noticed a secular man standing on the other side of the street, looking at me in a funny way. The phone was at the corner of Rechov Avitar HaCohen, just slightly before Rabbeinu Gershom, and the man was standing on Rechov Ohalei Yosef. It seemed to me that he was talking to himself. Afterwards, I realized that he was whispering into a kind of microphone, like the Shin-Bet people. That terrified me. I turned around and saw two other men who didn't fit into the neighborhood. They were walking toward me down Bar Ilan, from the direction of the bus stop. After a second, I heard a motorcycle ride up and stop in front of the big building—you know the one I mean? The building on the corner, with the courtyard. It was a police motorcycle of some kind."

"How scary," Chezky said, without a trace of the cynicism he had displayed just a minute earlier.

"I kept talking to the realtor," Miri went on, her voice trembling. "And then I saw, down the street in the direction of the Sanhedria intersection, a white car moving very fast. Someone in the back seat was looking at me.

"I hung up the phone, shaking with fear. I was in the heart of a religious neighborhood, just minutes from home, but I felt like a trapped animal. I looked up Rechov Avitar HaCohen—and suddenly there, too, on the sidewalk next to the clinic, was another motorcycle with two policemen.

"And then the phone rang. It was the realtor again. And he told me, "Miss, we got cut off so I called back the number you called from. When would you like to come see the property?"

"I was so scared, I couldn't say a word. After a second, I heard some whispering on the phone, and then he said—in a very different voice, very businesslike and decisive—'Okay, good-bye,' and hung up.

"At that same moment, like magic, all the people watching me, in every direction, disappeared. Really—they were gone within seconds. The white car continued on toward the Aperion, the man on Ohalei Yosef vanished into the courtyard, and when I looked behind me I didn't see a sign of any motorcycle. And I thought to myself: *Did it happen, or didn't it? Was it all just my imagination? Am I going crazy?*

"But then I heard the motorcycle inside the courtyard of the big building, and I decided—I don't know why—to go take a look. It was crazy. It was dangerous. But I didn't stop to think.

"I got there. There are a few steps at the entrance and I nearly fell, and then I saw a person running toward the playground and turning left. He looked familiar to me, but by the time I reached the playground he had disappeared in the direction of Or-Hatzafon. I sat down on a bench, breathing hard. I was positive that I'd recognized him, but I had no idea who he was. Only a few minutes later did it come back to me. I suddenly realized that it was Itzik Peled."

"Itzik Peled?" Both brothers shot up. "*He* arranged that whole chase? But why?"

"That's exactly what I asked him," Miri said.

"You asked Itzik Peled?"

"Yes. I called him up."

"*You called Itzik Peled?*"

Miri smiled weakly in the face of her brothers' amazement, but there was neither amusement nor joy in the smile.

"And what… What did he tell you when you called?" Avreimi asked, when he had recovered from the shock.

"He was very surprised that I'd noticed anything. He said that the whole thing had taken just two or three minutes, before the forces scattered."

"But why did they come? What happened?"

"He explained that Abba's workplace had not been so innocent. It was a cover for something else, better left unsaid. They had put up the 'For Rent' sign and a phone number in order to see who would call and to figure out if it was linked to the attack on Abba. The so-called realtor was someone who worked with them. That's why he dragged out the conversation, so that they could pinpoint the phone and trap whoever was calling. 'The minute I saw that it was you,' Itzik told me, 'I gave the order to disperse. But I didn't think you'd noticed us.'

"I asked him, 'Who's 'us'? The Shin-Bet? The police?' And he told me, 'No. Not the Shin-Bet, but something similar. I can't tell you, and anyway it's an organization you've never heard of and haven't read about in the newspapers. The less you know, the better.'"

"So even back then he was saying that someone attacked Abba?" Chezky asked.

"I asked him that. I was very upset to hear it. He calmed me down and said that it wasn't a certain thing. They only had suspicions and were trying to investigate."

"Sure," said Chezky. "I also 'suspect' that I got smacked today."

"Maybe that's enough already, Chezky?" Avreimi pleaded. Turning back to Miri, he asked, "But where did you find his phone number?"

"Where?" Miri repeated. "One day, Abba took me aside and said that he had something important to say. 'I'm talking to you,' he said, 'because you're the oldest one in the house today. Avreimi and Chezky are married and Ari is in yeshivah in Bnei Brak.' He gave me a telephone number and told me to memorize it. 'It's Itzik Peled's number,' Abba told me. 'He's an honest and trustworthy man, and if you ever need help you can turn to him with confidence.'"

Avreimi and Chezky were stunned.

"That's what Abba said?"

"Exactly that," Miri confirmed.

"When was this? When did he tell you that?"

Miri began to tear up again. Swallowing hard, she said, "About a week before he…" She couldn't finish the sentence.

How naïve Abba was, Chezky thought. But he was smart enough not to say it out loud.

And how naïve you two are, he continued his unspoken dialogue with his siblings. *Abba, who trusted Itzik with his eyes closed, ended up closing his eyes forever. Ima apparently learned her lesson and cut off contact with that traitor. It's a fact that she didn't share her plan with him, to go to Polowitz and fly from there to Ukraine. Ima and I—we're the only two who understand what's really going on here…*

Miri, in contrast, spoke out loud. Her voice was filled with tears.

"So what do we do about Ima?" she asked. "Itzik's gone and we're left here alone."

"He went away, but he's dealing with things," Avreimi comforted her.

"Sure," Chezky smirked. "We've seen how he *deals* with things…"

"So who *should* we trust?" Avreimi demanded. "Sean Mackenzie, the Englishman? Itzik, at least, is one of ours."

Chezky burst into loud laughter. Avreimi really cracked him up.

"Ours?" he mocked. "Tell me, are you blind? He's been tracking Abba for years. He pretended to be religious in order to get close to our family."

Avreimi closed his mouth and didn't answer. Unfortunately, he knew that this was at least partially true. Itzik himself had told him that he reported on their parents each year. In Itzik's best judgment, they hadn't embraced genuine religious faith but had only been a pair of very good actors. It was a good thing he hadn't shared *that* with Chezky…

"But you heard what Abba told me," Miri said in a shaky voice. "He said we can trust Itzik, and that he's an honest man."

Chezky was filled with compassion for his sister. Avreimi got on his nerves, but she was truly to be pitied.

"Miri, you have to understand," he said gently. "Abba said what he said, but he's not here. We have to deal with things ourselves."

"Abba's not here," Avreimi broke in, "but he left us instructions. He said that Itzik can be trusted. Do you know the meaning of the words, 'It's a mitzvah to carry out the wishes of the dead?'"

"You've run out of arguments, so you're recruiting words of Torah?" Chezky mocked.

Avreimi thought seriously before he answered.

"The Torah is the first argument," he told his brother—though he was not at all sure Chezky would understand what he meant.

"Anyway, who said that she's actually flown away?" Chezky asked. "Maybe she's fooling us about that, too?"

A painful silence ensued. No one had any ideas.

"There are Jews in Kiev," Avreimi said after a few minutes. "Maybe we can ask someone to go to the airport and see if she arrives?"

"First of all, who are you going to ask?" Chezky said. "And besides, it's probably a huge airport. How could someone locate one woman among tens of thousands of passengers?"

Miri shook her head. "Listen to how we're talking!" she wailed. "Trying to track down Ima…"

"Not tracking down. Protecting," Chezky told her. "If my instincts are correct, there's someone else who's tracking her."

Chezky's instincts, in this instance at least, had not deceived him.

53

THE EL-AL FLIGHT TO KIEV THAT WEDNESDAY HELD A MOTLEY assortment of passengers. At the front of the plane was a noisy group of Ukrainian tourists whose visit to Israel had made serious inroads into that nation's alcohol supply. Near the back sat a group of ultra-Orthodox Jews on their way to visit the holy graves of holy rabbis, looking fairly content for people on their way to pour out their hearts pleading for general and personal salvations. There were also some Ukrainian businessmen, a few Israeli students, and others.

In the center of the commotion, not far from the airplane's exit, sat a woman huddled over a book in her hands while her heart fluttered with fear. The flight was delayed for an hour, and each minute crawled past amid mounting worry. Now, finally, the doors had closed and the plane had begun to warm up its engines. But not until it lifted off and pointed its nose to the northwest would she be calm.

It would have been difficult to identify the woman, with her old wig and large, dark-framed plastic glasses, as Chana Kohlberg, veteran high-school secretary and the widow of R' Shlomo Kohlberg, z"l, who had tragically passed away less than thirty days earlier.

The start of the trip had been very successful; only later did the delays begin. When she had presented her passport at the control booth, ninety minutes earlier, the clerk had glanced at her briefly, compared her face to the one in the photograph, in which she appeared twenty years younger, and let her through without comment. Her airline ticket was also in perfect order. It had seemed to her then that she would shortly be leaving the borders of Israel behind.

Browsing in the duty-free shops didn't interest her, and she had taken along a suitcase simply not to stand out. She sat in a chair near the gate, waiting impatiently for the announcement to start boarding the plane. That was when the problems began.

She sat quietly in her place, trying not to draw any attention to herself, but the businessmen among her fellow travelers loudly demanded an explanation for the unexpected delay. They had no way of knowing, of course, that several of the intended passengers had received a last-minute request from the airline company to give up their seats because an important Israeli personality needed to get to Ukraine. At last, one Israeli tourist had agreed to postpone his flight in exchange for a major discount on his ticket price. Only when the seat became available for the important person did the boarding begin.

Chana Kohlberg attached no significance to the elderly-looking, coiffed woman waiting behind her in line. It was hard to believe that this was the "important Israeli personality" that had caused the maddening delay in the flight's departure.

Itzik Peled sat in his old Land Rover near the upper entrance of the Har HaMenuchos cemetery. The Jerusalem-Tel Aviv highway unwound below him, humming with vehicles, but where he sat all was blessedly quiet, with the peace that only the no-longer-living can bring.

From time to time, he checked the computer screen on the seat beside him, and the screen of the phone mounted in its usual place on the dashboard. By his calculation, it was time. The plane should have landed by now.

When he finally heard the ring, Itzik picked up quickly.

"Diana?"

"Yes," came the voice of the elderly, coiffed woman. "We landed fifteen minutes ago."

"I'm listening."

"Anna Aranowich is about twenty meters away from me."

"In which country?" Itzik asked impatiently, annoyed with Diana for providing an incomplete report.

"At this moment, Anna Aranowich is standing on Ukrainian soil."

Itzik Peled thought a moment. "I want to see," he said finally.

Diana, one of Shin-Bet's most veteran and experienced agents, needed no explanation. Though she had left the service some years before, she had worked with Itzik Peled long enough to be familiar with his eccentricities.

Using her phone camera, she quickly sent a photo of Chana Kohlberg—a.k.a. Anna Aranowich—from distant Kiev to Itzik Peled's phone screen in Jerusalem. Despite her strange wig and large glasses, he identified her with certainty.

"Okay, Diana. Thanks a lot. Enjoy the rest of your trip."

"Thanks," Diana said, and set out to find a way to reach R' Nachman of Breslav's gravesite in Uman.

Itzik made his next call while driving toward Ginot Sacharov on the outskirts of the city. Pressing "3" on his speed-dial connected him to Shaul Armoni.

"Shaul, I'm at the entrance to Yerushalayim," he said. "Where is he?"

"Still in the office," Armoni replied.

"I'll be with you in four minutes."

Armoni had been waiting for Itzik Peled for more than half an hour. His driver had parked the car near the Mossad Harav Kook building and Armoni used the time to peruse several documents. Now he got out and walked diagonally across the plaza beneath the HaMeitarim Bridge. Itzik pulled up at the curb and picked him up. A few minutes later, his car passed through the reinforced-steel gate to the Prime Minister's office building. In the parking lot he found the military secretary waiting. The young man greeted Shaul Armoni with unconcealed admiration. Armoni was considered a walking legend among people who were themselves walking legends.

"You'll have to wait a bit, I'm afraid," the secretary apologized as the three ascended to the second floor of the building. "He's in a cabinet meeting, and he also has a coalition crisis on his head. You must have heard about it in the news."

Shaul Armoni grunted, like a man who recognized the unavoidable limitations of politics.

Armoni and Itzik were ushered into a large, empty conference room. "Do you want something to drink?" the military secretary asked.

"No, thanks. There's no need," Armoni decided.

Ten minutes later, the secretary returned. "He's on his way," he said, and started to take a seat.

"Excuse me," Armoni said. "This meeting is for six eyes only. Is that clear?"

The military secretary, who held the rank of major-general in the IDF, gave the older man a long look, as though calculating the number of eyes in three people. Then he nodded in acceptance and left the room. Like so many in the intelligence community, he had worked under Shaul Armoni. Despite the considerable difference in their ages, and despite the fact that no one knew exactly what Armoni's position was today, the man still had the power to intimidate those around him.

Five minutes later, the Prime Minister entered the room—followed by his military secretary. Shaul Armoni didn't say a word. He merely looked penetratingly at the man.

"*Shalom*, Shaul," said the Prime Minister, who appeared preoccupied and harried. "I'm sorry about the circumstances, it's just..."

Armoni cut off the courtesies. "This is not a conversation for six eyes?" he asked.

The Prime Minister looked around, and then told Armoni with a smile, "If you want, I could leave..."

The military secretary, to his credit, maintained a sphinxlike expression.

Armoni swallowed his defeat. "This is Itzik Peled," he said.

The Prime Minister extended his hand. "I've heard a great deal about you."

Itzik shook his hand wordlessly. *Of course the Prime Minister had heard about him,* he thought. He'd heard that Itzik had been head of the security division until eight years ago. He'd heard that Itzik had been forced to leave under humiliating circumstances, and he had heard that Shaul Armoni had been employing him since then in his own small unit.

"What is this about?" asked the Prime Minister.

"Shlomo Kohlberg had a presidential pardon, so we couldn't touch him," Armoni said, to refresh the Prime Minister's memory. "But his wife definitely needs to be interrogated. We'd like to take her in."

"So what's the problem?" the P.M. asked, waving a hand in dismissal. "The *chareidi* MK's? We'll work it out with them. Believe me."

Shaul Armoni, with a glance, passed the floor to Itzik Peled.

"The problem is that she's succeeded in escaping to Ukraine," he said.

Two seconds of ringing silence filled the room.

"How did this happen?" asked the P.M.

"She's not a nobody, that woman," Itzik said ruefully. "She's crafty and sophisticated."

"We know that," the Prime Minister nodded.

"So Peled has an idea…" Armoni said.

"The most important thing to her is her children," Itzik said. "The Ukrainians are getting ready to kidnap one of the sons, and I think that that will bring her to her knees. To free her son, she'll agree to hand herself over."

"I want to restore Peled to the active service," Armoni said. "I want him to lead the operation tomorrow night. They know him, and they trust him."

The Prime Minister closed his eyes and mulled the idea over for a long moment.

"In principle, I can accept that—pending the Chief's consent," he said.

"Go'ash is in the building," the military secretary offered.

"Then let him come in. I'm going back to my business," the Prime Minister said. "Good luck."

Shin-Bet director Amos Go'ash was the same short, stocky, and bespectacled man that Itzik remembered from his time in the service. He'd only aged considerably.

"*Shalom*, Peled," he said, reacting with surprise to Itzik's ultra-Orthodox garb. He knew that Itzik Peled had married, but had not known that he had also decided to fall on his head...

"You claim that she's in Ukraine," said the Chief. "Based on what?"

Itzik Peled glanced at his watch. "I had an eyewitness report half an hour ago."

"Something that could be used as evidence in court?" asked the Chief.

"Absolutely." Itzik knew that Diana was completely loyal to him. He knew with certainty that Anna Aranowich was in Kiev right now.

"Maybe it would be better to search for her there?" Go'ash suggested.

"We don't have the time," Itzik said. "The deadline is noon tomorrow."

"And you're sure the Ukrainians are planning to grab one of the sons?"

"Trust me."

Amos Go'ash looked at Itzik. "Just don't pull another Nati Kahn," he snapped, referring to the episode that had led to Itzik's dismissal, after he had used a young Israeli citizen to further his own personal financial interests.

"I learned my lesson," Itzik said with deep sincerity.

"Good." The Chief thumped him on the shoulder. "You return to active duty tomorrow morning. I'll deal with the paperwork."

"Who's my opposite number?" Itzik asked.

"A fellow named Shachaf Gafni. I believe he was already around in your time. Don't let his name fool you—he's a good agent."

One half hour after the El-Al plane landed in Kiev, a young

woman by the name of Zeldy Bukshpan was wandering around Borispol Airport, searching for someone who matched the photograph in her hand. In everyday life, Zeldy was a crafts teacher at the local Jewish girls' school. Until two years earlier, she had lived near her parents in Givat Ze'ev. Then she and her husband were offered positions in the Kiev Jewish community. Since then, while he learned with boys in the yeshivah, she taught Jewish girls how to embroider challah cloths and make pillows for use on Seder night. No one had ever told her, however, that one day she would be given a mission that seemed to be straight out of the pages of some classic spy story.

She hadn't searched long before she located the woman who appeared in the picture. The woman was dozing on one of the benches on the second floor of Terminal D, near a small, non-kosher coffee shop.

Gently, she touched the woman's arm.

"Excuse me. Did you arrive with the group from Tzefas?" asked Zeldy Bukshpan. Her Ukrainian was flawless. She had always been told she had a knack for languages.

"No," Chana Kohlberg answered, in Russian. "I'm from New York."

"Oh. I'm sorry." The teacher smiled. "Because Tzefas is a beautiful city. It has good restaurants."

Chana Kohlberg smiled, too. "No restaurant makes schnitzel the way *I* make it!"

Then both women sobered. The code had been successful. The dialogue had been spoken exactly as had been established in advance: I say "Tzefas," you say "New York"; she says "restaurant" and you say "schnitzel."

Zeldy handed Chana Kohlberg a thermos of hot tea and a number of sandwiches that she had prepared for her. The women exchanged a few hasty sentences.

Five minutes after their meeting, they parted ways forever.

Evening descended on Jerusalem. The three Kohlbergs still sat in the empty house, waiting for something to happen.

"There's something unclear regarding Ima," Avreimi and Chezky explained to their respective wives. "I'll be home later, or maybe not till tomorrow. I'll be in touch."

Avreimi's wife requested, and received, his mother's name for the purposes of *tefillah*—Chana bas Henya—and passed it on to Chezky's wife.

Avreimi checked his watch and sat up in alarm.

"Look at the time!" he told Miri. "What about the kids?"

While he and Chezky had hurried to their parents' home after hearing that Sean Mackenzie was there, Miri had placed the younger children in the care of Mrs. Fink, their neighbor. It had still been light outside then.

Miri left immediately and knocked on the door of the neighbor's apartment, full of apologies.

The good Mrs. Fink calmed the girl and told her that she had put the children to bed when she saw how late it was. "I let them talk with your mother, and everything's all right," she said.

"You let them talk with my mother?" Miri echoed in surprise. "When?"

"About an hour ago."

Miri couldn't believe her ears. "Really? Ima called?"

If Mrs. Fink wondered why the girl was so agitated over a call from her mother, she hid it well. "She also asked me to tell you that she's been delayed and won't be home tonight. You're welcome to sleep here if you want."

When Miri reported back to her brothers, Chezky suggested, "Maybe you can ask Mrs. Fink where Ima called from. She can check the number." Immediately, however, he rejected that idea. They couldn't start running surveillance on their own mother...

"We'll sleep here tonight," the brothers decided.

"You can stay here or at the Finks, Miri," Avreimi said. "You have two apartments at your disposal."

"Are we dividing up the inheritance already?" Chezky quipped.

Avreimi stuck a friendly fist into his ribs.

"Oh, there's no help for you," he said, in smiling despair.

Modiin-Illit, 5772 / 2011

THE ROSH KOLLEL, ON HIS WAY TO THE BOOKCASE, HAPPENED to pass by Shmulik Mattias. The slender young man sat swaying over his *shtender*. It was 11:30 a.m.

"Where's Kohlberg?" the Rosh Kollel asked. "He did come in today, didn't he? I saw him earlier."

Avreimi Kohlberg was Shmulik's learning partner in the mornings. During the *shivah*, Avreimi had obviously been absent from the *kollel*, and in the ensuing days his continued absences were regarded with understanding and consideration. After all, his father had passed on suddenly, leaving behind a houseful of children, of whom Avreimi was the eldest. Many matters preoccupied him—not to mention many troubles—and he did his best to learn as much as he was able. After a number of days, during which his attendance had been sporadic at best, Avreimi told the Rosh Kollel that he would come in only on those days when he knew that he would be able to concentrate without disturbance during the learning *seder*. And that's what he had been doing.

Yesterday, Wednesday, he had been absent. But he had come today. The sound of his and Shmulik's Torah had joined with the other voices in the *beis medrash*. But an hour ago, strangely, he had abandoned his partner and disappeared.

"Something happened to him outside," Shmulik Mattias said, gesturing at the door.

The Rosh Kollel looked out. Kohlberg was sitting in the front passenger seat of a large, black, opulent rental car parked nearby. The driver was unfamiliar. Chezky, Avreimi Kohlberg's brother, sat in the back seat, leaning forward. The three—so it appeared from the distance—seemed to be conducting a friendly conversation.

"He's been looking very worried lately," Shmulik remarked, looking worried himself.

"Well, he has a lot on his head," the Rosh Yeshivah said with compassion.

Bright and early that morning, after a peaceful night, the Kohlbergs had woken up to find that their mother had not yet returned. Miri dressed the little ones while Avreimi and Chezky prepared sandwiches. With touching innocence, young Yoel asked if Ima had died, too, or if she had just gone someplace far away…

Miri went to school and they caught the bus to their own homes. Just before the Shilat intersection, Sean Mackenzie called Chezky's cell phone. The Englishman apologized for the conversation the day before, which had been cut off through no fault of his own, and said that he would be very happy to continue it at the earliest opportunity. Chezky consulted with Avreimi, who was seated next to him. Avreimi suggested that they meet during the lunchtime break.

During morning *seder*, Chezky had unexpectedly appeared with Mackenzie in the latter's rental car. He explained to Avreimi that he had pushed up the meeting because the Institute had called again—some new clerk whom he didn't know—to say that unless he appeared that afternoon for a personal interview with Dr. Laskin, the faculty coordinator, he would forfeit the entire semester and experience a delay in receiving his degree. Avreimi refrained from pointing out that the study of Torah was a bit more important than his degree. This, he knew, was not the time to dispense *mussar*.

So he got into Mackenzie's car, though he objected to the idea of "going somewhere for a cup of coffee." He wanted to stay close, so that he could return to the *beis medrash* the minute they were done.

"I already introduced myself yesterday," Mackenzie began. "I told you how your father managed to protect his life and his freedom despite the fact that he possessed the most highly classified secrets. I also explained that Israel and the Shin-Bet are working with the Ukrainians, and that you must not trust them."

Chezky demonstrated typical Israeli impatience: "You said that an email will be sent out tonight that will cause some sort of explosion. What were you talking about?"

Sean Mackenzie waved a hand dismissively.

"I was too worried yesterday. Forgive me for becoming overwrought. It seemed then that your mother might be cooperating with the Ukrainians, and that endangered both her and us. Now that she's back home, we're all calmer."

Avreimi and Chezky would later congratulate themselves on the self-control they demonstrated at that moment. Sean Mackenzie's casual words had floored them. On the one hand, he had confirmed what Itzik Peled had said: that his mother had flown to Ukraine. On the other, he had just informed them of her return. Nevertheless, neither brother batted an eye to indicate that this was news to them.

In the year 1993, the British agent related, he had been sent from London to Israel—more precisely, to Shin-Bet headquarters in Tel Aviv—to ask for help in a certain matter. During that same period, Iran had fallen to the ayatollahs, and the Revolutionary Guard ruled the country with an iron hand. Some years earlier the Soviet Union had also fallen apart, a factor that had not contributed to world peace and had played a role in his mission. Britain was interested at the time in the contents of a certain container that had been sent from Kherson, in Ukraine, to the port of Bandar-Abbas, Iran. In a normal country, a seaport is generally open to scrutiny, but it is impossible to move a stone in Iran without the authorities knowing about it. Every effort to penetrate the place through accepted channels failed. Finally, the decision was made to turn to

Israel for help. Israeli contractors and architects, advisers, security consultants, and intelligence personnel knew Iran well from the Shah's era.

"From the start, it was clear that the Shin-Bet wouldn't give us anything for free," Sean Mackenzie told the two brothers. "They operated with craftiness and finesse. First they stuffed us with irrelevant information that didn't help matters, and finally, with great courtesy, they hinted that they could ask the Mossad for help. That was where we finally received what we'd asked for—but they demanded certain information in exchange."

"And what was the trade-off?"

"The trade-off was your mother."

"Our mother?" Avreimi and Chezky repeated in amazement. "What did they want from her?"

"They wanted to use her to get to your father."

"Just a minute. Our parents were already in Israel?" Immediately, Chezky answered his own question. "Ah, of course. This was…. 18 years ago. I was five."

"But… what is your interest in our mother?" asked Avreimi.

Sean Mackenzie gave a half-smile. "Your mother, as you know, served in the KGB. All these years, she was a double agent."

"Double agent?"

"Certainly. All along, her true loyalty was with Great Britain."

"Great Britain?" Avreimi and Chezky looked at each other and burst out laughing. The shock was too great, their astonishment overflowing. What else was there to do but laugh?

Besides, which was preferable—their mother as a KGB officer or as a British agent?

Sean Mackenzie nodded his head in open appreciation. "She was not just an agent. She was an especially talented and clever operator. One who stood up to every test that the Soviets could devise, and earned praise and decoration. An agent who volunteered to work for us at the start of her journey, and rose in rank until she became an instructor in the most secretive unit in the KGB—the 'School for Foreign Cultures' in Kiev. There she received orders from on high to marry your father. And the rest is history…"

Now Avreimi and Chezky weren't laughing quite as hard. This reminder of the circumstances under which their parents had married did not exactly fill them with elation.

"Your mother was not the kind of spy you read about in books," Mackenzie continued. "The ones who take pictures of classified documents and pass the copies to their handlers on dark street corners. All through her service, she and her contact man met perhaps twice. Her contact man, by the way, was a Jew as well. She operated independently and yet managed to uncover a number of Russian spies who'd been sent over to settle in the West. You really don't know how smart your mother is. She developed a system, brilliant in its simplicity, whose code name was 'Fingerprint.'"

"Fingerprint?" Chezky spread his hand, which had at least five of them.

Sean waved his own hand. "I'm talking about a *mental* fingerprint. A consciousness fingerprint—a special sign by which she could recognize one of her students without their ever being aware that they were revealing themselves."

"How?"

"It worked like this: Your mother was in charge of helping her agents acquire Jewish knowledge. Because she was their only source of information, she made sure to plant a certain erroneous piece of information in each of them."

"Like what, for instance?"

"They were always trivial items, things which it would be reasonable to suppose the student would never need unless asked for directly. For example: she could tell one of the students that Don Isaac Abarbanel, a Jewish historical figure from the era of the expulsion from Spain, used to write with his left hand. Or that on the holiday of Shavuos, a certain Jewish ethnic group has a custom of frying pancakes in the shape of the number 4.

"She arranged the list of these 'fingerprints' in advance with her contact man. When your mother was about to receive her instructional post, she initiated a meeting with him, told him about her idea, and they arranged a series of ten special 'fingerprints' that she would plant in her students, one item each year. That way, she did not have to pass any names or lists on to London. Any person who was suspected of being a Soviet spy in those years, whether in Britain or in the United States, took the 'fingerprint' test. If he 'knew' that Don Yitzchak Abarbanel was left-handed—a completely false fact, incidentally—he was revealed as a spy."

"And were those really the 'fingerprints'? That someone was left-handed or fried pancakes in the shape of a '4'?"

Sean Mackenzie was amused. "No to both counts. Those were only examples that can be used to understand this chapter in spy school. The real 'fingerprints' were classified information of the highest caliber."

"And that's the secret information you were talking about?"

"Yes. The entire intelligence community—the British MI6, the Ukrainian SBU and the Israeli bureaus—have been pursuing those same fingerprints for more than twenty years now, ever since your parents left the Soviet Union."

"And who was her contact man?" asked Chezky.

"That, of course, is also classified," Sean Mackenzie answered.

Avreimi had been listening attentively, but something still wasn't clear to him.

"So you're claiming," he told the Englishman, "that our mother had information that could identify Soviet spies in the West."

"Exactly."

"And that information was also in the hands of the contact man, whoever he was."

"Correct."

"And the contact man was one of yours, from your organization?"

"You could say that."

"In that case," Avreimi finally succeeded in formulating the question in his mind, "you people already have all the details. So why is our mother important? Check your files, and you're done!"

Sean Mackenzie was enjoying Avreimi's analytical mind and quick grasp. "It's easy to see that you're your mother's son," he praised. "They say that the Jewish Torah sharpens the mind. I can see that's true… The answer is that all went smoothly until your parents got their last group of students. Six intelligent and outstanding agents who were dubbed the 'Six Wonders.'"

Half-an-hour's drive from the Kohlbergs, in the Unit of International Crime Investigations, the department charged with investigating serious international crime, 17-year-old Rotem Cohen, the young parking-meter inspector from Givat Shmuel, sat and enjoyed a milkshake and croissant that his aunt had bought him in the police station's cafeteria. The time was 11:45, and the senior officer who was coming from Jerusalem especially to hear his testimony was a little late.

Bored, Rotem memorized the list of police officers and captains of the Lahav 443 unit, whose pictures graced the walls. When it had all started that morning, he reflected, he had never believed things would work out this way. He'd simply caught his father before the latter left for his job at the municipality, and told him about the black Buick that he had seen near the religious institute. He showed his father the photo he had taken, and told him that a few minutes later he saw the same car with a different license plate.

Half an hour later, his father had phoned him from the train. "Rotem," he'd said, "the police want to talk to you."

Rotem had frozen in fear. He didn't like cops.

"I just hope I haven't gotten into trouble," he said.

"Some trouble," his father had joked. "Mordechai says that you demonstrated outstanding citizenship. He praised you highly."

Police superintendent Mordechai Cohen was Rotem's uncle, his father's brother, and served in the Givat Shmuel precinct.

"He said that this is linked to the Russian mafia, and that someone in the Unit of International Crime Investigations wants to talk to you," his father said. "Uncle Mordechai will pick you up in his patrol car soon, and will take you there. It's somewhere in the northern industrial region of Lod. Dress nicely."

Rotem was a little surprised by the senior office from Jerusalem, who was out of uniform and looked more like one of the Orthodox fellows from the institute. A cropped beard adorned his cheeks; he wore rimless glasses and a black *kippah*. He also preferred to talk with him in his car, a white Land Rover.

"Thank you for waiting," Itzik Peled told Rotem Cohen. "Tell me the whole story, from beginning to end."

Rotem told the story in detail, including the fact that he liked to slap a ticket on luxury cars, that the man in the Buick LaCrosse had looked like some senior man in a criminal organization, and that the man had spoken on the phone in Russian. He showed Itzik the picture he had taken, and the computer printout he had from the municipality, proving that the license plate belonged to a car that had been totaled in an accident two months before.

"Good work." Itzik Peled smiled at the youth. "You could be a detective yourself."

Rotem smiled proudly.

"What's your phone number?" Itzik asked. "I may need your help again."

Rotem nearly leaped out of his seat with joy.

"It's just that we have a shortage of manpower," Itzik explained with a wink.

Rotem laughed at the joke—unaware that Itzik had not been joking at all.

Kiev, 5737 / 1977

PROFESSOR WILLOTZKY WAS EXTREMELY PLEASED. THE SIX agents, the cream of the KGB crop, were progressing in a most satisfactory way. They had turned themselves before his eyes into Jews and Israelis, and had demonstrated both psychological and ideological strength.

Their mission would not be an easy one. They were about to be sent off to a primary location where they would operate as "sleepers" for an indeterminate length of time. They would have to integrate into the local social structure, find good jobs, and create a circle of friends. It would be preferable if they also married and raised families until they resembled Israelis in every way.

This stage of their mission was likely to last for a not-inconsiderable number of years, and it would be necessary to make sure that no one got lost along the way. There was always the danger that an agent would enjoy his new circumstances so much that he would forget who was paying his salary and providing him with such a good life… In the next stage, when the agents fit into their surroundings, the active part of their mission would commence: Some of them would remain in Israel, while others would immigrate to the U.S. or Great Britain. And then they would put into play the great goal for which this whole project had been created—a goal that Professor Willotzky had decided to conceal for the time being even from the cell's activators, the Arzi-Aranowich couple.

Each week, the Professor met with Momi and Anna to track each candidate's progress. More than once, they'd jokingly debated who was responsible for the project's success: himself, for providing such outstanding human material, or they, with the professionalism they brought to the candidates' training.

At a certain stage, the candidates began, one by one, to disappear from R-19. Each of them was to find his own way to Israel, whether as a new immigrant or under some other guise, and to begin building his new persona. Because of compartmentalization and security concerns, Momi and Anna did not know what each agent was doing, where he lived, or how he was succeeding in melting into his surroundings. At the right time, when Professor Willotzky so decided, they would be provided with methods to communicate with their agents. Nevertheless, one password had been established for use in an emergency—in the event that the handlers found an urgent need to meet with one of their agents.

Momi and Anna were the last to leave the compound on the outskirts of Kiev. The next day, bulldozers were brought to the site to begin what they did best: destroy. The R-19 stone building remained in place, but the Israeli compound known as the "School for Foreign Cultures" was razed down to its foundations and the ruins set on fire.

Momi, traveling through East and West Germany, reached Israel first. As he passed through Ben-Gurion Airport, he tensed slightly. But the papers that had been prepared for him by the KGB laboratories were flawless, and he entered the country without trouble. From Lod he traveled to Jerusalem and went directly to the Meah Shearim neighborhood, where he searched for a yeshivah that catered to people returning to their religious roots. He presented himself as Shlomo Kohlberg and spoke little about his past. Soon enough, he was an integral part of the community.

Anna's journey was longer and much more dangerous. According to the plan, she flew to Romania, where she took a series of trains and buses across the breadth of Europe in order to ensure that no one was following her. She used all the ploys she had been taught in KGB school, including the use of disguises and false identities. She never spent more than one night in the same place.

In London, she made a longer stop. She rented a room in a small hotel near the Wauxhall Bridge, which spanned the Thames. Now came the riskiest part of her journey. But it was for this part that she had come all this way.

Toward evening, she left her hotel room and walked along one of the city's main thoroughfares. London was bustling: speeding cars and buses, businessmen walking energetically, and young people passing by in a flash on their bicycles. Anna devoured the sights, strangely excited. The freedom of London intoxicated her. Even the dreary weather pleased her.

She entered a red telephone booth, closed the door behind her, and dialed the number for British intelligence headquarters.

"This is in connection to 'Fingerprint,'" she told the operator. She was certain this would bring immediate respect.

It didn't happen. Politely, the operator asked her who she was and what she wanted, please. The woman refused to pass Anna's call on to one of the senior agents, agreeing only to write down the hotel's address and phone number so that someone could get back to her if they deemed it necessary and proper.

The low-level agent who was sent over to hear what Anna had to say treated her a bit more seriously, and things started moving. Within three hours, she found herself sitting in the office of the secret service's assistant director, who listened with frank amazement to her tale of the "School for Foreign Cultures" in the KGB's Directorate R-19.

For two days, Anna was questioned. She handed over every scrap of information she recalled about the administration, including identifying details for scores of students who'd passed through her training program, now "working" in the West. She also offered the 'fingerprint' she had planted in each and every one of them, though she said nothing at all about her instructional partner, Comrade Momi Arzi.

The gracious British offered her a generous fee, which she refused to accept. "I didn't do it for the money," she told them. She also did not consent to continue working for them or to be available to them in the future. She did not tell them where she was headed or where she planned to settle. She wanted to put the intelligence aspect of her life behind her, she said. From now on, all she wanted was to lead a quiet, peaceful existence.

The trip from England to Israel took seven days. She now had to evade two intelligence bureaus: the KGB and MI6.

All the way, she couldn't stop thinking about the fate of her contact man. He had disappointed her. Why hadn't he done his part and transmitted the "Fingerprint" program to his secret service, as they'd agreed? Had he been captured by the KGB? If so, they would surely have extracted a confession from him which would have led them directly to her. Was it possible that the contact man had been tortured to death, protecting her secret at the cost of his life? Or perhaps he had simply fallen ill or become injured or died of natural causes? Or maybe he, too, had turned to MI6, only to be considered deranged or hallucinating—as they'd thought of her at first.

The program for female *ba'alei teshuvah* that she joined was located in Bnei Brak. She was careful not to be in frequent contact with Momi/Shlomo in Jerusalem, and their conversations were brief. In the Soviet Union, they'd both learned that silence was good for their health. No one could see what you were thinking, but anyone could hear what you said out loud.

Her contact man, Anna/Chana knew, had lived in Jerusalem in the past. She began making careful inquiries about him, fearing the worst, and was glad to hear that he was alive and well. Wasting no time, she went to see him. The man paled when he saw her standing in his doorway, as if he had suddenly glimpsed one of the walking dead.

The reason for this, she discovered almost immediately, was not his excitement at seeing a precious family member. "I decided not to turn to the British," he told her, "in order not to endanger you. If spies were to be exposed, one after another, the Russians would have pinpointed the source of the leak and easily found their way to you."

Her sense of betrayal was hard to surmount. Her contact man had, in one fell swoop, taken away the meaning of her life. She had known all along that she was a faithful soldier in the army of the free world, that she was fighting on the front lines against Soviet tyranny and Communist dictatorship. With his criminal omission, her contact man had stolen away the moral justification for everything that she had done.

There was no point in dramatic denunciations or heaping blame. She simply turned around and left. From that moment, she decided, she would erase him completely from her life. She would neither recognize him nor speak to him, for good or for ill. Ever.

One day, a rabbi from Shlomo Kohlberg's yeshivah approached him to say that a matchmaker in Bnei Brak had called to ask about him. "He spoke about a girl named Chana Aranowich," he said. "She's also a *ba'alas teshuvah*, talented, good-hearted, with fine *middos* and *yiras Shamayim*." After a few meetings, their engagement was celebrated with a modest party. Their wedding was held three months later. There were no relatives to attend it, but the *chasan's* and *kallah's* friends danced and rejoiced with them to the best of their ability.

It appeared as if Shlomo and Chana had reached the pinnacle of their contentment. They rented a small apartment in Jerusalem and tried to live a peaceful life.

One day, about half a year after they married, Chana heard a knock on the door.

In the doorway stood an elderly man in a long, shabby coat. At first, she thought he was looking for a donation, but then she heard the words that frightened her more than anything else: "The principal wants to let you know about a parent-teacher conference."

The man disappeared. Chana felt as if her entire world had collapsed on her head.

This sentence was the password for emergencies. It meant that her handler wanted to meet with her. Her handler, of course, was Professor Willotzky. What did he want now, so far ahead of schedule? Why had he initiated a meeting mere months after sending her off to her destination, before she or her fellow cell members had had a chance to put down roots?

Shlomo was not expected home until evening. Chana's thoughts took her to the most extreme and terrifying scenarios. Did Willotzky intend to summon them back to the Soviet Union? Or perhaps it would be sufficient for them to meet in some neutral country? Should she ask MI6 for help? It was possible, heaven forbid, that Willotzky's summons was connected to her London adventure. Maybe someone had seen her entering or leaving the intelligence headquarters. Or there might be a Soviet mole inside MI6 who had reported her actions to Moscow…

From hour to hour, the level of her fear rose. If summoned back to Moscow to provide explanations, Chana knew, she and her husband could end up in a prison cell or at the end of the hangman's rope.

When Shlomo returned home that evening and heard her news, his heart sank as well. Who, more than he, knew of the KGB's cruelty? Who, more than he, knew how cheaply they held human life? One day he had been walking down Rechov Malchei Yisrael and seen Zalman Berkovitch, the "recruit" he had brought to the KGB Zalman had not recognized him in his ultra-Orthodox garb—which was all to the good. But he, too, had hardly recognized Zalman, who appeared to be both physically and mentally ill. Zalman had been limping heavily and had looked rather less than sane. Indeed, Professor Willotzky had once mentioned that they had not succeeded in sending him back to Israel in exactly the same shape as he had been when they'd taken him…

The summons to meet their handler entailed a three-part procedure that had been arranged in advance: one messenger to announce the meeting, a second to transmit its location, and a third to inform them of the date and time. No messenger knew about the others or about the information they carried, thus ensuring the meeting's secrecy.

"Let's wait and see where he wants to meet," Shlomo told Chana, the tension clear in his voice. Once they knew that, they'd be able to assess the degree of danger preparing to ambush them, and could plan their moves accordingly. It was not easy to contend with the KGB, but one must not surrender.

What the Kohlbergs did not yet know at the time was that the British were furious with Anna/Chana and were seeking her assiduously.

Because, after their first excitement over the set of spies that she handed them on a silver platter—after they exposed a number of them and earned the gratitude of the United States—they learned through some means that she had "forgotten" to report a few others. Professor Willotzky's last six wonder agents had been conspicuously absent in her testimony to MI6. Their "fingerprints" had not been given to the British intelligence bureau, but had remained the private property of Shlomo and Chana Kohlberg.

To their vast relief, the next messenger, a Russian violinist in the Israeli Philharmonic Orchestra, told the Kohlbergs that the meeting was to take place not far from their home: at the rear of the Russian church in the Russian Compound in central Jerusalem. The date and time for the meeting were transmitted separately by a nun from the Ethiopian church, who knocked on their door the next day and handed them an envelope that contained a note: "Tuesday, 7 p.m."

Shlomo and Chana arrived, still anxious and apprehensive, at the small gate in the eastern side of the church's courtyard. An elderly gardener led them to a staircase that wound down to the church's basement. In a small room redolent of mold waited Professor Willotzky and a younger man. Both men, needless to say, had entered Israel under false identities and with forged passports.

"Know what I think?" Chezky told Sean Mackenzie with a laugh from the car's back seat. "You should have been a writer. You tell the story so well that I sometimes forget to translate it all for my brother."

Mackenzie looked at him in surprise. The comment seemed to be slightly detached from reality.

"What I mean is—did it all really happen?" Chezky clarified. "How do you know, for example, what happened down in the basement of the Russian church? Were you there?"

Mackenzie weighed his words before answering.

"Everything I'm telling you happened exactly as I've described it," he finally said. "In my line of work, every detail counts. We are careful to be precise with facts."

Avreimi, in the front passenger seat, turned his head toward Chezky for a translation of the dialogue, which had been conducted in an English that went right over his head.

"Okay, I'm sorry. We're listening," Chezky apologized to the Englishman.

"Well, then. The professor was very happy to meet your parents," Sean Mackenzie continued. "And they were relieved by the warm reception. He said that he had come to discuss something very important with them, but first he had brought them money with which to buy an apartment to serve the spy cell."

"Seriously?" Chezky broke in, wide-eyed. "Our parents' apartment was bought with Russian money?"

Sean Mackenzie gave a mischievous smile. "Suddenly you believe every word I say, eh?" He winked.

Chezky retreated, abashed. Mackenzie went on:

"The professor had not come, of course, just to give your parents a wedding present. He addressed the matter for which he had summoned them.

"Five of the agents were acclimating well, he told them. But Agent 6 was causing him many sleepless nights. That agent was a central pivot, without whom the mission would fail—yet Willotzky had not felt good about him for some time. That was why he had come to Israel in person, to hear their views. Because, after all was said and done, they were the ones on the dangerous front lines. If Agent 6 brought down the whole enterprise, they would be among the first to be harmed.

"Your parents asked the professor if there was any evidence of treachery, and he presented all the facts. Agent 6 had not been caught red-handed or anything close to that, but Willotzky had a gut feeling that he was a double agent working for the British. 'I haven't opened an official investigation or curtailed his authority,' the professor told your parents. 'At this stage, I've delayed sending him to his destination and signed him up for extra training, claiming that he needed more preparation for the mission. But if I am forced to give him up, this entire effort will have been in vain. The 'School for Foreign Cultures' will be considered a resounding failure.'

"Your parents considered all this carefully, and discussed it at length from every perspective. Finally, your father said that, in his opinion, Alexander Kittin—that was the agent's operational name, not his real one, of course—was completely trustworthy. Your mother joined him in this view and absolved him of all suspicion. Professor Willotzky relied heavily on their opinion, and was reassured. 'In any case, we're here in the field, and we'll keep an eye on him,' your mother told him. Willotzky issued a few more instructions to your parents, and they separated.

"Your parents emerged from that meeting with a huge bounty: the price of an apartment in Jerusalem, and total freedom from London's pressure."

"What's the connection?" Avreimi wondered.

"Even back in Kiev," Mackenzie explained, "your mother had had her doubts about Kittin's loyalty. She did not share her suspicions with anyone, for obvious reasons. But Willotzky had just, unwittingly, confirmed everything she had suspected. She did all she could to clear Kittin's name and restore the lost trust in him, for two important reasons: First, to save his life, and second, to save the lives of herself and her husband. Now she had a bargaining tool to use with British Intelligence. She had the means to put pressure on us. The equation was very simple: If you hurt me or my husband, your agent in the Soviet Union, Alexander Kittin, will pay the full price.

"This time, she didn't have to call headquarters and hope that someone would take her seriously. She simply sent a message to the higher-ups she had met in the past, and they understood her very quickly..."

"One thing bothers me," Avreimi said. "My parents exposed dozens of Soviet spies—but they protected the identities of those six agents?"

"That's correct."

"So my parents let six Soviet agents walk around free?"

Sean Mackenzie chuckled.

"You're forgetting that the Soviet Union disbanded long ago. That entire cell that Willotzky sent here never reached an operational stage. He himself was ousted from the KGB a short time later, and then died of an illness. The project was abandoned. Your parents benefited from the resulting chaos and were able to breathe easier."

"So why are we sitting here today?" Chezky asked.

"Because several years later, when they moved into their present apartment, your mother had a feeling that she was being followed. She was always on guard. Her senses were alert and sharp, and she knew how to notice things that ordinary people would pay no attention to. Perhaps there were strangers near the house, or an unfamiliar car parked across the street, or an odd look from a passerby. In any case, she came to two conclusions: First, that the British had discovered where she and her husband lived, and second, that Alexander Kittin had become too important to the British to leave the secret of his identity in the hands of a couple of KGB defectors who'd decided to live quietly in a distant land.

"Your parents were forced to contend with this new threat. The one who came up with the 'coiled spring' mechanism was your father. The basic idea was to create a situation that would deter an attack on them from fear of a retaliatory attack—and, of course, they made sure to let us know about it. At first it worked along tried-and-true lines: an envelope entrusted to a third party—a lawyer, apparently—who was instructed to put it in the mail on a certain date unless your father rescinded the order before that date.

In that way, your father insured his life and your mother's each month. Had we harmed them, the envelope would have been sent. Each month, he 'coiled the spring,' and at the end of the month he did it again.

"How did he transmit his instructions to the lawyer each month? That is something we don't know. But depend on your parents; they knew every trick in the spy handbook, including some that they invented themselves. Only years later, when your father began working in the computer field, did he develop a sophisticated program to coil the spring via electronic mail. The program was designed to transmit an email message at a specific future date. He was the only one who could prevent it from being sent, by way of a secret password. Each month he established a new date for the transmission."

"And what did the email message contain?"

"Just one thing: Agent 6's 'fingerprint.' The erroneous fragment of information that had been embedded in Alexander Kittin's mind twenty years earlier. A fragment that he himself was not aware was false. He didn't even know which area of knowledge it had been taken from."

"And who was the email supposed to reach?"

"The Ukrainian intelligence bureau, of course."

"So now that our father is no longer alive, there is no one to stop the message from being sent, and the Ukrainians will be able to expose him," Avreimi mused.

"Why—and I'm not trying to give you any ideas—didn't anyone try to get the information out of our mother?" asked Chezky.

"She doesn't have it."

"Why not?"

"Your mother hardly worked with Agent 6. Alexander Kittin did not require guidance in Jewish knowledge because he had acquired basic knowledge at home. The one who worked intensively with him was your father, who taught him about Israeli culture. That's why your father was the one who planted the false item of information in Kittin's mind."

"So our mother doesn't know it to this day? Our parents never talked about it to each other? Our father knew and didn't tell his own wife?"

"That was the way they worked: They preferred not to share their operational secrets with each other. That's far more secure for both sides. What you don't know can't hurt you."

"One of Abba's classic sayings, right?" Avreimi remarked as an aside to his brother. Chezky nodded.

"I'd like to point out," Mackenzie said, "that there was still some sort of system worked out between your parents. That system was designed to liberate the information, in the event that one of them was harmed and the other one wished to reconstruct it."

"Like now, for example..."

"Very true."

"And what was the system?"

"They called it the 'safes.' But I must confess that I, at least, don't know what was meant by that."

The first thought that popped into both brothers' heads was the secret hiding place that Itzik Peled had revealed to them just yesterday. But it had been completely empty, except for their father's passport.

"Could there be other safes in the house?" Chezky asked Avreimi quietly. Sean Mackenzie, though ignorant of Hebrew, grasped his meaning.

"These were not actual safes," he explained. "Just as no one *actually* coiled a spring, and no one really planted a fingerprint..."

Chezky nodded, slightly taken aback by the fact that the Englishman seemed to be able to read him like an open book.

"So you've come to us so that we can find the safes for you?" he asked.

"No, no," Mackenzie said quickly. "I've come to you only in order to find your mother. She wants no contact with us, and that places her in danger."

"So that she can give you Alexander Kittin's fingerprint?"

"Something like that."

"So who is Agent 6? That's the million-dollar question."

"The million-ruble question." Sean Mackenzie smiled.

"Or million-*hryvnia*, in this case."

"Ukrainian intelligence," the British agent continued, "has a few potential suspects. It could be, for example, a deputy-minister in your government, the manager of a government office, a large industrialist, or perhaps a military man. Outwardly, he looks like a loyal and devoted citizen, but in actuality he is working on behalf of British interests. You've surely grasped the importance that the Ukrainians attach to exposing him—and the 'fingerprint' that can identify him is in your parents' hands."

Chezky was confused. "Just a minute. Where, exactly, do the Ukrainians come into the picture?"

"An excellent question," said Mackenzie. "One evening, after a few years that passed peacefully and pleasantly for your parents and they became the parents of two sweet boys named Avreimi and Chezky, an uninvited guest arrived at their house."

"Professor Willotzky, returned from the dead," Chezky guessed in a dramatic voice.

"Not exactly," Mackenzie said. "It was a refugee from the KGB who was working for Ukraine's security service, which was founded in those days on the ruins of the Soviet Union. The man had taken stacks of files from KGB headquarters and gone through them. When he discovered that there were two senior agents in Israel, he decided to put them back in play and activate them for his own purposes.

"Your parents, of course, flatly refused. They saw themselves as absolved of all responsibility toward the KGB, which no longer existed. The Ukrainian did not give up. Fair play is not a commodity in the intelligence world; only the language of power is understood. He threatened to give them away to the Israeli Shin-Bet, who would be happy to accuse them of spying, contact with a foreign agent, and transmitting information to the enemy.

"Your parents fell back on the same defense mechanism that they'd used against us. They told the Ukrainian that, if he dared harm them, they would make sure that the list of five former Soviet agents—and their 'fingerprints'—would be sent to the Western intelligence bureaus. They assumed, they told him, that those agents were now part of the Ukrainian secret service. From that moment, the Ukrainians also had a good reason to keep your parents alive and free."

"So, at this point there are two intelligence agencies with an interest in protecting our parents," Avreimi summarized. "The British and the Ukrainians."

"And then the Israelis joined the party," said Sean Mackenzie.

"Naturally." Chezky grinned.

"It was in the year 1993. As I told you before, I was sent from London in search of information about the port of Bandar-Abbas, Iran. In exchange, the Shin-Bet demanded a meeting with your mother. The very next day, she was invited down to the Shin-Bet offices in Jerusalem."

"In other words, you 'sold' her," Chezky said accusingly.

An apologetic expression crossed Mackenzie's face. "It was not my decision. I was just a small cog in the system."

Chezky grimaced with clear distaste.

"And the Shin-Bet wanted to use her to put pressure on our father?"

"Correct. Because they couldn't touch him."

"Why not?"

"Because he had received a full pardon even before his return to Israel."

"A pardon? From whom?"

"I don't know. But it's a fact that they couldn't get close to him."

"Interesting…"

"In any case, she met with a tough Shin-Bet investigator by the name of Shaul Armoni, who demanded all the information she had about every topic under the sun, more or less. He threatened to make sure she sat in jail for the rest of her life—but he didn't know whom he was dealing with. Your mother did the same thing to him that she had done to the others."

"Which is…?"

"She described to him, in detail, the coiled-spring mechanism, and told him that it would be her great pleasure to add him to the good company of the British MI6 and the Ukrainian SBU"

"What information did your mother have against Israel?"

"That's what Shaul Armoni asked."

"And what was her answer?"

"That he should check out Dr. Ali Hamad, an expert in Arab culture and Islamic writings in Teheran University.

"Armoni stepped out of the interrogation room for a moment, made a phone call, and returned with an absolutely stunned expression on his face. Now he sang a different tune. 'What do you want?' he asked angrily. Your mother said that if he didn't leave her and her husband alone, she would inform the Iranian authorities about the veteran Israeli agent who'd been planted in their country for decades."

"And who was this Dr. Hamad?" Avreimi asked, hoping they were finally nearing the end of the saga.

"He'd worked for a time with your father, in the same KGB Directorate in Kiev, but returned to Iran not long afterward."

"An Iranian—working as an Israeli agent?" Chezky asked in astonishment.

"Certainly—in case you were wondering just how crazy the world of espionage can be. It was a very strange story. A KGB investigator once told your father that Dr. Hamad was a Jew helping the Soviet Aliyah *refuseniks*. Your father held onto that information, loyal to the principle of compartmentalization that he was so good at, and told it to your mother only when they had to exert pressure on Israel."

Avreimi and Chezky looked at each other helplessly. They knew Chana Kohlberg as a wonderful wife and mother, homemaker and beloved high-school secretary. The picture that Sean Mackenzie was painting depicted a ruthless, many-armed monster who threatened the whole world and did as she pleased with regard to intelligence bureaus.

"I know what you're thinking," Mackenzie said, "and that's exactly what Shaul Armoni told her. 'Mrs. Kohlberg, you would never give away Dr. Hamad and cause his death. You're a religious woman, aren't you?"

Avreimi and Chezky had not considered this aspect, but Armoni's question, asked years before, was an appropriate one.

"And do you know what she answered?" Mackenzie continued.

"What?"

"She said, 'Mr. Armoni, where I grew up there is no religion and no values. It's every man for himself. Let me be very clear: Neither my husband nor I are religious, so don't build up hopes based on our suffering consciences. If I feel that we are in danger, I will not hesitate to expose your man without batting an eyelash. Don't be fooled by our outward appearance. We are living in an ultra-Orthodox community only for reasons of convenience. This is simply a comfortable disguise. We have no connection to religion.'"

Chezky listened to this with relative equilibrium, but Avreimi turned pale as chalk. Of everything that he had heard these past few days, this frightened him more than anything. His mother had declared that neither she nor their father was religious… and Mackenzie wasn't their only source for this. This week, he had heard about somebody else who would report on his parents every year. And each time he had written that, to the best of his understanding, they were not really religious…

"So what happened all of a sudden?" Chezky asked.

"Very simple. A few weeks ago, Dr. Ali Hamad died in Iran. Your parents lost their leverage against Israel. Armoni, of course, was the first to find out. From his perspective, the whole game was starting over."

"By the way, who is this Armoni fellow?" Chezky asked.

"Don't ask," Sean Mackenzie said dryly. "He's vengeful and he's cruel. With him, everything is about plots and strategies and intrigues."

"What are you saying?" Avreimi was finding all this hard to believe. "Do you think he killed our father?"

"Let's analyze who benefits from the fact that there's no one to coil the spring," Mackenzie said, evading the direct question. "The Ukrainians have a clear interest, because the email, if sent, will expose Alexander Kittin. That will precipitate an international nightmare: a British agent in a position of power in Ukraine. Britain, incidentally, has been trying in vain to locate Kittin, to warn him that he's in danger. I can reveal to you that he has not been on active duty for many years now. We don't even know whether or not he's in Ukraine."

"Just a minute—their agents will be exposed, too."

"I told you yesterday: That's a price they're willing to pay. And agents can always be pulled out. They've probably already informed the five agents that they have until midnight tonight to drop everything and return to Ukraine."

"And what about Israel?"

"Israel has no problem with Britain being embarrassed. But that's not yet a reason to kill people."

"Then what is?"

"Shaul Armoni. In my view, he is the prime suspect. It would be just like him to let the Ukrainians finish off your father. Don't forget that your parents wounded his honor. He doesn't forget a thing like that."

"But who is he? Who is Armoni?"

"One of the most powerful figures in the Israeli intelligence network."

"Does he have a specific position? Is there anyone superior to him?"

"I can tell you this: He has someone beneath him. Someone who is his right-hand man and trusted confidant."

"And who is that?"

"Someone we all saw in action yesterday," Mackenzie said. "His name is Itzik Peled."

57

THE KOHLBERG BROTHERS STARED AT ONE ANOTHER IN shock. If Sean Mackenzie had meant to tarnish Itzik Peled's image in their eyes—he had succeeded in a big way. He had built a magnificent edifice of ideas, layer upon layer, concluding with an on-target suspicion of Peled's trustworthiness.

"Well, then…" Chezky sniped at his brother.

Avreimi looked even more stunned than Chezky.

"And you still believe him," Chezky said. "How gullible can you get?"

Avreimi's eyes were fixed vacantly on Chezky's face, but his mind was in full tilt. Things had not fallen into place for him. Something was still puzzling.

"What you've said is very convincing, Mr. Mackenzie," he said finally, while Chezky translated into English. "But perhaps *you* are also involved in all of this? After all, you were also there, on Rechov Malchei Yisrael, when my father died."

Mackenzie looked surprised.

"Who told you…?"

Chezky answered sternly. "No one told us. We saw several video clips from security cameras. We saw you pass right behind our father."

Mackenzie recovered quickly. "True. I was there," he admitted. "But I had a good reason. Your father asked me to meet him."

Chezky gave him a *who do you think you're fooling*? look.

"My father asked you to meet him," he repeated. "And now you remember to tell us about it."

"And if he invited you to a meeting, why didn't you speak to him?" Avreimi added.

Sean Mackenzie's answer surprised them: "Because, to this day, I don't know what he looked like."

This statement called for an explanation.

"I actually came to Israel to try to reach your mother. Your father, don't forget, never worked for us. On the other hand, we did have a responsibility toward your mother. When we heard about Dr. Hamad's death in Iran—we'd had a certain connection with him as well—we knew that she would be open to attack by the Ukrainians or the Israelis. The problem was that she refused to answer our calls or to contact us. Neither threats nor cajoling helped. When she wanted to, she knew how to be stubborn. In the end, it was your father who established contact, and asked me to meet him."

"How did he do that?"

"He sent a message through a third party, saying that he wanted to sit down for a few minutes and talk."

"Where?"

"In some bar at Rechov Malchei Yisrael 5."

Chezky nearly burst out laughing. "A bar? You mean, like... a pub? Near Kikar Shabbat?"

Mackenzie dug in his pocket and found a slip of paper. "It says, 'Paradise Bar.' Do you know it?"

Chezky glanced at Avreimi. "5 Malchei Yisrael," he mused out loud. "That's where Pitzuchei Gan Eden is, right?"

Avreimi shrugged. How would he know? All of Geulah these days sold *pitzuchim*... That is, where they hadn't yet opened a fast-food eatery or a clothing store...

"In any case, I wasn't able to find any bar and I didn't meet your father," Mackenzie said. "I figured that the middleman hadn't understood him, or else that your father had been delayed, and I began looking for him in other ways. I knew more or less where your parents lived, but I didn't know what they were calling themselves these days. I searched for an 'Arzi' family, and for 'Aranowich,' but I found nothing.

"Gradually, I came to the realization that they were living in an ultra-Orthodox community. The next day I was in Bnei Brak, and was amazed to see how many old contacts we also had there. Two days later, I had the name 'Shlomo Kohlberg' and the address—but when I got there, as you know, it was too late. I was in total shock. As I stood in the doorway of the apartment, I realized that something had happened, but I'm unfamiliar with Jewish mourning practices. When I heard that your father had died three days earlier, I understood that I'd missed him at the last minute."

His last words sent a shiver through the brothers. Was it possible that, if their mother had agreed to meet the Englishman, everything would have turned out differently? Could their father's life have been saved? Could they have gone on being the big, happy family they'd been before?

Fateful matters hung in the balance, yet ordinary life marched on. Avreimi had to pick up his little daughter from kindergarten. Chezky was in a hurry to reach the Institute. The secretary had phoned him again to remind him about his important meeting with Dr. Laskin.

"So what happens now?" he asked Sean Mackenzie.

"Without someone to re-coil the spring, the email messages will be sent out at midnight tonight. Regarding Alexander Kittin—either we'll be successful in locating him, or he's not in Ukraine at all, or he'll be arrested and gain international notoriety as a dangerous British spy. Regarding the five Ukrainian agents, it's not my job to worry about them. And as for your mother—it's truly a pity that she didn't want to meet with me. My only desire was to protect her and her family. In any case, extend her my condolences and those of the director of MI6—who, incidentally is the same low-level agent who came to see her in that modest hotel in London more than thirty years ago, when she escaped from the Soviet Union on her way to Israel."

"And you're going back to London?"

"There's nothing more for me to do here. I tried to help, and I failed."

Sadness was etched on the faces of the three men sitting in the car.

Sean Mackenzie waited a bit. The brothers were ready to leave, but he had one more thing to add.

"Look, I don't like accusing people without evidence, but it looks like someone chose to kill your father rather than let him meet me."

"Who could it have been?"

"I have a theory, but I won't share it with you," said Sean Mackenzie.

"Maybe you can change your mind?"

Mackenzie pressed his lips together. "When I said that I won't tell you, I meant it. But if you have access to video from the security cameras, why don't you get more clips and see who else was there at the time?"

Avreimi and Chezky didn't need to get anything. They were well aware of who had been there at the time: Itzik Peled. What they did not yet know was the nature of the new plot he was weaving.

As Chezky hurried to reach the religious institute in Givat Shmuel, Itzik Peled sat in his old Land Rover jeep a block or two from the men's entrance, waiting for him.

He was tense. At this stage of events he had neither a bagful of fancy technological tricks at his disposal nor a band of operatives worthy of the name. Where were the days when he had been able to rely on a battery of computer monitors to bring him photos from every arena—not to mention tiny microphones and GPS transmitters for planting on a subject, so that he could be tailed without his knowledge? He would have all those things later, during the official phase of the operation that the Prime Minister and Shin-Bet Director Amos Go'ash had authorized. But right now, at this early stage, he was doing something which, had they known about it, would have led to them hurling both him and Shaul Armoni down a flight of stairs…

Itzik picked up his phone and punched in a number.

"Where is the Russian?" he asked Rotem Cohen, the seventeen-year-old parking inspector, now an agent on Itzik's team…

"Facing the entrance, sitting in a Buick," the youth replied, excited by the mission in which he was taking part.

"If he moves, call me immediately," Itzik ordered.

So Oleg Marinov, SBU man and security officer for the Ukrainian embassy, was waiting to ambush Chezky Kohlberg at the Institute's entrance. Good.

But what does a non-Jew know about ultra-Orthodox students? Itzik thought with an inward chuckle. In the next few moments, it looked like the number-two man on his team would be called upon to go into action—to draw the bird into the cage.

The bus pulled up at the stop. Chezky glanced at his watch. There was still half an hour to go before his meeting with Dr. Laskin. Why not do what he usually did—slip into the nearest entrance and grab a cup of coffee and something to eat first? That way, he could ask his friends who else had been invited to the meeting, and what old Laskin wanted from them.

He cut through the women's entrance with a mischievous wink at the guard, and crossed the big, grassy lawn at the heart of the campus on the diagonal until he reached the best café in the neighborhood.

His phone rang. The number was protected.

"Hello?" Chezky recognized the voice of Itzik Peled's unknown messenger. "I have another disk that the boss sent me to give you."

Chezky tensed. More clips from security cams? That was good news. Though they surely would not contain evidence against the person who'd sent them, every additional detail could help.

"Where are you?" he asked the messenger.

The man paused a moment, as though seeking something. "Rechov Einstein," he said. "It says here, 'Men's Entrance.'"

Chezky hastened to that entrance. The man in the battered white Toyota was probably waiting for him as he had done several days earlier, with his weird baseball cap and sunglasses, and his collar turned up to conceal his face.

"Hey, Kohlberg, what's up?" called one of his friends, seeing him run out. Chezky motioned to him that he would be right back.

There was a minor human traffic jam at the narrow gate. A new guard was being scrupulous about checking bag after bag and asking everyone if he was carrying a weapon. Chezky waited impatiently, thinking, *Where do I know that messenger's voice from?* Then the traffic moved forward and Chezky walked through the gate, his thoughts jumping to another topic.

Itzik Peled's phone rang. "Chezky's going through the gate," said the owner of the white Toyota.

Another call was waiting: "The Russian is leaving his car," Rotem Cohen reported.

Chezky's phone rang again. The same hidden number.

"I had to get away," whispered the "boss's" messenger. "I noticed a troublesome individual come on the scene."

Chezky stood on the sidewalk, watching the white Toyota retreat up the street. *Which troublesome individual would that be?* he wondered. It was entirely possible that someone whom Itzik's man considered troublesome could be beneficial in Chezky Kohlberg's book…

At that moment, his eye caught a vaguely familiar figure. The man wore a good suit and walked like an athlete. Then Chezky recalled where he knew him from. He had seen him in the cafeteria on Monday, reading a Russian-language newspaper.

To his surprise, the man came closer and stuck out his hand. "Mr. Kohlberg?"

Chezky shook the outstretched hand. The man's grip was powerful. "Whom do I have the honor of addressing?" he asked, with a mixture of interest and suspicion.

"An old friend of your father's," said Oleg Marinov. "I knew him more than thirty years ago." He spoke very fluent Hebrew, though with a thick Russian accent.

"That was here in Israel?" Chezky probed, though he knew the answer.

"No. In the Soviet Union."

Unbidden, a sudden popped into Chezky's head. "Just a minute. Weren't you the one who came to our house when we were sitting *shivah*?"

Oleg Marinov nodded, and a small, apologetic smile crossed his face. "I looked a bit different then. I didn't want to upset any of you, so I dressed like a religious person."

"You were the one who asked if my father had continued being involved in archeology?"

"Correct." The Ukrainian's smile broadened and he looked much more pleasant.

"So what's going on? What's the story with archeology?"

The man motioned toward the Buick parked nearby. "Instead of talking in the street, maybe we can sit down somewhere? I have many things to tell you. Your father could have been a very rich man—and it's still not too late."

Chezky experienced a dilemma. What about his meeting with Dr. Laskin?

Then, as though directed by Heaven itself, his phone rang. On the line was the Institute secretary, all apologies. Dr. Laskin, she explained, had fallen suddenly ill and would not be able to make today's meeting. She very much hoped that he hadn't come to school especially for that…

The Ukrainian waited patiently for Chezky to finish his call. "I know a fine kosher restaurant in Tel Aviv, not far from the beach," he said. He pointed again at his gleaming car. "Can I invite you?"

In the old Land Rover, the cell phone rang. "The *dati* just got into the Russian's Buick," Rotem Cohen reported.

Itzik breathed a sigh of relief. For the first time since that morning, he smiled.

The operation had been crowned with success. Chezky Kohlberg was in the Ukrainians' hands.

C HEZKY JUST MANAGED TO STOP AN ADMIRING WHISTLE from escaping his lips. The Buick's interior was even more sumptuous than its exterior. The soft leather seats and gleaming wood dashboard took away his breath. They also caused him to lower his guard.

"Let's not waste time," said the Ukrainian. "We have a great deal to talk about." He turned away from Givat Shmuel, moving in the direction of the Gehah Highway.

"You are aware that your parents once worked for the KGB?" the Ukrainian security officer asked. Chezky was aware of this, as well as of the next items on Oleg Marinov's list: that his mother had designed the 'Fingerprint' system, thus exposing many Soviet spies to British intelligence.

"You must be asking yourself certain questions," Marinov continued. "First, whether your mother was born in Russia, and how she came to work for the British. Second, how it was that her betrayal was not discovered in time. And third, who was her contact man to the British? Perhaps there are also other things that you'd like to ask."

The Buick sped up, passing the Neve Achiezer neighborhood, the Coca-Cola intersection, and the Ma'ayanei Hayeshu'ah Hospital in a blur. Chezky took no interest in what was happening outside. His entire concentration was focused on the Ukrainian's words and the Buick's marvels. Traffic was heavy and he was no expert in surveillance, so that even if he had looked back, he would not have noticed Itzik Peled's vehicle following them. Oleg Marinov did notice, and was pleased.

"So—who was your mother, Anna Aranowich?" Oleg relaxed in his seat, one hand gripping the wheel. "In order to understand the story, we have to go back more than sixty years, to the period right after World War Two. Many young people throughout Europe were drawn to the Communist ideal. This is hard for us to understand today. In our eyes, Communism symbolizes dictatorship and tyranny and all the crimes that were perpetrated in its name. For you Jews, in particular, it symbolizes religious persecution and assimilation. But in that period after the war, people were disappointed with all ideologies and longed to build a new and better world. A world in which everyone was equal. A world without oppressors and the oppressed. A world in which everyone would work for everyone.

"In a small city not far from London, there lived a young Jewish girl by the name of Henya Aranowich. Her family had managed to escape from Poland before the war, but was subsequently split in half: Henya's father reached England, but his brothers ended up in the Soviet Union and stayed there. That young woman—who is actually your grandmother—was, like many other young people, a member of the local Communist organization. The authorities, of course, did not look with a kindly eye on groups of that sort, though they did not declare Communism illegal. Your grandmother studied nuclear physics in university, but when the time came to search for a job she was rejected because of the serious ideological stain on her character. Young Henya married a local Jewish boy, a fellow Communist member. He was a fellow who knew how to get by, and was also considered very capable compared to other young men his age.

"A number of months after their marriage, Henya opted to donate several years to the Revolution and the Party. She listened to political speeches about the beautiful life in the Soviet Union, where workers and farmers lived in harmony, and wanted to offer her knowledge by working there for a few years in the field of nuclear research.

"Her husband tried to dissuade her from carrying out her plan. He was less naïve than she was. In England, he made a living from various business enterprises, not all of them legal. In Russia, he knew, he would not be able to live as comfortably as he did in England. But his wife's ideological enthusiasm was unstoppable. When he refused to go along with her plan, she accused him of harming the Revolution and the Party. In the end, it was decided that she would go to Russia and he would follow at a later date.

"Through the intercession of the Communist Party in England, Comrade Henya was sent to Kiev, where she worked in the research department of the Stalin Physics University. Their daughter, Anna, was born in Russia. It didn't take long for your grandmother to realize that life in the Soviet Union was not the blissful existence that the Party said it was. There were days when they literally had no food, the heat didn't always work, and medicine for the child could be bought only on the black market. She was not even given a flat to live in as a token of appreciation for her dedication, but had to crowd into a small room in her aunt's flat—her father's sister—who was an ardent Jew despite the fact that religion had been declared illegal under Soviet law.

"Henya's husband, your grandfather and your mother's father, remained in England, waiting patiently until his wife saw the light and agreed to return. From time to time he traveled to the Soviet Union as a tourist, bringing some foreign currency and food products for his wife and daughter. The KGB turned a blind eye to his 'crimes' because it used him to pass messages from headquarters in Moscow to their branch in London.

"Finally, the time came when Henya decided that she had donated enough to the cause, and she wished to return to England. That was when, to her shock, she discovered that leaving the Soviet

Union was forbidden. In the framework of her work, she was told, she was in possession of important state secrets and could not be allowed ever to return to the West. No one suspected that she would betray them, they assured her, but British intelligence agents were known for their cruelty, and it must be feared that they would interrogate and torture her until she told them everything she knew.

"If Henya, your grandmother, had still had any faith in the Soviets, this turn of events would have shown her the enormity of her error. She was a 'prisoner' in the Soviet Union, raising Anna, her young daughter, with no hope of ever returning home. The Russians, of course, proposed that her husband come live with them, but he was not prepared to stick his head into the lion's mouth. The couple was forced to wait and see what would happen. She would remain in the Soviet Union while he endeavored to work on her behalf through British channels.

"It was in this complex situation that your mother grew up, with a mother who continued to hold a senior position and was required to demonstrate loyalty to the regime, but who lived with a terrible sense of bitterness that can only be felt by one who's stepped into a trap with her eyes wide open.

"Your mother received a good education. She studied in a fine school in Kiev and was an outstanding student. From her mother she inherited a good heart and a love of humanity, and from her father shrewdness, cleverness, and even a touch of slyness. She was quickly targeted by KGB recruiters, who sent her to the organization's academy. There, too, she stood out and was considered a prime candidate. Her mother tried to dissuade her, but Anna wouldn't listen. At the age of twenty-something she had already begun working in KGB headquarters in Kiev.

"The particulars of her life were, of course, well known to her KGB superiors. They knew that she lived in the same house as her uncle—a man whom many thought was her father, and who led a religious lifestyle. She herself, of course, was an exemplary Soviet citizen. A complete atheist who believed in no faith, who scorned Jews that clung to 2,000-year-old customs, and who believed that Communism would ultimately triumph... Not even the fact that her biological father lived in the West and came to visit from time to time slowed her rise up the ranks. Anna Aranowich passed every test with flying colors, passed muster in every investigation, and was considered a loyal worker, above suspicion.

"One day, in the year 1977, it was proposed that she join the most secret project in the KGB: the 'School for Foreign Cultures,' in which future Soviet spies would be educated before being sent to countries in the West. Anna Aranowich was very conversant in Jewish religious customs, and her job was to teach those agents-in-training whose cover story included some sort of Jewish background.

"But several weeks before that, there was a tragedy in the family. Henya, Anna's mother, was killed in a traffic accident. The driver escaped without a trace and police did not take too much trouble about tracking him down. When Anna went through her mother's things, she found—to her shock—her mother's repeated requests for permission to leave the Soviet Union, and repeated refusals by the authorities. Her religious uncle claimed that the accident had not been accidental at all, but part of a deliberate plot to get rid of Henya. Anna didn't believe him, and even accused him of slandering the regime, but she soon heard some casual talk in the corridors of the KGB which confirmed the story: The state had indeed killed her mother after Henya threatened to turn to parties in the West, tell her story, and demand an exit visa from the Soviet Union.

"Anna was distraught. Her world had crumbled around her. At first she thought about leaving the organization where she worked alongside her mother's murderers. Then she decided to do something better: to continue her work and cause as much damage as possible from within its framework.

"Her father, you will remember, would still sometimes travel from London to the Soviet Union. Anna decided to share her plans with him and use him to establish a connection with British intelligence. He had already moved to Israel, she knew, but he still had good contacts in London."

The black car turned west, toward Tel Aviv. Chezky was enjoying the smooth, silent ride. If there was money to be found in the archeological angle, he reflected, he would one day buy himself a Buick LaCrosse exactly like this one.

"So my mother's contact person was… her father?" he asked. Sean Mackenzie had told him and his brother that the contact man was a relative, but had not mentioned how close a relative…

"Exactly," said Oleg. "She waited for his next visit to the Soviet Union, filled with a desire for revenge. Then she showed him evidence of the fact that her mother, his wife, had been killed by Party operatives. He seemed as shocked as she had been, and asked what she intended to do. She told him about her new position at the 'School for Foreign Cultures' and about the plan she had devised—the 'Fingerprint' mechanism that would be able to pinpoint any student of hers who might be planted in a Western country in the future. Her father memorized the list of false items of information and promised to pass them on to senior people he knew in British intelligence. They agreed that he would stop visiting the Soviet Union in order to keep suspicion away from her, and that even if he had to travel there on his own affairs he would not visit her."

"By the way, when did he pass away?" asked Chezky.

Oleg glanced at him while driving.

"I take it that you have not figured out who I am talking about," he said with a smile.

Chezky wrinkled his brow in thought. No. He did not know who they were talking about.

"Because he is not dead," Oleg continued.

Chezky jumped. "He's alive? Our grandfather is alive?"

Oleg studied him out of the corner of his eye. "You really don't know?"

"No. Really."

"You're just pretending…"

"I am absolutely serious!" Chezky insisted. "Who is it?"

"It's amazing that your parents were able to hide it from you all these years," Oleg remarked, as though to himself.

By this time, Chezky was burning with curiosity.

"Because your grandfather," Oleg told him, "your mother's father, is the former orphanage administrator, Yechezkel Polowitz."

59

T HE ENORMITY OF THE SHOCK RENDERED CHEZKY speechless.

Over the past three weeks, he had become accustomed to surprises and turnarounds. He had thought that nothing had the power to surprise him anymore. But this was above and beyond anything. Yechezkel Polowitz, that elderly, questionable character whom the kibbutz secretary reported as having sold children from the orphanage—*he* was their grandfather? He was their mother's father? How was that possible?

So many questions whirled through his mind at once. First, how had it come to pass that their father had married—coincidentally or not—the daughter of the man who was responsible for his being raised in a completely secular environment? Second, what was the meaning behind their father's brief interchange with that same Polowitz on Rechov Ezer Yoldot, just minutes before Abba collapsed? And third, what was the connection between all of that and the missing page and documents about their father in the orphanage records?

Now Sean Mackenzie's words took on new significance. He had said that their mother was angry at her contact man and had cut off all ties with him. Indeed, she had spent all these years with her father living in the same city, and had ignored his existence! But if that was the case, why had she visited him yesterday? And why had she gone from his house directly into that black car?

And another question: If Yechezkel Polowitz—their grandfather (how strange it felt to call him that!)—was not suffering from senility or a faulty memory, had he recognized him and Avreimi when they'd come to see him to ask about an orphan from the past by the name of Shlomo Kohlberg? Had he realized that they were speaking of his son-in-law? Had he understood that his two grandsons were standing in front of him and decided to pretend he didn't know them? If that was the case, then it wasn't only their mother who had banished him from her life, but their grandfather who had excised her and her whole family as well...

The Buick was sailing along Sdereot Rokeach, between Luna Park and Ganei Yehoshua. Chezky's enthusiasm for the car had subsided beneath the force of his stunned confusion. *I have to call Avreimi*, he thought. He needed to let his brother know about this dramatic development. It completely changed the whole picture...

"Just tell me this," he told Oleg Marinov. "When did my mother find out that my father was a 'graduate' of her father's orphanage? Back in Kiev?"

"No," Oleg replied. "In Kiev, they agreed to keep from each other any information that there was no need to know. It was only when they arrived in Israel and married that they began to fill in the details for one another. Your father was surprised to hear that the man he had known as his father-in-law in Kiev was actually his wife's *uncle*—while his real father-in-law had been living in Jerusalem for several years by then.

"I don't have to tell you how stunned he was when he realized that his true father-in-law was none other than the administrator of the orphans' home who'd sold him to a kibbutz as a child and avoided him when he came, shortly before he moved to the Soviet Union, to find out who his real parents were. Only then did he learn that Polowitz had provided various services for the KGB. For example, he exposed Aliyah activists in their headquarters at 7 Mikelob Street, and it was he who sent Zalman Berkovitch back to Israel, to serve as a hold over your father and to ensure his loyalty."

"And did... our grandfather... know who his daughter had married?"

"Not at first," Oleg said. "He did keep track of your mother. He knew where she was studying and tried to send her money and help—which she rejected. He sent messages saying that he was sorry and regretted what he had done. He was prepared to buy them an apartment and support them, as long as they forgave him. Once, he even called up and cried over the phone, but she hung up on him. She was not able to forgive him.

"Incidentally," Oleg added with a sudden smile, "since we're on the subject—*I* brought your parents the money for their present apartment. A few months after they moved to Israel, I came here with one of the operation's supervisors and handed them a fat bundle of dollars..."

Chezky took his phone from his pocket and toyed with it. *I must call Avreimi*, he thought again. *He won't believe his ears.*

The Buick made a sharp left onto Rechov Ibn-Gabirol, and traveled over the Bar-Yehuda Bridge spanning the Yarkon.

"Are we close?" Chezky asked. He was hungry; also, he wanted to call Avreimi out of the Ukrainian's hearing, when they got out of the car and walked to the restaurant. The Buick turned right again, onto Rechov Usishkin—but then Oleg Marinov suddenly braked. A tall, broad-shouldered man stood waiting for them on the sidewalk. He opened the right rear door and got in. Chezky saw the left rear door open as well, and another man climbed inside. The car sped off again.

Chezky's heart began to speed up, too. Oleg's pleasant demeanor up until now would have led him to expect a courteous introduction of the two new passengers, but the Ukrainian's face wore a very different expression now, remote and detached.

Oleg drove a few seconds before he turned to Chezky and said, with a jerk of his head, "Give them the phone."

Chezky was frozen in shock. He was unable to utter a syllable or move a muscle. The change in the atmosphere was sudden and it was frightening.

"Give them the phone." Oleg Marinov raised his voice. He continued driving, both hands on the wheel and eyes facing front.

Chezky turned around, panic-stricken. The man seated on the right was fear-inducing. His body was a solid mass of muscle and his face was cruel. The one on the left, in contrast, looked like somebody's nice uncle…

"Give us your phone," said the man on the left. He had a soft voice and spoke Hebrew with a light Russian accent.

Chezky looked back at Oleg, in the grip of a deathly terror. "What is this?" he asked, his voice cracking. "You're kidnaping me?"

The Ukrainian's lips tightened.

"The doors are locked," he said dryly, as Chezky's hand inched toward the handle.

"Give me the phone," the man on the rear left repeated.

Chezky glanced outside. He was traveling through the heart of Tel Aviv. There were people all around, coming and going—and he had been kidnaped without anyone noticing!

"Give me your phone immediately," the man repeated.

Chezky was reluctant to obey. In the next instant, he felt two powerful arms grab him from behind and drag him over the front seat to the back. He was overwhelmed with a terrible fear. How had this happened? Why hadn't he suspected that this was a trap? Sean Mackenzie, the British agent, had told them that the Ukrainians were working hand in glove with the Shin-Bet—with Shaul Armoni and Itzik Peled.

Oleg looked at him in the mirror. "The less you resist, the less you will suffer," he said curtly.

The blood froze in Chezky's veins. Suddenly, out of nowhere, came an awful realization: He knew the identity of Itzik Peled's messenger. The man's voice had been familiar to him. How could it not be? They'd met early in the week, on Sunday. That's why the messenger had worn a baseball cap and oversized sunglasses. That was why he had also concealed the bottom portion of his face, which sported a beard. It was hard to believe that a religious fellow who appeared so gentle could participate in such a crime. The messenger had been none other than Moshe Sotzkover, Itzik Feled's son-in-law. Apparently, that rat had managed to corrupt *him*, as well.

Now all was clear. Now he understood why Sotzkover had been first on the scene to treat his father on Ashtorei HaParchi, with Itzik "coincidentally" wandering nearby. Sotzkover had indeed taken care of his father—though not in the way that is generally taught in first-aid courses…

Chezky's phone was now in the possession of the thug in the seat to his right, who had tossed it onto the front seat. The man also searched his pockets and clothing; Chezky's wallet and key ring soon rested beside his cell phone.

"We have no interest in hurting you," said the Hebrew-speaker to his left. "Just stay calm and you won't feel a thing."

From a hidden compartment in the car the avuncular man took a square, flat, metal container, placed it on a shelf that dropped at the back of the driver's seat, and swiftly opened it. The Buick, apparently, was large enough to allow kidnaping victims to be dealt with in comfort…

Chezky watched the man in undisguised fear. Inside the flat metal container rested a number of glass vials, and next to them syringes of varying sizes.

If Chezky thought about kicking the shelf, sending the container flying and shattering the vials, the man on the right with the grip of iron frustrated his plan. He took plastic handcuffs from his pocket and shackled Chezky's hands and feet.

The left-hand fellow began fiddling with the vials and syringes with deep concentration.

Chezky closed his eyes, in which tears had begun to form. How low he had fallen… He was barely a newlywed, he had not yet finished setting up their apartment, and he and his wife were expecting their first child, whom he would never see. They would probably name the baby Chaim Yechezkel, if it was a boy. Originally, they had planned on calling him Shlomo, after his father…

Twenty-three… was that any age to leave this world? What had he managed to accomplish in his brief lifetime? And how much more he could have accomplished… His friends from the Institute would come to the cemetery, neatly clad, earbuds in their ears and student backpacks over their shoulders, and would click their tongues over him. How tragic. How sad. What a waste… He was so close to earning his degree. Why, Dr. Laskin had invited him to his office to ask how he could ease his burden in light of his father's death… But he would be borne along among them all on a hard stretcher, wrapped in shrouds, listening to his mother and siblings cry, and thinking, *Degree, shmegree. Career, shmareer.* If only he could get up for one minute and scream at them, "Guys, wake up from your dream world!"

Because just as 23 years pass by, so do 70 or 80 years. And suddenly you find yourself staring up at a strip of pale sky from inside a deep hole, as they start to cover it up…

Abba would undoubtedly be there to meet him. They say that all fathers and grandfathers come to welcome the newest member of the family to join them up above. What an embarrassment! Abba would probably tell him, "Why did you get into that Ukrainian's car? Why didn't you realize that it was a death trap?"

No! That wasn't what his father would focus on. Abba would tell him, "Chezky, do you know why you got into that Ukrainian's car? Because the only thing that interested you was a shiny car or money that could be made from some archeological find. The vanities of this world and all of its nonsense and fleeting pleasures… But here, my dear Chezky, there are no cars and no money, no degrees and no titles. Here they ask you how much you managed to learn. How many mitzvos you did. How many times you triumphed over your nature. And how many times each day you thought about your Creator. I didn't merit the things that you had. I was raised on a Communist kibbutz and in the Soviet Union, because that's what Divine Providence decreed for me—perhaps only in order to let me meet your mother, she should be well and live 120 years, and merit bringing a family of righteous Jews into the world.

"Yes, Chezky. I did not merit achieving true understanding there on that world. I was a *tinok shenishbah* in the hands of Yechezkel Polowitz. But you, Chezky, were raised with Torah and *yiras Shamayim*. Your mother and I did everything in our power to make sure that no one ever knew it was all one big act. I kept the mitzvos, I prayed three times a day, I went to *shiurim* to learn Torah, and you and your siblings were sure that it was all real. You had all the conditions you needed to grow and flourish—and look what your goal in life was, and where they are. Avreimi is sitting and learning, and Ari is also okay (though, between us, he could stand to work a little harder). But you? What a pity. What a pity…

"And no, Chezky, I don't mean that you had to necessarily learn in a *kollel* all day for your entire life. Here, in the *Olam Ha'emes*, every person's capabilities are known. But even in law school you could have amassed plenty of mitzvos and good deeds. If you'd only gone there with the recognition that the first obligation you undertook in the *kesubah* when you married was to support your wife… If you'd only understood that your share in revealing the glory of Heaven in the world was to be a Jew who worked for a living and established set times for learning Torah… Take Sholom Widboski, for example. Yes, that Belgian fellow who sits next to you in class. The one whose rebbe sent him to study law, and who you laugh about because he insists on taking off his glasses during lectures on business law given by Dr. Rina Avigdor, despite an explicit promise by the administration that there would be only male lecturers. Or Shloimy Gross, who stays behind during breaks to learn the *daf yomi* while the rest of the class goes down to the cafeteria to while away the time. They provide *nachas* up here, even as they're studying *chukas hagoyim,* as Avreimi liked to put it—not that I approved of his mockery, either then or now. Avreimi was born with different abilities and different talents. It's hard to sit all day and learn without interruption, but that's not such a big *nisayon* for him, with his brilliant mind and incredible capacity for diligence…

"And do you know, Chezky, what I feel the most sorry about? Your last Rosh Hashanah. You didn't come to us because you said that you had to stay home. Down there, in the *olam ha'sheker*, I didn't know why. But here, there are no secrets. Here I know that you grabbed every free minute on that *Yom Ha'din* and... studied for your exam in Jewish law. You told yourself: This is Torah. What's wrong with learning this on Rosh Hashanah? What a pity, Chezky. What a pity... Had your Rosh Hashanah looked different, both of us could have been down there today, in the world that's full of emptiness but where you can accrue more and more merit...

"You were the lucky one, Chezky. They killed me quickly. It took a long time for you. You had time to think about how much you'd accomplished in your 23 years of life. Not much, in all. Ten years since your bar mitzvah... The suffering you underwent in those last moments will also stand you in good stead. What do you think I brought with me when I got here? A few people who saw them 'working' on me in the street and received a bit of *chizuk* or said a few *perakim* of *Tehillim*..."

Rechov Usishkin was crowded for some reason, and the Buick proceeded along slowly.

"*Mal'chik plachet* (the boy is crying)," the burly man told Oleg Marinov with a laugh. Chezky knew neither Russian nor Ukrainian, but it was clear that the man was making fun of the fact that he was sobbing, the tears running unashamedly down his cheeks.

The man on his left finished dealing with the contents of the metal box and picked up a syringe filled with some colorless liquid.

"You won't feel a thing," he told Chezky in his soft voice, while pulling up Chezky's sleeve and swabbing his skin with alcohol.

Chezky ignored him. He had more important things to do right then. He closed his eyes and focused his thoughts with all his might. What should he do now? What was his task at this moment? What did Hakadosh Baruch Hu want from him in these, his last minutes on earth? Should he say "*Shema Yisrael*"? And what, exactly, did it mean to say *viduy*? Was that like the "*al cheits*" of Yom Kippur? What was a Jew supposed to do before he went up to stand before the Heavenly Court? Old people no doubt took care to clarify such things while there was still time, but at the age of 23 that's not exactly one's primary concern.

"I knew your parents many years ago," the man with the syringe told Chezky. "I worked with them in Russia. Good people, all in all."

"Yompolsky! *Zatknis* (be quiet)!" snapped Oleg. But the man, Yompolsky, continued talking.

"They were an outstanding couple even back in Russia. We were friends. They never told you about Yevgeny Yompolsky?"

I have to fight back, Chezky thought. *I have to kick and scream and fight for my life. I can't just go like a sheep to the slaughter...*

"Hold him," Yompolsky told the second man, as though he had read Chezky's mind.

The man's steel hands gripped Chezky and seemingly welded him to the spot.

He felt the needle pierce his skin.

He felt the man slowly plunge the needle into his vein, and then remove it and clean the wound with a piece of cotton-wool dipped in alcohol.

Chezky started floating. Through the fog, he saw Yompolsky smile at him. "If you don't fight it, in two or three hours it'll all be over," his voice echoed as though from far away. "If you struggle, it'll only be harder."

I have two or three hours, Chezky thought with relief as he floated in the air. I have enough time to think about all the things that I never stopped to think about in 23 years.

But—no, he realized a second later. Apparently, not all the time was his to use.

"In a few minutes, you will fall asleep," Yompolsky said, gently kneading the injection site. Chezky began to feel an odd pressure inside his skull.

"Don't worry. It will be all right," Dr. Yevgeny Yompolsky soothed him.

But Chezky didn't need soothing. He wasn't worried. He felt calmer and more peaceful than he ever remembered feeling before. He had no questions, only the answer. All his fears and worries vanished. Everything was good, everything was nice. As nice as it could be for a mortal man in this humble world…

"WHAT ABOUT SHABBOS?" ASKED AVREIMI'S WIFE. IF necessary, she said, she would be happy to travel to Jerusalem the next day, Friday morning, and prepare everything for Shabbos there.

Avreimi had told her that his mother had been forced to fly out of the country on some matter and she understood that, even if she asked, he would not be able to explain. Miri and the children would be home, and perhaps Ari would also want to come in from yeshivah.

"It depends on Chezky, too," Avreimi said. "This is the last Shabbos before the *sheloshim*."

It would be best for the whole family to be together, he thought. And maybe—who knew?—Ima would be back by then. After all, Sean Mackenzie had told them that she had already returned from Ukraine, though she had not contacted or telephoned any of them. Perhaps she was in the country but hiding. Or maybe she had not returned, and the Englishman had been misinformed. The problem was that he had been trying to reach Chezky for the past two hours, with no success. His brother was simply unavailable.

"Have you tried him at home?" asked his wife.

"I did. His wife doesn't know any more than I do. She said that he had an important meeting at his school today, so maybe he turned off his phone."

Avreimi went to Jerusalem to spend the night with his siblings, more concerned about Chezky's disappearance than he had let on to his wife. There were several burning issues to discuss. The monument maker had said that, unless they sent him the final text immediately, the headstone would not be ready by Monday. R' Zerach had suggested that they conduct a *seudah* and a *siyum mishnayos* in shul on Sunday night. Avreimi had arranged to speak with Chezky this afternoon, when his brother was finished in Givat Shmuel, but his brother was nowhere to be found.

All the way to Jerusalem, Avreimi tried to reach Chezky—in vain. He also called Miri, at home, and asked if Chezky was there or if he had phoned.

He had not.

By the time Avreimi got off the bus on Sarei Yisrael, worry had begun to tickle him with cold fingers. *I've got to get Itzik Peled involved*, he thought. Itzik had told him not to call under any circumstances. So it would be necessary to visit his home. Avreimi decided to make a detour en route to his parents' house and make his way via Rashi and David Yellin Streets.

Itzik's wife, Brachah, was startled to see him at the door. A moment later she regained her equilibrium and asked how he was.

"*Baruch Hashem.* Is Itzik at home?"

"Ah, no. He went out around noon and hasn't been back."

"Does he have a cell phone?"

"I can send him a message if it's important."

"Yes, it *is* important," Avreimi said. "Tell him that Chezky, my brother, went to Givat Shmuel hours ago, and has been unreachable by phone since then."

"I'll tell him," Brachah said, and quickly closed the door.

Avreimi walked slowly down the stairs to the lobby. He was supposed to go to his parents' house now, but he didn't feel up to the task of pretending that everything was fine. He had planned to learn with Yoel and talk a bit with Miri, but they would notice at once that he was tense and anxious. What to do?

Then he remembered—Minchah! There was no better time for *tefillah*. He had no way of knowing what this day would bring. What could be more appropriate than *davening* and pleading for mercy for Chana bas Henya and for Yechezkel ben Chana… for what, exactly? Success? Good health? Salvation?

This was the first time since his father's death that Avreimi did not go directly to the *amud* to lead the service. His supplication would be very long today, and he didn't want to inconvenience the other worshipers. He called his wife to let her know that he would be turning off his phone and going to shul.

"Just remember to turn it on again afterward," she said. Then an idea occurred to her. "Your brother probably did the same thing before he *davened*, and forget to turn it back on."

"I hope you're right," Avreimi told his good wife, who never had to work hard to judge people favorably. In her view, they were always righteous, always deserving.

Forty minutes later, Avreimi's eyes were damp and his emotions still roiling, but a series of calls informed him that salvation had yet to arrive. Chezky was still unreachable, being neither at home nor at their parents' house. Even his wife was beginning to worry.

All at once, a thought popped into Avreimi's head. He suddenly realized what Chezky, his brilliant brother, was doing. He must have decided to work alone again, without letting anyone know. Exactly the way he had once gone to the orphanage archive, where he had found the English rabbi's letter. So what had he done this time? Avreimi tried to enter his brother's legal mind.

Yesterday, Wednesday, they had gone together to Yechezkel Polowitz's house. That is, Chezky had suggested going, and he, as usual, had not succeeded in dissuading him from the idea and was dragged along. The situation had become complicated when they saw their mother emerge from the building and enter a black car. Then they were rushed home by Miri, who'd opened the door to an unexpected visitor named Sean Mackenzie. Chezky must have decided to return to Polowitz. That would be just like him.

What to do now? Call Mr. Polowitz? Or maybe call his secretary, that strange guy with the gray beard? Not a good idea. The secretary had been hostile to them on their previous visit, and he would certainly not be very receptive over the phone. There was no choice but to get up and go. If Chezky was there then he, Avreimi, would be there, too.

He had a little cash in his wallet that an *avreich* in his position should not waste on a taxi. But he had even less time at his disposal—time that a brother in his position should not waste on a bus.

This time, Avreimi did not hide in the yard next door, but went straight into the lobby. He pressed the intercom for "Rabbi Yechezkel Polowitz" with a confident finger. His concern for his brother's welfare filled him with energy and a sense of urgency.

No answer came from the top floor. Apparently, no one was home.

Who was Yechezkel Polowitz, anyway? Avreimi wondered. And how had he suddenly appeared in their lives? His was a name they'd never heard before. Now he seemed to be present whenever there was a catastrophe at hand: Polowitz had headed the orphans' home from which their father was sold to a kibbutz; Polowitz had chatted with their father just moments before Abba's death; it had been from Polowitz's apartment that their mother had emerged, only to vanish again; and Polowitz—according to Itzik Peled—had been in Kiev during the same period of time that his parents were there.

Avreimi pressed the intercom button again, a longer jab this time. Still no answer.

Maybe he had gone away somewhere? Avreimi turned around and peered into the parking lot. There stood a black-and-beige Chevrolet, in all its glory.

At that moment, the elevator door opened. Yechezkel Polowitz and his ubiquitous secretary stepped out, the secretary pushing Polowitz's wheelchair.

Polowitz looked older than Avreimi remembered him from his visit nearly a week earlier, on the previous Friday. He felt a stirring of anger at him, and curiosity about the meaning behind his actions. But, most of all, Avreimi found Polowitz pitiable.

The secretary pushed his employer's wheelchair rapidly toward the car. Avreimi hurried to keep up.

"Excuse me," he panted, addressing the secretary. "Did you happen to see my brother? Chezky Kohlberg?"

The gray-bearded man glared at Avreimi and continued walking.

"He was on his way here," Avreimi added, though he was not sure this was so.

"The *rav* is in a hurry," the secretary snapped. The right-hand door of the car opened to let down a sophisticated wheelchair lift. The secretary wheeled Polowitz onto this, and it began lifting him into the car.

"Perhaps the *rav* saw my brother?" Avreimi asked Polowitz directly.

"Who is this?" Polowitz asked his secretary.

"Kohlberg. Kohlberg's son."

"What does he want?"

"Just wasting our time…"

Then Yechezkel Polowitz surprised Avreimi. "He wants to ask questions?"

The secretary seemed to have swallowed his tongue.

"The *rav* is tired," he told Avreimi finally, taking refuge in his usual ploy. He nudged Avreimi aside.

"I'm not tired," Polowitz said, raising his voice. "He wants to ask questions?"

So, thought Avreimi. *The old man is not so senile after all.*

"Your brother was not here," the secretary whispered to Avreimi in a suddenly helpful tone. "Save yourself that question."

Avreimi nodded in grateful surprise.

"I will answer a few questions, and that's all," Polowitz announced. Though he sounded hoarse and weak, he knew what he wanted. He motioned to his driver to get behind the steering wheel and be prepared to drive.

Avreimi's brain worked furiously. What should he ask the old man? What was the most important? What did he want to know more than anything?

"Did you hand our father over to the kibbutz?" he asked without thinking.

Yechezkel Polowitz looked at Avreimi through the car's right-hand window—the same window through which he had spoken to Avreimi's father less than one month earlier.

"Yes," he said in a pained whisper. "I gave him, and also other children."

Avreimi considered asking him if he regretted it, but the answer was obvious.

"And… what was our mother doing here yesterday?"

Yechezkel Polowitz's mouth began to tremble. He closed his eyes for a very long moment.

"She punished me, but I deserved it," he said, his voice breaking. "She lived here, not far away, but she didn't talk to me all these years. She didn't even invite me to your weddings…"

Avreimi didn't know what he was talking about. It seemed the old man was starting to ramble.

The secretary/driver was becoming impatient. He pressed lightly on the gas pedal and the engine roared softly, spurring Avreimi on.

This, he knew, would be the last question. He had tried their patience long enough.

"Was it you who took the records pertaining to my father from the orphanage archives?" he asked.

Yechezkel Polowitz leveled a look at him out of very aged eyes. "Yes," he said.

"Where are they?"

Polowitz sighed deeply. Then he motioned to his secretary, who leaned forward with blazing eyes toward a large leather briefcase resting beside the wheelchair. He withdrew a bundle of yellowing pages inside a plastic sleeve.

"This has to eventually be returned to the archive," Yechezkel Polowitz warned, handing Avreimi the bundle.

Avreimi stared wide-eyed at the item that he and his brother had been after for more than two weeks now. It was the original page that had been cut from the orphanage's record book: the page containing full details on Pupil 1065, the boy Shlomo Kohlberg.

The plastic sleeve also held a thin cardboard file, bound with an old piece of string. Avreimi looked at it and then up at the orphanage administrator. This man, Yechezkel Polowitz, had made very sure to conceal their father's past. When had he done so? Recently, or many years ago? And if it was done recently—was it before or after their father lost his life?

And what did all of this have to do with the conversation that Polowitz and his father had conducted in the last minutes of Shlomo Kohlberg's life?

Strangest of all, what was the reason behind this new, contrite attitude? Polowitz had more or less invited him to ask questions, and had volunteered to answer them without a fuss. What was going on? What had really taken place here these last few minutes…?

But Avreimi didn't have a chance to ask these questions. The Chevy's window glided closed and Polowitz's driver pulled away.

Avreimi was left in the building's parking lot, holding his father's past in his hand and wondering what awaited them in the future.

A<small>M I DEAD? CHEZKY KOHLBERG ASKED HIMSELF.</small>

It was reasonable to suppose that he wasn't, if only because Heaven was not supposed to be a place he shared with Oleg Marinov and Yevgeny Yompolsky... And besides, in Gan Eden one presumably did not lie on hospital beds with IV lines snaking out of one's arm...

"Dr. Yompolsky, *on otkryl glaza* (he opened his eyes)!" A nurse cried excitedly. Her name was Svetlana.

The two Ukrainian men stood over Chezky's bed wearing broad smiles, like a pair of happy parents gazing at their baby in his bassinet. Dr. Yompolsky, Chezky noted, looked tired and sweaty. The doctor lifted his eyes toward the ceiling and exhaled in relief, as though thanking Someone for a wondrous rescue.

"You gave him a dose big enough for a horse," the nurse hissed to the doctor. "He nearly died on us!"

Only now did Chezky learn that he had lost consciousness in the Buick, much to Oleg and Yompolsky's distress. This had not been planned. His body should have been able to handle the dosage that the psychiatrist had administered. The moment the Buick descended into the embassy parking lot, he had been taken by elevator to the infirmary on the third floor, where Svetlana—the nurse who'd been summoned for the procedure—waited. She had injected him with intravenous fluids and hooked him up to a monitor. After a quarter of an hour he had begun to move his hands, and ten minutes later he had opened his eyes—much to the medical team's visible relief.

Oleg tried to maintain a professional detachment. "Welcome to the Ukrainian Embassy in Israel," he told Chezky. "I thank you for agreeing to come to us."

Chezky was still too weak to speak, but his brain was functioning reasonably well. He grasped Oleg's meaning. An embassy is extra-territorial ground which, so to speak, did not exist within the hosting country's borders and therefore enjoyed diplomatic immunity. Oleg had decided for him, retroactively, that he had come here willingly and not as a victim of a kidnaping. Even if not everyone in the Shin-Bet was as corrupt as Itzik Peled and there'd be someone willing to rescue him, the matter would be problematic. One cannot invade a foreign embassy without such an action being considered a gross breach of international law.

The nurse brought Chezky something to drink. He asked if he could wash his hands first, then recited the *berachah* much more fervently than usual.

Oleg brought a high stool and sat by the bed. "You are no doubt wondering why we have agreed to host you here," he said without the glimmer of a smile.

Chezky nodded his head.

"Very simple. Because you are the only one who can save your mother from a fate similar to your father's," said Oleg Marinov.

Chezky narrowed his eyes in alarm.

"Your father, as you must surely know, has in his possession a certain 'fingerprint' that could help us expose a traitor in our country," Oleg said. "But he died, and your mother adamantly claims that she does not have the information. Perhaps she is telling the truth, and perhaps not. We can check that out with her, but it will be difficult, painful, and apparently also fatal."

Chezky's eyelids fluttered. Now he realized that he was incapable of speech, and that frightened him more than anything.

"So what does that have to do with you, you ask?" Oleg continued. "Very simple: your parents knew that one day, one of them would die, and that it would be best if the other knew the 'fingerprint.' So what did they do? They placed the information in something that they called their 'safes.' When one of them would die, the other could take the information out of the safe. Simple, is it not?"

Chezky had already heard about the safes from Sean Mackenzie. The British agent had told him and his brother that he had no idea what the term referred to. The Ukrainian, it seemed, did.

"And do you know what your parents' safes were?" he asked Chezky. "You children. You are the safes."

Chezky tried to ask what he meant, but the only thing that came out of his mouth was a peculiar squeak.

"Let me explain," Oleg said helpfully. "In the same way that your parents planted false information in the agents' consciousness, they did so with you children. Your mother—this is only an example—used to tell you a bedtime story about something that once happened in a Jewish town by the name of, let us say... Lemberg. From time to time, she would innocently repeat that this was a real town in Romania. You grew up with the knowledge that there is a town in Romania called Lemberg, but you are not even aware of how you have that knowledge. If one day you were to be asked about this, you would be convinced that you knew the answer. In reality, there is no such town. That's how a 'fingerprint' can be planted in someone's mind. There's nothing simpler.

"Your parents devised a system whereby they could extract the information from the 'safes' at need. The ideal thing would be if your mother would stand here and extract the fingerprint from your mind. There was a time when that was a relevant option, but right now it isn't possible. Therefore, you will provide that service in her place."

Chezky managed to understand the fact that the Ukrainian's explanation jived with Sean Mackenzie's. Mackenzie had said that their mother had gone to the Ukrainians intending to cooperate with them, and later changed her mind and returned to Israel. He finally managed to utter a complete word: "How?"

"I would like to reassure you." Dr. Yevgeny Yompolsky came closer to Chezky. "No physical or emotional harm will come to you. You will simply receive something that will cause you to chatter and will lead you back to an earlier stage in your life. The effect will pass within a short time."

Svetlana, behind the psychiatrist's back, twisted her mouth uneasily. She knew that the doctor was brazenly lying. Some of the people they'd treated in psychiatric hospitals had been left with irreversible damage after being used as his guinea pigs. The last one had been Barak Altman, a sweet 17-year-old boy from Tel Aviv, who'd been buried several weeks earlier in the locked ward, after Yompolsky had assured him and his mother, poor Leora, that he was going to administer some medications that would improve his situation wonderfully...

Chezky shrugged. He had no choice in the matter. He couldn't put up a fight. He lacked the strength to take a single step right now, and anyway he finally understood some things about life. He understood that he had no influence on his fate, and what is written on Rosh Hashanah is exactly what will occur, whatever one does or doesn't do.

Dr. Yompolsky took out the familiar metal box and took out another syringe. He handed it to Svetlana, who inserted the needle into the IV drip and increased its rate.

At first, Chezky didn't sense any change. After a few minutes, however, he began feeling very happy. He didn't know it, but within half an hour he was slated to return to the age of five, to speak in a childish tongue, experience childish feelings, and remember events that had taken place 18 years earlier as though they'd happened yesterday.

The results of the scientific experiment that Professor Andrei Willotzky had presented to Soviet President Leonid Brezhnev nearly forty years earlier, in 1973, had been extremely impressive. He had managed to return adults to their childhoods and bring about personality changes. No one knew the amazing results that could be achieved with this technique better than Yevgeny Yompolsky, who'd been a psychiatric student in the KGB's Directorate 19, and Oleg Marinov, who'd served as a counselor for a group of children. Unfortunately, the protocol was declared illegal a few years later, when psychological damage to the subjects came to light. No psychiatrist worthy of the title used this method—and anyone who did use it was unworthy of the title. Dr. Yevgeny Yompolsky had continued to refine the illegal protocol and to conduct secret experiments. He had made good progress, though the results were not yet incontrovertible.

"All I want from you," Yompolsky told Chezky, "is to tell me what you remember about a man named Yechezkel Polowitz."

"Yechezkel Polowitz?" Chezky repeated the name, watching the unidentified liquid streaming into his veins and checking to see if his mind was becoming clouded.

"Yechezkel Polowitz," the doctor confirmed. "Your grandfather. Your mother's father. What do you know about him? What do you remember?"

"Ye…chez…kel… Polo…witz," Chezky mumbled. His eyelids were growing heavy. "Yechz…"

The psychiatrist peered intently into Chezky's face, which was now calm and quiet. He gripped Chezky's shoulders and arranged him more comfortably on the bed. "Patience," he murmured to Oleg Marinov. "In half an hour, he'll start telling us everything he knows."

Oleg glared at his colleague. "Half an hour is a long time," he snapped. "Kiev is pressing hard on me. They're calling every five minutes."

SBU headquarters on Vladimirska Street, in the heart of Kiev, was indeed pressing hard. There remained less than four hours before the fateful emails were to be sent. Of the five agents, three had already died over the years, one was serving a jail sentence for tax fraud, and one was still in active service, planted in Washington D.C. in the guise of a lobbyist. He had already been warned to get himself and his family inside Ukraine's borders by midnight or run the risk of exposure.

But what was most important of all to the Ukrainians was the fingerprint of Agent 6, Alexander Kittin. They knew that the British were doing everything in their power to locate him, and they very much wanted to reach him first.

"Relax, Oleg," said Dr. Yompolsky. "Relax, and let me do my job."

An hour later, no one in the room was relaxed.

Chezky's body shook uncontrollably, and beads of sweat stood out on his forehead as he murmured truncated syllables of gibberish. Oleg Marinov appeared to be on the verge of apoplexy. "Don't kill him!" he screamed at the psychiatrist. "I need him alive, understand? There's nothing I can do with a corpse!"

Dr. Yompolsky was out of ideas. From a professional perspective, he knew, there was no problem. He had gone through this with scores of patients and none of them had died. Perhaps a little irreversible brain damage here and there, but definitely not death. True, all his other experiments had been conducted on adolescents, while the current patient was 23 years old, but the problem was different. The more he tried to extract information about Yechezkel Polowitz—the more the patient refused to speak at all. Gradually, Yompolsky upped the dosage. But Chezky still wouldn't talk.

"Either he doesn't know anything, or his body is somehow resisting the effects of the substance," Dr. Yompolsky told Oleg in a troubled voice.

The calls from Kiev had grown increasingly more agitated. Less than three hours remained before the emails went out.

"Who is Yechezkel Polowitz?" Yompolsky asked. He leaned closer to Chezky, who'd begun frothing at the corners of his mouth.

"What does the word 'orphanage' mean to you?"

"Have you ever heard your mother speak about her father?"

At the psychiatrist's instigation, Chezky returned to his childhood, was brought back up to adolescence and then back to babyhood.

Dr. Yompolsky slammed a fist into the wall. "The guy is strong!"

he said. "He's managing to keep his mouth closed. You can tell that he is the son of spies…"

Avreimi traveled from Bayit Vegan to Geulah in a state of anxiety tempered by relief. Chezky was still missing, and his mother had yet to contact them, but the strange meeting with Yechezkel Polowitz had filled him with a feeling that something positive had happened.

He couldn't stop himself: While still on the bus, he began flipping through the yellowed pages.

"What's new?" he asked cheerfully as he walked into the house.

Miri looked at him suspiciously. "What's gone wrong now?" she asked cynically.

"Nothing's wrong," Avreimi laughed. The next words flew out before he could stop them: "At least, not at this stage…"

"Where have you come from?" Miri asked, glancing at the bundle of papers in his hand.

"Yechezkel Polowitz's house," Avreimi said, surprised that he no longer considered any of this especially dramatic anymore. "He gave me the pages that were missing from the orphanage archive."

Miri had been filled in on her brothers' adventures in the orphanage.

"Is there anything new?" she asked as she went into the kitchen to prepare supper for everyone.

"Not much beyond Rav Shabsai Gordonsky's letter," Avreimi said, talking a seat at the kitchen table. He scanned the file, summarizing as he read. "Abba was the son of a French partisan named Maurice. Maurice was born in Germany and fled to France before the war, in the year 1939. There, he joined some organization with a name I don't recognize…"

"The Resistance." Miri smiled, facing the sink.

"Something like that," Avreimi agreed, and continued his summary. "Then he joined a cell that attacked the Germans. The cell blew up a train bridge. It doesn't say which year…"

"Forty-four," Miri said, and continued chopping vegetables.

"Five cell members were caught by the Nazis. Only Abba's

father managed to escape from France. At the start of '45, he came to England…"

"Does it mention the breakout from jail?" Miri asked.

"Maybe. It says a lot of things here."

"Because our grandfather was already in Nazi hands," Miri said. Now she turned to face Avreimi. "They interrogated and tortured him, and then the Resistance sent him a secret message through a French lawyer who pretended to cooperate with the Nazis. They blew up the outer wall and rescued him. That's how he was saved and managed to escape to England."

"Some grandfather we had…"

"We deserve a grandfather at least on one side, don't we?"

"But… just a second! How do you know all that?"

"Abba once told me."

"Really?"

"Yes. In fifth grade, we had to do an assignment about our family history, and Abba told me the whole story. I got a good mark, I remember."

"Interesting that he never told us."

"He told me that you boys were in yeshivah then, sitting and learning," Miri told him. "You didn't have to know about such acts of heroism, which would distract you."

"Interesting…"

"I must have the assignment somewhere. I even remember its name: 'Jewish Heroism in Marseille.'"

"Why Marseille?"

"Because that's where they blew up the bridge."

"That's funny. It says here that it happened in Lyon."

"No, it was Marseille. I'm positive."

"So let it be Marseille. Lyon, Marseilles, Bordeaux, Paris… Why are we sitting here chatting, when Ima's dropped out of sight and now Chezky's gone, too…?"

"He's not talking," Oleg yelled into the phone. "Yompolsky hasn't managed to get a word out of him."

The psychiatrist glared at the security officer in mingled fury and fear. Oleg was speaking with headquarters in Kiev and placing all the blame squarely on his shoulders. But he had done everything in his power! Was it possible that the young man *really* didn't know anything about Yechezkel Polowitz?

Silence filled the room. Oleg listened to the decision coming through from the Ukrainian capital. Even he, in whom compassion was not a strong point, found it hard to believe what he was hearing.

"I want him to hear this," he told the speaker, and passed Yompolsky the phone.

Yompolsky's eyes opened wide in shock when he heard the instructions from Kiev.

He passed the phone to Svetlana. She listened in silence, and then began to cry.

"The Prime Minister has authorized increasing the dosage without limit," the head of Ukraine's intelligence service said. They all knew what that meant: by evening's end, someone was likely to leave the room no longer among the living.

Absolute silence held the room, except for Chezky's faint snoring.

Yompolsky drew a double-dose of the chemical into a syringe and handed it to Svetlana.

The nurse wiped her tears and injected the contents of the syringe into the IV drip.

Now it was necessary to slow the pace of the drip. In five minutes, the trio knew, Chezky would begin to talk about everything. But ten or twenty minutes after that, he would not be capable of talking about anything, ever again.

"What is he saying?" Oleg asked. "What is he mumbling over there?"

Dr. Yompolsky leaned closer to Chezky and listened intently. Then he straightened and said in a dismissive tone, "Doesn't sound significant to me. I managed to isolate a few Hebrew words: '*Beyadcha afkid ruchi...*'"

"OLEG, TELEPHONE!" DR. YOMPOLSKY DIRECTED HIS colleague's attention to the device ringing on the table. The name on the screen was unfamiliar. Oleg took the call with a questioning look.

"This is Itzik Peled, of the Shin-Bet." The name was known to him, if not the voice. "We've been informed that an Israeli citizen is being held in your embassy, and we demand his immediate release!"

Instinctively, Oleg moved to the window to scan the surrounding area. The street on which the embassy stood was bustling with life, as it was every Thursday afternoon. From his vantage point on the third floor he noticed no suspicious activity. The restaurant across the street was crowded with a loud group of patrons; three elderly women sat on a bench nearby, chatting together; a bus stopped at the corner had poured out a group of young Americans; Tel Aviv parking inspectors energetically filled out their tickets. A day like any other.

"No one is being held here against his will," Oleg answered carefully.

With this Peled character, he reminded himself, it was necessary to exercise caution. He was on their side and working with Shaul

Armoni—but he had to play the game and do his job, in case there were ears listening in on the embassy line.

"Can I speak with him?" Itzik Peled asked.

"Speak to whom?" Oleg asked.

"Listen to me well." Itzik's voice rose. "If anything happens to that kid, I will personally hound you until your last day on earth, understand? Now, put him on immediately!"

"Don't threaten me," Oleg snapped. He was furious. "I'll let you talk to whomever I want, when I want, and *how* I want!"

He was well aware that Peled was helpless. He was not allowed to stick so much as a toe inside the embassy gates. Besides, he wasn't really worried about young Kohlberg. He was simply behaving the way any Shin-Bet man was required to behave in the event that an Israeli citizen was being held in a foreign embassy. After all, it had been Peled himself, Oleg mused, who had knowingly driven the kid into his arms and even followed them to the embassy. Maybe that's what's bothering him, Oleg concluded. He was afraid that the kid would sustain some irreversible damage and Peled would be held accountable both to the government and to the family, who considered him a friend.

"Let's de-escalate this," Peled surprised him by saying. "I have a proposition for you."

"What kind of proposition?"

"Someone is prepared to give himself up in exchange for the boy."

Yevgeny Yompolsky didn't recall ever seeing such an expression of utter astonishment as the one that crossed Oleg Marinov's face at that moment.

"Give himself up? Who?" Yompolsky heard him ask. Then he saw Oleg's jaw drop in even greater surprise when he heard the answer.

"How soon can you get here?" he asked.

The answer—no more than an hour—satisfied him completely.

"But there's one condition," he emphasized. "The exchange must be approved at the highest level."

"No problem," replied Itzik Peled. He took into account the

fact that the Ukrainian relied on Shaul Armoni more than he did. Armoni, after all, had been working with him for long years…

The infirmary suddenly turned into a war room. Dr. Yompolsky and Nurse Svetlana began racing around in a frenzy to carry out the prescribed emergency measures. Chezky Kohlberg's life—which, until a moment before, had been considered about as important as a garlic peel—was now more valuable than gold.

"Get rid of the IV!" the doctor shouted.

Svetlana pulled the needle from Chezky's arm, to spare him the small amount of fluid that was still in the line ready to enter his bloodstream. She quickly inserted a different fluid into his other arm, and set the stream to a more rapid pace.

The psychiatrist stood by, ashen with tension, facing the monitor to which Chezky was attached. Intently he studied the patient's heart rate, blood pressure and oxygen saturation.

Then he opened his metal box and chose a vial with a pale hue that he had not used until now.

"Twenty cc's, quickly," he urged the nurse.

Svetlana took a syringe and drew a precise measure from the vial. Chezky felt neither the prick nor the insertion of the drug.

All this time, Oleg Marinov paced the room like a caged lion, with clenched fists and gnashing teeth.

"What's happening? What's happening?" he asked again and again. But neither the doctor nor the nurse was able to promise anything yet.

"You have to save him!" Oleg roared, and pounded the wall with his fist. "I need him alive!"

Half an hour later, Chezky discovered that his time to pass into the "world that is all good" had not yet arrived. He was still in this world, which was crawling with Ukrainians, psychiatrists, and traitorous Shin-Bet agents.

Oleg was the happiest of men. Contrary to all expectations, the operation seemed poised for success. He would return to Kiev crowned with glory. But he had to take care of his partners as well. He descended one floor, entered the First Secretary's office, and instructed him to see to Yompolsky and Svetlana's hasty departure from Israel. Both of them must be on the first plane to Ukraine, where they, too, would receive lavish praise from the service chiefs and even the Prime Minister.

"Do you want something to drink?" Svetlana asked Chezky.

Chezky sipped water through parched lips with the aid of a straw.

"What happened?" he whispered. He was still suffering pain and chills.

"There are people who love you," she replied with a smile. Immediately, she bit her lip in alarm. She had just said something she was forbidden to say.

From the other side of the room, Dr. Yompolsky shot her a baleful look. Oleg had explicitly ordered that the patient be told nothing.

Despite his weakness, Chezky tried to protest. After a second, he collapsed under a fresh wave of pain.

"Relax," said Dr. Yompolsky. "Everything will be all right."

"No, no," Chezky groaned. The nurse had said that he was to be released and that there were people who loved him. The conclusion was clear: Someone was preparing to give himself up in his place. Chezky did not want that to happen at any price.

"Calm down. Calm down," Svetlana urged. But Chezky did not feel calm.

Oleg returned from the First Secretary's office.

"What happened?" he asked, seeing Chezky groaning and protesting.

On the spot, Dr. Yompolsky improvised a version of the last few minutes:

"While still unconscious, he apparently heard that we're going to exchange him for somebody else," he whispered to Oleg. "He doesn't want that."

Oleg Marinov approached Chezky's bed and pinched his cheek with feigned affection. "We didn't ask your opinion when we brought you here," he said, "and we're not going to ask you when we give you back."

Now that he knew he had viable merchandise to exchange, Oleg called Kiev to announce the dramatic new development:

"One of the big shots called me up and proposed bringing me the original instead of the copy," he reported.

Kohlberg, Jr., really didn't know anything, the Ukrainian concluded to himself. With a set of parents like his, who'd turned compartmentalization into a fine art, it was no wonder that he had lived in the same city as his grandfather for more than twenty years without ever hearing his name. But the kid was no longer necessary. Who needed the piggy bank, when the real treasure was on its way here—thanks to the generosity of Shaul Armoni and Itzik Peled.

Leaving Chezky in the company of the doctor and nurse who were supervising his recovery, Oleg went down to prepare for the exchange. He stood in the embassy courtyard and watched the usual activity taking place all around. One person went into the embassy and another came out. Anyone observing the scene would never know that he was witnessing an intelligence deal of global proportions involving powerful parties on all sides.

He used the established methods to scan the embassy's environs. He knew every inch of the area within a 100-meter radius. He identified two or three Shin-Bet men, unfamiliar to him, as they took their places in advance of the coming exchange. It was only natural, he reflected, that Armoni and Peled wanted to increase their forces slightly around the exchange site, in case matters took a turn for the worse.

He picked up his phone and called Yompolsky, three stories above.

"How's the boy doing?"

"He's agitated," Yompolsky said. "And he is unable to walk."

Indeed, every inch of Chezky's body ached. His head thrummed with pain, he was dizzy and nauseous, and his heart rate was erratic. In addition, he had lost some sensation in the left side of his body. Dr. Yompolsky's drugs were powerful stuff.

"Where's my phone?" Chezky mumbled, moving restlessly in his bed. "Where is my phone?"

I have to call Avreimi, he thought in terrible distress. He had to tell his brother that they'd kidnaped their mother and were bringing her here. He had suddenly realized what the nurse had meant when she had said that there were people who loved him: Ima was about to hand herself over to save his life. But she didn't know what she was walking into. Those cruel thugs would have no pity on her. She would not leave this place alive.

Where was his phone? Was there a phone in the room?

Svetlana hurriedly reported Chezky's preoccupation to the doctor, who summoned the fellow with the steel arms to stand guard and make sure Chezky didn't do anything foolish.

"You'll be leaving us in twenty minutes," Svetlana told Chezky sweetly. "Do you want to get out of bed? Want to try?"

Her words floated past Chezky, who was thinking, *How do I save Ima? How do I prevent her from falling into the same trap that I fell into?*

"He needs a wheelchair," the nurse told Oleg over the phone. "He can't walk."

Oleg Marinov smiled. "You'll find one in the supply room. On one of his visits to Dr. Yompolsky's hospital, from which he had taken an IV stand and various other pieces of medical equipment, he had thrown in a brand-new wheelchair as well.

Ten minutes before the appointed hour, Chezky sat in a wheelchair in the embassy lobby. Behind him, like proud attendants, stood Dr. Yompolsky and Nurse Svetlana.

Through the glass Chezky could watch the Tel Aviv street, now draped with long shadows as evening drew in. Carefree people passed by; stores were open and people came and went in them. Would any of them dream of what was taking place just a few meters away? A son was about to have his life saved—at the price of his mother's life!

What could he do? How to prevent it?

He had an idea. When he saw her, he would simply cry out, "Ima, run! Ima, look what they did to me! Look at me sitting in a wheelchair. Look at me, a broken vessel. Run! Run while you still can..."

An ambulance glided up the street and stopped in front of the embassy entrance. "You're going to be all right," Dr. Yompolsky said, with a thump on Chezky's aching shoulder. It finally occurred to Chezky that the ambulance was for him.

Oleg's phone rang. Itzik Peled was back on the line.

"That's our ambulance," he said. "I understand that the kid requires medical evacuation. Do you want to make sure everything's all right?"

Oleg accepted this suggestion. He went into the courtyard, stepped out into the street and approached the ambulance. A pair of rear doors opened to greet him. Inside the ambulance were a paramedic, a doctor, and a driver. Oleg nodded curtly and turned around to return to the embassy. There were no Shin-Bet men there, or police. No surprises.

He signaled Dr. Yompolsky in the building. Five minutes.

Chezky was out of ideas. Now that he was feeling a little better, he was even more acutely aware of his situation and of his mother's grave danger. Maybe he should simply start yelling his head off when he reached the street? He could attract the attention of passers-by. But where was the exchange slated to take place? Could they be bringing his mother in right now through the underground parking lot, the way they said they'd brought him?

Excited whispers made it apparent that something else was happening outside. Chezky lifted his eyes, and his heart froze in his chest. He saw Itzik Peled's car. The familiar white Land Rover. What was *he* doing here?

Oh, no! It had been Itzik, together with his corrupt son-in-law, Moshe Sotzkover, who'd helped Oleg trap him and bring him to the embassy. Apparently, Itzik was not yet satisfied. It was not enough that he had handed him over to the Ukrainians; now he was about to do the same to Chezky's mother. Curse that man! How his father and mother had helped him. How they'd cared about him. How they'd thought of him all those years. . . What terrible ingratitude. Only a Divine punishment could repay him for his evil misdeeds.

Itzik's vehicle pulled up behind the ambulance, but not too close. Chezky looked at it with loathing. Everyone else was looking, too, their curiosity mixed with excitement. The right-side door opened. Out stepped a tall, elderly man with a vigorous air and thick white eyebrows. With the aid of a cane, he walked up to the embassy.

Even without being told, Chezky knew that this was his family's enemy, Shaul Armoni.

63

"WHY IS HE PARKING THERE?" MARINOV GRUMBLED. HE was back in the building by this time. Those Israelis… acting like they owned the road…

He was picking up the phone to call again, when another car drove up, making three in all. This one parked a short distance behind Itzik Peled's.

The third vehicle was partially hidden from Chezky's view. He wheeled himself slightly forward—a sign of progress that afforded the doctor and nurse much satisfaction—and was stunned to see whose car it was. It was the black-and-beige Chevrolet belonging to Yechezkel Polowitz. What was his *grandfather* doing here?

Even without being a law student, Chezky would have been able to connect the various dots of circumstantial evidence into an impressive visual tapestry. If his mother had left from her father's house before flying to Kiev, as everyone claimed, and she had arrived in his car to turn herself in, then Polowitz must have some serious role to play in all of this. Yesterday afternoon she had apparently decided to cooperate with the Ukrainians, as Sean Mackenzie had told them, but then she regretted the decision and came back.

Both Mackenzie and Oleg Marinov had somehow known that she had returned to Israel. Now, apparently, she had once again decided to hand herself over—this time, through the good offices of Shaul Armoni and Yechezkel Polowitz.

Itzik Peled got out of his car and joined Armoni on the sidewalk by the embassy gate. From the distance, Chezky saw him dial a number; a moment later, Oleg's phone rang.

"The exchange will take place at the gate," Itzik Peled said. "Take Chezky down the stairs and walk with him across the courtyard. Stop when you are one meter in front of the gate."

"We're coming!" Oleg said happily.

Svetlana didn't say a word. Yompolsky squeezed Chezky's shoulder, leaned down, and whispered, "Send my regards to your mother."

Oleg pushed the wheelchair through the embassy's front door. The muscled bodyguard easily lifted Chezky down the seven steps, to the level of the courtyard and sidewalk and went back inside the building.

What to do? Chezky head spun. Shout? Run? Jump? He had to prevent his mother from being taken. He must sabotage this smooth, sterile exchange, which was taking place without the slightest disruption.

Exerting a mighty effort, he stuck his foot out and pressed it down, hard, on the floor. The wheelchair halted momentarily.

"What's the matter with you?" Oleg snapped, and easily overcame the resistance. He jerked the chair backward, and Chezky's legs flew up in the air.

"I don't want to trade places with my mother!" Chezky said, raising his voice.

Oleg chuckled as he walked.

"Who said you're trading places with your mother?"

Chezky didn't have an answer to this, nor did he have time to think of one. Oleg had reached the meeting-point: a meter before the gate, a meter-and-a-half away from Polowitz's car, and the same distance from Shaul Armoni and Itzik Peled, who stood, like the wicked men they were, outside the gate.

Oleg inclined his head at Armoni, as though to say, *I've done my part.*

Armoni looked at Itzik, who signaled to someone seated in the rear seat of the Chevrolet.

It wasn't the gray-haired secretary, Chezky noted, because he was sitting up front, beside the driver, and nervously chewing his nails.

Both of the Chevrolet's back doors opened wide. A sophisticated wheelchair lift emerged and began descending to the pavement. The car door blocked Chezky's view of the person seated on the chair.

Chezky strained his burning eyes and tried to focus through the pounding in his head. From the shoes and trousers, he could see that it wasn't his mother. So who was it?

A moment later, Chezky's heart lunged against his rib cage. No! No, no! It wasn't his mother… it was his grandfather! Yechezkel Polowitz sat in the wheelchair. *He* had offered to hand himself over in exchange for Chezky's freedom. He was stepping right into the lion's den…

The man in the baseball cap waited for the lift apparatus to fold itself up and be swallowed inside the car. The two primary figures in the exchange faced each other across a gap of two meters, wheelchair to wheelchair.

Chezky's emotions were in violent turmoil. A profound sense of gratitude filled him completely. His grandfather had volunteered to put his head on the guillotine in his place. After all, he was the one the Ukrainians had been seeking all along. Oleg Marinov and Dr. Yompolsky had asked incessant questions about him, though Chezky had been unable to supply any answers. Now he was serving himself to them on a silver platter, and they would not handle him with silk gloves… Chezky's eyes filled with emotional tears. His grandfather had rescued not only him, but also Chezky's mother—his own daughter—whose trust he had betrayed and whose plans he had thwarted, thus earning a decades-long banishment from her life. His grandfather had decided to make one last gesture of love, sacrificing his life to save those of his daughter and grandson.

Polowitz, too, appeared to be on the brink of tears. He was breathing heavily, with a hand over his heart in the classic pose of a person who fears the worst.

For a few seconds, the scene seemed to freeze. Oleg didn't stir from his place behind Chezky's wheelchair near the embassy gate. On the sidewalk outside the gate stood the young man in the baseball cap, behind Polowitz's back. Both of them looked at Shaul Armoni and Itzik Peled, waiting for the signal.

It came in the form of a tiny nod.

Oleg stayed where he was. The other man began pushing Polowitz's wheelchair toward the gate. Then both chairs were lined up beside one another, the first facing outward and the second facing in.

"*Saba* [Grandfather], thank you so much," Chezky said sincerely, though the words paled beside the intensity of his emotion.

Polowitz's response stunned him. The old man seemed to rouse from his frightened stupor. He looked at Chezky and said, "*Saba*? Whose *Saba*?"

Chezky stared at him in disbelief. "*Saba*..." he repeated.

But Polowitz cut him off again. "I'm not your grandfather!"

Chezky felt as if the world around him had suddenly halted in its orbit. "You're not... my grandfather?" he asked in wonder.

Despite his pain and fear, Polowitz appeared to be slightly amused.

"Whoever gave you *that* idea?"

Chezky stared at Oleg Marinov, who appeared no less shocked than he. "*He* told me," he said, gesturing feebly with his hand.

Polowitz lifted his gaze to the Ukrainian security chief. "I'm his grandfather? Where did you get that story from?"

Almost of their own accord, Oleg's eyes went to Shaul Armoni in a piercing glance. "He told me," he said through his teeth.

Polowitz turned to the suspect of the hour. "So you're the one with the imagination, Mr. Armoni?" he asked with a trace of mockery.

Shaul Armoni was pale with fury. Slowly he swiveled his head to lock eyes with Itzik Peled. "You snake," he hissed.

Itzik appeared nonplussed. He nodded in Chezky's direction. "He told me," he said defensively.

Chezky, who'd been following this bizarre script with a sense of shock, felt as if Itzik had just slapped him again. What a liar! What a scoundrel! Now he was dumping everything on his shoulders...

He opened his mouth, intending to repudiate this with all his strength. But the stunning sequence of events had temporarily robbed him of his powers of speech.

With astonishing speed, Armoni's hand went to his gun holster. Before Chezky could lift his arms to protect himself, he saw a gun appear in Itzik's hand as well.

At that instant, the air was rent by a loud commotion. The young man in the baseball cap, standing behind Polowitz, whipped out a gun of his own and screamed, "Drop your weapons! I said, *drop your weapons*!"

The three old women sitting on the bench leaped to their feet and began racing for the embassy gate. As they darted forward they drew submachine guns from their shopping baskets, yelling in the voices of young men, "Hands up!" The doctor burst forth from the ambulance, along with the driver and the paramedic; four diners in the restaurant abandoned their table without leaving a tip and raced across the street, as did the parking inspectors and "Discovery" tourists. Dozens of fighters appeared out of nowhere before Chezky's befuddled eyes.

"Drop your weapons!" the young man behind Polowitz's chair shouted again at Armoni and Peled.

Armoni looked around at the circle of fighters surrounding them, and then turned to the young man in the baseball cap. "Etzioni, that's enough. You're making a mistake."

"Drop your weapon, or I'll shoot," Chanan Etzioni demanded, waving his gun. But Armoni still did not seem to get the message.

"Don't you point a gun at me!" Armoni snapped. "Do you know who I am? Do you know who this is?" He gestured at Itzik Peled.

"I know that both of you are suspected of cooperating with a foreign power and selling state secrets," Etzioni replied. "All weapons on the floor! *Now*!"

Left with no choice, Shaul Armoni bent down and placed his gun on the pavement. Itzik Peled did the same.

Without understanding exactly what had happened, Oleg Marinov realized that the exchange deal had fallen through. With feline speed, he shot back into the building and vanished behind the glass doors. Shaul Armoni and Itzik Peled stood with immobile faces and slumped shoulders. The silver-haired secretary got out of the passenger seat and hurried over to his agitated employer.

"Can you move a little closer to me?" the Shin-Bet man with the baseball cap asked Chezky, who'd been left abandoned in his wheelchair. With alacrity, Chezky wheeled himself out of Ukrainian territory and onto the Tel Aviv sidewalk.

The three original ambulance crew members burst out of a nearby music store, from which they'd watched events unfold. They pulled out a stretcher, placed Chezky on it, and prepared to bring it into the vehicle.

"Don't get scared, but we're taking you to a psychiatric hospital. They wouldn't know what to do with you in an ordinary ER."

Itzik Peled was placed inside a white Shin-Bet car, hands manacled behind his back. Shaul Armoni was led away to a different car. He was not handcuffed, but his demeanor was defeated.

At that moment, a cry came from Polowitz's secretary. The old man was white as chalk. He was clutching his chest with both hands and appeared to be in the midst of a heart attack. The medical crew raced over and began to examine him. A second ambulance was hastily summoned to take him to the nearest hospital.

Chanan Etzioni, the operation's commander, approached Chezky. He removed his baseball cap to expose a head of curly hair topped with a knitted *kippah*. "May you have a *refuah sheleimah*," he said, and shook Chezky's hand.

"*Amein*," Chezky said emotionally. "But I still don't have a clue about what just happened here."

"We'll talk about that later," Etzioni said. "I'll send someone over to explain everything to you."

"At least it won't be Itzik Peled," Chezky murmured, half to himself. "Finally, his true face has been revealed."

The Shin-Bet man tilted his head, his expression thoughtful. "No one knows what Itzik Peled's true face looks like."

"Do you know him?"

"I knew him in the past… But enough of that now. I came to tell you that you may not tell anyone except your immediate family what happened here today. And even to them, do not say anything about my security people until after you've been briefed."

"Okay," Chezky said, his mind on other things. "Where did you know him?"

Etzioni looked around. "I used to work for him ten years ago," he said. "In Amsterdam. It turned out to be his last mission."

"And since then?"

"Since then, he left the Service and became a *ba'al teshuvah*. No one really knows what's in his mind."

"*I* know," Chezky stated flatly. Then he stopped short and corrected himself in mid-speech. "That is, I *think* I know," he finished in a much gentler tone. Suddenly, he felt no hatred toward Itzik Peled—only pity and compassion.

64

CHEZKY WAS RELEASED FROM THE HOSPITAL ABOUT TWO hours later. He recovered with remarkable speed, though the doctor at the psychiatric facility warned him that he was likely to suffer additional bouts of dizziness and instability when walking, thanks to Dr. Yompolsky's not-so-friendly drugs.

Avreimi nearly cried when he received an unexpected phone call from his lost brother. All Chezky could tell him was that he had been through some harrowing adventures but that he felt much better now—and that someone from the Shin-Bet would be coming to brief them and issue instructions regarding the future.

"Who's home?" Chezky asked.

"Miri and the children."

"So Ima's not back." Chezky was silent for a moment, and then told his brother that he had another question. "I didn't *daven* Minchah today. Can I say the Ma'ariv *Shemoneh Esrei* twice?"

"It seems clear that you can," Avreimi said. "It was unintentional."

"But that's just it. It may fall under the category of *'techilaso b'peshiah v'sofo b'ones'*—something that starts out intentionally and later becomes unavoidable. Could you ask a *rav* for me, Avreimi?"

Avreimi was both astounded and moved. In his brother's 23 years of life, he didn't remember Chezky ever asking a question like this. He had apparently been through a truly remarkable experience today...

"Listen, Chezky," he said. "I'm ruling that you can *daven* twice. The *'aveirah'* is on me... And if you have any more *'aveiros'* like that—send them all my way!"

At eleven p.m. that night, the three oldest Kohlbergs waited in their parents' house. Ari was still in yeshivah, with no idea of what had been taking place at home. The youngest children had been placed in the tender charge of their good neighbor, Mrs. Fink.

"The mission leader was religious," Chezky remarked. "I wonder if he'll come here himself to talk to us."

When a knock sounded on the door, the trio tensed. Their astonishment was boundless when they found that the person on their doorstep, wearing a broad smile, was none other than Itzik Peled.

"They told us that... someone from the Shin-Bet would be coming," Chezky managed to choke out.

"Well, here I am." Itzik took a seat at the head of the table and looked around. "Now, is this any way to receive guests?"

Without a word, Miri went into the kitchen to fetch the refreshments she had prepared. She heard Chezky ask, hesitantly, "You're not... under arrest?"

And she heard Itzik ask in a mocking tone, "See how it goes? These days, with a little *protektzia*, you can get out of anything!"

Avreimi shrugged with incomprehension and took a chair near Itzik's. Chezky took the seat farthest from the head of the table. He was swamped by new fears. His brother and sister had believed in Itzik Peled all along. Even now, they had no idea what he had been up to. Chezky was not allowed to tell them that Itzik Peled had brought about his kidnaping by the Ukrainians, nor about how sly and deceitful he had been. But, with all that, the past day had taught him that he neither knew nor understood everything... Though he still harbored deep suspicion about Itzik's motives, he was determined to hear him out fully before deciding what he thought of him.

"Let's begin with a few updates," Itzik said. "First of all, Shaul Armoni is under arrest, and I'll explain why in a minute. Second, Israel has expelled Oleg Marinov, who'll be flying back to Ukraine tonight. Third, Dr. Yompolsky and the nurse, Svetlana, have been up before a judge and will be held in custody until the proceedings are over. They've been charged not only with the events at the embassy, but also with conducting medical experiments on humans who were admitted to the psychiatric facility where they worked. And, fourth—not such good news—Yechezkel Polowitz is in the Intensive Care Unit at Ichilov Hospital, and his condition is not encouraging."

"So, is he our grandfather or not?" Avreimi asked, while Miri asked his name so she could *daven* for him.

"Yechezkel ben Margaret," Itzik said.

Chezky looked at him suspiciously. Suddenly, light dawned. "Yechezkel?" he asked. "That's *my* name, too!"

Itzik laughed out loud. "Good morning!" he crowed. "You just realized that you have identical names? And you want to be a lawyer…"

"Does that mean he's *not* our grandfather?"

"You tell me…"

Chezky thought. "Maybe Ima was so angry at him that she gave her son his name as though he were dead?"

"A nice idea, and an original one," Itzik said with approval.

"And correct, too, for a change?"

Itzik turned sober. "To answer that, we'll have to start the whole story over from the beginning," he said. The three Kohlbergs leaned forward intently.

Itzik poured himself a drink.

"What you're about to hear will be outrageous and infuriating," he said. "But you have to know the truth, even though it's not pleasant."

Avreimi inclined his head, and gestured at Itzik as though giving him the floor.

"Well, as you know, your father collapsed on a Sunday, one month ago," Itzik began. "A few days after he had 'coiled the spring.' The emails will be sent out to their recipients at midnight tonight, as there is no one around to rescind the message.

"The ones who are most threatened by this are the British. Their man—Agent 6, Alexander Kittin—may be exposed in Ukraine and denounced as a traitor."

"But the Ukrainians have something to lose, too," Avreimi pointed out. "Their agents will be exposed as well."

"The Ukrainians—or, to be more precise, the heads of the SBU—were prepared to sacrifice even more in order to expose Kittin. They're been seeking him a long time. They narrowed down a list of suspects, and were ready to interrogate each one as soon as the email arrived. But that wasn't enough for them. They were afraid that Kittin was not on the suspect list, and then they would lose their chance because the British could simply tell him what his 'fingerprint' is. The Ukrainians became determined, therefore, to obtain Kittin's fingerprint before anyone else.

"Oleg Marinov, chief security officer at the embassy and seemingly charged with protecting the diplomatic staff, has been under suspicion by the Shin-Bet for some time as an Ukrainian intelligence agent, but he's been careful enough and clever enough to conceal his illegal activities.

"He visited your home during the *shivah* in Orthodox garb, in order to form an impression of your family and try to establish a connection. When you told your mother about a strange Russian, a *ba'al teshuvah*, who asked if your father was still involved in archeology, she knew very well who you meant. She was alarmed by the fact that the Ukrainian intelligence bureau was still sending its tentacles out to her. But she also knew that she had nothing to worry about."

"Why not?"

"Because the whole race centered on Alexander Kittin's identity, and everyone knew that his fingerprint was known only to your father and not your mother. Kittin, if you'll recall, was a Jew, and needed no instruction in basic Jewish tradition. He took lessons only from your father, who was an expert in various aspects of Israeli culture. Therefore, your father was the only one who could have implanted his fingerprint."

"But there were also the 'safes,'" Chezky remembered. "Ima could have taken the information from them if necessary."

"True," said Itzik. "But it's obvious that your parents told no one about the system of safes, since that would have put you children—the safes—directly in the line of fire."

"But you knew about the safes?" Chezky asked.

"I did," Itzik acknowledged. "Though I only found out recently."

"Wait a minute," Avreimi said. "Mackenzie knew."

"And so did Oleg Marinov," Chezky added.

"First of all," Itzik said with a chuckle, "notice that the two of them did not have identical information. The Englishman knew only that there was a general concept of 'safes,' while the Ukrainian already knew that you, the children, are the safes."

"So when did they find out?"

"Ever since I told them," Itzik said, and threw a challenging look at Chezky.

Chezky bit his lower lip with all his might. A muscle in his jaw twitched. He held his tongue—but it cost him. He had resolved not to heap accusations on Itzik, but it was hard. Oh, how hard it was!

Itzik looked down, a bit surprised at Chezky's self-control.

"Let's go back to the *shivah*," he said. "Not only Oleg Marinov, but also Shaul Armoni went into action. He had been after your parents for many years, and not even your father's disappearance from the arena stopped him. He knew that your father was the only one who could 'coil the spring,' and he also knew that the computer that held the program that did it was one that your mother had no access to. After a great deal of thought, a solution to the riddle suddenly occurred to him: The program must be on one of the computers in your father's workplace, to which neither your mother nor anyone who was unauthorized could gain access."

"So Abba's work really belonged to the Shin-Bet?"

"Not the Shin-Bet, exactly, but your father did work for the government in a certain sense. It all connected back to the pardon he was granted in the past, after he was instrumental in freeing some Jews from the Soviet Union… but that's for another time. In short,

Armoni closed the place down and confiscated all the computers for a thorough investigation."

"That's why the place was empty when I went there," Miri realized.

"Correct. Nothing, by the way, was found on the computers, but Armoni didn't give up. He was still convinced that your mother knew something. That's why we hung a 'For Rent' sign on the door…"

"*We* hung?" Chezky stressed the first word.

Ignoring the interruption, Itzik continued his sentence: "…with a phone number that we used in our operations. Armoni believed that your mother would fall into the trap and call the number, but it soon became clear that the daughter had more initiative than the mother…"

Miri blushed slightly.

"The call you made from the public phone," Itzik told her, "got our whole team hopping. When I realized it was you, I ordered them all to disperse. You have very sharp eyes."

Chezky leaned toward his sister with a grin. "Do they have a course in spying at your school?"

Miri answered at once: "Yes, they do. But I'm not allowed to talk about it…"

"And then," Itzik said, bringing the conversation back to serious lines, "last Friday, just before Shabbos, Polowitz called me, completely hysterical. He told me, 'The boys were at the orphanage, and Chezky found out about his grandfather.'"

"How did you know Yechezkel Polowitz?" Chezky asked.

"Up until that minute, I *didn't* know him. But your father had told him—as he had told a few other people—that if he ever had a problem, he could call me."

"So I guess he's not that senile after all," Chezky remarked.

Itzik Peled smiled.

"I think Yoni Schlusserman, who now runs the orphans' home, hit the nail on the head when he said that Polowitz is 'half-senile.' Polowitz really is half-senile—but he decides when to be which half…

"Anyway, I cut Polowitz off at once—there's nothing less secure than a phone line—and drove over to his house. (I had to walk back home on foot, because by then it was already Shabbos.) By that time, from what I understand, you boys had already begun digging. You'd visited Chacham Reuven, seen Zalman Berkovitch and spoken with R' Allon Koler, your father's commanding officer in the army. By Motzaei Shabbos I realized that I had no choice but to get in touch with you—basically to keep an eye on you from up close, to prevent things from spiraling out of control. And on Sunday you went to see Moishy Sotzkover, my dear son-in-law, who directed you to me."

"Just a second. Excuse me." Chezky raised a protesting finger. "We reached Moishy through a news item that appeared on a certain site. It directed us to a Tzvika Rothman, owner of a printing firm. He was the one who sent us to Moishy."

Itzik chuckled softly. "And who do you think made sure that you'd see that news item on that site?"

Chezky's eyes narrowed, and his smile was skeptical. It seemed to him that Itzik was going out on a limb with his last statement.

"You know what? I have an idea for you," said Itzik. "Go ahead and see if you can find that news item again. Believe me, you won't find it anywhere. The item was written specially for you—and there was also Someone who made sure that you'd stumble across it while searching the web."

The smile died on Chezky's lips.

"Really?" he asked weakly. "Someone can hack into my computer and…?"

Itzik Peled raised his voice and chanted, "*Ayin roeh… v'ozen shoma'as… v'chol ma'asechah b'sefer nichtavim…*" *An all-seeing eye, a hearing ear, and all your deeds are written down in a book…*

"I don't believe it," Chezky whispered, shaken to the core.

"Believe it." Itzik winked at him. "Belief is good for your health."

Avreimi intervened. "So what did your son-in-law mean when he said that our father hadn't collapsed in the street, but had been brought there?"

"That was a foolish move on his part," Itzik complained, "and

I told him so. He was looking for a way to send you to me, but there was no point adding to your stress… In any case, the important thing was that you came, and I heard you out, and we went together to Ashtorei HaParchi in search of security cameras. In reality, I didn't need you and I didn't need the video clips. The idea was to get you to trust me and to view me as a professional who could be depended upon."

With difficulty, Chezky held back a snort of derision.

"On Monday," Itzik continued, "I sent you a bunch of video clips from the many that I had in my possession. But I made two mistakes that day."

"Tell that to Chezky," Avreimi said with a mischievous smile.

"First of all," said Itzik, "I didn't notice Sean Mackenzie on Rechov Malchei Yisrael. That's not like me. Apparently, I'm also getting older… When you showed him to me on the screen, I was shocked. I knew that the British were meddling in the matter, but I didn't know that Mackenzie was the man. Up to that point, I'd considered Oleg Marinov the villain of this story, but in my view Mackenzie was no less cruel and wicked. Under the façade of the British gentleman is a cold, cynical agent to whom human life counts for very little."

"And the second mistake?" Chezky asked.

"My second mistake derived from the fact that I didn't know about the unique look of Polowitz's car, and unwittingly exposed you to the meeting that he had with your father on that fateful day."

"But what is Polowitz's part in all of this? Is he good or bad? A traitor or a fine family man?"

Itzik leaned back and heaved a theatrical sigh. "*Ai, ai, ai…* Polowitz is like the rest of us in this world: trying to repair the things we did wrong."

"Meaning…?" Avreimi prompted.

"Well," Itzik said uncomfortably, "this is no time to point an accusing finger at a person who's hovering between life and death. Still, there were a few things in that man's life that were really not so praiseworthy. In the fifties, he handed dozens of children over to secular kibbutzim, in return for money or favors. He was up to his neck in all kinds of shady deals. For all his long beard and ultra-Orthodox clothes, he was a member of the Communist Party in England and made connections with people in the Soviet Union. He accrued power for himself, but paid for it in coins of blood. His name has been linked to the arrest of Jewish Aliyah activists, and he was apparently also involved in the death of your grandmother, Henya Aranowich."

The three Kohlbergs stared at him.

"No wonder Ima never forgave him," Miri said.

Itzik compressed his lips in thoughtful silence.

"On the other hand," Chezky said, "he did volunteer to switch places with me at the embassy. They could have killed him there."

Itzik's eyes met Chezky's in a rare moment of accord.

"I haven't always been the biggest *tzaddik*," Itzik said suddenly. "But as long as the candle is burning, there's still time to remedy matters. I've spoken a great deal with Polowitz over these past few days. He told me that he had the biggest shock of his life when your parents moved to Israel. Suddenly, he saw them as religious people—especially your father, whom he had handed over to the secularists. From that day, he began trying to repair the damage he had done. He did his best to track down the orphans he had sent away to various places, and tried to be *mekarev* them. Some of them became *ba'alei teshuvah*. He rented apartments for some of them, and assisted them financially. One of them, by the way, was Zalman Berkovitch, whom you've already met."

Avreimi, Chezky, and Miri gaped at one another in astonishment. Now they saw Yaakov the grocer's story in a different light. He had told them about all the grocery bills that their father used to pay for other people…

"So… Abba was working with Polowitz?" Avreimi asked hesitantly.

"Yes," Itzik affirmed. "Your father was his messenger in that mitzvah."

"Really? And Ima knew about it?"

"Your mother knew, but it didn't affect her feelings about Polowitz."

The Kohlbergs were silent for a long moment.

"And what about the video clip from Weill's bookstore?" Avreimi asked finally.

"That was also my initiative," Itzik said. "I wanted to arouse suspicion against me, after which I would perform wonders to show you that you were embroiled in a situation in which I was the only one holding out a life jacket. The only one you could trust."

"Avreimi trusted you. Me, not so much," Chezky admitted.

Itzik smiled forgivingly, and continued his story. "The big mess began the next day, on Monday. Something aroused the suspicion of a parking inspector by the name of Rotem Cohen, from Givat Shmuel. He issued a report on Oleg's car, a handsome Buick LaCrosse parked outside the famous religious Institute."

Chezky wrinkled his brow, trying to reconstruct events. "Monday? He was sitting in the cafeteria, wasn't he? I saw him."

"Correct," said Itzik. "He went there to speak to you. He planned to start a conversation with you, but for some reason was summoned back to the embassy in a hurry.

"When I received that information—it doesn't matter how—I was alarmed to realize that the Ukrainian was on your tail. It took me back to my phone conversation with Polowitz on Friday. Your name, if you'll recall, was mentioned then. Polowitz had said that 'the boys were at the orphanage, and Chezky found out about his grandfather.' It made me think that Oleg was aware of that conversation, and that that was what had brought him to you."

"How did he hear the conversation?"

"That's exactly what I asked myself. My house, as you'll have noticed, is completely impervious to eavesdropping and electronic bugging. And no one was interested in Polowitz's house. There was only one way it could have happened: all my conversations are recorded and kept in a special file. The only one who had access to that file was Shaul Armoni. The conclusion was that Armoni had transmitted the information to Oleg Marinov."

"Who *is* Armoni, really?"

"I can't tell you much, except that he's one of the most veteran members of our intelligence network. For some years now, I've been serving under him in a small, secret unit. One of my jobs was to keep track of your parents…"

Chezky shot Avreimi a look that said, loud and clear, "I told you so!"

"But the job turned into a friendship," Itzik continued. "I also merited becoming a *ba'al teshuvah*. And, with regard to the matter at hand, a long time ago your father and I began to suspect that Armoni had questionable ties with Ukrainian intelligence, and now my suspicions were strengthened. I was worried and out of ideas. Things were spiraling out of control. If Oleg got his hands on you, we'd be in big trouble. On the other hand, Mackenzie was no saint himself…

"And then I decided to seek advice from the smartest, cleverest person I know in the field. Your mother."

"At first, she was terrified. She'd known Oleg from their Kiev days, and knew how cruel he could be. But when it came to Sean Mackenzie, she calmed me down. Without going into too much detail, years before, I'd suspected him of giving away an Iranian student who'd been helping us at the time. But your mother said that Armoni had admitted openly to her that *he* had been the one to betray the student. Your mother heard all the details, thought about it a bit, and then came up with a simple and brilliant plan. From that moment, Tuesday morning, I've been operating on her instructions.

"The first change involved you two. From that point on, we were not going to try to hide your parents' past from you anymore. You would be told everything. I invited both of you to come to my house, but you, Chezky, preferred to stay away and only Avreimi came. I started outlining your father's history: his youth, his military service, and then his recruitment by the KGB. I related that your mother was also a KGB agent and devised the 'fingerprint' system. I reached the point where they'd come to Israel as a pair of young *ba'alei teshuvah*. It was getting late by then, and you, Avreimi, went home.

"The following morning, Wednesday, you, Chezky, insisted on speaking with Yechezkel Polowitz, and Avreimi joined you.

There you saw your mother leaving Polowitz's house, speaking in Russian, and getting into a car from the Ukrainian embassy."

"So they really were Ukrainians?"

"Absolutely. Meanwhile, however, Miri called you urgently because Sean Mackenzie had come to visit. I rushed over to the house because I thought the visitor was Oleg. If I'd known that it was Mackenzie, I wouldn't have bothered to come."

"How did you know that anyone had come at all?" Chezky asked curiously.

"I can't tell you that," Itzik said. He sounded apologetic. "In any case, Mackenzie told you about the 'coiled spring' mechanism, about the Ukrainian-Israeli-British balance of fear, and about Dr. Hamad, who'd died in Iran. Mackenzie knew that your mother had flown to Ukraine. As a very senior agent, he has access to flight information and passenger manifests. He came to the natural conclusion that your mother was cooperating with the Ukrainians, and he told you so.

"For me, the move came as a complete surprise. Your mother hadn't told me her plan in advance, and it aroused my suspicion. Had she deceived me, too? Was she operating behind my back? What was her reason for taking that flight? While I was talking to you, if you'll recall, I received a phone call and stepped out onto the balcony to take it."

"Right."

"It was your mother. She explained why she'd had to take the flight, and also gave me the secret code for the safe in the light fixture of her room…"

"But the slap on the face was your own idea," Chezky interposed.

Itzik looked at Chezky and let some air escape his lips. "You have no idea how angry you made me. I was turning the world over to save you, and you were ruining everything. But I shouldn't have lost control. That wasn't right."

Taken aback, Chezky lowered his eyes and said nothing.

"The fact that your mother was out of the country created a possibility that I hadn't considered before. I went with Shaul Armoni to see the Prime Minister, requesting his authorization for the operation that took place outside the embassy gates today. I was able to look the Prime Minister right in the eye and declare that Anna Aranowich was not in the country, and then propose a way to draw her back into the trap. At that stage, Armoni was convinced that I was working hand-in-glove with him. The P.M. put me back on the active list, and I began planning the operation with two men I'd known from my own days in the service, Shachaf Gafni and Chanan Etzioni.

"In coming to your *kollel* this morning, Avreimi, Sean Mackenzie did my job for me. If he hadn't come, I would have had to be the one to finish the story of your parents' lives. And, apart from that, Chezky seemed to believe that stranger more than he believed me…"

"While the two of you sat with Mackenzie, I made plans to drop you, Chezky, into Oleg's hands. At that stage of the operation I was not using people from the service, because this mission was neither legal nor, apparently, legitimate. My 'team' consisted of Moishy Sotzkover, Rotem Cohen the parking inspector from Givat Shmuel, and… Brachah, my wife."

"Brachah?"

"She was the 'Institute secretary' who called you to set up a meeting with Dr. Laskin… a meeting she fabricated." Itzik laughed at the shocked expression on Chezky's face. "The minute you entered the institute grounds, the official mission began. You were taken to the embassy, and then I called Oleg and proposed the hostage exchange. I worked things out so that you and Polowitz would meet side-by-side. All I wanted was to create a situation where you would call him *Saba*."

"But—why?"

"Why? Because Polowitz is *not* your grandfather."

Ukraine, 5772 / 2011

THE MAIN BRANCH OF THE TRANS-YOKO FIRM TOOK UP EIGHT floors of a handsome office building in the heart of Kiev's commercial district. The firm was involved in various enterprises, from lumber, to quarrying for metal, to tourism and hotels. On the top floor was the office of the firm's owner, Misha Chernowsky, a man of modest habits. Relatively speaking, of course. He rode around in an armored Mercedes only as a precaution against an attack by gunmen in the hire of his rivals. His private plane had been acquired second-hand and was slightly used; and his home was spacious but by no means breathtaking.

Misha Chernowsky was a hard-headed businessman known for his negotiating skills, and like all businessmen he had given a share of his earnings to philanthropic and charitable works. He had donated money, for example, to erect a chain of public health clinics in Kiev's suburbs, and to found a chemistry department in Odessa University. His favorite contributions, however, were the ones he gave to Jewish causes. He gave to all the various groups without discrimination. Still, everyone knew that he fell into the category of a "minor" donor, and was not a source of enormous sums such as might be extracted from an honor-seeking oligarch.

By the nature of things, he had various social obligations as well: one day a restaurant meal with investors, another evening a reception at the French embassy to mark Bastille Day. Tonight he had been invited to a new museum opening, to be attended by Foreign Minister Victor Yankovich and many other guests.

"The Minister's office called to confirm that you'll be coming," his secretary told him as evening drew near. He stifled a sigh. He would come; of course he would come. He had to, in order to end the nightmare that had begun three days before, with a call to his cell phone at a number that few people knew.

He didn't recognize the voice, and the number was unlisted, but the words he heard froze the blood in his veins. "The principal has announced a parent-teacher conference," said a female voice—and Misha knew that everything he had built up over the past thirty years was about to crash down with a mighty roar.

He was incapable of action. He canceled all his meetings and sat in his office, paralyzed with fear. How had this happened? He had been out of this business for years. No one in the world—including his wife—had any idea that he had once been a KGB agent. No one knew that he had been recruited as a young man into a secret project for R-19, of whose very existence few were aware. No one knew that he had been called Alexander Kittin then, and that he had been one of six agents, the crème de la crème, who'd trained for months for a mission of unparalleled sensitivity. And, of course, no one knew about the procedure by which his handlers could summon him to an emergency meeting: an innocent sentence about a principal inviting his faculty to a parent-teacher conference…

No one knew? Not exactly. There were two people who knew: his two handlers, Momi Arzi and Anna Aranowich. They must have been the ones who'd sent him the message. Where had they been all this time? And why had they surfaced so unexpectedly now, when the Soviet Union no longer existed and the KGB had vanished as if it never was? Even they were unaware of his greatest secret. They had no clue that he had not been faithful to the KGB, but had been working for the British all along.

The blind obedience instilled in him by his trainers so many years ago still held sway over Misha. He knew that he would receive another message specifying the time of the meeting. And then a third message would arrive, at precisely the same interval, regarding the location.

Half an hour later, he received an email message informing him that the meeting would take place the following morning. Exactly thirty minutes later, his fax machine spat out the third message: The meeting would be held on Rechov Bayit Vegan, Jerusalem, Israel.

The location was actually less surprising to him than the rest. He assumed that Momi and Anna were living in Israel, where the great mission had been intended to be played out. His five fellow spy-cell members had, in due time, been dispatched to their destinations; only he, for some reason, had been told to remain in the Soviet Union. After continuing to play a role in KGB activities for a time, he had been told to establish an ordinary life, to find some sort of job and await orders. He had been annoyed at first, but had soon come to appreciate the peaceful lifestyle to which he had been "sentenced."

The years had flown by, the Soviet Union had fragmented into its component parts, and he had cut off contact with the British MI6. He soon integrated into the business arena, where he rose in meteoric fashion. He had thought all the rest had been put behind him.

It had not. In the shadow-world, the world of spies and intelligence, one's past never dies. Even after 34 years, even after whole nations have been wiped from the map and clandestine organizations are borne away to the graveyard of history, there's someone holding on to information and waiting for the right moment.

What was this about? wondered Misha Chernowsky. *Financial blackmail? Or could Momi and Anna be working for some sort of bureau that was interested in recruiting him? Perhaps they were in trouble and seeking to save themselves through him? Perhaps handing him over was the price of their lives and liberty.*

Gradually, his initial panic dissipated and he was able to think in a more organized fashion. If, at first, he had thought about how to catch a flight to Israel and what pretext to use to cover his absence from home and office, now he remembered that he was no longer a young and impressionable agent, eager to please his handlers. He was Misha Chernowsky, a powerful and influential millionaire. He had connections, he had friends high up in government circles, and there were plenty of people who owed him a favor. Instead of letting that despicable spy duo attack him, he would attack *them*. He would return their fire.

He had twelve hours left to alter the balance of power and to make them regret that they'd dared disturb his peace.

Jerusalem, 5772 / 2011

The three Kohlbergs were completely baffled.

"So Yechezkel Polowitz is not our grandfather? Is that definite?" Chezky asked.

"He's not your grandfather," Itzik Peled replied. "But, apart from that, all the rest is accurate: He really was her contact man to the British; he really refrained from transmitting the 'fingerprints' to the secret service in London; and your mother really met him in Israel and was so angry at him that she cut off all contact."

"That means that she really was born in Russia."

"Yes. Your grandmother, Henya, was an ardent British Communist in her youth, and innocently went to help the Revolution. Only when she reached the Soviet Union did she discover, to her dismay, that it was a one-way ticket. She married a man there named Avraham Aranowich and your mother was born in Kiev."

"Avraham Aranowich?" Avraham repeated.

"That's right. He's the grandfather you're named after. A man who kept the mitzvos with *mesirus nefesh* under the Soviet regime."

"Then who is Yechezkel Polowitz?"

"He's actually your mother's uncle."

"An uncle?"

"Indeed. Her mother's brother."

"And why did you want me to call him *Saba*?" Chezky asked.

"Let's go back to your mother's brilliant plan," said Itzik. "All I had to do was tell Armoni that I'd discovered something stunning: Yechezkel Polowitz, whom we'd known until then was related to the family somehow, was actually your grandfather, and that this fact had been concealed from you all your life. He would connect that with Polowitz's hysterical statement that 'Chezky had found out about his grandfather.' That way, Armoni would be convinced that Kittin's 'fingerprint' was somehow connected to Yechezkel Polowitz."

"In other words," Avreimi summarized in a learned sing-song, "Polowitz meant that Chezky had learned about his *Kohlberg* grandfather, but you let Armoni believe that he had discovered his *Polowitz* grandfather."

"Well put." Itzik nodded approvingly. "So we reaped two benefits. First, we turned Armoni away from the real meaning of Polowitz's words and directed his attention to Chezky, who did not have Kittin's fingerprint. But there was something even more clever at play here. We'd laid a real trap: If and when we learned that Oleg thought of Polowitz as your grandfather, we would know for certain that he had received that knowledge from Shaul Armoni—because there was no other source for that false tidbit of information."

"In other words," Miri remarked, "it was the same system that our mother always used. She planted false information in Armoni, a kind of 'fingerprint' that eventually came out through Oleg Marinov."

"Precisely," Itzik agreed. "And, *baruch Hashem*, we got even more. Oleg said on the scene that Armoni had told him that, thus incriminating him explicitly. At that moment, the arrest took place."

Chezky was still thinking things over. "What I don't understand is why Polowitz got so upset when I found my Kohlberg grandfather's letter?"

Miri's face suddenly shone. "I know!" she cried.

But Itzik Peled put a finger to his lips to silence her. He glanced at his watch. "It's a quarter to twelve," he said. "You can talk about it only after midnight. After the emails have been sent to their destinations."

Miri subsided with a secretive smile. Itzik's response had confirmed her guess. Chezky and Avreimi, on the other hand, gaped at her curiously.

"While we're waiting, maybe you can explain Polowitz's helpful and remorseful attitude when I came to see him this afternoon," Avreimi said.

Itzik chuckled. "Very simple," he explained. "Before his visit to the embassy, I prepared him for what would happen. He was apprehensive, and kept asking me what he needed to do. I told him that his mission was very simple: All he had to do was to answer honestly any question that Kohlberg's son put to him. I was referring, of course, to Chezky. But before he set out for Tel Aviv, you surprised him in his parking lot. He got mixed-up and encouraged *you* to ask questions, so you benefited from his confusion. But he was in a remorseful mindset already…"

Chezky had missed that encounter, and Avreimi quickly filled him in. Then he showed his brother the file folder containing the missing page from the orphans' book, and the other documents about their father that had vanished from the archives.

Chezky was excited. "Look at this!" But Itzik dampened his enthusiasm. "Guys, we've waited a month, and we can wait ten more minutes. You never know who's watching or who's listening."

"Even here?"

"Especially here."

"The all-seeing eye and ear, eh?" Chezky tried to joke.

But Avreimi's demeanor was serious. "Can we talk about the big question before midnight? The question of whether or not our parents were really *shomer mitzvos*?"

"By all means," Itzik assented.

"Because you told me something troubling…" Avreimi slanted an uneasy glance at his sister. He and Chezky were used to earth-shattering revelations by now, but Miri…

"Yes. I told you that, each year, I reported to my superior Shaul Armoni that the Kohlbergs were living in the guise of a *chareidi* couple, while actually not adhering to a religious lifestyle. It was merely camouflage."

Miri stifled a gasp.

"Allon Kolar disagrees with you," Chezky said.

"*Harav* Allon Kolar, if you don't mind," Avreimi corrected him. Chezky, to his surprise, reacted with only a nod.

"What do you mean?" Itzik asked.

"He said that he's sure he sensed something stirring in Abba on that long-ago Yom Kippur in the bunker on the Suez Canal."

"I'm not arguing with that," Itzik surprised him by saying. "It started then, and it continued in the Soviet Union. Your father was very disillusioned with the Communist way of life, and his dream-bubble burst. Ironically, he acquired his knowledge of Judaism from the *sefarim* which the KGB had supplied him. He learned about the mitzvos from your mother, with some help from Zalman Berkovitch.

"It was for that reason, of course, that your mother arranged to marry your father in an authentic Jewish ceremony. They married again here in Israel. The only person with whom they shared their unusual circumstances was the *rav* who served as their *mesader kiddushin*, since it has halachic ramifications… The *rav*, by the way, Avreimi and Chezky, was your Rosh Yeshivah."

Avreimi and Chezky were stunned. "Really? Rav Moshe Aryeh Steinhertz?"

"None other," Itzik said with a smile.

"So why did you keep reporting to Armoni that they weren't religious?"

"Because that's what kept them alive."

"What?"

"It's very simple. The underlying threat that they held over Israel's head was their ability to expose Dr. Hamad as an Israeli spy in Iran. Armoni had scoffed at the threat, telling your mother that she would never expose Dr. Hamad to the authorities because he was a Jew. Your mother replied that she and her husband had never cared about their religion, and that they would give Dr. Hamad up in a heartbeat if they felt threatened. My report backed up that claim. I was someone whom Armoni trusted. To this day, he thinks that my whole lifestyle is just a disguise for the purpose of carrying out my mission. He had known me in my earlier incarnation—and, believe me, a more anti-religious fellow you've never met…"

"So you told Armoni that our parents are *not* religious, and you're telling us that they *are*?" Avreimi asked.

Itzik Peled consulted his watch. Midnight was fast approaching. He could take a risk. "I have much better proof," he said.

From his pocket he took a scrap of newspaper and placed it on the table. Three young heads bent over the paper. It showed a picture taken at a *Hachnassas Sefer Torah*. One of the faces in the photo had been blackened with a marker, and a few words had also been censored.

"Two months ago," Itzik said, "your parents saw an announcement about a *Hachnassas Sefer Torah* in Kiev. They looked at the face of the donor—a local Kiev businessman—and suddenly recognized him."

"Alexander Kittin," Chezky guessed.

"Correct," Itzik affirmed. "And at that moment, they knew that their lives had changed. They had discovered the identity of Agent 6. The stand-off was beginning all over again. They would resume their battle positions, and this time they were assured of success."

"So who *is* Kittin?" Chezky asked.

"I can't give you any identifying details," Itzik said. "But yesterday morning, just as you were coming to speak to Yechezkel Polowitz, your mother came out of his house to meet Alexander Kittin."

"After cutting off all ties with Polowitz for twenty-five years, she went to his house?"

"Yes. That's why she was so emotional."

"So Alexander Kittin was waiting inside that black Mercedes?" Chezky asked.

"That's what your mother assumed. She'd summoned him for a meeting, but he's no fool, either; he sent someone in his place. Inside the car your mother found the Ukrainian ambassador to Israel. Accompanying him were two armed guards who 'invited' her to get into the car in a way that didn't leave her much choice…"

"The Ukrainian ambassador?"

"In person. He, by the way, had no idea what was going on. He had simply received orders from on high to go to a certain street in Bayit Vegan and tell the woman who would approach him that, if she was interested in the meeting she had asked for, she would have to fly to Ukraine. Which she did."

"Wait a minute," Miri interrupted. "Ima took along her passport and prepared enough food for a week. She knew she would be traveling."

"She didn't know. But she anticipated such a move, and came prepared."

"So why did both Oleg and Mackenzie say that she had returned to Israel? Where is she now?"

Itzik smiled. "'Anna Aranowich' did return to Israel, but Chana Kohlberg is still in Kiev. She's about to board a flight to an unknown destination."

"*What*? What are you talking about?"

Itzik leaned slightly forward, as though about to reveal a secret. "Your mother stayed in Kiev, but a woman by the name of Zeldy Bukshpan—who happens to be my wife's niece—volunteered to fly to Israel on your mother's diplomatic passport, so that her trail would disappear."

"What? Why?"

"First, so that Alexander Kittin would also think that she got cold feet and left Ukraine. And, second, to confuse the *satan* named Oleg Marinov."

"I don't understand anything," Chezky complained. "Why did Ima stay in Kiev? Why did she want to meet with Kittin? And what brought her to Yechezkel Polowitz's house after twenty-five years?"

"I'll put it this way," Itzik said. "In order to meet Kittin, she had to go through Polowitz."

"Why?"

"Because the information that she wanted to give Kittin was on the computer in Polowitz's house. Which was the same computer, by the way, that your father used for his 'coiled spring' program."

"Aha!" Avreimi smiled with pleasure.

"What? What?" Chezky was having a hard time keeping up with his brother's agile mind.

"That was something Armoni didn't think of," Itzik said. "The computer was in a place where your mother was prevented from going—not your father's workplace, but Polowitz's house, which she had stayed away from all those years. Incidentally, Zeldy Bukshpan undertook a great risk. The Shin-Bet and other organizations are searching for 'Anna Aranowich,' and Zeldy walking around the airport—using someone else's passport, no less…"

Avreimi sat back, as though trying to obtain a broader perspective of the whole picture. "Just a second," he told Itzik. "You need to explain two things. Where is the proof? And how will any of this clear our parents' name?"

Itzik swallowed a smile. The sharp-witted Avreimi always knew the right questions to ask.

"I spent years reporting that your parents were capable of giving up Dr. Hamad without blinking an eye, right? Now your mother proved that she's willing to risk her life to save a Jew whom she barely knows—a Jew whose alias is Alexander Kittin."

"Then the whole trip was for the purpose of giving him his fingerprint?"

"Precisely."

"So maybe you'll finally tell us what that fingerprint is?"

Itzik Peled looked at his watch. The big hand and the little hand had met at the 12. At this moment, three electronic messages were being sent to their destinations. A new era was dawning for the Kohlberg family.

Misha Chernowsky, in faraway Kiev, tried to appear cool and collected, but he was sweating profusely beneath his expensive suit. It was about to happen now. In the next few minutes he would be put to the test that would determine his life or death, his freedom or a humiliating public trial. And, of course, there would be those who would use the fact that he was a Jew to fan the flames of anti-Semitism that always roiled and hissed beneath the surface. If he was denounced as a former KGB agent, and if it came to light that he had done a not inconsiderable amount of work for

British intelligence, it would negatively impact the whole Jewish community.

The tables set in the museum's vestibule were laid with a variety of alcoholic beverages and costly hors d'oeuvres. With the official program behind them, the guests were circulating and chatting in small knots.

"Dr. Vasily Platyev," a short man introduced himself to Misha Chernowsky. "University of Kiev."

If Misha was not sure that the fellow actually received his salary from that academic institution, he showed no indication of it.

"They did a nice job here," the short man said, gesturing at the new exhibit of the Second World War. "Museum displays these days have to be more accessible and user-friendly than in the past. People have no patience anymore."

Misha Chernowsky murmured in agreement. "Yes, yes, the younger generation…"

"The problem," continued the historian, "is that the viewer gets an overly simplistic picture that does not go into detail. Take France during World War II, for instance. What do you know about the topic?"

Misha hoped that the fellow—who was clearly no historian, but an executioner—didn't notice that he had turned pale. "The Nazis conquered France, didn't they?"

"And have you heard about the Resistance?" the man challenged him.

"That was an anti-German underground movement, wasn't it?" Misha said. "I read about it somewhere."

"And do you know what they did?"

"I certainly know less than you, Doctor," Misha said, with a forced laugh.

"People think that they only hung up signs and distributed propaganda leaflets. Not many know that they had an actual terrorist cell that carried out attacks and sabotaged the German war effort."

"That's right, that's right," Misha said, as though he had just remembered. "I heard about that."

"Really? That's very good," the short man complimented him.

"Those are things that the average person doesn't know. It's good to occasionally meet an individual with a broader horizon."

"Thank you, Doctor," Misha said modestly.

"I look at all these guests," grumbled Dr. Vasily Platyev, "and I see people with no historical knowledge, no appreciation for the past. Empty, shallow people."

"Sir, you're making me blush…"

"They were a cell of six members," the man said, as though imparting a great secret, "and they carried out many missions. But one mission changed the face of the war. Do you know what it was?"

Misha knew very well.

"Remind me," he said, wrinkling his brow as though trying to retrieve a morsel of information from the depths of his memory.

"They blew up the railroad bridge by which the Nazis ferried out minerals and other quarried substances that they'd robbed from France," said the "historian."

"You don't say!" Misha marveled.

"But where did it take place…?" The man scratched his forehead. "The name escapes me…"

"It was in France, no?" Misha was beginning to enjoy this.

"But in which city?"

Misha smiled with enjoyment. "Perhaps Paris?"

"Quarries and minerals—in Paris?"

"Then it must be toward the south," said Misha. "That's where the mines are."

"Perhaps Marseille?"

Misha wrinkled his brow. "No… impossible. It must have been… Lyons."

He had a hard time hiding his smile at the sight of the "historian's" face, which crumpled like a punctured balloon…

Jerusalem, 5772 / 2011

"I know what the fingerprint is," Miri said, and got up to go to her room.

Avreimi, meanwhile, pulled the pages out of the folder that contained their father's documents. He showed Chezky the section that described their grandfather, Maurice Kohlberg, and the attack that his cell had carried out in Lyons. Then he compared it to the historical background that Miri had heard from their father, which placed the attack in Marseille. Itzik was on the phone, his expression gloomy.

"So you were the 'safe' for Kittin's fingerprint," Avreimi said in wonder.

"That's why Polowitz was so upset," Itzik said. "He had been given the job of concealing your father's past, and suddenly Chezky came along and found a letter with the most important detail in the whole story…"

Chezky looked at Itzik suspiciously. "What do you mean, 'he had been given the job'?" he asked.

"Look," said Itzik. "The situation after Dr. Hamad's death was untenable. The big fear was that Armoni would simply 'sell' your father to the Ukrainians: allow them to snatch him and take him to a foreign country, where they could question him with their well-known methods. Or they could simply have kidnaped one of the children and squeezed the information out of him…"

"So our father's death solved all the problems?" Chezky asked cynically.

"You could say that," Itzik acknowledged.

"Just don't tell us that he sacrificed his life to save the family," Avreimi said.

Itzik paused before he spoke. "I think that, had it been halachically permissible, he would have considered that option. But of course there's no permissible way for a person to commit suicide."

Chezky's face suddenly took on a comprehending expression, and his eyes spewed sparks of anger. "It was not permissible for him to commit suicide—but for you and Polowitz to help him die—was permissible?"

Itzik slowly spread his hands in a gesture of apology.

"That makes both of you… murderers." Chezky's voice shook. The calm that had enveloped him all evening had vanished.

Itzik lowered his eyes. "Let's leave Polowitz out of it for now."

"I hope he never makes it out of the hospital alive." Chezky's voice rose. "And you'll pay the price, too!"

"What could we have done?" Itzik's voice was low. "What choice did we have?"

"I don't know. I don't know…" Chezky's face was white with fury.

"Just like that, to kill a Jew? A family man? Your friend? And we're supposed to thank you for 'saving' us?"

Avreimi put a calming arm around his brother's shoulder, but Chezky shrugged it off. A new idea had sprouted in his brain.

"You could have simply staged his death," he lashed out at Itzik.

Itzik waved his hand dismissively. "What do you mean by 'staged'? Have you ever tried to fake a death, my young friend?"

"I don't know…" Chezky was beside himself. "He could have collapsed in the street and been taken to the hospital, where word would go out that he had died. Then the British and the Ukrainians would have believed him to be dead, and everything would have been all right."

Itzik gave Chezky an odd look. "Do you think we didn't consider that?"

"Well?"

"It was impossible—and also hopeless. First of all, it's impossible to fake mourning. Anyone who would have come to the funeral would have seen that it wasn't genuine. Anyone who came to pay a *shivah* call would have seen the family laughing instead of crying."

"So we didn't have to be told," Chezky expostulated. "We could have been let in on the secret a few weeks later."

"Oh, really? And where would we have found a body for burial? And which doctor would have signed the bogus death certificate? Which Chevra Kaddisha would have agreed to bury a non-Jew in a Jewish cemetery? And how, exactly, would your dead-alive father have left Israel? A story like that would have put ten people in prison for the rest of their lives."

Chezky fell silent, though the gaze that rested on Itzik Peled was filled with loathing. How could the man be so equable when he had caused the death of another human being?

The silence that filled the Kohlberg living room was thick and stifling. No one looked directly at anyone else. Miri mopped her eyes, which streamed with nonstop tears.

"Leave it alone, Chezky," Avreimi said softly. "It happened, and that's that. Why ask questions? We don't know how things are calculated in *Shamayim*. Abba apparently completed his mission in this world, and at the same time had the merit of rescuing his family. I'm sure he's content now, and that things are good for him in the *Olam Ha'emes*—a lot better than they are down here in this *Olam Ha'sheker*."

Chezky didn't respond. His eyes had also begun to tear. Usually, when Avreimi began to spout his *"emunah"* talk, Chezky would feel annoyed. Tonight it was actually comforting, and served as a salve on his festering emotional wounds.

"One more thing interests me," Avreimi said. "What would have happened if Polowitz hadn't called you?"

Itzik pressed his lips together hard. There are some things that are very unpleasant, he thought, but one must speak of them. That's what Shlomo Kohlberg, his friend, would have wanted him to do.

"The question isn't what would have happened if he hadn't called," he said, "but what would have happened if you boys hadn't started rooting around in your father's life."

Chezky straightened up with a jerk. The criticism was aimed at him, as was Itzik's hard stare.

"It seems to me that your older brother begged you to leave the whole matter alone," Itzik said. "You acted without your mother's knowledge or consent. You visited the orphanage, and then Reuven Dalel in the south, and then Sonia Arzi in Kibbutz Tel-Chana, and who knows who else. You practically woke the dead, and you certainly aroused suspicions in all sorts of quarters."

Chezky clamped his jaw in an effort not to hurl himself at Itzik. "It's my right to know what happened to my father!" he said, voice shaking.

"No! It's your job to listen to those who are older and wiser than you," Itzik said firmly. "To know that you aren't the smartest person in the world."

"You're talking almost as if that would have restored our father to life," Chezky said between clenched teeth.

"Not that, no," Itzik agreed. "Nothing can bring your father back to life. But if you hadn't done what you did, your mother wouldn't be forced to escape from Ukraine to some country that doesn't have an extradition treaty with Israel. Your younger siblings wouldn't have to join her soon and live in a place that doesn't even have a Jewish community. Your brother Ari wouldn't have to be a 'living orphan' with no home to return to during *bein hazemanim*. And Miri, if she wants her mother to walk her down to the *chuppah*, wouldn't have to get married in Zimbabwe or the Congo or some such place."

"So that's the reason for the slap, eh?" Chezky's face was distorted with anger.

"Yes! And you deserved it!" Itzik blazed. "I couldn't hold myself back any longer. The stupid things you did could have caused terrible and even catastrophic damage. *Baruch Hashem*, they only caused terrible damage…"

"You're so smart," Chezky muttered.

"No, *you're* the smart one," Itzik retorted. "You're studying law, aren't you? You're a lawyer. No one will be able to tell you what to do, because you'll know better than them all."

"You could have told us…"

"Told you? I *did* tell you! But you wouldn't listen. You thought you knew everything, when in reality you didn't even see a tiny fraction of the whole picture. Listen to me, Chezky—if you don't learn to listen to those who are greater than you, you won't get far. And I believe I'm speaking for your father when I say that."

Chezky stood up in a rage. "You killed him, and now you're speaking in his name," he spat out. "Very nice."

Avreimi looked at the two sparring men and the words died on his lips. His heart went out to Chezky, even as he pondered the meaning of Itzik's actions. Something still wasn't clear. He had a strong sense that there remained more to be said, that all the cards were not yet on the table.

"There's something I don't understand," he said. "Why does our mother have to go to a place that has no extradition treaty with Israel? What crime could she be charged with?"

Itzik checked his watch and took some time out for thought. He wasn't sure if their mother had left Ukraine's border yet. On the other hand, how long could he continue to string these confused young people along?

He took a deep breath and looked at Avreimi.

"She can be charged with everything I said earlier," he replied. "Persuading a doctor to sign a false death certificate; burying an anonymous body under a forged name; and helping an Israeli citizen leave the country by illegal means... along with a few other not-insignificant crimes."

Avreimi's face turned as white as a corpse's.

Chezky turned to stone, and stared at Itzik in disbelief.

Miri still needed a few seconds to digest what she had heard.

It was Avreimi who recovered first. In a shaking voice, he said, "So you're saying that..." He couldn't finish the sentence.

Tears stood out in Itzik Peled's eyes. He nodded his head.

"So it was all..."

Itzik did his best not to burst into tears, without much success.

"And Ima knew all along?" Avreimi asked, his throat choked with tears.

Itzik shook his head. He swallowed hard and tried to gain control of his emotions.

"She didn't know until yesterday," he said in a voice that was remarkably steady. "My son-in-law and I were the ones who cooked this up with your father—may he live and be well!"

"But... how? How?"

Itzik was himself again. "That's something you'll never know. People risked their lives; people committed serious crimes. But your mother has undertaken full responsibility in the event that it ever comes to light—which we hope it never will."

Itzik's cell phone vibrated in his pocket. He picked it up and listened to the caller for a few seconds. Then he hung up and turned back to the Kohlbergs.

"Instead of laughing with joy, you're crying?" he asked with a smile, as he wiped away the last of his own tears.

"But Abba… will never be able to come back again?"

"I don't know what your parents will decide," Itzik said. "But, right now, he has to disappear from the face of the earth for an extended period of time."

"Then he *won't* be at my wedding," Miri said, halfway between laughter and tears. "Because I'm not getting married in Zimbabwe!"

"Not openly, certainly," Itzik told her. "But maybe, if it's completely secure, you'll see some unfortunate, tattered beggar there—and only you, and a select few, will know that your happy father came from a distant land to be at his daughter's wedding."

Chezky still resembled a pillar of salt. He could neither move a limb nor utter a sound.

"And Polowitz?" Avreimi asked. "When did he find out?"

"That's something I don't know," Itzik said. "Your father asked him to come to Rechov Ezer Yoldot without telling him why. He gave him the access code for Alexander Kittin's fingerprint, but not the code for the coiled spring. Polowitz contacted your mother a few days ago. I don't know if he guessed, or knew, or suspected, but he behaved exceptionally up until the last minute."

"The last minute?"

Itzik nodded his head, finding it suddenly difficult to speak. He dabbed at a few tears that had sprung up anew.

"A few minutes ago," he said at last, "Yechezkel Polowitz returned his suffering and purified soul to its Creator. Chanan Etzioni was with him. He's a religious boy; I've known him for a number of years. He recited *viduy* and *Shema Yisrael* with him. Polowitz's last words were: 'I repaired what I could. May my death serve as atonement for my sins.'"

EPILOGUE

Jerusalem, Har HaMenuchos, 5772 / 2011

AVREIMI, CHEZKY, MIRI, AND ARI STOOD FACING THE monument that marked their father's empty grave. The monument manufacturer had worked hard to have it ready on time for the family's visit to the cemetery on the thirtieth day after their father's death. That's what it's like with families, he had sighed to himself with typical graveyard humor. They have a lifetime to prepare the text for the stone, but always wait until the last month...

Itzik had instructed the brothers to behave as usual: to continue davening for the amud, to say Kaddish, and to visit the grave on the thirtieth day. "There's no halachic problem with saying Kaddish, or with reciting a few chapters of Tehillim in front of a stone over an empty grave," he had said. "The only possible problem was saying the berachah of 'Dayan Ha'emes' at the levayah. But, according to your father's research, that wasn't a berachah in vain because you had received grievous news and needed to recite the berachah."

"And, for heaven's sake, don't joke around while you're up there," he had cautioned that morning.

"Don't worry. We'll safeguard the mission," Chezky said, and broke into liberating laughter.

Their younger siblings had flown to Ukraine. Their mother had been in touch with educational and professional people about how to break the news that their father had been resurrected from the dead. Itzik hadn't come to the cemetery, though he had said that he was sending a number of young men to complete the minyan.

"Well, you were right. We didn't have to run after Abba," Chezky told Avreimi.

Avreimi merely looked at his brother in silence.

"So, the kollel man outwitted the law student, eh?"

Avreimi's expression changed to one of surprise.

"The 'traditional' son got the better of the 'modern' one," Chezky continued, his tone bitter.

Avreimi grasped his brother's sleeve and turned him around to face him. "You're talking nonsense," he said. "If you want to speak that way, then say that da'as Torah triumphed over thinking that we know it all ourselves."

Chezky pondered this for a long moment.

"Da'as Torah..." He looked into his brother's eyes, as though he had finally realized something.

"Of course," Avreimi said, with no trace of victory in his voice. "How can a person possibly cope with issues of life and death without consulting a rav?"

"So you did talk to the Rosh Yeshivah."

"Yes. I did."

"And what did he say?"

"He was adamant that I not take any initiative. But if you were determined to forge ahead, I should stay with you all the way."

Chezky was suffused with a deep shame, untouched by even the tiniest trace of anger.

"And did he also say that Itzik Peled was a person who could be trusted?" he asked.

"No," Avreimi replied. "The Rosh Yeshivah just said that we should do whatever we are obligated to do, simply and wholeheartedly."

"And what are we obligated to do?"

"Keep the mitzvos. Without making calculations."

"What do you mean? Which mitzvos?"

"For example: 'It is a mitzvah to fulfill the wishes of the dead.'"

Chezky fixed his eyes on the ground.

"Because Abba told me, and Miri, and you," Avreimi continued, "that Itzik Peled can be trusted."

Chezky bit his lip. His brother's rebuke was veiled, but clear. And he, Chezky, had earned it.

"How do you know he told me?" he asked weakly.

"I just know…" Avreimi did not elaborate.

Chezky found the courage to meet his brother's eyes. "Abba did say that to me," he confessed. "But I thought I knew better…"

Avreimi nodded silently.

"So you summoned Itzik when Sean Mackenzie came to the house," Chezky now understood.

"Among other things," Avreimi said, with a faint hint of a smile.

A sea of silence filled the cemetery, where the marble tombstones surrounded them like islands. Chezky approached his father's unoccupied grave, tears filling his eyes. Here lies R' Shlomo Kohlberg, read the inscription. May his soul be a link in the chain of life…

"Tell me," Chezky said, turning to his brother. "Do you think Abba consulted the Rosh Yeshivah before he concocted his whole plan?"

Avreimi took two steps forward to stand beside Chezky. "I have a feeling he did," he replied. "In fact, I was a little forward yesterday and actually asked him that question."

"And what did he answer?"

"The Rosh Yeshivah smiled," he said. "And then he said something that I'm sure you'll recognize. He said, 'Even if your father did ask me, I'd have to tell you that he didn't. So even if I tell you that he didn't ask, you wouldn't be able to believe me'…"